The Hall of Worlds
The Beginning of the End

by Todd Weitzel

Dedicated to Cordelia.
Life isn't the same without you.

Prologue

Water trickled down the cold, moss-covered stone wall and onto the cheek of a frantic middle-aged man. He wore something resembling a tattered burlap sack with holes ripped out for his head and arms. His eyes darted from left to right, then up and down, as if someone – *or something* – might be coming at him from any direction. He stood at the intersection of three hallways. The hall to his right was the hall from which he came. It was a dark corridor housing several dimly lit cells. Large wrought-iron doors, locked with heavy chains, framed each cell. The chain and metal lock that had held him captive in one of the cells lay on a pile next to his cell. A narrow hallway led off to the left, ending in a small wooden door with a large black lock upon it. Directly ahead of him was a wide corridor ending in two large wooden doors held shut on the opposite side by a heavy log. Although he had managed to escape from his cell, he was still very much trapped.

An ornate stained-glass window in the shape of a large, red bird was cut into one of the dark walls. The bird's eyes were bright orange and flames shot from its mouth. In its large claws it held a dead rabbit. The man leaned against this window, catching his breath and steadying his weak legs. In his dirty, bloody hand he clutched a small metallic object. The object was shaped like a key with a small green gem inlaid on the end of the handle. It had no teeth, just a smooth cylindrical golden shaft; its beauty was marred only by the drying blood upon its surface. He clutched it tightly, for his life depended upon it.

He looked around again, took a deep breath, and heaved himself from the window. He limped toward the small wooden door down the hall to his left, dragging his injured left leg. Blood stained the burlap around his left side and ran in lines down his leg to his bare feet. He had to use both of his hands to help lift his leg while he walked, occasionally leaning on the wall to rest briefly before pushing onward again. He left bloodstains on the floor and the wall as he slid along its surface toward the door. He knew these marks would lead his captors to find him more easily, but he simply hadn't the strength to walk without support. He had not eaten for some time and the physical torture he endured at the hands of his captors left him weak and severely injured. His only hope now was to escape and find refuge where he could rest and heal. Then he could return and finish his mission.

Paintings of a regal-looking gentleman in various frumpy outfits lined the walls of the hallway. He had a diamond shaped head with beady little eyes. He sported a curly, handlebar mustache, and his chin came to a point with a black triangular goatee. A crown rested regally upon his head, and rings encrusted with jewels of all shapes, sizes and colors covered his slender, dainty fingers. As the man moved past the paintings toward the door at the end of the hallway, something caught his attention. He stopped to look more closely at the one nearest the door. In this particular painting, the man wore a bright coat with a puffy yellow shirt beneath. Ruffles of yellow fabric pooled around his wrists and neck. A golden crown with sapphires about the pinnacle rested atop his head. He had a smirk of arrogance on his face. But it wasn't any of those things that grabbed the injured man's attention. It was the eyes. He shifted his weight onto his good leg and stared closely at the painting. As he moved to the right, the eyes of the painting followed him. He shifted to his left leg, momentarily forgetting it was injured and nearly fell. The eyes followed him to the left. The man backed up in terror, shaking uncontrollably as he realized that his escape had now been detected. The guards would be upon him at any moment.

In his haste to back away from the painting, he failed to see a large trunk resting on the floor behind him. He struck the corner of the trunk with his right leg and fell to the stone floor, further injuring his leg and side. He cried out in pain and grabbed his side, putting pressure on the wound beneath his ragged clothes. Breathing hard, he tried to regain control of his limbs. The guards were coming. It was imperative that he get up immediately. No sooner did he think this than he heard the faint sound of footsteps coming toward him. Holding his breath, he listened hard to determine from which direction the footsteps were coming. As the steps grew louder, he could not believe his ears. The footsteps appeared to be coming from *inside* the trunk!

Using his right hand, he grasped the stone wall and pulled himself up. The trunk vibrated with the sounds of footsteps. He moved as quickly as possible toward the door and away from the trunk. The trunk began to buck and jump, as if something were banging on it from the inside, trying to escape. Reaching the door, he examined the cast-iron lock that barred his entrance. It was about six inches wide and very thick. He held up the metallic object he was carrying and rubbed the green jewel. The jewel began to glow. He placed the object into the lock and rubbed the jewel again. Heat radiated from the object as it grew thicker and heavier. He could hear metal moving against metal inside the lock. When the sounds stopped and the object began to cool, he turned it to the right. The lock sprung open and fell to the floor.

The banging in the trunk stopped. The man turned to look at it. Desperate fear danced in his eyes. The spring inside the lock of the trunk clicked, and the lid popped open. In the dim light of the hallway, he could see something emerge from the depths of the trunk. It was a hand – a bluish-green hand!

He turned quickly, threw open the door he had just unlocked, and stepped into the tiny room beyond. He closed the door behind him, hoping that whatever was attached to the hand in the box had not seen him enter the room and that he had at least a few seconds to find an escape. The room was dark as pitch. He rubbed the gem on the object again, so that its green light lit up the room. Quickly surveying the room, he saw no other doors or windows through which he might escape. The room was about twenty square feet in size with a small cot in one corner. A small wooden nightstand sat next to the cot. A candelabra sat on the surface, and it contained one tiny drawer. A broken spinning wheel lay in the other corner next to a pile of old clothes. A picture of a stately woman and a small child hung on the wall. The child in the picture had the same diamond shaped head as the man in the paintings in the hallway. He stepped away from the door and toward the nightstand. The gem in the metallic object began to pulse a brighter green. Footsteps echoed in the hall. They stopped at the door, and he heard someone pick up the metal lock that had fallen from the door. He had only seconds before they would find him.

The door swung open and five armed guards entered the room. Their skin was a bluish-green and they had large black, shiny eyes. They resembled giant salamanders that could walk on two legs. They wore tight body suits and armor. Their swords were drawn. Two bore torches to light the way. They spread out to search the room. One guard approached the spinning wheel and pile of clothes. He poked the pile of clothes with his sword to see if anyone was hidden under them. He pushed his sword all the way through the pile until the tip met the stone floor with a metallic clink. He scattered the clothes to reveal nothing hidden below. Three of the guards went toward the cot. They raised their swords and plunged them through the mattress and wooden bed-frame to the stone floor. If the fugitive was hiding under the bed, he would surely be stabbed. They knelt down to look under the cot and found nothing. The room was empty aside from the broken spinning wheel, the pile of scattered clothes, the painting, the mangled cot, the candelabra, and the nightstand with a drawer slightly ajar. The fugitive had escaped, but they knew not how. They looked at each other with quizzical expressions.

"Where did he go?" asked the guard closest to the spinning wheel. "Is this the wrong room?"

"No. This is the room Count Milton told us to enter. Somehow he has managed to escape us," said the bewildered guard who had led them into the room.

"How?" asked another guard.

"I do not know, but Count Milton is not going to be pleased."

Chapter One

Rays of sunlight sliced through the partially closed blinds of Ms. Zipple's fifth grade classroom and fell upon the desks of the students sitting nearest the windows. Xachary Biddle was one of those students. The shadows between the vertical bars of white light that fell upon his heavily smudged and eraser-torn paper resembled the bars of a jail cell, trapping his math homework behind them.

If only all math homework could be locked away in a jail cell, Xachary mused, *never to harm or torture another student again...never to torment me with its fractions and integers, angles and equations...never to cause me headaches and frustration.*

It was no secret that Xachary did not like math. In fact, math was his **least** favorite subject. Each night's math homework presented an endless struggle for him. No matter how much help he received from his parents, the fundamental logic behind the numbers was baffling and humiliating. He much preferred science, English, and reading and excelled in these subjects. He was looking forward to the day's reading lesson, because his group was reading a science fiction story about space travellers lost in an unfamiliar galaxy populated with strange and fascinating creatures.

The real world, or more specifically the world of elementary school, was not Xach's favorite place to be. Since the older boys teased him for being young and for his unusual appearance, he much preferred to retreat into the recesses of his imagination to escape that torture. Although Xach had just celebrated his tenth birthday a few months ago, he was still one of the youngest boys in his class. However, even though Xach was younger than most of his peers, he was taller and slimmer. His mother was fond of telling everyone that Xach had a "growth spurt" the moment he turned ten, just like his father had when he turned nine. In addition to his father's height, he inherited three other traits that made him a target of ridicule. The first and most noticeable was his bi-colored eyes. Xach's right eye was blue, and his left eye was green – a rare genetic condition called *heterochromia.* The second thing he shared with his father was large lopsided ears. His ears were presently a little too large for his head. He hoped he would grow into them, but when he looked at his father, he knew he never would. In addition to the size of his ears, they were misaligned on his head. His left ear was a quarter inch lower than the right one, so that every pair of glasses he put on looked crooked or only rested on one ear. The third thing he shared with his father was a cowlick that refused to be tamed. These traits did not render Xach unattractive by any means – just "different" – and anything different was subject to ridicule in the juvenile society of elementary school.

Today's cowlick had been particularly stubborn and defied even the strongest of styling products. It stuck straight up on the left side of his head like a wiry tuft of grass missed by a lawnmower. Upon returning to the classroom after lunch, Peter said that Xach's hair resembled a shark fin. He asked Xach if it helped him cut through the air more quickly, before he broke out in a roar of laughter that drew others to the attention of it. Xachary fought the urge to respond in kind with a snarky comment about the volcano-like pimple on Peter's forehead and how he looked like a unicorn, but felt it was better to avoid confrontation. He slipped into the seat behind his desk and started drawing three-eyed aliens in the margins of his math homework, quickly losing himself in another daydream as Ms. Zipple began the Math lesson.

"Xachary, would you please come to the board and demonstrate how to properly answer question number three?" asked Ms. Zipple.

Xach didn't hear her. His mind was lost in a daydream concerning a gargantuan, lime-green, gelatinous, three-eyed alien with a laser cannon firing upon one of the astronauts trying to rescue his comrades. The astronaut dove to safety, barely escaping the sizzling blue electric bolt that issued from the cannon. Instead, the bolt hit the statue of an evil looking bird perched on a human skull behind which the astronaut had been hiding. The statue exploded into a thousand pieces and rained down upon…

"Xachary Biddle," interrupted Ms. Zipple's stern and angry voice. "I will not ask you again. Come to the board and show us how you solved question number three."

Torn from his exciting daydream and slammed once again into the harsh reality of math class, Xach looked up from his doodles with glazed eyes.

"Number three on the board, Mr. Biddle," Ms. Zipple repeated curtly.

Xachary blinked twice, picked up his homework, and slowly walked to the front of the room, his cowlick waving in the breeze of his forward momentum. Although he had not been paying attention, he was partially prepared for this. Ms. Zipple had not called on him all day, and it was about time for his daily dose of humiliation. Everyone knew that Xachary generally struggled with his math homework, and Ms. Zipple tended to call on him more frequently during the math lesson because of this. His classmates whispered and snickered behind him, as he shuffled toward the blackboard and inevitable humiliation.

It had been like this since Day One at Barker Elementary – the day Ms. Zipple had found a snake in her desk drawer. She mistakenly blamed Xach for the snake's presence in her classroom and managed to find ways of humiliating him at least once a day in retribution for the horror inflicted upon her. Xach navigated his way through the maze of desks toward the blackboard, but his mind was not focused on math. His mind raced back to that fateful day and those preceding it.

****

The "snake incident," as it had come to be known, happened within minutes of entering his new school, but his troubles actually began about three months prior to that fateful first day. Xachary and his family had been living in Bangor, Maine where he attended King Elementary School. During the third week of summer vacation following his completion of the fourth grade at King, his father announced to the family that they would be moving from their comfortable home of fifteen years to the city of Philadelphia in Pennsylvania. In fact, his father made the announcement just three days before Xach's tenth birthday, making his birthday party on June 25th a going-away party. In one short week, the Biddles had all their possessions in boxes and trailers, and Xach found himself unpacking into their new home in Upper Darby, a suburb of Philadelphia.

Mr. Biddle was very aware of Xach's anger over having to leave his friends behind, but he had been given little choice in the matter. The company for which he worked was forced to downsize as a result of out-sourcing. As he was exceptionally good at his job, they offered him a choice of moving to Philadelphia and working at company headquarters or taking early retirement with a less than generous severance package. He chose the only option that allowed him to continue providing for his family. In a very short period of time and working with very limited funding, their real estate agent found them a nice house in Upper Darby, a suburb of Philadelphia, that would allow Mr. Biddle to work in the city while providing a more suburban lifestyle and education for his children.

Xach was very apprehensive on his first day at Barker Elementary. His mother smiled warmly and encouraged him to have a good day, but he knew she was struggling with their new surroundings just as much as he was. He put on as brave a face as he could muster. Despite the potential for ridicule, he allowed his mother to kiss him goodbye and hand him his lunch bag before exiting the car. He took a deep breath and walked past the different clusters of students toward the large glass doors at the school's entrance.

While this was not a city school by any stretch of the imagination, one could easily tell that some of the city was creeping into the neighboring suburbs. He was at once struck with the many differences between his old school and this new one. The biggest difference was the student body. A large percentage of the students were African-American and Hispanic, making *him* the minority. Two very large African-American guards in blue uniforms stood directly inside the doors. King Elementary had not needed guards, and the implication was extremely upsetting. As he walked through the door, his eyes darted from left to right, taking in the frightening aspects of this unfamiliar environment. He must have looked suspicious, because one of the guards stepped in front of him and motioned for him to stop.

"Open your bag, son," he said gruffly.

Xach did as he was told. The guard inspected the contents of his backpack and seemed satisfied that it contained no weapons.

"Place the bag on the floor. Spread your legs and arms, please."

Xach complied. He heard the students behind him chuckling and whispering to one another. His face flushed with embarrassment as the guard swept a wand over his torso, arms, and legs.

It was at this very moment, when Xach and the guard were completely distracted, that Bobby Brenner, one of the boys waiting behind Xach, slipped a snake into Xach's backpack that rested open on the floor beside him. Bobby melted back into the crowd to tell his friends about the joke he played on the new kid. They all giggled and watched Xach intently, waiting for the joke to pay off.

The wand made a few beeps, but nothing significant enough to warrant further search. The guard motioned for him to continue into the school. Xach grabbed his bag and zipped it quickly, failing to close the zipper entirely, as he moved past the guard and into the main hall.

Xach stopped the first teacher he saw to ask directions to Ms. Zipple's room.

"Excuse me, sir," Xach said politely. "Could you please direct me to Ms. Zipple's classroom? This is my first day, and I don't know where I'm supposed to go."

"Welcome to Barker Elementary," the young man said cheerfully. "I'm Mr. Brown. This is my first day here as well. I think I have a map of the school in my pocket. I'd be happy to help you find your way."

He patted his pants pockets and jacket pockets, feeling for the folded lump of paper that was his copy of the school map.

"I have a copy of the map right here," said Xach. He set his backpack on the floor, unzipped the front pouch, and withdrew the map. He handed it to Mr. Brown, who studied it to locate their position and their destination.

The snake chose to make its escape at this time. It wriggled out of Xach's bag and slithered toward the open space between Xach and Mr. Brown. Having an unnatural fear of snakes, Mr. Brown screamed the moment he saw it over the corner of the map. He threw the map into the air and leapt backward in an attempt to distance himself from the scaly creature. Unfortunately, he was standing beside a trashcan, which he summarily knocked over, falling head over heels into the pile of scattered rubbish.

Several girls screamed and ran from the scene, but most did not. A large group of students quickly gathered to laugh at Mr. Brown as he lay on the floor surrounded by trash. The snake glided across the floor in search of a hiding place, and chose the first place it could find – Mr. Brown's left pant leg. Mr. Brown let out a high pitched squeal and jumped around like a man on fire, beating his pants and screaming like a girl.

Luckily for Mr. Brown, the snake was just a garden snake and was not venomous; otherwise his attack on the serpent slithering around in his pants would have caused it to bite him. The snake retreated from Mr. Brown's pummelling fists, dropped from his pant leg, and slipped into the crowd of on-looking teachers and students in search of less threatening place to hide. The crowd parted like the Red Sea, allowing the creature free passage to less populated areas.

Attempting to regain control, Mr. Brown smoothed his jacket and tie and tucked his shirt neatly beneath his belt again. However, when he spoke, his voice betrayed his calm looking façade. In a high-pitched, breathy voice he told the crowd around him that he had everything under control and that they should go to their classrooms. He grabbed Xach roughly by the arm and walked him directly to the principal's office. Xach attempted to explain that the snake did not belong to him, but Mr. Brown ignored him.

Amidst all the confusion and commotion associated with Mr. Brown hauling Xachary through the crowd toward the principal's office, no one but Bobby's friends noticed the snake's true owner move from the crowd and capture the serpent. He gathered it into his hands and slipped it into the pocket of his jacket. He and his friends made their way to Ms. Zipple's classroom. Ms. Zipple smiled and greeted them as they entered the room. Bobby made his way toward the teacher's desk. Although the incident with Mr. Brown had been extremely amusing to him and his buddies, he knew there was still a great deal of fun to be had with his little pet. While Ms. Zipple greeted a loud group of girls entering the room, Bobby slid open the first desk drawer and dropped the snake inside. He quietly took a seat near the back of the classroom with his friends who were laughing heartily and smiling with giddy anticipation.

Meanwhile, Mr. Brown dragged Xachary into the waiting area of the main office. He directed Xach to sit on a small, uncomfortable chair outside the principal's office while he spoke with Mrs. Wilson, the principal's secretary. She was an older woman with silver hair and distinguished features who appeared to be in her sixties. She wore a red knit shawl over her white polyester dress. A pair of black rimmed spectacles hung from a gold chain around her neck. She spoke to Mr. Plether, the elementary school principal, through a small microphone box on her desk and then ushered Mr. Brown into the office when instructed to do so. Through the closed door, Xach heard Mr. Brown excitedly recount the horrors of the snake in his pants.

"The snake fell out of the boy's bag and attacked me! It...it tried to strike me, and I...I fell over a trashcan and it slid up my pants! **Up my pants!** I beat it away, but...but everyone was laughing and pointing...and this is **not** a good way to start my first day here at Barker, Mr. Plether. This...this totally undermines my authority. They were all laughing at me...who'll respect me now?"

"Mr. Brown," responded Mr. Plether in a calm, almost uninterested tone, "I understand that this has been upsetting for..."

"*Upsetting?* **Upsetting?!?** Of course it's upsetting! What will I do? How can I go to class covered in garbage…after they heard me scream, after they saw…"

"Mr. Brown," the principal interrupted forcefully. "You will simply go to the faculty room, clean yourself up, and pull yourself together. You have all year to change the students' impressions of you."

"Yes, but…but first impressions are…"

"Are easily forgotten, Mr. Brown. Now please, go clean yourself up and get a drink of water. You have a class full of students waiting to learn. I will deal with the hooligan who perpetrated this incident."

"But sir, I fell…I screamed…they laughed…"

"Mr. Brown," he sighed heavily, already bored with the conversation. "I assure you, this boy will wish he never set foot in this school today. Everyone will know what happens to children who mess with my teachers."

Xachary shifted uncomfortably in the tiny chair.

Realizing that Mr. Plether had uttered his final words on the subject, Mr. Brown bowed his head and left Mr. Plether's office to seek sanctuary in the teacher's lounge, where he hoped the other teachers might be more sympathetic to his plight. He did not even look at Xach as he brushed past him, mumbling under his breath. Mr. Plether appeared in the doorway. He was a short, stocky man about five feet tall. His face was ruddy, and he sported a large graying beard and mustache. He was bald except for a band of hair around the base of his skull that connected his left ear to his right ear and a few long strands combed over the top.

"Son," he said in a gruff voice. "Come into my office."

Xach slowly raised himself out of the chair and walked into the large, dark room. It reminded him of a cave. The ceiling was high and looked even higher because of Mr. Plether's short stature. Tall brown-stained wooden bookshelves lined both sides of the room from the door to the small window behind Mr. Plether's huge mahogany desk.

"Have a seat son," he said, motioning toward a large brown leather chair placed directly in front of the desk.

Xach did as he was told, perching himself on edge of the leather cushion, feeling very small and anxious. Mr. Plether walked around his desk, disappearing from view as he passed behind a pile of books and papers on the corner of his desk that were stacked higher than his diminutive frame. He reached his chair and sat down. From his seat, Xachary could only see the top of Mr. Plether's head; his disapproving eyes and bulbous nose were all Xach could see. The man's mouth was hidden beneath the desk's horizon. He stifled an involuntary giggle at the sight of the tiny man seated behind the gigantic desk. It reminded Xach of the old ladies he often saw driving around his neighborhood. They were too short to see over the steering wheels of their cars, their eyes just barely peering over the dashboard as they barrelled down the crowded suburban streets.

"What's your name, son?"

"Xachary Biddle, sir."

"And how old are you Mr. Biddle?"

"Ten years old."

"So you're old enough to know that a school is no place for a snake. You're old enough to know that scaring a teacher and students with said snake is going to get you in a great deal of trouble. What do you have to say for yourself, son?"

"The snake wasn't mine sir. I don't know where it came from."

"Mr. Brown said it slid out of *your* backpack. How did it get in your backpack if it wasn't yours to begin with?"

"I don't know sir. But I'm telling the truth. It wasn't my snake."

"Well, truth or not, the fact remains that it came from *your* bag. Therefore, you are responsible." Mr. Plether paused, as if waiting for Xachary to protest.

Xachary said nothing. It was clear that he would lose any argument he mounted, just as Mr. Brown had been forced to curtail his protests under Mr. Plether's insistence. He decided to keep quiet and hope that this unpleasant experience would end quickly, so that he could just get through the day, return home, and hide in his room.

Mr. Plether continued speaking. "So you have nothing else to say?"

"No sir. If I can't convince you that the snake wasn't mine, I see no reason to argue."

"Are you getting smart with me Mr. Biddle?" Mr. Plether said, raising his voice and standing up so that Xachary could see his entire red face.

"No, sir. I..."

"I can see we're going to have a problem, Mr. Biddle," Mr. Plether cut in. "Just sit here quietly and don't touch anything. I'll be back in a moment."

He moved from behind his desk, his face pinched in an angry stare. He moved past Xach and exited the room. Xach put his head in his hands.

I am in so much trouble, Xach thought. *It's my first day at this new school and I'm in more trouble than I've ever been...and it wasn't even my fault! Why did we have to move to this place? If we hadn't moved here, I would be sitting in Mrs. Walter's fifth grade class with all my friends. Instead I'm here, sitting in the principal's office waiting to hear how I'm going to be punished for something **I didn't even do**! Who's going to be friends with me now?*

Mr. Plether returned to the room, carrying a folder. He stood next to Xachary, leafing through the pages of the file. "So, Mr. Biddle...you are a new student in this school. And this is how you spend your first day here?"

"No sir, like I said..."

"Let me tell you something, son," Mr. Plether interrupted again. "I don't like trouble-makers."

Mr. Plether leaned in toward Xachary's face for emphasis. The unpleasant smells of peppermint and onions invaded Xach's nostrils. Mr. Plether's breath mints obviously weren't working.

"According to your file, you weren't a trouble maker at your other school," he said looking Xach over with a furrowed brow. "So why are you starting out so poorly here?"

Xach said nothing, figuring it was just another of Mr. Plether's rhetorical questions. He assumed he would just be interrupted again.

"Nothing to say for yourself? Well then, we'll make this quick. I'm assigning you a week's detention with Mr. Brown, starting tomorrow after school for half an hour each day. You will help Mr. Brown with whatever he asks. I will be checking with him every day to see if you have served your time and done what he asked. If I get *any* kind of negative report from him, your detention will be doubled. Any questions?"

"No, sir."

"Good. Now get to class. My secretary, Mrs. Wilson, will write you a pass. I hope I don't see you in my office again. If I do, I'll be contacting your parents."

Xachary stood up and started toward the door.

"Son," Mr. Plether continued, "welcome to Barker Elementary. I hope you turn things around."

Without turning around, Xachary mumbled, "Thanks. We'll see."

Before Mr. Plether could say anything else, Xach closed the door and walked over to Mrs. Wilson's desk. She smiled at Xach and handed him a slip of paper.

"Here's your pass, Xachary. Do you know where your class room is, dear?"

"No, ma'am. This is my first day. I was asking Mr. Brown where my classroom was when that snake scared him. But I don't know where it came from, honest!"

Mrs. Wilson leaned forward and whispered, "I know, Xachary." She smiled and stood up. "I'll show you to your classroom. Follow me."

As Xachary followed Mrs. Wilson through the halls, she talked to him about the school, pointing out certain rooms and mentioning teachers' names. Turning a corner they came to a room with the number 126 on the door. She stopped and smiled again.

"This is Ms. Zipple's room. She's a nice lady. I'm sure you will get along well with her."

"Thank you, Mrs. Wilson."

"You're very welcome Xachary. Being a new student is pretty tough. Stop in and see me anytime if you need anything. I'll do whatever I can to help you find your place."

"Thanks again."

"Don't mention it," she whispered, patting him on the shoulder. She turned and knocked on Ms. Zipple's door.

A tall, skinny woman with a pinched face and long black hair came to the door. An elegant silk black shawl of delicate lace flowers was draped across her shoulders and a sleeveless mint-green dress that ended above her knees. Her face was naturally soft and pretty, but sharpened because of the dark rouge on her cheeks and the bright red lipstick on her pursed lips.

Mrs. Wilson smiled and said, "Ms. Zipple, this is Xachary Biddle. He's a new student in your class. He's running a bit late."

"Ah, yes. He's the one who brought the snake to school."

"Well, I don't know about that," Mrs. Wilson said. "I just thought I'd show him around and bring him to class." She turned to Xachary and winked. "He's a very nice young man. I'm sure you'll have a wonderful year together."

"We'll see," Ms. Zipple said, looking down her nose. "Thank you, Mrs. Wilson. I'll show him to his seat."

"Have a good day, Xachary," Mrs. Wilson said, as Ms. Zipple led him into the room. Xach smiled and mouthed "thank you" again.

Instead of leading Xachary to a seat, Ms. Zipple led him to the front of the class. He stared out at the sea of unfamiliar faces. All of the students stared at him intently, their eyes assessing his worth by appraising his clothes, backpack, and school accessories.

This is so embarrassing, Xach thought. *Why can't she just let me sit down?*

"Class," Ms. Zipple said in a high nasally voice, "this is Xachary Biddle. He is a new student who will be joining our class. From where do you come to us, Xachary?"

"I...uh...used to live in Maine," Xachary replied quietly.

"Speak up, I can't hear you."

"Maine," Xach said louder.

"Ah, a New Englander," she said. "And why did your family move to the Philadelphia area?"

Xachary cleared his throat and responded, "My dad had to move here to keep his job. His company told him he had to move closer to the main office in Philadelphia, because they closed his office in Maine."

"Very interesting," Ms. Zipple said in a tone that suggested it was anything but. "Does anyone here have any questions for Xachary before we continue with the lesson?"

Xachary blushed bright red. *Is this woman insane? Doesn't she realize how terrifying this is? I just want to sit in the back of the classroom and wait for this horrible day to end. I don't want to tell my life story to a bunch of strangers.* He looked nervously around the room. . *Maybe I'll get lucky and no one will ask any questions.*

He was horrified to see several hands go up.

"Yes, Miranda. What is your question for Xachary?"

A small Asian girl with long black hair put her hand down and spoke. "How old are you?"

"Ten," Xach replied.

"Kevin, what is your question?" Ms. Zipple asked, addressing a chubby, blonde boy with glasses and freckles seated in the front of the room.

Kevin put down his hand and asked, "Um, where do you live?"

"My parents bought a house on Evergreen Terrace."

Ms. Zipple pointed and nodded at a tall, African - American boy in a bright orange jacket. He put down his hand and said, "Do you have any brothers or sisters?"

"Yes, I have a baby brother and an older sister."

Ms. Zipple, already bored with the Q&A said, "We'll take one more question. Bobby, what would you like to know?"

Bobby said in a loud clear voice, "Do you like snakes?"

The class erupted into boiling laughter. Xach even heard Ms. Zipple give a little snort of laughter.

"Bobby, that was not funny," she chided with a smirk. "Settle down everyone. Settle down. Okay, let's get back on track, shall we?" Ms. Zipple tapped Xachary on the shoulder and pointed to an empty desk on the right side of the room near the window. Xachary took his seat; his face blazed red, mortified with embarrassment. Ms. Zipple began writing something on the board about history. Xach took a notebook from his backpack and started taking notes, intensely focusing his anger and embarrassment into the scribbling of his pen.

"Before we greeted our new student, we were discussing the topics we will be studying this year to prepare you for middle school next year," she said as she wrote on the board. "We will be studying American history, beginning with the pilgrims." She turned to face the class. "What do you know about the pilgrims?"

A blonde girl in hot pink overalls with ponytails raised her hand.

"Yes, Cindy. What can you tell us about the pilgrims?"

"The pilgrims were people who came to America so they could worship without prosecution."

"*Per*secution, Cindy. They came to escape *per*secution. Very good!" She turned and began writing the word "persecution" on the board, but her piece of chalk broke in the downward stroke of the "t." Without missing a beat, she continued talking as she turned around and walked over to her desk to retrieve a new piece of chalk from one of her desk drawers. "The pilgrims came from Europe on a ship called the Mayflow-AAAAHHHHH!" She lurched backward from her desk, her scream echoing around the classroom.

The students looked at each other in surprise and panic, except Bobby and his friends who started laughing uncontrollably. Ms. Zipple tripped over the leg of a table along the front wall and fell to the floor. From behind the desk slithered the very same snake that caused Mr. Brown to fall in the trash and hop around like a clown. Some of the children in the front of the class screamed and jumped on top of their desks. Ms. Zipple grasped the edge of the table and pulled herself to a standing position. She told the class to settle down, but no one heard her over the girls' screaming. Determined to regain control of her class, she grabbed an umbrella from the closet and started hitting the defenseless snake. A boy wearing a jean jacket with a picture of a race car painted on the back, jumped up and grabbed the snake by the tail. He carried it quickly to the window, opened it, and dropped the snake into the bushes below. The girls stopped screaming and returned to their seats. Ms. Zipple returned the umbrella to the closet and quickly glanced at her reflection in the mirror on the inside of the closet.

Straightening her dress and fixing her hair, Ms. Zipple turned to the boy and said, "Thank you, Jeremy." She wheeled around on her heels to face Xachary. Her eyes blazed with anger. "Young man, do you remember the way to the principal's office?" Xachary nodded. "Then I suggest you go there immediately. I do not want you back in my classroom until your parents have been contacted."

The class erupted in laughter once again.

"But Ms. Zipple, I didn't do anything. That's not my snake," Xachary protested.

"Young man, I do not want to hear excuses. The whole school knows you were responsible for what happened to Mr. Brown this morning. I don't know what you were like at your old school, but it is apparent that you enjoy tormenting teachers. You are to report to the principal's office immediately!"

"But Ms. Zipple, how could I…"

"Mr. Biddle, I am about to lose my temper," she said, her voice warbled higher in decibel and pitch. "Report to the principal's office *immediately*, or I will call for an escort."

Realizing he was fighting yet another losing battle, Xachary picked up his backpack and notebook and headed toward the door. His fellow students laughed and whispered to one another as he walked past them. The only one who wasn't talking was Jeremy, the boy who had rescued the snake from Ms. Zipple and her umbrella. He smiled at Xach and nodded knowingly toward Bobby, who was laughing so hard he was holding his sides from the pain. Xach exited the room, and Ms. Zipple closed the door behind him. He heard her trying to regain control of her class, but she wasn't having much success. Over the quieting laughter, he heard her pick up the phone, dial Mr. Plether's extension, and tell him to expect Xachary's arrival for another snake incident.

Xachary headed slowly down the hall toward the principal's office, his head hung low. *I've already been assigned a week of detention for scaring Mr. Brown. What am I gonna get for scaring Ms. Zipple? It just isn't fair! Why can't she see that it couldn't have been me? I didn't even know which room was hers, and even if I did, I was sitting in Mr. Plether's office the whole time! How could I have put that snake in her desk? From the way that kid, Bobby, was laughing at Ms. Zipple, it's gotta be his snake. He must have been the one who put the snake in my backpack this morning. Why would he do that to me? I don't even know him! What did I do to him to deserve this?*

He entered the office through the double doors. Mrs. Wilson looked up from her desk to greet him.

"Xachary, what a pleasant surprise! What can I help you with?" she asked.

Before he could answer, Mr. Plether stormed out of his office.

"Mr. Biddle! Get in my office at once!" he yelled.

Xachary hung his head, sighed, and walked into Mr. Plether's office for the second time in less than two hours. He expected to be read the riot act for being back so soon. He took a seat in the leather chair and awaited his doom. He waited…and waited…and waited some more. Mr. Plether did not enter the room. Xach directed his attention to the doorway through which he could hear Mrs. Wilson and Mr. Plether talking. He couldn't catch every word, but the gist of their conversation concerned the snake in Ms. Zipple's desk. After what seemed like an eternity, Mr. Plether entered his office followed by Mrs. Wilson.

Mr. Plether began. "I understand that there was a snake in Ms. Zipple's desk. Do you have any idea how it got there?"

Xach looked at Mrs. Wilson who smiled encouragingly. He decided to try telling the truth, even though he figured neither would believe him.

"No, sir. I don't know how the snake got into her desk."

This time Mrs. Wilson spoke. "The snake isn't yours, is it?"

"No, ma'am. It isn't. I believe I might know who…"

"We're not interested in heresay," Mr. Plether interrupted. "Just answer the question."

Mrs. Wilson continued. "Did the snake come out from under Ms. Zipple's desk or did it come out of her drawer?"

"It came out of her top drawer when she opened it to get a piece of chalk. You can ask her. She'll tell you which drawer it came out of."

Mrs. Wilson addressed Mr. Plether. "You see, Mr. Plether, the snake was in the top drawer. There is no way the snake could have gotten into that drawer unless someone put it there. Snakes can't climb up desks and open drawers. Mr. Brown said he escorted Mr. Biddle directly to your office after the snake attacked him. Therefore, he could not have taken the snake to Ms. Zipple's room and placed it in her desk. He never left the sight of Mr. Brown, Ms. Zipple, you, or me. Furthermore, he didn't even know where Ms. Zipple's room was until I escorted him earlier this morning. Therefore, the snake must belong to someone else. This person must have placed the snake in poor Xachary's bag as a prank. Then after it attacked Mr. Brown, he or she must have hidden it in Ms. Zipple's desk. I tell you, this poor boy is just a victim of a heinous prank and should not be held responsible." She turned to face Xachary with a huge grin on her face.

Mr. Plether was silent for a moment, trying to wrap his mind around the brilliant deductions of Mrs. Wilson. Apparently realizing the validity of her statements, his face turned a deep crimson. He looked like he was about to pop. He wanted to yell but realized this would be inappropriate, because he would be yelling at the wrong person.

Finally he spoke in the most controlled voice he could muster. "Well, um, Mr. Biddle, it would *appear* that Mrs. Wilson…" he paused and exhaled loudly "…is correct. Please accept, um, my apology." He hung his head a little as he said this, embarrassed that he had to concede to Mrs. Wilson. He adopted the demeanor of a scolded puppy, and his uncomfortableness with this fact was palpable.

"Yes, sir. Thank you, sir," Xachary said with a huge smile on his face. He hoped this meant that he would not have to serve the detention he was assigned earlier in the day and that his parents would not be called, as Mr. Plether had threatened during their earlier encounter.

Seeming to read Xachary's mind, Mrs. Wilson asked, "I suppose this means that Mr. Biddle will *not* have to serve that detention you assigned him this morning? Is that correct, Mr. Plether?"

In an almost inaudible whisper, Mr. Plether replied, "No, I suppose not."

"Well then, Mr. Biddle, I guess this whole thing is straightened out," she said with another big smile. "I'll take you back to Ms. Zipple's classroom and explain what happened. Mr. Plether, perhaps you should try finding out who the snake actually belongs to."

Mr. Plether mumbled something and retreated to his office to lick his wounds.

"Thanks for your help," Xach said. "That was amazing!"

Mrs. Wilson winked at Xach. "Well my dear, Mr. Plether might hold the "title" of principal, but I have a great deal of power as well!"

Mrs. Wilson returned with him to Ms. Zipple's classroom and explained to her that Xachary was not responsible for what happened with the snake. She assured her that Mr. Plether would find the party responsible for this incident and deal with them appropriately. Xachary noticed that Mrs. Wilson looked directly at Bobby when she spoke of the "party responsible for this incident." She told Ms. Zipple to allow Xachary back into her classroom. With a frown and a stern look, she reluctantly allowed Xach to return to his seat.

Even though Mrs. Wilson cleared Xach's name, many still believed him to be the culprit behind "the snake incident" – most importantly, Ms. Zipple. From that day forth, Ms. Zipple "had it in for him." She always called on Xachary to answer the most difficult questions, so she could correct him when he made an error. She frequently requested that he explain the hardest homework problems on the chalkboard. She had him read aloud, and she was very quick to correct even the smallest mistake.

****

The events of his horrid first day and the subsequent trials in Ms. Zipple's class flooded his mind once again as he trudged toward the looming darkness of the blackboard. He had grown so accustomed to the snickering of his classmates, that he hardly noticed their teasing any longer. Xachary's parents did everything they could to correct these injustices, but they met with little success. His parents were very involved and concerned, but the myriad of parent-teacher conferences did nothing to change Ms. Zipple's opinion of him. He had no real proof that she was targeting him, and so things continued as they always had. Today was just another example of this prejudice.

"While we wait for Xachary to reach the board and show us his answer to question three," Ms. Zipple said to the class, "I want you all to work on the sample problem in the margin of your textbook."

Question number three gave Xach a great deal of trouble the night before. He worked on it for over twenty minutes and came up with two different answers. He wasn't sure if either of them was right, and he wasn't sure what he should put on the board. He half-wished another snake would come out of Ms. Zipple's drawer or some other catastrophe would occur that would interrupt class and keep him from having to complete his problem on the board.

And I'd probably get blamed for it, Xach thought darkly. *Best to just get it over with and do my best.*

He started to copy the problem from his paper onto the board when the chalk he was holding inexplicably began to shake. He tried to write the number 5, but the chalk was shaking so much it resembled a backwards 7. He looked around to see if anyone had noticed, and then he realized what was happening. It wasn't just his chalk that was vibrating; it was *everything*! The potted plant hanging from the ceiling bounced up and down on its hook. Books slid off their shelves and onto the floor. Ms. Zipple's nameplate rattled off her desk and fell to the floor with a clang. Then it got worse.

The hanging plant bounced off its hook and landed upside down on Ms. Zipple's head. For a moment before she fell to the floor dazed, she looked like a strange version of Carmen Miranda, with ferns and ivy sprouting from the top of her head. She collapsed forward, hitting her face on the floor. With her head under the spilled contents of the flowerpot and her butt in the air, she resembled an ostrich with its head buried in the ground.

The shaking of the floor caused the students' desks to bounce and slide across the floor in different directions, eliciting a volley of screams from the girls. They ricocheted off one another as their classroom turned into a nightmarish bumper car ride. Xachary stood as still as possible, watching the chaos that conveniently saved him from question number three.

Let's see her pin this one on me, he chuckled to himself, as the floor lurched to upward, cracking the tiles beneath his feet and sending him stumbling to the right.

The lights flickered like a strobe light. Ceiling tiles jostled from their holders and fell onto the jumble of students and desks that amassed in the center of the room. Most of the students freed themselves from overturned desks, brushed off pieces of ceiling tile, and ran from the room into the hallway. Children screamed in the halls, and teachers barked orders above the din in a vain attempt at maintaining control.

As the world shook and broke apart around him, Xach managed to recall a television show he had seen about earthquakes on the Discovery Channel and remembered that doorways were the safest places to be during an earthquake. The closest doorway to him was the one that led to Ms. Zipple's closet. He took a wobbly step toward the closet, as the chalkboard disengaged itself from the wall and fell to floor with a loud crash. It split down the middle. One part fell against Ms. Zipple's desk and shattered. The other part leaned toward Xach. He leapt toward the closet door as it slammed to the floor, missing him by mere inches and kicking up a cloud of dust and debris. He grasped the doorknob and turned. It was locked.

Of course, Xach thought. *It's always locked.*

Ever since "the snake incident," Ms. Zipple had taken to locking everything to avoid another fright from some unknown creature lurking amongst her things.

Jennifer ran screaming from the room and bumped into him, knocking him off balance. He maintained his grip on the doorknob, but the muscles in his shoulder screamed as he lost his footing and fell to the floor. As he fell, the handle on the closet door mysteriously turned, and the door swung open. Xach released the knob and slid into the doorway, feeling a little safer. In the flickering light, he surveyed the destruction that had occurred in the classroom. The blackboard lay in pieces on the floor. The papers, books, and other objects formerly on Ms. Zipple's desk were strewn across the floor next to her unconscious body. John Quinn was hiding under Ms. Zipple's desk, while the other students who hadn't run from the room cowered under a large wooden table in the back corner of the room. Books, desks, and broken ceiling tiles lay in various piles around the room, and jagged cracks zig-zagged through the walls and floor. Most of the blinds covering the shattered and cracked windows had fallen to the floor or hung twisted and tangled from the wall.

The vibrations in the floor quickly dissipated, but Xachary remained braced in the doorway to the closet. He was so intently focused on the destruction in his classroom that he failed to notice movement from within the dark closet behind him. A blood-covered hand emerged from the darkness and grasped his ankle tightly. Before his mind could register what was happening, he was on his stomach being pulled into the closet. Instinct took over as he twisted his leg and ankle free of the hand and kicked away from its grasp. He felt his foot hit something solid. He rolled over in time to see the bloody hand retreat into the darkness of the closet. He pushed himself back from the doorway and jumped up to face his attacker. An arm shot out of the darkness and grabbed his ankle again. It pulled so roughly and with such strength that Xach pitched backward, lost his balance, and crashed to the floor on his back. The shock and pain of hitting the floor temporarily dazed him. He frantically grabbed for anything onto which he could hold, but the only thing he could reach was the closet door, which began to swing closed as the hand pulled him into the dark recesses of the closet. He let go of the door, just before it slammed shut on his fingers. The darkness swallowed him as the hand moved up his leg toward his throat.

Chapter Two

Xachary felt the hand release its grip on his ankle and climb its way toward his stomach. He tried to scream, but the noise stuck in his throat. He tried to move, but he was paralyzed by fear. He lay there silent and rigid as the hand moved closer and closer toward his face. Then a second hand grabbed a hold of his shirt and pulled him into a sitting position, so that he was facing his unseen attacker.

"Don't be frightened, child," said a voice from the darkness. "I will not harm you." The voice sounded like it belonged to a male, but it was weak and strained.

Xachary found his voice and stammered, "Wh-wh-who are you?" He strained his eyes to see the man in the darkness, but he could not see a thing. "I c-can't see you."

"Let me fix that," whispered the voice.

Xach heard some rustling in the dark, and then a faint green light began to glow in front of him. As the light grew stronger and his eyes adjusted to the darkness, he could make out the shape of a man crouched in the corner. The man held the green light in his hands.

"Who are you?" Xach asked.

"My n-name is…Gerald M-M-Milton, nephew…of the great…and t-t-terrible…C-Count Milton," responded the man in a hushed, breathy tone.

"Who is Count Milton?"

"I haven't…m-m-much time, ch-child," the man continued, as if he hadn't heard Xach's question. "I am injured. C-c-can you help me? Is this place…safe?"

"What, the school? Safe from what?"

"I must…find s-s-someplace…to h-h-hide."

"You *are* hiding. This is a closet. No one can see or hear you, except me."

"No…I need to g-get…as far away…from here as p-p-possible. He m-may…have f-followed me."

The man collapsed forward into Xach's lap, unable to maintain consciousness. He dropped the green light. Xach scrambled backward, kicking the man from his lap. He slid backward until he was pressed firmly against the closet door.

The man slumped to the floor beside him and remained motionless. Xach tapped the man's shoulder cautiously with his shoe, but he did not move.

"M-mister, are you okay? Mister?"

When the man failed to respond, Xach began to feel a bit more curious than frightened. He picked up the light and examined it. It seemed to radiate heat. It was some sort of key with a green light on the handle. He held it close to the man's face, so that he could get a better look at him. The man looked to be close to his father's age – somewhere between thirty and forty Xach guessed. His face was dirty and thin. He had dark circles under his eyes, and his hair was a dirty, ratty mess. Upon closer inspection, Xach could see that the man was wearing a burlap sack as clothing.

Xach stood up and turned to leave the closet, when he realized the floor had stopped rumbling. The earthquake had ceased. He glanced down at the man on the floor. *This guy is obviously crazed or possibly dangerous,* Xach told himself. *It would be best to get as far away from him as possible.* Without realizing it, he slipped the key-thing in his pocket and opened the door. The classroom was deserted, except for Ms. Zipple who still lay unconscious on the floor. He heard a lot of voices in various levels of distress coming from the hallway. He walked to the door and looked to see if an adult was nearby who might be able to help his teacher. Through the shattered doors at the end of the hall, Xach saw a large group of students standing on the lawn in front of the school. The teachers had corralled the frightened students onto the lawn and were attempting to take a roll call. He saw Mr. Brown coming around the corner, heading toward Ms. Zipple's room.

Xach ran to Mr. Brown and said, "Come quick. Ms. Zipple is hurt!"

With a bit of trepidation, Mr. Brown followed Xachary into the room. His eyes darted suspiciously around the room and back at Xach. Ever since "the snake incident" he had made a concerted effort to avoid Xach. He did not trust him, and he was especially angry that Xachary had not been punished for the snake. Despite the fact that Xachary had been cleared of all suspicion by the principal, he nonetheless remained wary of him. He saw Ms. Zipple and rushed to her side. He knelt down next to her and felt her neck for a pulse.

"What happened?" he asked.

"During the earthquake, the plant fell off its hook and hit her on the head. She fell down and didn't get up," Xach explained.

"Go find another teacher and tell them to call an ambulance. I'll stay here with her," said Mr. Brown.

He brushed the dirt away from Ms. Zipple's head and removed the plant from her hair. Xach left the room and went toward the office. Along his way, he saw that the earthquake had done a great deal of damage to the school. Some of the lockers were twisted and hung open. Trashcans had fallen over, spilling refuse about the floors. A few of the light fixtures hung from wires in the ceiling, and several large cracks zig-zagged down the walls. Floor tiles buckled and cracked. The glass doors to the main office were completely shattered. He pushed the door open, carefully dodging pieces of falling glass and the shards on the floor.

Mrs. Wilson knelt on the floor, collecting the objects that had fallen off her desk. She turned toward the door when she heard the tinkling sound of glass falling on the floor.

"Oh, be careful, dear," she said. "Don't cut yourself."

"I'm all right, Mrs. Wilson, but Ms. Zipple is hurt. Mr. Brown told me to find someone who could call for an ambulance."

"Oh my! What happened to her?"

"A plant fell on her head and knocked her out."

"My goodness! How awful! Stay here, I may need your help to answer some questions."

She picked up the phone and dialed 9-1-1.

"Yes. This is Mrs. Wilson at Barker Elementary School. We need an ambulance sent over right away. A teacher has been injured in the earthquake." A strange look came across Mrs. Wilson's face as she listened to the person on the other end of the line. "Yes. I said 'earthquake.' We just experienced a severe earthquake at Barker Elementary School. Certainly you must have felt it!" Again she looked perplexed and concerned. "Well, nonetheless, we have at least one injured person here, and we need an ambulance and some assistance. …I don't know; hold on?" She turned to Xach and asked, "Is Ms. Zipple conscious?"

"I don't believe so. She wasn't moving when I left."

"No, she is not conscious," she said into the phone. "Yes, I understand. Yes, that is the correct address. Okay. I will. Yes. Thank-you." She hung up the phone, but she still looked confused. "The gentleman with emergency response said they didn't experience an earthquake. How odd?" She paused, thinking about the implications of this information. She shook her head. "Oh well. We'll worry about that later. For now I need you to go tell Mr. Brown that an ambulance is on its way."

"Ok."

"Thank you, dear."

Xach returned to Mr. Brown and relayed the message. Mr. Brown thanked him and told him to join the students outside on the lawn.

Xach paused. *Should I tell him about the guy in the closet? What if Mr. Brown doesn't believe me? On the other hand, the guy was hurt badly…what if he dies? I don't want to be responsib…*

"Xachary," Mr. Brown said gruffly, "I told you to go outside with the other students. Get going!"

"Um, sorry Mr. Brown, but…"

"Yes?" he asked impatiently.

"I don't know how to say this so you'll believe me, but there is a guy hiding in the closet who is really hurt."

"What are you talking about? This is no time to be making up stories. Your teacher is seriously injured, and you should be outside with the others."

"I'm not making it up, sir. I hid in the closet during the earthquake, and this guy was hiding in there too."

"That's enough! Go join the students on the lawn and stop lying to me."

"I'm not lying. I'll show you!" Xach walked over to the closet and opened the door. The light from the windows revealed…***nothing***! The closet was empty!

Where did he go? Xach thought. *Did I imagine the whole thing?*

"Listen, son, I am sure you were scared by the earthquake…or maybe you're just a little too *stimulated*, but I have *no* time for your stories or games right now. Now *please* join the students on the lawn and allow me to care for your teacher."

"But…"

"No 'buts,' just go!"

Xachary walked into the closet to get a better look. On the floor was a smudged pool of blood, as if someone had dragged a bloody body across the floor. The bloodstain wouldn't be enough to convince Mr. Brown that the man had been there, but it was enough to convince Xach that he wasn't crazy. He hadn't imagined it.

He turned to leave the room, and something caught his eye. A red stain streaked across the windowsill of one of the broken windows. It was a bloodstain! *The man must have jumped out the window after I left to get Ms. Zipple some help. I guess he wasn't dead.*

Xachary left the room and headed toward the main doors leading to the front lawn. He put his hands in his pockets and realized that he still had the man's key-thing. He pulled it out of his pocket and examined it. It looked like a gold key without the teeth on the end. The handle had a green stone in it. *That must have been what was glowing in the closet,* Xach thought as he put it back in his pocket and walked out into the afternoon sunlight. *I wonder what it is? What made it glow in the dark? I bet it's valuable? What if the man comes looking for me to reclaim it?*

As if in answer to his question, Xach saw someone out of the corner of his eye limp behind a blue car in the parking lot on the left side of the school. He didn't get a good look at him, but the dirty, tangled hair and red stained burlap were enough evidence to convince him – it was the man from the closet. He watched the parking lot intently, trying to determine what direction the man would go, but the man did not move. The tuft of tangled hair remained immobile just above the roof of the car. Xach moved a little deeper into the crowd of children and teachers, occasionally glancing back at the parking lot to see if the man had moved. He didn't. The man remained motionless – his staring, unblinking eyes trained intensely on Xach!

Chapter Three

Jeremy Jones searched the crowd of anxious students for his best friend. He couldn't find Xach anywhere. He weaved in and out of the chattering clusters of frightened students, wondering why he couldn't find him. He was so preoccupied with his search that as he craned his neck to see over the crowd he didn't look where he was going and bumped into Bobby Brenner.

"Watch where you're going, Germ!" Bobby said, shoving Jeremy in the shoulder.

Jeremy shuffled backward and likely would have fallen if he hadn't bumped against someone else.

"S-sorry, Bobby. I wasn't watching where I was going."

"Obviously, dweeb."

Normally, Jeremy did everything he could to avoid Bobby or engage him in conversation, but he was worried about Xach. Without really thinking, he blurted out, "H-have you seen Xach?"

"No. Did you lose your boyfriend?"

Bobby's friends erupted into waves of laughter. Jeremy turned bright red and looked away.

"Don't cry, sugarpuff," Bobby said effeminately, playing it up in front of his friends. "Maybe Xachy found himself another guy?"

Jeremy knew it was pointless to even respond. He learned a long time ago that any response would only add fuel to Bobby's fire. He ground his teeth, turned, and walked back into the crowd.

"Wipe those tears away," Bobby yelled after him. "You'll find someone else...maybe."

Bobby and his friend's laughter felt like fire on the back of his ears, but Jeremy did not look back or even acknowledge him. He found it best to ignore him whenever possible. More often than not, Xach and Jeremy were together when Bobby decided to act out, making his ignorance a little easier to tolerate. It helped having a kindred spirit around in times of torment, and this is perhaps the main reason Jeremy befriended

Xach in the first place. Jeremy was the only student in the class who believed Xach's innocence in "the snake incident," largely due to his suspicion that the snake belonged to Bobby. He saw a commonality in Xach and offered his friendship during recess that first day; Xach was quick to accept. They bonded quickly and were rarely apart, both in and out of school. He wasn't sure how they had been separated during the quake. It was all a big blur of screams and broken objects. He was worried.

As he wove through the crowd, a flash of light temporarily blinded him and drew his attention to the front of the school. The door opened, reflecting the early afternoon sun directly into his eyes. When his vision returned, he saw Xach emerge from the school. He sighed with relief and pushed his way through the crowd until he was standing behind him.

"Dude, where have you been? I've been looking all over for you. I bumped into Bob..."

Xach did not turn to greet his friend. Instead he stood very still, staring into the parking lot. It was almost like he didn't even realize Jeremy was there.

"Xach?" Jeremy grabbed his shoulder and shook him a little. Xach remained still and focused. "What's wrong with you? Are you ok?"

No answer.

"What are you staring at?" Jeremy asked quietly.

Without breaking his stare on the man in the parking lot, Xach replied, "You're not going to believe me if I told you."

"Try me."

"I'm being followed. I mean *watched*."

"By who?"

"By that guy in the parking lot." He extended his arm and pointed to the blue car and the man crouched behind it.

Jeremy turned to see where Xach was pointing. "I don't see anyone."

"Behind that blue car. His hair is sticking up a little over the roof."

Jeremy looked more closely. He saw the messy hair and followed it down to the dirty, staring face behind the window of the car. They made eye contact, but the man remained immobile, fixed on Xach and his location.

"Who is he?"

"I don't know."

"So, why is he following you?"

"That's the part you won't believe. During the earthquake, I tried to hide in the closet, because a doorway is the safest place to be during an earthquake. Instead of being locked like always, it was open. When I opened it, that guy pulled me inside."

"That guy hiding behind the car over there was in Ms. Zipple's closet? How'd he get in there? What was he doing in there? That makes no sense."

"I told you you wouldn't believe me."

"I didn't say I didn't *believe* you. I just said it didn't make sense. Tell me what happened?"

"He pulled me in the closet and told me not to be afraid of him. He said that he was being chased by someone and that he was hurt. Then he passed out. He had this thing in his hand that glowed in the dark, and I took it from him when he passed out. I didn't mean to keep it, but I put it in my pocket by accident when I left the closet. When I opened the door, I saw Ms. Zipple was unconscious on the floor, so I got Mr. Brown to help me. I told Mr. Brown about the guy in the closet, but when I opened the closet door, the guy was gone. There was blood on the floor and the windowsill, so I'm guessing he jumped out the window when I left the room to get Mr. Brown. That is why I didn't come outside when everyone else did. I had to go to the office to tell someone to get an ambulance, because Ms. Zipple was hurt. And now this guy is following me, because I think he wants the thing I took from him."

"Ok. Let's assume for a moment that I believe you. What did you steal from him?"

Xach reached into his pocket and withdrew the object. Without breaking eye contact with the man in the parking lot he handed the object to Jeremy. Xach saw the man's eyes widen at the sight of the object.

"What is it?"

"I don't know. It looks like a key, but it doesn't have any of those key-thingies on the end of it."

"You mean teeth?"

"Yeah, it doesn't have teeth – the things that open the lock mechanism of a door. And it's got this jewel on it that looks pretty expensive. I'm not sure, but I think that's what was glowing in the closet. It wasn't very bright, but it was bright enough to see the guy's face and clothes in the dark. It was sort of like a glo-stick."

Xach looked at Jeremy for the first time since the beginning of their conversation, and he realized that Jeremy was hurt. He had a small cut on his forehead that was bleeding. The cut didn't appear to be deep, but it had bled enough to make two red lines down the side of his face.

"Oh my God! You're bleeding! Are you all right?"

"Huh?" said Jeremy. He touched his forehead and felt the sticky, half-dried blood. "I guess I was cut by one of the falling ceiling tiles. I didn't even know I was bleeding." He handed the object back to Xach and pulled a tissue out of his pocket to wipe his forehead.

"You have blood all down the side of your face, too," Xach added.

After Jeremy was cleaned up, as best as a dry tissue would allow, Xach turned his attention back to the object.

"I'd return it to the guy, but I don't know if he's dangerous or not. He didn't hurt me in the closet. He seemed really weak and injured. He passed out from the pain. I'd rather give it back to him with someone else around so that if he tries to do something then I've got backup…just to be on the safe side."

Xach put the object back in his pocket and looked back at the parking lot. The man was gone. Jeremy noticed as well.

"Where did he go?" Jeremy asked. "I don't see him."

"I don't know. I don't see him either, but I'm sure he didn't go far. I think he wants that thing back."

"What are you going to do?"

"I don't know. I'm not sure I should tell anyone else about this – especially my parents or any other grown-ups.

They probably wouldn't believe me, and if they did, they'd be freaking out that some guy was hiding in the teacher's closet."

"You're probably right."

"For now, I just want to get home and hide this thing. If I don't have the object on me, then he can't hurt me even if he does find me. If he hurts me, then he'll never find it. As long as I'm around other people, I should be safe. Besides, he doesn't know who I am or where I live, so once I leave here I don't think he'll be able to find me."

The sounds of police sirens, fire engines, and ambulances filled the air. The parking lot filled up with cars, vans, and emergency vehicles. News crews unloaded their equipment and began taking pictures and interviewing students and teachers. Parents jumped out of vehicles and ran around trying to locate their children. Things were degenerating into chaos. The group of students broke up as parents pulled their children toward their cars.

"I hope Ms. Zipple is okay," said Jeremy when he heard the sirens. "I saw the plant fall on her head, but then someone knocked me out of my chair. When I got up, she was on the floor. Then the ceiling tiles started falling on my head, so I just ran outside. I didn't even look to see what happened to anyone else."

"I don't blame you. If I hadn't been pulled into the closet, I might have run out with you."

A microphone appeared between the two boys, and an excited reporter with a camera crew in tow started squawking questions at them.

"Excuse me boys, could I have a word with you?" Without waiting for an answer or any indication that they would be open to being interviewed, he continued, "What happened here today?"

Xach didn't want to be bothered. He was too busy scanning the crowd and the parking lot for the mysterious man. He tried his best to ignore the reporter, but the reporter kept sticking the microphone in his face.

"What was it like being in the school during the earthquake?" He paused, breathing heavily. Xach and Jeremy just looked at him, saying nothing, so the reporter started talking again. "This is John Heinz reporting live from Barker Elementary School where a strangely localized earthquake has just rocked the school. I am standing here with two of the survivors. One of them has obviously been injured. What are your names, and where do you live?" He thrust the microphone in their faces again. They responded with their names and hometowns. Sensing that Jeremy might be a little more apt to talk to him, the reporter began directing most of his questions toward him.

"What was it like in there, Jeremy?"

"It was like an earthquake."

"What happened exactly?"

"The floor shook. The chalkboard fell off the wall. The windows and walls cracked. Books fell off the shelf. You know, the kind of stuff that happens in an earthquake."

Dissatisfied with Jeremy's comments, he directed his next question to Xach.

"Xach, how did you get out of the school?"

"I walked out those two doors," he said, pointing to the main doors.

The reporter put his hand to his throat and made a sawing motion, signifying that the camera man should stop rolling tape.

"Look boys, this is television. You want to be on TV right? Of course you do. All young boys want to be on TV. I'm trying to get some exciting stories here, and yours are, well…boring. Is there anything exciting you can tell me?" Pointing at Jeremy, he continued. "You were hurt. What happened to you? Did you see anyone else get hurt?"

"I wasn't hurt that bad. A ceiling tile fell on my head," said Jeremy, "but my teacher got hit on the head."

"Great!" he said, motioning for the camera to start rolling tape again. His enthusiasm over another person's misfortune was a bit upsetting. He continued with his report. "What happened to you in there, Jeremy? I see you have a cut on your forehead."

"When the earthquake hit, the ceiling tiles started to fall down. One hit me on the head and must have cut me. I didn't even know I was cut until I got outside."

"Was anyone else hurt during the earthquake?"

"Yes, my teacher was hurt."

"My goodness!" said the reporter with fake surprise. "That must have been scary for you?" he asked with a condescending tone, as if he were talking to a five-year old. Jeremy scowled at him, but the reporter just kept on going. "And is your teacher all right?"

"I don't know," Jeremy said curtly. "They're wheeling her out to the ambulance right now."

Jeremy pointed towards the parking lot, where Ms. Zipple was being wheeled toward the ambulance on a gurney. She had padding around her entire head and much of her face seemed to be bandaged. She appeared to be awake and was moving her legs.

The reporter spun around and left as quickly as he had appeared. The boys watched him dash up to Ms. Zipple and shove the microphone in her face. It was obvious that she was struggling to speak. The reporter followed her all the way to the ambulance despite the EMT's attempts to shoo him away.

"That guy was a jerk!" Jeremy said emphatically.

"Yeah, I thought he'd never leave. Now that he's gone, I have to try to find out where that guy went."

"JEREMY JONES!" screamed a female voice from within the throng of people outside the school. "JEREMY JONES, WHERE ARE YOU?"

"Oh God, it's my mother," groaned Jeremy. "I'M RIGHT HERE, MOM!" he yelled.

A skinny woman with a large nose and teeth that stuck out like a rabbit's burst from the crowd. She had her hair in a bun on top of her head and wore an apron over a bright yellow dress. Her face was smudged with flour. Apparently she was baking when she heard the news about the earthquake and did not stop to clean up before rushing to the school. She ran to Jeremy and threw her arms around him, squeezing him so hard his eyes seemed to bulge.

"Oh thank God, you're all right! I was so worried!" She started crying, and the tears made streaks in the flour on her cheeks. She kissed and hugged him. The more he tried to release himself from her grasp, the harder she squeezed him.

When she finally released him, she noticed the cut on his face and the screaming began anew.

"OH MY GOD! YOU'RE HURT!" she cried, touching his forehead. "What happened? Are you dizzy? Does it hurt?" She pulled a tissue from a pocket in her apron and pressed it against his forehead.

"Ow!" said Jeremy, trying to pull away. "That hurt."

"Oh, my baby is hurt!" she continued. "Keep applying pressure so you don't bleed to death!" She began hugging and kissing him again. "It'll be okay. Don't panic."

"Mom. It's okay. Mom, let go," Jeremy said, trying to maintain his calm, even though he was embarrassed beyond belief. She seemed to ignore him and continued fawning over him to the point that he yelled, "MOM, LET ME GO!"

She released him and stepped a few inches back. She looked as though Jeremy had slapped her across the face and spit on her. Xach thought she looked like she was going to cry.

"See, Mom, I'm fine. I'm sorry for shouting, but there is no need to get so excited or upset."

He looked around nervously to see if anyone had seen his mother's overly affectionate greeting and concern. Several of the girls nearby were smiling and whispering to each other. Jeremy blushed and groaned.

"Well, I'm sorry if I embarrassed you darling, but I was worried." She couldn't stop touching his face. "I heard on the radio that the school nearly fell down from an earthquake. I rushed right over here to make sure you were all right."

"I'm fine," said Jeremy, pulling a few more inches away from her. "I just need a band-aid. That's all. How's our house?"

"Our house? Why? Our house is fine. The reporters said that the school was the only building that was affected." She paused a moment, looking perplexed. "I guess that is a little weird, huh? Well, let's go. We need to get you cleaned up and bandaged. Plus, I have baking to finish."

Jeremy rolled his eyes.

"Good-bye Xach. See ya tomorrow. Good luck with that *thing*."

"Thanks! See ya later," said Xach, waving his arm. "I'll call you later!"

"Okay!" Jeremy shouted over his shoulder, as his mother pulled him toward the car.

Xach looked around, hoping to catch a glimpse of the man from the closet, but there were just too many people. *He could be anywhere*, he thought. *He's probably getting help from the doctors for that injury or getting as far away from this commotion as possible.* He leaned against a tree, watching the events in front of him. *Mom will probably be here soon. I bet she's as freaked out as Mrs. Jones was.* Xach smiled, remembering the sight of Jeremy's mother with the tear stripes in the flour on her face. *At least I won't have to walk home alone if...*

A hand slipped over Xach's mouth, and another gripped his arm. In a flash he found himself being pulled behind the tree and dragged into a large flowering bush on the edge of the park that was next to the school. With all of the commotion, no one noticed.

Chapter Four

Xach struggled against his attacker, but the grip on his arm and mouth were too strong. Terror seized him, as he was dragged into the bushes. Although he could not yet see his attacker, he figured it was the man from the closet. This didn't make him any more comfortable with the situation. The man hadn't hurt him upon their first meeting, but Xach felt he might be a little less cordial since he had stolen the key-thing from him. The branches of the bush scratched his face and arms, as he was pulled into a small clear area between bushes. Xach kicked his legs and squirmed, but all he managed to do was bang his leg on a rock and rub dirt and leaves under his pants and shirt. The only option he could think of was to bite his attacker's hand and hope he released him long enough to scream for help. He pushed forward against the man's hand and tried to open his mouth enough to get a finger or two between his teeth. He bit down hard. He could feel the man's arm tense against his ear as if in pain, but he did not remove his hand.

Once hidden from the view of everyone in the park and the schoolyard, the man attempted a different restraint. He rolled Xach onto his chest and straddled Xach's torso, pinning his arms to his side. To do so, he had to remove his hand from Xach's mouth. Xach screamed for help, but he could not be heard over the sirens and commotion in the schoolyard. Xach struggled and tried to wriggle out from between the man's knees, but he could not move. The man tore a piece of burlap from his clothes and stuffed it in Xach's mouth. He remained still for some time, collecting his energy and catching his breath. Eventually, he leaned closer and whispered in Xach's ear.

"I will remove…the gag…if you p-promise…n-not to scream. **cough** I do not w-wish…to harm you, but…I will to protect myself…and the Hall **cough** at any cost. If you understand…and agree,…n-nod your head."

He paused again for a few moments, coughing uncontrollably. Xach could feel the man's entire body shake violently. Xach nodded his head and stopped squirming. When his coughing had subsided, he continued.

"I'm g-going…to remove…the gag now. **cough** If you scream,…I will s-s-slam your f-face into the ground." He slowly pulled out the foul tasting fabric and coughed again. Xach lay still, afraid to move or speak.

"Good," said the man, clearing his throat. "N-now we need…to t-talk."

"Can I get up please?" asked Xach.

"I w-would…prefer you remain in this position… **cough** …until I have s-secured the k-k-key and explained myself."

"The key is in my left pocket. I'm sorry about taking it. I didn't mean to steal it. I just put it in my pocket without thinking," rambled Xach. "It was an honest mistake. I'm not a thief." He felt the man's hand on his left hip, feeling for the key in his pocket.

The man began to cough again. This time he didn't stop. The man's weight shifted to the right, and he fell over, releasing Xach from his restraint. Xach quickly rolled onto his back and sat up. He held up his fists, ready to defend himself in case the man tried to hold him down again, however, the stranger did not move. He was lying unconscious on the ground again, grasping his bloody side. The blood was wet and oozing between his fingers, and Xach figured that his physical exertion must have aggravated the wound.

Xach pushed aside the branches of the bush and ran out into the school yard again. He entered the crowd and made sure he was surrounded by people, before turning to see if he had been followed. Even though this man had basically attacked him twice that day, he didn't appear to be malicious in nature. Xach felt sorry for him. The man was obviously very hurt, and his parents always taught him to help those in need. *Besides*, Xach thought, *if I hadn't taken the key thing, he might just have run away when he jumped out the window instead of coming back for me.* He turned around and made his way toward the emergency vehicles in the parking lot. As he passed one of the ambulances on his way to talk to a police officer, an EMT grabbed Xach's arm.

"Are you okay? Do you need medical assistance?"

"No. I'm fine. I need to talk to that policeman."

"If you're fine, then why are you covered in blood? I need to examine you!"

Xach looked down at his clothes. His shirt and the top half of his jeans were saturated with blood – the stranger's blood. To anyone unfamiliar with Xach's day, it looked as though he'd been seriously injured. Before he could explain that the blood was not his, the EMT carefully lifted Xach's shirt and began inspecting his side for cuts or puncture wounds.

"You're not cut or bleeding. Where did this blood come from?"

"The blood isn't mine. It's from a man lying in the bushes over there." Deep down inside, he strongly believed that the man had meant him no harm, so he told a little lie to keep the man from getting into trouble. "I found him lying in the bushes. I tried to help him, but I couldn't. I wanted to talk to that policeman over there and tell him that the man needs help."

"Don't worry son. I'll take care of it." The EMT whistled and motioned for another EMT to follow him. "Can you show us where the man is?"

"Sure. Follow me."

Xach led the EMTs to the bushes and parted the branches so that they could see the man lying on the ground.

"There he is," he said as he pointed to the bloodied body within.

"I see him," said the EMT. He pushed Xach aside and entered the clearing between the bushes. His partner stood on the outside, waiting for instructions.

Xach heard the EMT gasp. Then he began yelling. "Eugene, we have a serious bleeder here. I need several rolls of gauze and a gurney. We need to get this guy to the hospital immediately, or we're gonna lose him."

"Ok, Tim," said Eugene. He turned and ran toward the ambulance. He talked to another EMT and the two brought over a gurney with a medical kit. They returned to the bush and started bending and breaking the branches of the bush to clear a path for the gurney. Xach tried to see and hear what was going on, but the three talked so quietly and quickly to one another that he couldn't understand them. They bandaged the man's wounds and placed him on the gurney. Eugene and his helper picked up the gurney and carried it through the crowd to the ambulance. They lifted the gurney into the back of the ambulance and closed the doors. Eugene hit the door twice, signaling to the driver that the patient was secure and ready. The ambulance sped away toward the hospital as Tim surveyed the ground in the clearing, writing some notes on a little notepad.

"Son, do you know that man?" Tim asked, as he exited the bush.

"No sir."

"Do you have any other information about him that might help us care for him?"

"No. I first saw him in the school, and then I saw him in the bushes lying on the ground."

"Ok. Then all I need is some personal information from you. What is your name?" Tim asked.

"Xachary, with an 'X'."

"Can you spell that for me?"

"X-A-C-H-A-R-Y. The X is pronounced like a Z. My parents wanted to be different."

"And your last name?"

"Biddle. Like *riddle* but with a *b*."

"And where do you live?"

"247 Evergreen Terrace."

"And your phone number?"

"863-934-8935."

"Ok, Xachary. Thank you very much for your help. You just may have saved that man's life. We'll be in contact if we have any further questions." Tim returned to the ambulance and began helping other people with their injuries.

The sun passed overhead and was heading toward the west. Xach glanced at his watch. It was 2:00 pm. That meant that even if his mother had not heard the news about the earthquake, she would be here soon anyway. The school day regularly ended at 2:25 pm. The group of teachers and students had greatly lessened over the past hour. Some of the students had slipped out of the schoolyard when the teachers weren't looking, but most of them had been picked up by their parents or guardians. With all the emergency vehicles in the area and policemen and EMT's running around, it would have been easy for a student to slip into the park and disappear. Even though Xach could have walked home in twenty minutes, he knew that his mother would be frantic if he weren't there when she came to pick him up at 2:30 pm, so he waited.

****

Nancy Biddle was hard at work on a presentation for the latest Zipp Cola campaign with her business partner, John Pendelton, when her secretary barged into her office, talking frantically about an earthquake at the Elementary School. Panic set in immediately. She tried to call the school several times, but the line was continuously busy. She needed to make sure Xachary was all right but felt badly about leaving all the work for John. He assured her that he could handle the remaining details and that she should go pick up Xachary. So, twenty-six minutes later, she arrived at Barker Elementary. A police officer directed her to the far side of the parking lot. She parked her large, black SUV where she was directed, taking up two parking spaces. She opened the door and stepped down using the running board. She was a petite, short woman who looked even smaller than she actually was when standing next to such a large vehicle. She enjoyed owning a large vehicle, even if she looked like she was too small to drive it. It made her feel bigger and a little more powerful. She wore a black suit jacket, cream colored silk shirt, skirt, and sneakers. She found driving in high heels to be uncomfortable and impractical, so she kept a pair of sneakers in her car to wear to and from work. Her long red hair hung in curls past her shoulders. She scanned the crowd for her son as she walked toward the school.

"Can I help you little girl?"

She turned to face the rotund police officer in a gray uniform who addressed her. His smile faded the moment he realized that she was not a little girl. His cheeks flushed and he stammered, "Oh, I-I'm s-sorry ma'am. I thought you were one of the children."

Nancy frowned, working the situation to her benefit. She was often mistaken for a little girl because of her size, and she had learned over the years that most men were extremely embarrassed and helpful once they realized their mistake. She did not respond to him immediately, drawing out the uncomfortable silence. The police officer began fumbling with something on his belt.

"I am really sorry, miss. Can I help you with anything?"

Feeling that he'd suffered enough, she responded with a smile, "Yes, you can. I am looking for my son, Xachary Biddle. Do you know where Ms. Zipple's class is?"

"Biddle, you say?" said the officer, scratching his head with his pen. "Why do I know that name?" he mumbled to himself, taking out a small notebook from his right breast pocket and leafing through the pages.

"Is he all right?" she said, immediately concerned. She felt that if the officer knew Xach's name, then something must have happened to him.

The officer stopped leafing through his notebook and began reading aloud. "Xachary Biddle of 247 Evergreen Terrace?"

"Yes?"

"I believe he was taken to the hospital…near fatal wound to his side and leg. The EMT over there," continued the officer, pointing at Tim, "was the one to take his statement. You can talk to him."

Nancy heard nothing after the words "near fatal wound."

"Near fatal…?" she whispered as the words caught in her throat. She couldn't breathe. Darkness began to envelope her from all angles. Before she could sit down, she lost consciousness, falling forward onto the surprised police officer. Her forehead struck the badge on his left breast pocket. He dropped his notebook in surprise and managed to grab Nancy's arm before she fell onto the asphalt parking lot. He gently laid her on the pavement and yelled to Tim for assistance.

"Tim! I need help here! This woman fainted!"

Tim grabbed a medical kit from the front of the ambulance nearest him and ran to aid the officer. He put the kit on the ground next to Nancy and grabbed her wrist to feel for a pulse.

"What happened, Harold?" Tim asked.

"She just passed out. I was telling her that her son was hurt and that you had taken his statement. The next thing I know she fell over."

"Who's her son?" asked Tim, as he removed a little tube of smelling salts from the kit. He broke the inner seal and held it under Nancy's nose.

"Xachary Biddle. You said he was wounded and taken to the hospital."

"Biddle? No, Harold, he's the kid who found the guy in the bushes. Xachary is fine."

"Oh. My bad."

Xachary had seen his mother pull into the parking lot and walked toward her waving his arms in the air to get her attention. He saw her talking to the police officer, when she just fell over! He ran over to where she lay on the ground, just as Tim revived her with the smelling salts.

"Mom?! Are you all right?" asked Xach, kneeling next to her on the ground and taking her hand.

"Uhhhh," she groaned, as the pungent odor of the smelling salts pierced her nostrils. The darkness faded from her eyes, as she tried to sit up. "Xa-Xach?" she stammered.

"Yes, mom. Are you okay?"

Nancy rubbed her eyes as Tim helped prop her up against a car. "Xach? What happened? Where am I?" she said groggily.

"You're at my school," responded Xach.

"You passed out, Miss Biddle," said the officer.

"How do you feel?" asked Tim.

Nancy looked from the officer to the EMT to Xach. When her eyes rested on Xach, she smiled and reached out a shaky arm to touch his shoulder.

"Hi hon…" her voice cracked as her eyes took in the full picture, including the blood all over Xach's shirt and pants.

"OH MY GOD! YOU"RE BLEEDING!" she screamed. The memory of what the police officer had said about Xach being fatally wounded flashed into her mind. She panicked and began to hyperventilate.

"Mom? I'm okay. Really," said Xach, as his face began to blur and fade into the darkness of Nancy's vision.

She slumped to the right and passed out again.

Tim was quick to put the smelling salts under her nose. This time she sat up quickly and appeared lucid immediately.

"XACH! Are you okay?" she asked frantically.

Xach squeezed her hand, physically reassuring her that he was fine.

"I'm all right, mom. I'm not bleeding. It's someone else's blood."

"Your son may have saved a man's life," added Tim. "He found an injured man bleeding in the bushes and tried to help him."

Nancy looked slowly from Xach to Tim and back to Xach again. Xach smiled and nodded his head.

"I'm sorry, Miss Biddle," said the officer. "I misread my notepad and told you that your son was hurt when he wasn't. I'm very sorry."

Finally understanding what happened, Nancy smiled and gave Xach a hug. "I'm so glad you're all right."

"Are you okay, mom?"

"I'm feeling much better now," she said, trying to stand up. Xach and Tim helped her stand. Xach put his arm around his mother's waist for support. "Let's go home, Xach, and you can tell me all about what happened, okay?"

"Okay," he said, leading her to the SUV and helping her into her seat.

"Thank you for your help," she said to the officer and Tim.

"No problem," they responded in unison.

"Take care, Xachary," said Tim.

Xach walked around to the passenger side and climbed in. He slammed the door, receiving the same disapproving look he usually got for such an action. Simultaneously, the tailgate door flew open, surprising both of them. The key-thing in Xach's pocket began to vibrate.

"Don't worry, Miss. I'll get that," said Tim. He jogged around to the back of the vehicle and lowered the door back into its latched position.

"Thank you, Tim," she said with a smile. "I guess I hit the release button." She knew she didn't.

"No problem. Have a safe drive home."

"Thank you again for your help."

He smiled and walked away. Nancy looked at the tailgate in the review mirror, pursing her lips. Xach was more concerned with the key-thing, but tried his best to pretend it wasn't there.

"A-are you sure you're all right to drive, mom?" Xach asked.

"Uh, sure, honey," she said, shaking her head and smiling. "I feel fine. It was just the shock of hearing that you were hurt and then seeing you with all that blood..." Her voice trailed off as she recalled the horror that had overtaken her system. "It's a horrible thing to hear that your child was injured and might be dead." She turned to face Xach and smiled a very warm smile, as a tear rolled down her cheek. She wiped it away quickly, sniffed, and put the key in the ignition. She started the SUV, checked her mirrors, and backed out of her parking space.

As they rode out of the parking lot and down the street, neither said a word for a while. Each was thinking about the events of the day. Nancy's head was filled with thoughts of losing her son, while Xach was wondering if he **could** or even **should** tell his mom the truth about the day's events and the object that was vibrating in his pocket. Finally, Nancy broke the silence.

"So what happened today?"

"Well, Ms. Zipple called me to the board to do a math problem when the earthquake happened. The chalkboard fell off the wall. Books fell off the shelves. The desks started moving around. Everyone freaked out and ran out of the room. Some walls and windows cracked, and the ceiling tiles and lights fell down. I remembered a show we saw on TV about earthquakes and figured the closet doorway was the safest place to be."

"That was very smart," she said, giving him a quick smile. "Was anyone hurt?"

"A flower pot fell on Ms. Zipple's head and knocked her out."

"How terrible!" she said, raising her right hand to her chest as a sign of concern. "Is she all right?"

"I don't know. I saw them taking her to the ambulance on a stretcher. She didn't look too good."

"Maybe we should go visit her this evening once you've gotten cleaned up and had some dinner. What do you think?"

"I guess that would be okay," said Xach reluctantly. He hoped she would forget to go later that night. He didn't really want to go visit her in the hospital. It's not that he didn't like her, but she certainly didn't like him. He didn't see the point in going to visit someone who didn't like him, but he decided it wasn't worth arguing about it.

"And what about the guy you helped? The EMT said you might have saved his life? Who was he?"

"I don't know," said Xach, rubbing his hand over the vibrating key-thing in his pocket. "I saw him lying in the bushes. He was bleeding pretty badly, so I called the EMT over for help. They rushed him to the hospital, but they didn't think he would make it."

"That's a shame. I wonder what happened to him and how he ended up in the bushes? I would hate to think that something violent happened in the park next to the school. I wouldn't feel very safe sending you to school. As it is, I doubt you'll have to go for a while. They will need to clean up after the earthquake and make sure it's safe to allow students inside again. You said some of the walls cracked?"

"Yeah. It didn't seem that bad."

"It may not have looked that bad, but it will have to be inspected and declared 'safe' before I let you back in that building!"

"Jeremy's mom said that the school was the only place affected by the earthquake. Isn't that a little weird?"

"Now that you mention it, I guess it is." She was silent for a few moments pondering this bit of new information. "Actually, that is *very* weird. I hadn't thought about it, because I was too much in shock over the incident and my concern for you. Earthquakes usually aren't localized in such a small area. I guess we'll have to watch the news tonight and see if they have an explanation."

"I might be on TV tonight," Xach added, remembering the annoying reporter from earlier. "Some obnoxious reporter interviewed me and Jeremy, but I don't remember what news channel he was from. I was too busy watching…" He caught himself before he inadvertently told his mother that he was watching the guy from the closet. That wouldn't have matched with his story thus far, so he quickly thought of something else to say. "…um, I was too busy watching them carry Ms. Zipple to the ambulance."

"Oh that poor woman! We should stop and get her flowers or a card when we go to see her later tonight."

"Yeah," said Xach. "That would be nice." *I guess I'm not going to get out of visiting her tonight,* he thought. *At least I probably won't have school tomorrow. Maybe Jeremy could come over and…*

His thoughts were interrupted when the key-thing in his pocket became instantly warm and vibrated even more violently! He put his hand over his pocket and could feel it moving or changing! There was definitely heat coming from it, because the skin on his leg felt like it was burning. He wanted to take it out of his pocket, but then his mother would see it. It got hotter and hotter. Panic set in. *What if it burns a hole in my pants?*

"Are you all right, Xach? You look a little worried."

A thump sounded from behind the back seat. Xach heard it, but he was more concerned about the burning key. Nancy looked in the rearview mirror to see if she had hit something.

"No. I'm okay," he said, trying to cover the fear in his voice. "I- I guess I was just thinking about Ms. Zipple. I hope she's all right." As he said this, the object started to cool down and shrink in size. It returned to its mild state of vibration.

Maybe it wouldn't be such a bad idea to visit the hospital, he thought. *Maybe I can find the guy from the closet and return his key-thing. I'm not sure I want it. What the heck is it, and why did it just do that?*

"Well, we'll go visit her tonight," she said, turning the SUV into the driveway and parking in front of the garage.

The Biddle house was a two-story brownstone house with ornamental shrubbery and a pristine flower garden in the front. Flowers in all the colors of the rainbow sprouted from beds lining the front of the house. Each bed was surrounded by a small white picket fence and neatly mulched to keep weed growth to a minimum. Mr. and Mrs. Biddle spent an inordinate amount of time working on the lawn and the flowerbeds. They took great pride in their beautiful lawn and gardens. It looked very picturesque and had even been photographed several times for the local newspaper. A stone walkway led from the driveway to the front door and had little lights evenly spaced on either side, so one could see his or her way in the dark.

Nancy put her hand on Xach's leg and smiled warmly. "I'm sure she's okay. You go get cleaned up, okay? I'll make dinner. How about hamburgers and macaroni and cheese for dinner?"

"Yeah, that sounds great!"

"I'll get started while you get a shower. Bring your clothes down to me, so I can pre-treat them. Otherwise that blood will never come out."

They walked to the front door, and Nancy unlocked it. Xach ran inside and up the stairs to his room. She clicked the button on her key fob, setting the SUV's alarm system. The alarm beeped, and she went inside.

"And don't put those bloody clothes on the carpet or your bed!" she yelled after him. "I don't want them staining anything!"

"Ok, mom!" he yelled back as he entered his room.

Movie posters lined the walls of the room, most of them science fiction or horror related. A poster of a green glowing alien making a peace sign with his three fingers hung over his cluttered desk. Action figures from science fiction movies lined his bookshelves and lay amongst the mess on his desk.

His bed was unmade and clothes were strewn all over the room – hanging off the bed post, lying on the floor, crumpled on a pile near the window, and hanging off the door knob. Xach wasn't the neatest of children.

He closed the door behind him. He fished in his pocket and withdrew the object. From the moment he entered the house, the vibration had ceased. Even though it moved and got hot in the car, it looked no different than when he put it in his pocket. He expected it to be longer and fatter, but it wasn't. The gem glowed faintly. He opened the top drawer of his desk and took out a tin box about the size of a deck of playing cards. He emptied its contents onto his desk – a few role playing dice and some marbles – and put the key-thing in the box. He put the box back in his desk drawer.

An alarm sounded outside his window, startling him. It was his mother's car alarm. He heard his mother shout something from downstairs. He heard the front door open and close, before hearing the alarm chirp off. When they first got the vehicle, Xach remembered it going off in the middle of the night; it woke the entire household. He chuckled to himself as he slid the desk drawer closed and set about getting himself cleaned up.

He took off his shirt and pants, turning them inside out and balling them up so that they would not stain anything. He placed them on his desk chair. He rooted around in his dresser for a clean pair of underwear, found one that looked clean, and sniffed it. It was good. He took his dirty clothes and clean underwear to the bathroom. He put the dirty clothes on the tile floor near the laundry basket, figuring he would get in trouble if he allowed them to ruin any of the other clothing already in the basket. Before jumping in the shower he caught a glimpse of himself in the bathroom mirror. He realized that the man's blood had stained his skin red. He took a long, hot shower and washed away the dirt, blood, and stress of the day. However, despite all of Xach's scrubbing, he could not fully remove the stain of the stranger's blood. A pink ghost-stain remained on his skin.

He dried himself off and returned to his bedroom. After a small amount of searching and the usual sniffing, he found something relatively clean to wear from his bedroom floor. He selected a pair of wrinkled jeans and a black t-shirt with a skull and cross-bones on the back. He dressed himself quickly, returned to his desk, pocketed the metal tin containing the key-thing, and ran downstairs for dinner.

Chapter Five

After a filling meal of hamburgers and macaroni and cheese, Xach and his mother headed off to the hospital. Mrs. Biddle had arranged for Brandon, Xach's one and a half year-old brother, to stay with the babysitter until Mr. Biddle could pick him up after work. Leesa Biddle, Xach's fifteen year-old sister, had called and asked for permission to visit her friend Jane after school. Mrs. Biddle agreed under the provision that she would finish her homework before returning home. This freed up her schedule to take Xachary to the hospital to visit with his teacher. They made a quick stop at the corner grocery store to pick up flowers for Ms. Zipple.

The ride was quiet; neither having much to say to each other, until Mrs. Biddle's cell phone rang. She glanced quickly at the caller ID screen, saw that it was her business partner, John, and flipped open her phone to speak.

I forgot my phone and my backpack, Xach thought to himself, when he saw his mother pull out her cell phone. His mind had been focused on one thing – the key – and he forgot everything else. *Oh well, it's not like I'll need it.*

"Hello, John. What's up? We're fine, thanks. ...Yes. We promised them that we'd have a rough copy of the promo ready for Monday. ...No. I didn't authorize that. ...No! Definitely not. We can't afford to do that pro bono. ...Ok. Yes, if they agree to cover those expenses, we can do it. Tell them that we'll negotiate prices for filming at the meeting. ...Yes. ...Um, yeah. ...Ok. ...No. ...All right. You have it under control then? I don't want you working too late. ...Ok. I'll see you tomorrow. Call me if you have any problems. My son and I are going to the hospital, but I have my phone with me. ...No, I told you, he's fine. We're going to visit his teacher. She was injured in the earthquake. Yes, ok. Later."

She ended the call. She looked a bit frustrated.

"Everything okay, mom?" Xach asked.

"Yes, I just don't like leaving big projects in the hands of my assistant. He's a good guy, but John hasn't had enough experience to make split-second decisions. He'll end up costing us too much, or he'll cause us to lose the account. At least he was smart enough to contact me instead of making a decision on his own."

"Uh-huh," Xach mumbled, not really caring about or understanding what she was talking about.

"Our client, Zipp Cola, decided at the last minute that they didn't want an animated commercial. They decided they wanted to do a live spot with model, Daria Loofa. That is all well and good, but we did not budget for film or her salary. That would change our entire bid on the project, and John was ready to just switch gears and go with it! He hasn't had enough time to learn pricing, billing, or quoting for large corporate projects like that."

"Ok."

"It cost us a few thousand dollars already to hire the animators to…" Xach started to tune her out. She often started talking about work and would just talk and talk and talk. It seemed as though she thought everyone in the house understood the intricacies of the advertising business, but Xach and Leesa both began to ignore her after she started in on a lengthy discourse on one of her projects. He turned his attention toward the sights outside his window. Occasionally he would say something to let her think he was listening like "ok" or "yeah" or "uh-huh." She would just continue rambling on.

Mrs. Biddle stopped the car at a traffic light, and Xach's attention was drawn toward an old woman attempting to cross the road with several overstuffed bags and packages. With almost every shaky, slow step she took, something would fall out of one of the bags. She would stop, put down the bags, retrieve the item, put it back in the bag, pick up the bags, take another step or two, drop another item, and repeat the process. The traffic light turned green, and the woman had only made it one quarter of the way across the road. People waiting impatiently in their cars began honking their horns and shouting out their windows at the frail, old woman.

"What a shame," his mother said, distracted from her tirade about Zipp Cola's unreasonable timetable.

"She could use some help," Xach said.

Mrs. Biddle pulled the SUV to the side of the road and out of the line of traffic as best she could.

"Go ahead, son."

Xach jumped out and ran to help the old woman. The woman was bending over to retrieve a can of peaches that was slowly rolling away from her. Xach stopped the can with his foot and picked it up for her.

"Can I give you hand?" he asked with a smile.

"Certainly, young man. Thank you!"

Xach placed the can of peaches back into one of the bags she had placed on the pavement. He picked up two of the bags, leaving the woman to carry one bag and two small boxes. He quickly crossed the road to the corner and put the bags down. He returned to the woman and asked for the remaining bag. She handed it to him and walked with her to the corner. Cars sped past them even before they stepped onto the corner. Some of the drivers yelled and cursed at them as they flew past. Xach attempted to ignore them, but he was extremely annoyed with their ignorance.

"Thank you, son," she said. "I bought too much at the store, and I can only carry three bags. They are just a little too full. I guess I should have made two trips, but I'm expecting my daugher and her husband for dinner."

"Do you live near here?"

"Yes," she said and pointed to a building a block and a half up the street. "I live above that antiques shop."

Xach looked over his shoulder at his mother, waiting patiently in the car. He motioned toward the antiques shop with his arm. She nodded, understanding that Xach meant to help her carry the bags to her home.

"I'll help you get them to your house, if you'd like," he offered.

"Why certainly! Thank you so much!"

Xach picked up two of the bags and held them in front of him.

"If you'd like, you can put those two boxes on top of the bags, then you only have one bag to carry."

As the old woman carefully balanced the two boxes on top of the bags, she studied his face closely.

"Do I know you? Have we met before?" she asked.

"I don't think so, ma'am."

"My name is Xach."

"Nice to meet you Xach, my name is Gladys. That is curious though," she said. "You look very familiar to me. Oh well. When you're as old as me, you've met so many people that everyone looks like someone else."

She turned toward her apartment and picked up the remaining bag. As Xach followed her, he felt a distinct vibration in his pocket. It was coming from inside the tin box. The vibration continued to grow stronger, when all of a sudden he felt a hand shoving him forward.

Behind him, a high-pitched, nasal male voice full of arrogance said, "Get out of my way, boy."

The packages fell backward into his face, as he lurched forward. Losing his balance, he fell head-first toward the ground. Not wanting to crush the old woman's groceries, he threw the bags forward, spilling the contents onto the sidewalk. He put his hands out to stop him from slamming his head onto the pavement. Gladys gasped and dropped the bag she was holding to try and help Xach. She was too slow, and Xach hit the ground. He rolled onto his side, allowing him an opportunity to catch a glimpse of the man who pushed him.

The man was wearing a black cape and shiny black boots. Despite the fact that he was a diminuitive man in general, he had a small head for his body size. Atop his head of long black hair, glittered a jeweled beret of some kind. Xach could partially see that the man had a handle-bar mustache, because the hair stuck out from the side of his face. His fingers bore several gold and jeweled rings. He looked like one of those silly corner magicians who were all spectacle and no talent. The man did not turn to see if Xach was all right but continued walking away quickly, occasionally flailing his arms in effeminate frustration.

"Are you all right, dear?" Gladys asked.

Turning his attention back to himself, Xach responded, "Yes. I'm fine." He pushed himself up and brushed the dirt off his hands. The vibration in his pocket lessened and stopped. "I'm sorry about your groceries. I didn't want to drop them, but I was afraid I'd crush them."

"Oh, I'm not worried about my food. Are you sure you're okay?"

"Yes. Just a little dirty is all."

"What an incredibly rude man," she said. "Some people should never be allowed to leave their house."

"Yeah. He didn't even ask me to move before he pushed me."

"Someday he'll get his," she said with disgust in her voice. "They always do."

"XACH! Are you all right, honey?" It was his mother. She had witnessed the whole incident in the rearview mirror and came running to his aid.

"Yeah. I'm okay. He just pushed me; he didn't even ask me to move!"

Mrs. Biddle did a quick inspection of her son to make sure he was not hurt. She turned to the old woman and offered her hand. "I'm Nancy Biddle, Xach's mother."

"Nice to meet you. My name is Gladys Simpson," she said, shaking Mrs. Biddle's hand. She glanced toward Xach and said, "Your son is such a nice young gentleman."

Xach blushed and started collecting the groceries that were scattered about the pavement.

"Thank you so much for your help!"

"No problem," said Xach, collecting the final item and putting it in the bag. He put the two boxes on top of the bag in front of him. "Now let's get these home before anything else happens!"

Each picked up a bag and headed toward the antique shop. As they walked, Gladys told them that she had been living above the antique store for fifty-three years. She used to run the antique shop with her husband, Henry, but she hadn't opened the store since he disappeared twenty-five years ago during a secret military mission. Bill, her son in-law, had wanted her to sell the store, but she couldn't bear to sell it. She admitted that she always hoped her husband would return, even though that seemed less and less likely with each passing year. She wanted the store to be there for him if or when he did return. So, Bill had convinced her to let him sell the items from the shop on the internet. The profits from those sales and the money left by her husband had been enough to keep her living well enough. She explained that she usually doesn't buy so many groceries at one time, but she was planning to make a late dinner for Bill and her daughter, Sue.

"Here we are," said Gladys, as they approached the storefront of the antique shop. A dented metal security gate with graffiti upon it hung in front of the store. "We can get in around back. Then I won't have to open the gate to the store." She led them around the side of the building through a narrow alley to a rickety metal fire escape. She slowly climbed the stairs to the second floor. Xach and his mother followed carefully behind her, both fearing their combined weight would cause the stairs to collapse. When she reached the top of the stairs, Gladys put down the bag she was carrying and withdrew a ring of keys from her pocket. She unlocked the door, pushed it inward, picked up her bag and entered the apartment. They followed her inside. The apartment smelled a bit musty but with a hint of cinnamon.

"Can you put those bags on the table here," Gladys said, putting hers on the dining room table. "Thank you so much. I really appreciate it."

"It was our pleasure," said Xach. "Take care and have a nice dinner with your family."

"May I offer you anything to drink before you go?" she asked, clearly wishing to prolong their visit.

"No thanks," they both said. They turned to leave, but Gladys put a hand on Xach's shoulder.

"Wait here a minute, Xachary. I have something for you."

"That's not necessary."

"Nonsense!" she said. "You were very kind to help an old woman. Most people wouldn't have stopped to help a stranger. We need more people like you in this world. I have something I'd like you to have."

She went to a door in the middle of the hallway between the living room and what Xach assumed was her bedroom and bathroom. She disappeared down the stairs into the antique shop. Xach turned to his mother, who was just standing there smiling at him.

"Are we going to be too late to get to the hospital?" Xach asked.

"No dear. We can spare a few minutes. I'm proud of you. We should all take time out of our busy lives to help others. We're always rushing around from place to place, worried about our own little lives. We seldom take the time to help others with theirs."

Xach looked around Gladys' home as he waited for her return. The walls were papered in a dingy yellow and green patterned wallpaper. Several pieces of old cherry furniture lined the walls; the largest was a china closet in the dining room that was almost overflowing with plates of all sizes and colors. Old pictures and paintings hung on the walls. In the living room hanging above an old television was a portrait of a young woman and a man in uniform. Xach moved a little closer to examine the picture. He assumed the woman in the portrait was Gladys as a young woman with her husband. As he studied the picture, Gladys reappeared at the top of the steps. She was out of breath and paused to collect herself.

"That's my Henry," she said, once she caught her breath. Her voice was sorrowful with a tinge of pride. "He always looked so handsome in his uniform. That picture was taken right after he returned from World War II." She paused, lost in her reminiscence.

"It's a very nice picture."

"Yes. It was a beautiful day." She paused, lost again in her memories. "Well," she said, almost as if she were just waking up. "I guess you would like to be on your way, so I'd like you to have this." She extended her hand toward Xach. In her hand she held a shiny silver medal bearing the imprint of an eagle grasping several arrows in one claw and an olive branch in the other. The medal hung from a silver band with a pin on the back. Xach recognized it as the medal on the jacket of Gladys' husband in the picture they were just discussing.

"I can't accept this," said Xach, turning toward the picture. "Wasn't that your husband's medal?" He pointed at the picture.

"Yes, Xach. It is his medal, but I would like you to have it. You have many of the same qualities that Henry had. He was a kind and generous man. You remind me a great deal of him. This medal belongs with someone like him. I'm sure he would want you to have it as well."

Xach looked to his mother for approval. He realized the immense significance this medal must have for Gladys, and he didn't want to take it if his mother thought he should not. She just smiled and nodded, wiping a tear from her eye. He took the medal from Gladys' hand.

"Thank you very much."

"No, thank *you*!" said Gladys. "I appreciate you taking the time to help me with my packages. The world needs more people like you and less of the ones like the one that pushed you over. It was a genuine pleasure meeting you. I know you have somewhere to be, but you're welcome to stay for dinner if you like."

"No thank you," Xach said politely. "We already ate. It was a pleasure meeting you as well, Gladys." Xach slipped the medal into his pocket next to the tin box containing the key-thing. "But we really should be going. We have to get to the hospital before visiting hours are over."

"I do hope everything is all right."

"Yes, we are going to visit my teacher. She was injured in the earthquake this afternoon."

"Ah, yes. I heard about that on the news this afternoon. It's curious that it was localized only to the school." She paused, studying his face again. "That's it!" she said suddenly. "I knew I recognized you! You were on the afternoon news being interviewed about the earthquake with another young man, weren't you?"

"Yes, I was. That was my friend Jeremy. I didn't get to watch the news, so I didn't know if they aired my interview or not. We DVR'd it, so I can watch it tonight."

"Yep. They aired it," she said with a big smile. "I knew I recognized you," she said again. "I guess I'm not losing my mind after all." She winked at him.

Xach just smiled, not knowing what else to say. He looked at his mother, who was checking her watch to see the time.

"Well, I better let you go. I wouldn't want to be responsible for you missing visiting hours at the hospital. I'm sure your teacher will enjoy a visit." She turned to Xach's mother. "It was very nice to meet you. It's good to know that some women are still raising children with manners."

"Take care Gladys. Have a nice evening with your family," said Mrs. Biddle.

"You too," said Gladys as she saw them to the door. She watched them walk down the fire escape and waved to them as they turned the corner.

"What a nice woman," said Mrs. Biddle. "It makes me wish that your grandmother and grandfather had lived long enough for you to get to know them." She fell silent for a moment, remembering her parents and the accident that had claimed their lives. She often regretted not being able to see them or talk to them before they died. Thoughts of them and their horrible pain and suffering always made her melancholy.

Attempting to distract herself from such horrible memories, Mrs. Biddle tried to think about something else. "May I see the medal she gave you?"

Xach fished it out of his pocket and handed it to his mother.

"This must be worth some money," she said. "Not to mention it must hold a great deal of significance for her emotionally. You should be proud to wear this," she said, handing it back to her son. "Please make sure you take good care of it and don't lose it."

"I won't," Xach said, putting the medal back in his pocket. "She seemed awfully lonely."

"Yes," she sighed. "It's hard living by yourself after a loved one passes away. Yet she can't even be sure that he is dead. I wonder what happened to him? How can someone just disappear? I can't imagine what it must feel like to wait for someone who is Missing in Action...to hope they're alive but fear each passing day that they're probably dead, but not to know for certain…it's just awful. I don't know what I'd do if your father passed away."

Xach shuddered at the idea of his father dying. *What would we do if dad died? What would mom do? Who would pay the bills? Mom makes good money, but would it be enough? Would we have to move back to Maine?*

His mind raced with thoughts about what life would be without his father, and these thoughts of death reminded him of the man who attacked him in the closet and the bushes. *I wonder if he has a family? What if he dies from his wounds? Who would he be leaving behind? And what about me and the key-thing? I'll never learn what it is or where it came from? I hope he didn't die. I hope I can find him and give this thing back to him. I hope we're not too late for visiting hours.*

"Do you think we'll be able to get to the hospital before visiting hours end?"

"It's nearly six o'clock. Visiting hours should be until seven at least…I hope. I think we'll make it."

"Good."

Chapter Six

The remainder of the ride to the hospital was uneventful. Xach spent the time devising ways to slip away from his mother and find the man who attacked him without getting in trouble. He figured faking a need to use the bathroom would be his best bet at leaving the room without his mother following him. His biggest concern was finding the man's room and getting enough time to talk to him...*if* he was even still alive. The medics who had taken him to the ambulance seemed to think he was in a serious condition.

Mrs. Biddle pulled into the hospital parking lot and stopped at the security gate. She took the parking ticket from the machine. The the electronic arm raised, allowing her entrance into the parking garage. She parked her SUV and locked it, before heading toward the hospital entrance. Xach was carrying the flowers they purchased at the store. He kept switching the boquet from one hand to other, because the palms of his hands were sweating profusely. The closer he and his mother got to the actual hospital building, the more anxious he became. The automatic doors slid open releasing a gust of warm, sterile smelling air into their faces. Xach never liked the smell of hospitals.

When he was five years old, he spent about two weeks in the hospital with a severe case of pneumonia. His lungs kept filling with liquid, and he needed constant supervision. By the time he left the hospital with a clean bill of health, his clothes smelled like the hospital. It took several washings before he could no longer smell it on certain articles of clothing that he wore during his stay. Ever since that ordeal, he felt uncomfortable in hospitals, and the smell made him a little anxious. He tried to remind himself that he wasn't there for himself; he was there just to visit. However, this did little to mitigate his anxiety.

Mrs. Biddle walked up to the receptionist's desk and asked for information on Ms. Zipple. The plump nurse behind the counter, whose nametag said Betty, told her that Ms. Zipple was in Room 407. She said that visiting hours would be over in 45 minutes. Mrs. Biddle thanked the nurse, and they went in search of an elevator. They found one, and Xach pushed the up arrow for the elevator, fidgeting impatiently as they waited. An old man wearing a light blue bathrobe and matching slippers joined them in front of the elevator. He was holding onto a rolling metal pole with his left hand. A bag with clear liquid hung from the top of the pole and was connected to the man's wrist by way of a thin clear tube. The man smiled at Xach, revealing his toothless gums. Xach smiled uncomfortably and looked away. Seeing the bag and tube reminded him of the catheter he had to get when he was in the hospital with pneumonia. He had been poked and prodded with needles so many times he had developed a real phobia of them.

The bell on the elevator rang, and the doors slid open. The old man walked onto the elevator first; Xach and his mother followed. The man asked for the second floor, so Xach pushed the buttons marked two and four. The doors began to close when Xach heard a voice yell, "HOLD THAT ELEVATOR PLEASE!" Xach quickly put his hand in between the closing doors to trigger the electric eye and stop the doors from closing. As the doors re-opened, a young male nurse in scrubs poked his head into the elevator car. Behind him was a man on a rolling stretcher.

"Is there enough room in here for us?" the nurse asked.

"Sure," said Mrs. Biddle, moving to the right of the car to make room for the stretcher.

The nurse got behind the gurney and pushed it onto the elevator. He joined Xach in the front of the car near the button panel as the doors slid shut.

"Fifth floor, please," he said to Xach.

Xach pushed the button with the number five on it, and the elevator started to move upward. Xach could feel his stomach turn with that usual moment of motion sickness that occurs when an elevator begins moving. Xach focused his attention on the rising numbers so that he would not have to look at the man on the stretcher.

The display changed from G to L to 1 to 2. The elevator came to a stop, and Xach's stomach came up into his chest.

"This is my floor," said the old man.

"Oh," said the nurse, realizing that he would need to move to allow the man a clear path to exit. He walked out of the elevator, followed by Xach and his mother. The old man rolled his cart around the gurney and through the door. He thanked them and continued on down the hall. The nurse entered the car first, aware that Xach and his mother would be getting off on the fourth floor before he and his patient got off on the fifth. Mrs. Biddle entered. Xach followed but tripped over the gap between the floor and the elevator, losing his balance. Without thinking, he grabbed a hold of the gurney to stabilize himself. He righted himself and his gaze fell on the man lying before him. He quickly withdrew his hand as if he had been stung by a bee and stood in shock in the doorway of the elevator. The man on the gurney was the man who had attacked him at the school!

"Are you all right honey?" asked Mrs. Biddle, putting her hand on his shoulder.

"Oh, uh, yeah," said Xach, regaining his composure. "Sorry. I just lost my balance." He took his place beside the gurney, and the doors closed.

The man from the school was wearing a hospital gown and was covered with a white blanket. His face and hair had been cleaned, but it was obviously the same man. Xach quickly tried to memorize as much about him as he could, so he could find the man again when he got away from his mother. He examined the nurse. He looked to be in his twenties with short black hair and blue eyes. He had an identification tag hanging from the bottom of his shirt. His name was Stephen Block. A clipboard with medical information hung from the front of the gurney. The name on the paper was John Doe, signifying that the hospital had not yet been able to determine the man's identity.

Xach felt his stomach lurch, and the elevator stopped on the fourth floor. Xach exited slowly, as he tried to read the clipboard. Since he obviously had no medical training in how to read hospital forms, he was unable to decipher anything useful. His mother exited behind him and then took the lead. He followed his mother to Room 407. A small piece of paper on the door had the names Zipple and Harvey hand-written on it. His mother rapped lightly on the door and entered the room.

The first bed in the room was occupied by an old woman with curly white hair, presumably with the last name of Harvey. She appeared to be asleep. A respirator was hooked up to her nose and several tubes and monitors were connected to her at various points on her body. Beyond the curtain in the middle of the room, Ms. Zipple lay on her bed. She had a thick wad of gauze on her temple. It was held in place by a bandage that wrapped around her head and under her chin. Tufts of hair protruded from holes in the bandage. She wore a neck brace around her neck, and her nose was bandaged as well. She had dark black circles under her eyes. She was staring at the television that hung from the ceiling, watching the local news. Her eyes were glazed, and her mouth hung open a bit. It looked as though she were in a trance. To Xach, she actually looked rather scary, in a deranged mental patient kind of way – like some of the characters in the horror movies he often watched.

"Ms. Zipple?" Xach asked tentatively, afraid to disturb her. "Are you all right?"

She slowly turned her head toward Xach's voice and blinked. The glazed look slowly left her eyes, as she forced herself to become lucid for her guest. "Xachary! What a pleasant surprise!"

"Hello, Ms. Zipple. How are you?"

"I'm okay, but I'm in quite a bit of pain. Apparently I fell on my nose and broke it. I must look awful."

"You look all right," Xach lied. "My mom brought me here to check how you were doing."

Ms. Zipple extended her hand toward Mrs. Biddle to greet her. "Yes, I remember you from parent teacher conferences. Nice to see you again."

"Likewise," replied Mrs. Biddle. "My son told me all about the horrible earthquake and your accident. I thought it would be nice if we checked in on you."

"These are for you," Xach said, offering her the flowers.

"Thank you," she said, sniffing them with her broken nose. "They are beautiful." She placed them carefully on the rolling table on which her half-eaten dinner still remained.

"That was very kind of you. I understand that it was Xach who found help for me when I was unconscious on the floor. Thank you, Xach."

"Allow me to put those in some water," offered Mrs. Biddle, reaching for the bouquet.

"Thank you again," replied Ms. Zipple.

"You're welcome." She unwrapped the celophane from around the bouquet and placed the flowers in one of the plastic water pitchers provided by the hospital.

Xach just smiled at Ms. Zipple, not really knowing what to say. Both watched silently as Xach's mother attended to the flowers.

"Please forgive me if I seem a little out of it," she continued. "They gave me a number of painkillers for my head and nose. I'm a little groggy."

"That's fine," said Mrs. Biddle.

Another slightly uncomfortable pause arose in the conversation. Not wanting to appear rude to her guests, Ms. Zipple attempted to make conversation by addressing the news report on television.

"Did you hear about that scientist that disappeared?"

"No," replied Mrs. Biddle, relieved that there was something new to talk about.

"They say that it happened this afternoon around 1 pm. He just vanished into thin air! He was giving a lecture to some students in his laboratory when he just disappeared. It's been on all the news channels this evening. All of his students gave the same story, but no one knows where he is or how it happened. They don't know if it was a publicity stunt or a prank of some kind. Everyone is baffled. I think his name was Cornelius or something strange like that."

"That's very odd," said Mrs. Biddle. "It seems like a lot of odd things are happening today, like the earthquake being localized only to the school grounds and no where else in town."

"Yes, I heard that on the news as well. Very curious. Which reminds me, Xach. I saw you and Jeremy on the news tonight. Were you hurt? I remember seeing a lot of blood on your clothes. Forgive me for not asking sooner, but I'm not thinking too clearly on these meds."

"It's okay. I wasn't hurt. It was someone else's blood. A man was hurt in the earthquake."

"Is he alright?"

"I don't know," Xach said. "They took him to the hospital, so I guess he's here somewhere."

Xach glanced at the clock on the wall. Visiting hours would be over soon, and he needed to find the man and return the key-thing to him. He decided to put his "bathroom plan" into action.

He turned to his mother and whispered that he needed to go to the restroom.

"It's just down the hall, I think," she whispered in return.

"Ok. I'll be back in a little while." He turned to Ms. Zipple and said, "Excuse me a moment, I'll be right back."

As he left the room, he could hear his teacher say something about Xach's good manners. He walked briskly toward the elevator. It occurred to him that Ms. Zipple was being unusually nice to him and seemed genuinely happy to see him. Considering how she treated him in class, he half expected her to tell him to leave her alone. She never complimented him on his manners, even though he was always polite and respectful to her. He chuckled a bit to himself as he thought *perhaps the bump on her head messed up her memory. If that's all it would have taken to change her attitude toward me, I would have hit her on the head months ago!*

He pushed the up arrow for the elevator and waited anxiously for the doors to open. He kept his eyes fixed on the doorway to Room 407 to make sure that his mother didn't come out and see him waiting for the elevator. The door finally opened, and he stepped inside. A family of four and a woman in a wheel chair were already in the elevator.

"What floor would you like?" asked the woman in the wheel chair.

"Five, please," responded Xach.

The woman pressed the button for the fifth floor, and the doors slid shut. Xach felt his stomach churn more violently as the elevator moved up toward the fifth floor. It wasn't often that he purposely deceived his mother, and he felt very guilty and anxious.

One time when he was seven years old, his mother had refused to buy him a toy he wanted at the grocery store. He couldn't even remember exactly what toy it was anymore, but he had stolen it and hidden it in his jacket. A few days later his mother had seen him playing with it and asked where he had gotten it. He lied and told her that his father had bought it for him the other day when they had gone to the grocery store. She checked with his father, of course, and Xach had found himself in a heap of trouble. Not only did his parents make him return the toy to the store and apologize to the store manager, but they grounded him for a month. That wasn't the worst of it though. What bothered him the most was the fact that his mother and father seemed distrustful of him for quite some time after that. It was many months before he felt that his parents trusted him again.

He hated to betray that trust now, but he felt as though he had no choice. If he told his mother why he wanted to see the stranger, she would refuse to let him go near him and might even have the man arrested for attacking him. He knew that his mother would have been furious at him for taking the man's key-thing, even if it had been an accident. If all went well, he planned to find the man, return the object, and rejoin his mother in Ms. Zipple's room within a few minutes.

The elevator came to a stop, and the doors slid open. Xach exited the elevator and walked briskly toward the information desk. A large African-American woman sat behind the counter, typing something into a computer as she talked to someone on the phone through a headset microphone. Xach approached the desk and smiled at the woman. She smiled and held up a finger, signaling for him to wait a moment. Xach glanced nervously around the hall as he waited.

"Can you hold on a moment, sir," the nurse asked the person on the phone. "Thank-you."

She twisted the microphone away from her mouth and addressed Xach. "What can I do for you sweetheart?"

"Betty from downstairs told me that Stephen Block brought John Doe to the fifth floor, but she didn't tell me what room he was in."

She typed something into her computer and said, "The John Doe's in Room 555. Who are you?"

"Me?"

"Yes, you. We don't know anything about this guy. You're the first person to ask about him. The police and hospital administrators will want to speak with you."

I don't have time for that.

Thinking quickly, he said, "Oh, yeah, my name's Jeremy. I spoke with the police downstairs. They told me to talk to Stephen Block, the nurse who brought John Doe up here to his room. They said he could put my information on John's chart."

"Wait a minute. The man's name is actually John?"

"Huh?"

The phone on the nurse's desk began to ring incessantly as three calls came in at once. "One moment," she said to Xach. She pushed the microphone back in front of her mouth. "Yes sir, I haven't forgotten about you. Can you hold one more moment? Yes, I have your wife's test results. They just came up from the lab a few minutes ago." She turned slightly to the left to pick up a folder in a wire basket next to her computer. "If you can just hold for another minute, I'll get them." She turned back to face Xach, but he was gone.

He used her moment of distraction to his advantage and ducked below the counter. He looked for a sign on the wall indicating in which direction Room 555 might be. A sign hanging from the ceiling indicated that Room 555 was down the hall to Xach's right. Trying not to draw attention to himself, even though he was walking hunched over to avoid being seen by the nurse, he walked into the hall and around the corner. Once out of the nurse's sight, he stood up straight and almost sprinted down the hall. *It won't be long before that nurse sends someone to look for me,* Xach thought. *I gotta hurry!*

He looked at the numbers on the doors as he passed them. They appeared to be ascending by odd numbers on his right, meaning that Room 555 would be closer to the left end of the hall. He kept peering over his shoulder to make sure that he wasn't being followed. Near the end of the hall he found Room 555 and ducked inside. Poking his head partially out the door, he checked one last time to see if anyone was following him. Aside from a few people and nurses who appeared to be occupied with their own business, it seemed he was in the clear.

He took a deep breath and turned towards the beds in the room. The room smelled heavily of disinfectant and soap. The first bed was empty, and the curtain was drawn around the second bed. Xach felt along the curtain for a break. Finding one, he pulled the curtain aside and stepped inside.

The man lay on the bed completely motionless with his eyes closed. He appeared to be sleeping. His body was wrapped tightly in a white sheet, and his arms rested beside him. A myriad of tubes were attached to his arms and nose; Xach assumed these were to help him breathe and to keep him medicated. His tangled hair had been cleaned, cut, and combed. His face was clean-shaven and no longer dirty. A padded wire was attached to his chest that monitored his heart rate. He looked very peaceful and calm, quite unlike Xach's previous encounters with him.

Xach slowly and quietly approached the side of the bed and tapped lightly on the man's right hand. The man did not respond. Xach tapped him a little harder and still got no response. He leaned in over the man's torso and said quietly, "Hey Mister…" There was no response. He said it again, a little louder, while poking the man's shoulder. The man remained motionless.

Oh well, thought Xach. *At least I tried.* He reached in his pocket and pulled out the silver tin containing the key-thing. He opened the lid and slid the object into the palm of his hand. Carefully he turned the man's hand slightly to the side so that he could place the key-thing in the man's palm. He curled the man's fingers around it and returned his hand to its resting place by his side. He slipped the tin back into his pocket and turned to leave, when he felt a hand grasp his left forearm. The heart monitor in the corner started to beep louder and faster. He turned to see the man sitting up in bed. He grasped Xach's arm with his left hand. His eyes were open very wide, as was his mouth. Yet he made no sound and did not release Xach's arm. Xach tried to pull away, but the man would not let go.

On any other person, the man's facial expression would have evoked fear, but for Xachary, who found himself in the same position with this man for the third time that day, it only resulted in startling him. Sensing that the man wished to speak but couldn't, Xach tried to explain his presence in the room.

"There is no need to get excited Mister. I returned your key-thing. See, it's in your hand," he said, pointing to the man's right hand. "I didn't mean to steal it. Honest! I was looking at it in the closet when you grabbed me the first time, and I just put it in my pocket without even thinking. I am really sorry." Xach realized that he was babbling. "So I just came to return it to you. Now that you have it, can I go?"

Xach waited for the man to respond, but he seemed frozen in a state of mid speech. Then the man slowly closed his mouth and blinked. He blinked again...and again. It was as if the man was waking up from a year-long coma and needed to remember how to move and talk. He looked around the room and at Xach. A look of fear and disorientation spread over his face like that of a small child waking up in a strange place.

"Mister, are you okay?" Xach asked. "Can you let me go please?"

The man looked at his hand, which remained clamped on Xach's arm. Xach could feel the pressure of the man's grasp pressing into the muscles of his arm. A dull pain began to radiate through his arm.

"I won't go anywhere. I promise. You're kind of hurting my arm," he winced, as he tried to twist free of the man's iron-grip.

The man blinked twice and slowly released Xach's arm. Xach turned around fully to face him.

"Thank you," said Xach. "I guess you've had a pretty traumatic day, huh? Did they fix up your injury?"

The man continued to mutely stare at him and his surroundings, moving slowly and stiffly like a robot.

Trying to fill the awkward silence between them, Xach continued to babble. "I came back to return your key-thing." Xach pointed again to the man's right hand, indicating the location of the object. "I didn't mean to take it from you. It really was an accident."

Bending his neck slowly, the man turned his attention to his right hand. Then as if reacting to an electric shock, the man jumped and his arm jerked upward. His fist unfurled, releasing the key-thing into the air. Acting on pure instinct, Xach reached out with an extended hand and caught it. It was vibrating furiously, as if it were trying to escape from his fist. He had to squeeze his fingers tightly around it to keep from dropping it. It was vibrating, just like it had earlier that day during the car ride home and when that man knocked him over on the sidewalk as he was helping Gladys with her groceries.

The man's face took on a look of shock and frantic horror. His eyes darted from Xach to the door.

"What's the matter? Why is this thing vibrating?" Xach asked.

The man did not respond but began furiously pulling the wires and tubes from his body. When he ripped the IV from his arm, blood sprayed across the curtain and his bed from the open holes in his arms. Xach watched in horror as blood splattered across the front of his shirt. The man struggled with the sheets that were wrapped tightly around his body. By the time he freed his legs and swung them over the side of the bed, the sheets were wet with blood.

Xach stood frozen in fear. It was like he was standing in the middle of a horror movie. He had never seen so much blood in his life. Then to make matters worse, the bloody stranger grasped Xach's shoulder and tried to stand up. The man's legs, weak from surgery collapsed under his weight, and he pitched forward into Xach's arms. Xach tried his best to keep the man from falling.

Eventually, he found his voice: "M-Mister, I-I don't think you should be getting up. You're bleeding pretty bad."

For the first time since waking up, the man spoke: "M-m-must get a-way. D-danger."

The man struggled to stand. He grasped the curtain behind Xach and tried to pull himself into a standing position. The curtain rings snapped, bringing both to the floor. Xach helped him onto his knees.

"He's very c-c-close," the man stammered.

"Who's close?"

Xach helped push the man to a standing position. Now his shirt was completely covered in blood. *Mom's going to be furious!* he thought. *My clothes are ruined. SHE'S GOING TO FIND OUT I LIED! How am I going to explain what happened?*

Before Xach could begin to formulate an answer to this question, the stranger dragged him across the room. He held Xach's arm tightly as he limped toward the door. He grasped his side, which was bleeding heavily. Xach surmised that either the doctors had not been able to repair the wound, or in getting out of bed the man managed to tear it open again. Xach didn't know what to think, but he knew enough to believe that the man should not be walking. Blood dripped from between the man's fingers and left a small splatter trail across the floor.

"Hey, let go of me! Where are you taking me?" Xach asked, more out of curiosity than fear. He realized that he was in a heavily populated hospital, and he was fairly certain that it would be hard for a limping, bleeding man to abduct him. *All I need to do is to scream loudly,* Xach resolved. *Someone will surely come running to help me.*

"Let go of me, or I'll scream," Xach warned the man, as they reached the door to the hallway. He released Xach's arm and gripped the doorframe to support his weight. Xach took a few steps back to distance himself from the man, in case he tried to grab him again.

"M-must be quiet. M-must g-get away," the man whispered.

"Away from what? Where do you intend to go? You're bleeding all over the place."

"N-n-not important. M-must pro-protect the k-key."

The man glanced at Xach's fist which held the key-thing. Xach realized that in addition to vibrating violently it was once again getting hotter. The man leaned against the doorframe, catching his breath. Slowly he peered around the corner into the hallway. From the look on the man's face when he turned back, Xach was certain the man had seen something in the hall that he didn't like. The color had drained from his face, and he looked as pale as a ghost. The man closed his eyes tightly and scrunched up his face – he was either thinking really hard or in excruciating pain. Xach wasn't sure. After what seemed like many minutes, but was in reality was only seconds, the man's eyes flew open. A look of determination spread across his face.

"Give me the key," said the man in a steady voice.

Xach extended his arm toward the man and released his fist. The key-thing jumped from his palm and into the man's outstretched hand. His fingers tightened around the shaft. Extending his index finger, he began rubbing the jewel at the end of the key-thing. The jewel began to glow faintly.

"What are you doing?" Xach inquired.

"I do not have time to explain. I need your help. Count Milton stands beyond this door. He comes for the key. He must not get it! There is an exit not far from here, however Count Milton must not see us. If he sees us, we will never make it."

"*We* are not going anywhere. I have to get back to my mother. I am not going anywhere with you," said Xach as sternly as he could, taking a few more steps backward from the man.

The man frowned and paused. "Very well, child. But will you help me?"

"What can I do? I'm just a kid?"

"You know this world better than I. How may I get across this hall without being seen by Count Milton?"

"I don't know. Where is he?"

"He stands yonder speaking with the large dark female."

"Dark female? What are you talking about?"

"Look for yourself, but quickly please. He may come at any moment."

Xach poked his head into the hallway and looked down towards the nurse's station. He couldn't believe his eyes. The man with the handlebar mustache and magician's cloak that knocked him down on the street earlier that day was standing at the nurse's station talking loudly to the large African-American nurse who helped him find John Doe. She was no longer behind the desk and was using her considerable size to block the hallway and hold back the tiny man. He was gesticulating violently, obviously very angry about something. Two security guards that had been standing near the desk began to approach him in an effort to calm him down.

Xach turned back toward the man.

"Is Count Milton the guy dressed like a magician?"

"Yes, but do not be fooled by his diminutive stature. He is a powerful and dangerous wizard."

"There are no such things as wizards," said Xach incredulously.

"Perhaps not in this world, but he followed me here. Look, young one, I do not have time to explain. We must escape before he finds us."

Xach peeked out into the hallway again. The guards were now holding Count Milton's arms, attempting to escort him from the building.

"I would go now," Xach said. "Count Milton is being detained by security right now."

They both peered into the hallway again and saw the two security guards lifting Count Milton off the floor and carrying him toward the elevator. Since Count Milton was so short, it was easy for them to do so. Count Milton screamed and kicked his feet. His face turned beet red, and Xach expected smoke to start pouring from his ears like in the cartoons. He had never seen anyone so angry!

"Come child," said the man, grabbing a hold of Xach's arm again. "We will go now."

"I told you to let go of me!" said Xach in a moderately loud voice.

A nurse and some people standing in the hall watching the commotion at the nurse's station turned to see who was yelling.

"Quiet boy!" the man hissed.

"LET GO OF ME!" yelled Xach again as loudly as he could.

The man let go of his arm. Xach was about to run in the opposite direction when he heard someone else yelling. It was Count Milton.

"THERE HE IS! LET GO OF ME, YOU CRETONS! GERALD, BRING ME THE KEY AND YOUR SUFFERING WILL BE MINIMAL! I MUST HAVE THE KEY!"

At that moment, the elevator opened, and Nancy Biddle walked into the scene. Her face was full of worry and concern. She had excused herself from Ms. Zipple to look for Xach when he hadn't returned. A gentleman had searched the bathroom for her and found no signs of Xachary, sending Mrs. Biddle into a panic. The nurse at the registration desk said she had seen a young boy get on the elevator. She hadn't been sure which direction to ride the elevator until she heard screaming coming from the floor above her. Though she prayed Xachary had nothing to do with the commotion above, she figured it was a good place to start searching.

Upon exiting the elevator on the fifth floor, she came face to face with the red, fuming face of Count Milton. He was yelling so violently that spittle was flying from his mouth. She stopped dead in her tracks and leaned backward to avoid being hit in the face by a flying gob of spit. She slid past the guards and up the hall, catching a glimpse of Xach in the doorway of a room near the end of the hall.

"PUT ME DOWN IMMEDIATELY! HE'LL GET AWAY!" screamed Count Milton. Realizing that the security guards were not about to release him, Count Milton fell silent. He relaxed his body and went limp. He closed his eyes and began chanting quietly.

"Arum nexus protor..."

"XACHARY BIDDLE," his mother yelled. "What are you doing down there? Get over here immediately!" She started to move down the hall toward him, swinging her purse wildly as she walked.

Before he could answer or even move toward her, Xach felt the man that Count Milton called "Gerald" grab his arm again. He had forgotten the man had identified himself as Gerald Milton during their first encounter in Ms. Zipple's closet. He tried to pull away, but Gerald's grip was firm. He pulled Xach toward Room 256 – the room directly across from the room they just exited.

Count Milton's chanting became louder, reaching its crescendo with "PARLAY TEMPUS FROVAR!" There was a blinding flash of green light followed by ripples of blue sparks that flowed throughout the entire hallway. Xach instinctively covered his eyes, but just enough so that he could still see what was going on. As the blue sparks began to dissipate, he realized that the people in the hallway had stopped moving. In fact, everything around them seemed to be frozen!

Before the explosion of light a little girl in a light pink dress had been drinking water from the water fountain. She now stood motionless, bent over with her mouth open in a small "O" to slurp from the stream of water from the fountain that touched her lips but did not flow. Little droplets of water were suspended in mid air. The guards that had been dragging Count Milton were frozen like statues in mid stride, their left legs raised slightly forward off the ground. By all accounts of physics, they should have toppled over, but they did not. Xach's mother was immobilized with her arms bent and raised slightly at her side. With her purse hanging in mid-air horizontal to the floor, she looked a bit like a bird trying to flap its wings. Everything and everyone were frozen in their tracks, *except* Xach, Gerald, and Count Milton.

Count Milton opened his eyes and twisted his head around to look directly at Gerald and Xach.

"I see you have a helper," Count Milton sneered. "No matter. I can dispense with the both of you once I've gotten the key." He closed his eyes and began chanting again. "Murmur leviar wentum."

Xach watched in disbelief as Count Milton's body began to rise into the air. His arms slipped from the frozen grips of the security guards as he levitated toward the ceiling. Once he was free from the grasps of the guards, he floated back down toward the floor.

Gerald pulled Xach from the hallway and into Room 256.

"Wait a minute..." Xach began.

"Hush child. There is no time!"

"But my mother...what happened to her! Why didn't we freeze? Why do you keep pulling me with you?"

Gerald surveyed the room. It was identical in design to the room they just left – two beds, two curtain-dividers, two closets, two bedside tables with a phone, a bathroom, and a TV suspended from the ceiling. He held up the key and waved it slowly about the room.

Lying in the beds were two patients – one young male and one older male. They too were immobile, frozen in the acts of eating their dinners. The young man had been pouring himself a glass of water. The water pouring out of the pitcher was frozen in mid air in an arch toward the cup. The older gentleman had been spooning green Jello into his open mouth. A clump of it had fallen off his spoon and now hovered above his chest, stopped from falling by Count Milton's spell.

As Gerald waved the key around the room, Xach noticed that it began to glow more brightly when pointed toward the closet at the far end of the room. Gerald noticed this too and began moving toward the closet, pulling Xach behind him.

"Hey, where are you taking me?"

"An exit!" Gerald exclaimed. "How fortunate to have one so close!"

The closet door was slightly open, and Xach could see the old man's jacket and a few shirts hanging on a hanger. His pants lay folded on top of his shoes on the bottom of the closet. Gerald closed the closet door and held the key level with the small keyhole embedded in the door next to the handle. He rubbed the brightly glowing jewel with his thumb, and the key started to reshape itself. The shaft extended to over six inches and teeth grew on the end.

Xach could hear the clicking of Count Milton's boots moving toward them up the hallway.

"Gerald, there is nowhere to hide this time. Give yourself up, and I will make your suffering less profound," Count Milton sneered.

The key stopped growing and shaping itself, so Gerald slid it into the keyhole. He turned it counterclockwise as if he were locking it. Then he turned it clockwise to unlock it. He withdrew the key and pulled open the door.

"What are you do...?" Xach choked back rest of his sentence in disbelief as he stared into the closet. The man's shirts, jacket, pants and shoes were gone! In fact, the interior walls of the closet were gone! The only thing Xach could see inside the closet door was a black, seemingly endless void!

Xach heard a noise behind him and turned around just in time to see a vase of roses tip off the edge of an end table and fall to the floor. The vase shattered and water splashed in every direction. He thought maybe he or Gerald had bumped it, but neither was close enough to the end table to have bumped it.

"How'd tha...?" Xach started to say as he turned back toward Gerald and the closet, but he never got to finish his question. A strong force hit his shoulder and pushed him toward the closet. Xach tumbled head over heels into the darkness. As he rolled into the void, he caught glimpses of Gerald walking through the closet door and pulling the door shut behind them, sealing them in darkness.

****

Count Milton entered Room 256, his cloak billowing behind him like a diminutive superhero.

"Now Gerald, you shall pay for..."

The room was empty except for the two patients frozen in their beds. A small trail of blood drops led to the closet farthest from the door. He approached the closet quietly and swung open the door.

"A-HA!" he shouted.

Hanging from a rod running across the top of the closet were a man's jacket and some shirts. A pair of pants was folded atop a pair of shoes.

"Blast!" he exclaimed slamming the closet door. "BLAST! BLAST! BLAST!" He stomped around the room in a small circle, kicking over a chair and pushing over a rolling food tray. He waved his arms in the air like a child throwing a temper tantrum, his face as red as a beet. This break in his concentration broke the spell he had cast to freeze the hospital. The green glob of Jello fell into the old man's lap, and the younger man continued to fill his glass with water. Shocked by the appearance of Count Milton, he gasped and dropped his glass, spilling water all over himself.

"Hey Tom, look there," said the younger man. "Did you see that? That little guy just appeared in our room!"

"Uh-yeah," said the old man, Jello dribbling out of the corner of his open mouth. He had forgotten to close his mouth or chew at the appearance of the little stranger in magician's garb.

"That there's one heck of a trick, little man! Are you here to entertain the patients?" asked the young man.

"Entertain?" responded Count Milton arrogantly. "LITTLE MAN?" he roared. "You insolent toad! How dare you imply I might serve the likes of you! Allow me to demonstrate who is the *superior* being in this room."

He pointed at the door to Room 256 and said, "Cemente indente insurate." It slammed shut and sealed itself. Almost instaneously, the screams and pounding of Mrs. Biddle and the security guards could be heard on the other side of the door, having also been unfrozen when Count Milton's concentration broke. He turned back to the young man, pointed at him, and shouted, "IRENTUS CORUNT IMMENDIUM!"

Orange sparks flew from his index finger and landed on the young man. The young man's skin bubbled and turned green. His eyes bugged out and his fingers elongated. Webbed skin grew between his fingers, and his jaw stretched and protruded outward.

The old man watched in horror as his roommate shrank in size. The young man's skin became dry and lumpy and turned a dull greenish brown; his hair fell out. In moments the transformation was complete, and the young man was no more. Sitting upon the wet sheets was a lumpy, little toad.

"And what of you, old man? Do you wish the same fate?"

The old man just stared at the toad in amazement and fear.

"Speechless, I see. A good quality in a subject. I shall spare your life, but I can't have you telling others what you've seen this night." He pointed his finger at the old man and whispered, "Seraptious correntum laureli!"

Wisps of white smoke issued from Count Milton's finger and swirled around the old man's head. Tendrils of smoke like tiny hands slid around the man's mouth and burrowed into his lips. The man tried to scream but found that his lips were being pulled shut. The smoke wove up and down between his lips like a tailor closing a hole with a needle and thread. Reaching up with a trembling hand, he felt for his lips but found only skin. His mouth had completely vanished!

Smiling wickedly, Count Milton turned toward the toad. He scooped it up in his hands and carried it to the bathroom.

"Now this will be *entertaining*!" he said as he dropped the toad into the toilet and pulled the handle. Water flooded the toilet bowl and washed the poor toad down the drain. "I may not have gotten the key, but I somehow feel a little better. Now to find another door into the Hall and finish this!"

He closed his eyes and placed his fingers on his temples.

"Irrasible ocularus entiendum," he whispered three times slowly. He opened his eyes, catching a glimpse of his disappearing reflection in the mirror.

He exited the bathroom and murmured, "Insurata indente cemente." The seal on the door to Room 256 was released. The door flew open and a nurse ran into the room, followed by a security guard and Mrs. Biddle. A quick survey of the room brought Mrs. Biddle to the stark realization that her son was not within. He vanished along with the strange man with whom he entered the room. A scream of utter loss and anger escaped from her throat as she collapsed against the wall and fell to the floor sobbing.

Count Milton stayed a moment to enjoy the pain and chaos of the moment, and then exited Room 256. A nurse rushed past him to aid the man with no mouth, and the two guards ran over to offer Mrs. Biddle some comfort. Invisible to all around him, Count Milton strolled quietly and quickly down the hallway and out of the hospital, leaving behind the frantic hospital staff and the hysterical Mrs. Biddle who cried and screamed inconsolably for her son who disappeared without a trace.

Chapter Seven

After tumbling head over heels a few times, Xachary came to a stop when his body rolled into a wall, but it wasn't so much a wall as a firm, spongy surface. He felt around in the dark for something with which to steady himself. The tumbling messed with his sense of balance, and he felt a little dizzy. The complete and total darkness surrounding him only compounded his disorientation, as he could not see anything to steady his vision. He placed his hand against the wall and stood up. He could feel his feet sink a little into the spongy floor. It was kind of like trying to stand on one of those carnival moonwalk rides where the floors and walls are inflated with air.

"Gerald? Where are you?" Xach asked uncertainly. "Where are we?

Gerald said nothing. Xach strained his ears to hear something in the dark. He heard shallow, uneven breathing coming from a few feet away. Holding his arms out in front of himself, so as not to bump into anything, Xach shuffled his feet slowly along the springy floor toward the breathing sound, which he hoped was coming from Gerald. He felt his foot bump into something. He leaned over and felt around. His hand brushed what felt like hair, so he felt below it in hopes of finding Gerald's face. Below the hair he found a nose and beard stubble. Xach knelt next to Gerald and felt around for the key. He found it on the floor a few inches from Gerald's right hand.

He picked it up and rubbed the gem as he had seen Gerald do. The gem began to glow with a faint yellow-green light like a glo-stick. Xach brought the key closer to Gerald's face. His eyes were closed, and he was not moving. Waving the key across Gerald's torso, Xach was able to see that Gerald's side was bleeding heavily again. A small pool of blood was collecting on the floor. It looked black and viscous in the green glow. *Gerald needs medical attention,* Xach thought. *And I need to get home.* He began searching the dark room for an exit. Having his senses restored to him, Xach realized that although they entered through a closet door they could not possibly be in a closet. The space was too large.

Whatever magic Gerald used to hide us in the hospital closet must be reversible, Xach thought. *Whatever he did, it's got something to do with this key. Perhaps it will re-open the doorway and get me back home.* Holding the key above his head, he set about determining the dimensions of the black room. From end to end it seemed to be about fifteen feet long. The width and height of the room were about ten feet in each direction. *There should be a door where we entered*, Xach thought. He held the key close to the wall where Gerald had stepped through the doorway of the closet, but there was no door. It had vanished as soon as the door closed. *Where did it go? It was just here a moment ago!* He began walking along the perimeter of the room, using the key's light to search for another door or opening of some kind. As he approached the far end of the room, the outline of a door began to glow faintly, as if a bright light were shining behind it and showing through the cracks. He felt along the sides for a door handle but found none. *Perhaps it's a swinging door and will open with a push,* he thought. He put the key in his pocket and placed his hand upon the soft, squishy door. He pushed and felt his hands sink into the door. He pushed with more strength until his palms met with resistance. The door swung open into what appeared to be a dimly lit hallway.

He stepped into the hallway and looked around. To his left the hall stretched as far as his eyes could see. Lining the hall on each side were hundreds of doors similar to the one from which he had just stepped. To his right were several more doors and a larger arched door at the end of the hall. As his eyes adjusted to the dim lighting, he realized that there were thousands upon thousands of stars providing the light for the hallway. The walls, the ceiling, and the doors were made of a squishy translucent substance that acted like a window and allowed the stars behind them to shine through. *Am I in space?* Xach wondered. *If I am in space, how can I be breathing? What is this structure?* Xach looked at his feet, and immediately felt a sense of vertigo. It looked as though he should be falling into space. It was like standing on air. Panic crept into his mind as he realized that "home" was much farther away than he thought. He closed his eyes and tried to relax as his frantic mind spit out questions he could not answer. *Where am I? How am I going to get home? WHERE exactly IS home? What is this place?*

"Welcome to the Hall of Worlds," whispered Gerald from within the darkness. Xach jumped a little, startled by Gerald's sudden speech. He thought Gerald was unconscious. Xach stepped back into the darkness and knelt near Gerald's body.

"Are you all right?" Xach asked.

"No, my child." He coughed and gasped for air. "I believe I am dying," he replied in a quiet whisper.

"So how do we get back? You need a doctor, and I need to get back to my mother before she has a total conniption."

"I'm afraid…that's not possible at the moment," Gerald continued. He paused to cough. It was a horrible rattling cough that shook his entire body.

"What do you mean that's not possible?!? Where am I? What have you done? Where is my home? My mom?" Xach rambled. "If you die, I'll be trapped here…wherever HERE is…all alone!"

"I know you have many questions, my child. ***cough**cough*** I am sorry you were involved, but ***cough*** we must get to someplace safe immediately. ***cough**cough**hack*** Then I will tell you what I can."

Gerald attempted to sit up, but immediately grasped his side and fell back against the wall, moaning in agony. Xach watched in silent disbelief. With each passing moment, the dire reality of his situation began to sink in. He was trapped in this place and his only hope of ever getting back home lay with a dying man. Tears welled up in his eyes, and the floor beneath his feet seemed to drop away. His head began to spin. Thoughts of loneliness and despair circled in his head, and he felt sick to his stomach. The darkness of the room made him feel very claustrophobic, so he stepped back into the hallway.

With his vision blurred by tears and his entire system immobilized by fear and doubt, he hardly noticed a distinct increase in the brightness of the stars lighting the hall. The stars sparkled and dimmed twice, followed by a low rumbling sound like thunder. The floor shifted up and down as if waves of water were moving underneath his feet. Xach wiped the tears from his eyes and saw that the ripples were not just in the floor but on the walls and ceiling as well. It was as if the entire structure in which he stood was made out of water and someone threw a pebble into it, causing ripples outward from the point of impact. The ripples were coming from behind a door further down the hall on the opposite side.

"Child," Gerald coughed, "from where do these vibrations originate?"

"From down the hall," Xach said, choking back his tears and pointing toward the door about thirty feet away.

All of a sudden, Gerald seemed to be stronger and more forceful, just as he had been when they were being chased by Count Milton in the hospital.

"Quickly child, help me up," he directed. "We must hide quickly. He'll be here momentarily."

"Who?" said Xach, moving back into the room toward Gerald.

"There's no time to explain. Help me up, NOW!"

"Ok. Calm down," said Xach. He put his arm under Gerald's and helped him into a standing position.

Gerald groaned loudly and grasped his side. For a second, Xach thought he might pass out again, but somehow Gerald managed to remain conscious. They staggered toward the hall. Xach peered around the corner and checked the hall. It was empty.

"Quickly now," said Gerald as he shuffled into the corridor toward the right, dragging Xach along while using him as a crutch. "We must reach **cough** the end of the hallway before he *ack* finds us!"

They reached the door at the end of the hallway and stopped. Gerald's body stiffened.

"Where is the key? I've lost the key!"

"Oh, I have it," said Xach. He reached into his pocket and withdrew the key. He handed it to Gerald. Gerald rubbed the gem, and it began to glow green again. At the same time, light began to shine around the doorframe, as it had for Xach when he found the door in the dark room. Gerald leaned his body against the door and used his body weight to push it open.

They stepped through the doorway and into a much larger hall. Xach turned around slightly to push the door shut behind him. Before the door closed completely, he saw someone emerge from a door thirty feet from the room that somehow connected to the hospital closet. He saw a shiny, black leather boot emerge into hallway. His heart sank a little as he realized the leg must belong to the same little man who chased them out of the hospital and into this place.

Count Milton purposefully stepped into the hallway and quickly surveyed it, hoping to catch a glimpse of Gerald and the boy. Luckily for Xach and Gerald, Count Milton turned first to his left and did not notice the main hall door closing.

Gerald felt Xach's hesitation as he watched Count Milton and admonished him to move faster. "Come quickly child! We haven't much time!" he urgently whispered.

He pulled Xach along into the larger hallway they had just entered. This hall was four or five times the size of the other. It was made of the same translucent, squishy material and was lit by millions of stars. The hall had a vaulted ceiling, and the doors were arched and much larger.

"Come along boy! Stop dawdling and move quicker! Count Milton is near, and he *hack* means to kill us!"

Back in the first hallway, Count Milton looked to his right and saw an open door about thirty feet away. He turned on his heels and swooped toward the open door, his cape billowing behind him like a super hero in flight.

In his haste to catch his prey, he did not notice Gerald's blood on the floor. He planted his foot squarely in the center of one large pool. His forward momentum propelled his foot out from under him. He pitched backward and hung awkwardly in the air for an instant before falling solidly on his back.

"Blast!" he yelled. The fall scared him more than anything, because he was not physically hurt in any way. The cushiony material of the hall provided a comfortable fall, but his cape and suit quickly absorbed the copious amounts of blood on the floor.

He stood up and effeminately wiped the blood from his hands onto his suit jacket.

"Ewwww," he whined, flapping his arms and hands in total disgust.

In the main hall, Gerald hurried to the right, urging Xach to follow. There were many more doors in this hall – so many that Xach thought there must be millions! The hall stretched endlessly in each direction. Through the door to the hall they had just left, Xach distinctly heard Count Milton yell, "Blast!" He quickened his pace to match Gerald's.

Gerald came to a sudden stop before one of the doors. He touched the key to the surface of the door and watched impatiently as the symbol on the door and the edges of the door began to glow faintly. The symbol on the door looked like a capital letter "B" with two dots in the center and some lines coming off the center like a ray of light.

"This will do," Gerald mumbled, glancing nervously over his shoulder toward the door separating them from Count Milton. "Hurry now," he said, pushing the door open.

The two stepped inside and quickly closed the door behind them. Before them lay another smaller hall with hundreds of small doors like the one into which they first stepped from the black antechamber of the hospital closet.

"Let's find a door that works and **cough, choke** get out of here before he finds us."

Back in the first hall, Count Milton was still mumbling curses under his breath as he tried to clean the blood from his outfit. Then he realized that this unfortunate and foul occurrence might actually be a blessing in disguise. He peered into the dark room and found nothing. He formulated that this must have been the anteroom to the closet exit Gerald and the boy used to escape from the hospital. Following the trail of blood from the room led him to the great arched door at the end of the hall. *With one of them bleeding this much,* thought Count Milton, *they can't have gotten too far. This is fortunate, yet a bit disappointing. I won't have the pleasure of torturing and killing the both of them myself. Oh well, I guess I'll just have to torture the one who lives,* he thought as an evil grin spread beneath his curly handlebar mustache. He withdrew a gold key from his cloak and waved it in front of the door. Light shown through the cracks around the door, as it had done for Gerald, but instead of being a consistent soft light, the light pulsed sharply. He pushed open the great door, and it swung open.

"I know where you are Gerald," he taunted loudly. "I know one of you is seriously injured. Just give me the key and I promise to help you...*help you die quickly instead of slowly and painfully*! Ah-ha-HA-HA!!"

Although the walls and doors muffled sound, Xach and Gerald could hear Count Milton yelling and laughing.

Who is this guy? thought Xach, as he tried to keep up with Gerald's pace. *He's totally deranged!*

Gerald was almost running down the hall, holding the key in front of every door he passed. As they passed the eleventh one on the right, the gem on the key glowed.

"Here!" Gerald gasped.

He waved the key in front of the door and its edges glowed. He pushed it open and pulled Xach inside. Xach tripped over Gerald's dragging feet, and the two tumbled into the dark room.

At that very moment, Count Milton entered the hall and saw the two of them fall through the doorway. "I see you!" shouted Count Milton. "At last I've caught you!" He sprinted toward the open door.

"Close the door!" yelled Gerald.

Xach raised his leg and tried to kick it shut, but Count Milton was too fast. He stopped it from slamming and pushed it back open. He stood in the doorway watching Xach scramble to his feet and try to help Gerald stand again. However, Gerald's body was limp; he passed out again.

"Hello nephew," cooed Count Milton. "This ends now!" he growled and leapt into the room.

Reacting on pure instinct, Xach dropped Gerald to the floor and delivered a swift, hard kick directly to Count Milton's groin. Milton doubled over, screaming in pain, clutching his crotch. Xach threw his body against Milton, hoping to push Milton backward toward the open door and into the hallway. Instead, Milton toppled sideways, knocking the door closed. He fell to the floor in a fetal position. The moment the door sealed, the three of them were enveloped in total blackness.

"Great!" mumbled Xach, as he felt around in the darkness for Gerald's body. Upon finding him, he felt for the key and pried it from Gerald's clenched hand. He quickly waved it around the dark room in search of the exit. Directly opposite the entrance another doorway began to glow. Xach shoved it open, flooding the room with bright orange light. He put the key in his pocket and rushed back to Gerald. He hoped that if he got Gerald through the door and closed it that Count Milton would not be able to follow them just like in the hospital. He hooked his arms under Gerald's and backed into the open doorway, dragging Gerald's limp body with him.

Xach stood on the threshold of the exit with Gerald's body entirely within the anteroom as Count Milton began to recover from his kick to the groin. Milton struggled to stand up, glaring in fury at Xachary. He could not yet stand up straight, so he lurched toward them in a crouched manner, comically reminding Xach of a hunchback. Whatever humor he found in Count Milton's hobbling movement instantly melted away as he realized Count Milton was moving faster than he was.

As if by divine intervention, Count Milton did not properly negotiate his footing and once again stepped in a pool of Gerald's blood. The following moments seemed to progress in slow motion. Milton's foot slid backward on the blood, and his body tipped forward as both of his feet left the ground. He flew through the air headfirst toward Gerald and Xach.

Milton's forehead made contact with Gerald's chest with enough force to knock Xach and Gerald through the exit and onto the ground. Xach landed on a cushion of grass; Gerald landed on top of Xach. Xach rolled Gerald off his chest, jumped up and over Gerald's motionless body and grabbed hold of the door, which from his side looked like the wooden door to an outhouse. Count Milton lay on the floor of the anteroom, his arms outstretched before him. He grabbed Gerald's leg with his right hand and tried to pull himself through the exit. Xach threw his entire weight against the door to close it. He hoped the door would hurt Milton's arm enough for him to withdraw back into the anteroom momentarily, so that Xach could securely close the door and seal him inside.

Count Milton screamed in pain as the door made contact with his arm. The door slammed in his face. He felt a hot, searing pain in his arm just below his shoulder. He screamed in agony as pain radiated through his entire body and darkness enveloped him as the door shut tightly.

Xach heard Count Milton's cry of pain as the door made contact with his arm, but it was cut short and simply disappeared when the door closed completely. Just to be sure that Count Milton and the anteroom had indeed vanished, Xach opened the door quickly and peeked inside. A gust of warm, stale air carrying the stench of feces and urine hit Xach in the face. The room inside was a small wooden cubicle with several half-foot holes cut into its wooden floor. The putrid stench of waste rose up through these holes in the floor. Although it looked nothing like any outhouse he'd seen before, it was definitely an outhouse. He could not begin to understand how it might be used as such, but he quickly decided that was a question he really didn't need answered at this time. He closed the door and rested his back against it, breathing a sigh of relief as he slid down the wooden surface and sat on the blue grass next to Gerald's motionless legs and Count Milton's arm! Count Milton's arm lay on the ground, neatly severed just below the shoulder, still gripping Gerald's ankle.

****

In the pitch-black anteroom, Count Milton writhed in pain. He tried to push himself up using his right arm, but he felt no movement, only pain. He rolled onto his back and sat up. He couldn't feel or move his right arm, yet it was tingly with pain. He tentatively drew his left hand to his right side to feel for his non-responsive limb and felt nothing! He reached for his shoulder from which the dull pain radiated and felt a smooth surface where his arm should have been. His arm was *gone*!

"NOOOOOO!!!" he screamed, jumping up and pounding on the door with his one good arm. "GIVE ME BACK MY ARM!"

The door would not open. It was sealed tightly, locking him in the darkness with his insurmountable anger. Half crying and cursing the darkness, Count Milton swore that his nephew and the meddling boy would pay for his injury and humiliation with more than their lives.

Though temporarily defeated and in severe pain, his anger gave him newfound energy. He awkwardly stood up and began searching for an exit. He obviously could not follow Gerald through the door once it was closed, so he needed to get back to the Hall of Worlds and find another door. However, he found that this door was also sealed. He waved his gold key over every wall in the room and found the same result. Not a single door would open. He was trapped!

A hysterical, almost primal scream of total madness rose in his throat, and he plunged the key into one of the walls. It sunk several inches into the squishy material. Tiny red bolts of lightning hissed from the hole and snaked across the walls of the chamber. The alarming appearance of these electrical currents did little to curb his unbridled rage and frustration. He continued howling and punching holes in the wall until he was able to press his hand into one of the ragged and sparking holes.

He tore the wall apart, piece by piece, until he was able to crawl through into the adjoining antechamber. He hardly noticed the sting of the electricity coursing over his body; his adrenaline and anger provided an almost superhuman tolerance to the phenomenon.

He wobbled into a standing position. With as much dignity as he could muster, he took a deep breath, and smoothed his clothes. The red lightning blazed furiously around the giant hole through which he had pushed himself, and it lit up the room like a demonic strobe light.

Count Milton waved his key around the room. The door to the new world and the door to the Hall of Worlds lit up intermittently. He briefly contemplated entering the new world, so that he might track down Gerald and the boy and kill them slowly and painfully. However, one small rational part of his otherwise incapacitated psyche told him that his present physical condition coupled with the likelihood that he might emerge on the new world thousands of miles from Gerald and the boy might result in failure. Failure was not an option. He pushed open the door leading back into the Hall of Worlds and headed back toward the Great Hall, mumbling and giggling incoherently as he nursed the shoulder of his missing arm and plotted his revenge.

Behind him in the room he had just exited, the shredded wall continued to spark and crackle with ever increasing intensity. A moment later, a small piece of the wall along the tattered edge of the hole fell to the floor and exploded in a puff of red sparks. Moments later another piece fell and vanished in a brilliant flash of tiny red fireballs. This was followed by another and another as the entire wall began to crumble and erode.

Chapter Eight

Count Milton's arm twitched and shook as it lay on the ground, still gripping Gerald's ankle. Xach reached out his hand and poked it in the forearm section. He half expected it to release Gerald's ankle and attack him, as severed limbs so often did in horror movies, but it did not. He knelt closer to it and examined the area cut by the door. He saw the pink and red muscle tissue surrounding the white bone center, but it was not bleeding. The cut was smooth and precise. It somehow cauterized the wound and kept it from hemorrhaging whatever blood remained in the arm.

Xach had not intended to cut off Count Milton's arm; he just wanted to escape from him. He realized, at least to some degree, that Count Milton wanted to kill them, so he shouldn't feel badly about injuring him in this manner. Having never been placed in a life or death situation before, he had no real concept of what one was capable of when placed in mortal danger or what one would feel. His life had become one crazy roller coaster ride of events ever since the earthquake and his first encounter with Gerald. He could hardly believe that it was still the same day! So much had happened since he got up this morning – the earthquake, the hospital visit, the Hall of Worlds, and Count Milton's attack. He wasn't entirely sure why Count Milton wanted to kill him, but he was an intelligent young man and assumed it had something to do with the key. Nonetheless, he still felt a little guilty about cutting off the man's arm.

Just like most young boys his age, Xach often dreamed of an adventure that would take him away from his boring life and protective family. He read comic books about superheroes and watched horror and sci-fi movies about creatures and alien worlds, wishing he could experience the thrill of the unknown. Yet, now that he seemed caught up in just such an adventure, he began to long for his normal life with his parents and siblings. Moreover, he wished Jeremy were with him to share in the adventure. It was one thing to be abducted from his home and family and stranded in a strange place with no idea of how to get back, but it was quite another thing to be stranded in a strange place without a friend or family member to rely upon for help and support. He felt very lonely, even though Gerald was with him. Gerald's presence was not much of a comfort. If Xach failed to revive Gerald and find someone to heal his injury, he would be totally alone with no way of getting back home. The wave of frustration and desperation that caused him to break down in the Hall of Worlds washed over him again, but he took a deep breath and held back the tears.

"Oh well, what's done is done. Best to keep moving forward," Xach mumbled to himself as he set about disposing of Count Milton's arm and helping Gerald.

Count Milton's hand was tightly clenched around Gerald's ankle, but Xach was able to pry each finger loose one at a time. Once it was detached from Gerald's leg, he gingerly picked it up by the wrist and lifted it off the ground. He held it away from him at arm's length, just in case it were to become reanimated and try to choke him like in the horror movies his mother had always forbidden him to watch. The arm wriggled a little in his hand, but it made no sudden movements. Using his free hand, he took a deep breath and opened the outhouse door. Leaning forward into the humid, smelly darkness of the wooden shack, he dangled the arm above one of the holes in the wooden floor. Without a second thought, he released his grip and watched Count Milton's arm disappear through the hole. Xach heard the arm hit the bottom with a *sploosh*. He closed the door quickly and took a deep breath of fresh air.

He surveyed his surroundings. For the first time he realized that he was in a strange place that looked similar to Earth but was most definitely **not** Earth. For starters, the grass under his feet was not green – it was a bright, electric blue. Looking up into the sky, he could see floating clumps of earth like islands in the sky. There were no clouds, just the floating clumps of dirt. Two suns shone brightly in the sky. One was very large and green in color. The other was about two-thirds the size of the green sun and shone bright pink. Xach had to hold his hand over his eyes to look at the smaller sun, as it was so intensely bright that he was nearly blinded just by looking in its general direction. Bird-like creatures with large wingspans and dangling tails floated through the air, landing on the floating dirt piles to rest. One particular bird, sporting silver feathers, landed squarely on one of the floating islands and was attacked by something Xach could not see. With a howling squawk and flurry of feathers, the magnificent bird disappeared from Xach's view. Feathers floated to the ground like large silver snowflakes, landing on the strange landscape around him.

What looked like upside down trees grew out of the ground with their roots stretching into the air. Bushes of every color – red, orange, yellow, purple, and green – dotted the horizon, but he could not clearly focus on any of them, as if they were vibrating or moving. He squinted and tried to focus on a large purple rock, which he assumed was stationary. As he watched the rock, he saw a green and a red bush moving toward the rock, while a yellow one appeared to be moving away from it. As the extraordinary strangeness of his surroundings sank in, Xach questioned where exactly he was? *What is this place? I am certainly not on Earth, but where am I? Where did Gerald bring me?*

Something brushed against his arm, startling him and causing him to sidestep and trip over Gerald. He landed on his tailbone quite hard. Xach shook his head and looked up to see a purple bush moving toward Gerald's body. He watched in disbelief as the bush sidled up to Gerald's body and appeared to reach outward toward Gerald's side where he was bleeding profusely.

The purple leaves quivered, and Xach thought he saw things moving along the branch toward the end of the bough. He leaned forward to look more closely, and his tailbone screamed in pain. He rubbed his sore butt, as he watched the things move uniformly along the branch. His curiosity got the better of him, so he got on all fours and crawled over to the branch to get a closer look.

The bush teemed with what looked like insects – much like an organized ant colony. They moved in a straight line across the bough toward the leaves closest to Gerald. Xach squinted and knelt closer to the branch, and he realized that the creatures were not insects or ants at all. They were extremely tiny, red-skinned people! If he had not just been kidnapped by a stranger, brought through a closet into the Hall of Worlds, and cut off the arm of a man trying to kill him, Xach might have thought he was hallucinating. If he had been older, he might have met these fantastical things with stubborn disbelief, but being a ten year-old boy, he was fascinated and exhilarated by what he saw.

He watched silently as the tiny red creatures, no larger than a centimeter or two, made their way towards the ends of the leaves. He assumed they were male in gender, because they did not have breasts or hair. However, contrary to his male gender theory, they lacked any discernable male genitalia. They appeared genderless. Their skin was smooth, red, and shiny, like a candy apple or the glossy red paint on a wagon. As they moved, he saw no moving musculature, so he assumed their skin was hard, like the exoskeleton of most insects.

They walked upright like a human on what appeared to be two legs, but they had two sets of arms on each side of their torsos. One set ended in what looked like fingers, and the other set looked like pincers of some kind. Their heads resembled a human's in that they had two eyes, a nose, and a mouth, or so it seemed to Xach. He assumed the two large black, glossy discs atop their heads were eyes and that the three tiny black slits below the discs were nostrils. Beneath the slits was a tiny circular opening he assumed was a mouth. Xach could detect no protuberances that might be construed as ears, and they were hairless. The green and pink suns reflected off their shiny heads as light might reflect off a highly polished stone. Along the backs of their legs were spines or spikes of some kind, and Xach wondered if they were for protection, hearing, or something else entirely.

The tiny red men marched in single file to the edges of the leaves. Each line of men held onto a silken thread that originated from somewhere within the bush. When one of the men reached the end of a leaf, he stepped off, keeping hold of the thread as he fell, like a mountain climber repelling off a rocky overhang. The others in the line held the line steady, so that the one who jumped did not plummet to the ground. Instead they slowly lowered the men down onto Gerald. One by one they jumped off the bush and landed on Gerald's side. Once securely upon Gerald's body, each creature released the thread, coiled it neatly on a pile, stepped away towards Gerald's wound, and waited for the next one to come down.

In minutes, several hundred of them swarmed around the blood soaked patch of cloth covering Gerald's wound. Xach didn't know what to do. He didn't know if they were trying to help or hurt Gerald. His first instinct was to swat them away as he would swat a fly or mosquito that landed on him or buzzed in his face, but since this wasn't Earth, he didn't know what to do. *Besides,* he thought, *Gerald is almost dead, and I certainly can't do anything to help him. Maybe these guys can? They certainly can't make things any worse, can they?* The little people didn't seem to notice Xach or care that he was so close, so he decided to just let them continue doing whatever they were doing. *If it seems like they're hurting Gerald, I can just squash all of them with my hand. They have to realize that I could harm them if I wanted, so they must be trying to help him.*

As Xach looked on, the little red people bent over, placing their sets of pincer-hands on the cloth of Gerald's robe. They formed a circle around the bloodstain and began moving in a clockwise direction, all the while keeping their hands on the cloth. After a few seconds, Xach saw the cloth of Gerald's robe fall away from the edge of the circle. Their pincers acted like scissors to cut the fabric away from the wound.

After the cloth was removed, they moved in to inspect the wound. There was a large oozing cut in Gerald's side. All of the walking, pulling, and twisting that Gerald did to escape from the hospital and bring Xach to the Hall of Worlds wreaked havoc on the hospital stitches. Xach saw where the hospital stitches were made, and it looked as if most of them ripped. The stitches tore through Gerald's skin, leaving the edges of the wound ragged, raw, and bloody.

Blood flowed in a steady stream from the wound, and the little people seemed to know that this was a bad thing. They formed lines leading from the coiled threads they used to repel from the bush to the edges of Gerald's wound. They moved with lightning-quick speed, feeding the thread along the lines to the person closest to the wound. Using their pincers like needles, they perforated the skin surrounding the laceration in Gerald's side. They slipped the thread in and out of these perforated holes and wove them back and forth across the expanse of the gaping wound. Once the wound was crisscrossed hundreds of times by the gossamer threads, the line of little men tugged strongly on the thread, tightening the weaving they performed over the wound. The skin on either side of the wound drew tightly together like a bodice, leaving little or no space for any blood to escape.

The little red people were so intent on their medical procedure and Xach was so mesmerized by their speed and skill that neither noticed something swoop down out of the sky until its shadow fell over the tiny community of helpers moving about on Gerald's body. It let out a loud, shrieking squawk that startled Xach and caused the little red men to scatter in all directions.

"SKREEEEAWWWK!" cried the bird-creature as it swooped down on the red people. Panic and confusion erupted throughout the group as the bird glided down with its claws stretched out and snatched several of them from off of Gerald's chest. Xach heard the quiet screams of those carried away. Some managed to squirm free of the bird's grasp, only to fall twenty feet to the ground as the bird took to the sky.

Xach watched in muted horror as the bird flew up toward one of the floating islands and hovered over what looked like a nest, dangling the tiny red men over its opening. Small bird heads popped up out of the nests, their mouths open wide as they cried for food. The bird released the helpless red beings, and they fell into the hungry maws of the tiny birds. The tiny birds swallowed them whole or fought over them, pulling them apart with their beaks. With a massive flap of its wings, the giant bird lifted itself into the air and dove toward Gerald's chest for another attack.

Xach looked at the group of people frantically running about Gerald's body. Some scrambled back up the threads and retreated to the dark interior of the bush from whence they came. Others tried to hide under the folds of Gerald's robe, while others took shelter in Gerald's nostrils, ears, and hair.

Xach heard them screaming as they careened into one another looking for a place to hide. It was complete pandemonium!

The bird was nearly upon them, but Xach was not about to let any more of them get snatched up and eaten. He stood up and straddled Gerald's body, waving his arms and yelling, "GET BACK! STAY AWAY!" Startled by Xach's sudden and loud movement, the bird veered to the right. It avoided a direct collision with Xach and managed to escape the encounter with a minor swat to its tail end. This minor contact did not result in any notable pain for the creature, as it did not squawk, but it did send the bird into an uncontrollable tailspin toward the ground. It crashed awkwardly in a flurry of feathers, dirt, and grass.

After a moment, the bird stood up and shook itself to release any loose feathers and dirt that were stuck in its disheveled coat. With a strong flap, the bird took flight again and flew several feet away before it turned and circled Gerald again. This time its circular path was much larger. It kept its distance. Xach continued to stand over Gerald, keeping his eye on the circling bird. Eventually, it realized that it would be unable to make another surprise attack and retreated to the floating island that held its nest and the babies that squawked for more food. It perched on the edge of the island and watched Xach intently to see if he would move.

Xach decided to remain standing over Gerald, but he returned his attention to the group of people remaining on Gerald. He could hear murmuring amongst the group as they stared upward at the towering figure above them. Those who took refuge under Gerald's robe or in one of his orifices crawled from their hiding places and rejoined the group. They too murmured and pointed and looked upward fearfully, as if they were uncertain whether Xach had just saved them from the bird or if he had just scared off the bird so that he might eat them himself.

"It's okay," Xach said to the group of little men. "I won't let the bird get you again." He pointed at the bird perched on the island. "I'll protect you. I mean you no harm."

What are you doing? Xach asked himself. *These creatures aren't human. You're on an alien world talking to aliens in English. How could they possibly understand you?*

The red congregation on Gerald's chest stared silently at him.

Of course they don't understand you, you idiot! What are you gonna do now? He looked bewilderedly off into the distance, as if an answer lay in the distance hills. He scratched his head and looked down at the little men. He was surprised to see that they reorganized themselves and were busy finishing their stitching on Gerald.

Did they understand me? Xach wondered. *That can't be possible. It's a little too much to hope that they'd understand English! I don't even understand English sometimes. Maybe they understood my body language and realized that I was trying to scare the bird away and help them? Who knows? How could an alien from some planet I don't even know about possibly understand English? Then again, it is distinctly possible that Gerald is not from Earth either, and he spoke English. He looks human, but his blood **did** stain my skin. Maybe he's an alien too! And if he is, he spoke English and understood it, so maybe these guys can too?*

Xach's mind began to spin at the thought that Gerald might not be from Earth. He became acutely aware that things were not at all what they seemed. He determined that if he was going to survive on this world or any others in the Hall of Worlds, he was going to have to be open to almost anything and attempt to expect the unexpected.

He turned his attention back to the tiny red beings working on Gerald's wound. They were almost finished. They knotted the threads and tied off the ends. The bleeding almost stopped, blocked by the intricately woven threads and stretched skin. Xach watched as they collected their scraps of thread, climbed back up the bush, and filed into its interior out of Xach's sight. Once everyone returned safely to the bush, the bush moved away from Xach towards Gerald's head.

"Thank-you," Xach said, still unsure as to whether they even understood him or not, but he felt it was worth a try.

However, the bush did not leave. Instead it moved into a position directly in front of Gerald's head. Again the streams of little red people carrying thread lines left the bush and repelled off the branches onto Gerald's shoulders. Marching in a straight line, they walked down Gerald's shoulder, through his armpit, and returned on the other side. Once fully around his shoulder, they tied the end of the thread to the line leading to the bush, thereby creating a harness of sorts. Once they had ten to fifteen thread loops tied to each shoulder, they returned to the bush.

What are they doing now? Xach wondered. The bush began moving again, pulling Gerald across the ground behind it. Since they just stitched his wound, Xach was fairly certain that the creatures meant Gerald no harm by dragging him. Xach followed along behind, thankful that he didn't need to carry Gerald. Besides, he was certain he could rescue Gerald if the bush dragged him into any kind of danger. He glanced briefly over his shoulder at the bird to see if it was still watching them, but it had gone. Apparently, it saw no gain in attacking the bush any further. Xach took this opportunity to observe his new surroundings as he walked.

The suns in this world were so bright that Xach had to walk with his hand held over his eyes like a visor. He half wished Gerald had kidnapped him from school or his room, so that he would have been able to grab his backpack with his sunglasses and other stuff. His attention was continually drawn to the bushes that moved slowly from one place to another like grazing chickens or cows, seemingly without purpose. He noticed that they clustered quite often near the large purple boulders that dotted the landscape. Just ahead of him, he could see a group of yellow and red bushes milling around a purple boulder that was about the size of a small car. The bush dragging Gerald made its path near the car-sized rock, so Xach was able to look more closely at the bushes' behaviors.

The yellow and red bushes moved around the rock. Periodically they stopped and extended their branches toward the rock's surface. The little people living within the bush walked out on the branch, dragging small cocoons behind them. Xach could not see what was in the cocoons, but they ranged in size from that of a mouse to as large as a small rabbit or hamster. The little red people deposited the cocoons on the surface of the rock and retreated back into the bush. After the bush retracted its branch, the rock surface changed. It became less solid like it was made of a viscous fluid similar to pudding. It bubbled up around the cocoon, folded over it, and enveloped it – much like an amoeba would absorb and digest food.

Out of the corner of his eye, Xach caught a glimpse of one of the bird-like creatures as it leapt off one of the floating islands and swooped down toward the little people who struggled with dragging a large cocoon toward the rock surface. Xach cringed, fearing he would witness the deaths of several more little people, but just as the bird came within five feet of the rock, it was stopped in mid flight by the rock itself! An arm like an octopus tentacle shot out of the rock with amazing force and speed, smacking the bird out of the air. A cloud of feathers drifted slowly to the ground around the dazed bird. It stood up, shook itself, and hobbled away, temporarily unable to fly due to a sprained wing and mild concussion.

The little people went about their business of feeding the rock as if nothing had happened. *This must be some type of symbiotic relationship. In exchange for protection from the birds, the little people capture and deliver food to the rock creatures. Ms. Zipple would have been fascinated by this*, Xach thought. It reminded Xach of Ms. Zipple's lesson on the symbiotic relationship between sharks and the small "cleaner-fish." She spoke with great enthusiasm about the sharks and other dangerous fish who have their teeth and gills cleaned by smaller fish. In exchange for the cleaning, the larger fish do not eat the little ones, and the little fish arc fed by whatever they clean off of the large fish's teeth and gills. His teacher also made reference to the moral implications of such animal kingdom behavior. She said that "a helping hand, receives one in return."

I wonder how she's doing, Xach thought, as he returned his attention to Gerald and the bush that dragged him. *I wonder if she's still in the hospital?* Thinking of Ms. Zipple opened a floodgate of thoughts about school, Jeremy, and his family. *I wonder how they're handling my disappearance? Is the school open after the earthquake or am I missing a free vacation from school? What will Jeremy do now that I'm gone? I wish there were some way I could let mom and dad know that I'm all right so they don't worry about me.*

He was so consumed with his thoughts about home that he didn't realize the bush stopped pulling Gerald and was resting near a pool of pink sparking liquid. He tripped over Gerald's leg and found his face rushing toward the ground as he fell forward. He tired to break his fall with his arm, but he only managed to get his right arm partially out, causing his full weight to fall on his wrist. His wrist twisted inward and broke his fall. He cried out first in alarm, but his cries quickly turned to those of agonizing pain when his wrist bent the wrong way. He rolled on his back and grasped his injured wrist with his left hand, trying to relieve the pain shooting from his wrist into his upper arm.

Tears welled in his eyes and the emotions of the past several hours took over. He was lost in a strange world with his nearly dead kidnapper and an injured wrist. He wanted to be home in his bed. He didn't want to be **here**. He didn't want **any** of this! Tears streamed down his cheeks as he sobbed. At that moment he felt like an abandoned baby, lost and ineffectual, unable to communicate or fend for himself. After all, he was only a ten year-old boy, not an adult with years of life experience and the emotional development to cope with such fantastic and unusual events. The twisted wrist was the proverbial "straw that broke the camel's back," and Xach simply gave into the despair and fear he was suppressing since his abduction.

Through his sobs, he failed to hear the tiny, quiet voice that asked him if he needed help.

Chapter Nine

Xach continued crying for a few minutes until he began to feel a little tired from exerting the amount of energy it takes to maintain a good long cry. As his sobs subsided, he became distinctly aware of a quiet voice whispering in his ear. He choked back a sob, closed his wet eyes, and concentrated on listening closely to the tiny voice.

"…stop crying and tell us how we may help you, Oh Great One. Tell us what hurts so we may mend it and repay you for your kindness in saving our people from the quarken."

Xach opened his eyes and wiped away the tears with his left hand. His nose was running, so he sniffed it back. He turned his head toward the voice and came face to face with a group of tiny red people standing on a leaf of the purple bush. The one in front of the group stepped forward and spoke in a quiet feminine voice. It was larger than the others and more purple than red in color.

"Oh Great One, how may we help you?"

"You speak English?" Xach sniffed in surprise.

"I do not know what 'English' is, but we speak our language, Zindi."

"But you spoke English just now. I heard you and understood you."

Xach sat up and cradled his injured wrist.

"I do not understand," the woman continued. "You have been speaking Zindi. That is why we understand what you have been saying."

"I mean no disrespect, but you are clearly speaking what I call English," insisted Xach. "Perhaps our languages are exactly the same but called different names?"

"Perhaps," she said, "but this discussion is irrelevant. We do not have time to discuss semantics. My people need to know if we can help you. We can not afford to stand out in the open too long or we risk attack from the dreaded quarken. Plus, we must continue with our harvest. Are you injured in some way that caused your crying? May we be of assistance?"

"Actually," said Xach, looking down at his already swollen and purple wrist, "I fell on my wrist, and it hurts quite a bit."

"If you would be kind enough to watch for quarken and to ward off any that might attack, my people will attempt to help you."

Xach was not sure *how* he knew that a quarken was the silver bird that attacked the tiny red people, but he just seemed to inherently *know*. He nodded acceptance of her offer. She turned toward the group of people behind her and nodded. A few retreated into the bush's interior and returned with a cloth of woven thread.

"You may use this to wipe away the liquid that is dripping from your face," she said, gesturing toward the cloth.

"Thank-you," said Xach and accepted the cloth with his good hand. He wiped his eyes and blew his nose. The cloth was very soft and almost silky in texture. It felt like he was blowing his nose on a rose petal. Yet for all its delicate texture, it was amazingly strong and resistant to moisture.

"Thank-you again," he said after he'd finished cleaning his face.

He didn't want to litter and didn't want to give the soiled cloth back to them, so he put it in his pocket.

The red people softly wove a series of criss-crossed threads around his swollen wrist. The threads resembled the design of a fisherman's net. They walked very gently across his skin, creating only the slightest sensation on the surface of his skin like puffs of air. The creatures appeared to be very dense and solid, yet they didn't have the weight he expected. Two groups of several men were on the ground holding the two loose ends of the threads.

"Oh Large One," said the female on the leaf, "we are about to fix your wrist. This may hurt a bit."

"All right," said Xach. "Thanks for the warning." He grasped Gerald's leg and squeezed, preparing for whatever pain might be coming.

Each group of little men holding the ends of the threads began to pull away from each other, tightening the threads around Xach's wrist. As they pulled harder, the tension on the threads became greater and the pressure on Xach's wrist grew exponentially. In an instant of blinding pain, the threads pulled so tight that the fractured bone in his wrist was pulled back into place. Tears welled up in his eyes, but once the bone was in place, the pain subsided significantly into a dull throbbing.

"My apologies for the pain, Oh Great One," said the woman. "But I believe we have fixed the problem. Please do not move while we set your arm and finish our repairs."

Xach nodded, wiping his eyes with his left hand. He watched closely as the little red men quickly wound the silky thread around and around his wrist, hand, and lower arm, forming a fibrous cast around his fractured wrist that was both solid and soft to the touch. When they were finished, they began to weave a sling for his arm by pulling threads out of the bush and tying them around his neck and arm. Xach was amazed at their speed and agility, but even though he was fascinated with their skills and wanted to see all that they were doing, he kept glancing upward to scan the sky for quarken that might try to attack his new friends. As each man finished his job, he returned to the bush. When all were safely inside the bush, the female returned to speak to Xach.

"Your arm is repaired to the best of our abilities, Oh Great One."

"Thank-you. You can call me Xach."

"Xach?"

Yes, that's my name. It is what I'm called. What is your name?"

"I am called Queen Zini."

"Thank you, Queen Zini, for you and your friends' help. I can't thank you enough for fixing my arm and patching up Gerald's cuts."

"You are quite welcome, Xach, and we thank *you* also for warding off the quarken. Is there any further assistance you require?"

"I don't think so, but could you tell me where I am?"

"You are in the land of Zindartha on the continent of Neu Quarta. We have not seen anyone like you or your friend for quite some time, but our historical records tell of your kind visiting here several hundred years ago and observing my people. They bore witness to our way of life and the lives of other species on this planet. They presented no danger to our society and conversed with my people at length about our lives and practices, so we perceived them to be friends. That is why we came to your assistance when we detected that your friend was injured. Should you require any further assistance, simply tap on one of the bushes and ask for help. I will alert the other colonies to your presence. Presently, we must be moving along to complete some harvesting for the long night ahead of us."

"Long night?"

"Yes, when the two suns set, it will become very dark for several days. During this time, we are unable to harvest food. The quarken can see quite well in the dark and are able to catch and eat us with almost no trouble."

"How long before the suns set?"

"The suns will set in about three hours or so. I don't want to be rude, but we really must be going. My colony has not yet finished harvesting," she said, turning around and walking toward the interior of the bush.

"Ok," said Xach, "sorry to keep you. Thanks again for your help."

Queen Zini disappeared from Xach's view, and the bush slowly ambled away from him and Gerald. Xach knelt down next to Gerald and put his ear on Gerald's chest. He could hear a faint heartbeat. He held his hand under Gerald's nose and felt the whisper of his shallow breath against the back of his hand. He placed his hand on Gerald's shoulders and shook gently, hoping that might wake him. It didn't.

Xach looked at the pool of pink water and wondered if it was poisonous or not. It looked like fluorescent Kool-Aid. *If he remains in a coma, he's no help to me,* Xach thought about Gerald. *He's not getting any better just lying here, so what can it hurt to have him try the water?* He cupped his hand and dipped it into the pool of pink water. It felt quite cool, considering that the pool was not shaded by a tree and open directly to the two suns above. He brought his hand over Gerald's face and released the water. As the cool droplets hit Gerald's face, Xach saw the muscles in his cheeks spasm and his eyes twitch. Pleased that this elicited some movement,

Xach continued to scoop water from the pool and drop it on Gerald's face.

After several splashes, Gerald snorted air from his nose and mouth. The snorting turned to coughing, and he opened his eyes. He blinked several times, attempting to adjust to the brightness of the two suns. Xach could tell Gerald's mind was racing as he tried to figure out where he was and what had happened. He lifted his head slightly and slid his arms backward, so that he was resting on his elbows and partially sitting up. Upon seeing Xach, he smiled.

"Are you all right?" Xach asked. "Do you know who I am and what happened?"

"Yes," Gerald replied slowly. "Your name is Xach, right?"

"That's right. How do you feel?"

"Very tired and weak. Where is Count Milton?"

"I don't know where he is. I guess he's still in the Hall of Worlds." Xach lowered his head and started swishing his finger nervously in the pink pool. "Um…there was kind of an accident."

"What kind of accident?" said Gerald in a concerned tone. He sat up abruptly and immediately grasped his side as his wound telegraphed a painful reminder that it had not yet healed. "Uhhhhh," he groaned, and fell back into a horizontal position. He tried to catch his breath as the pain subsided. "He didn't get the key, did he?"

"No, I have it," said Xach. He fished in his pocket and produced the key. He offered it to Gerald, but Gerald shook his head, indicating that he didn't want it. Xach put it back in his pocket. He figured Gerald wanted him to hold it since he had no pockets.

"So, what kind of accident occurred?"

"Well…um…I…ahhh…kind of…cut off Count Milton's arm," Xach said quickly. "I didn't mean to do it. It just sort of happened," he rambled. "He was grabbing your leg through the doorway, and I slammed the door on his arm. I just wanted to hurt his arm, you know, so he'd let go of you. But I guess I pushed too hard or something, and it cut off his arm. I didn't mean to hurt him. I've never hurt anyone in my life! I feel so terrible…I just…" Xach trailed off, not sure of what else to say or how else to effectively express his regret, when he realized that Gerald wasn't even paying attention to him.

At some point during Xachary's rambling discourse of shame, Gerald began giggling. He reached a point of near hysteria when Xach ran out of words. His hardy laughing caused his side to hurt again, bringing an abrupt end to his guffaws and reducing him to quiet giggles. His eyes began to tear up from the pain and humor of it all. Xach thought this was extremely inappropriate, but he decided to let it go on account of Gerald being injured.

Once Gerald had composed himself and wiped the tears from his eyes, he questioned Xach again.

"Explain to me again how this happened."

"You passed out in the Hall of Worlds, and I had to drag you through the doorway. Count Milton reached through the doorway, grabbed your leg, and was trying to pull himself through the doorway. I wanted to get him off of you, so I slammed the door on his arm. I expected that the door would hit his arm, and that he'd release you. But the door just kind of went *through* his arm and cut it off. Once the door closed, I opened it, but the Hall of Worlds and Count Milton were gone. His arm was still gripping your ankle."

A large grin spread across Gerald's face as Xach recounted his ordeal for a second time. Xach could tell that he was trying very hard not to start laughing again.

"Why do you find that so funny? I cut off a man's arm!"

"Count Milton is not a man!" Gerald said gruffly. "He's a monster, and he deserves all the pain and suffering he gets. I just wish it had been me who delivered that blow! Good show!"

"You're actually happy that this happened?"

"Yes, my dear boy, Count Milton would have killed both of us if he had been able to get through the door. Not only did you injure him quite severely and possibly delay him in his pursuit, but you saved both our lives! Bravo!"

"Well, I can't say I'm as happy as you are that I did this to him. But I guess that doesn't matter. What does matter is that we're *here*… and *here* is not where I belong! I'm not even so sure that *you* belong here."

"Well, Xach, you're partially right. I don't really *belong* here, but it is my job to be here from time to time."

"What does that mean?"

"I'll explain all in good time. What happened to your arm?"

"I fell. I think I sprained or broke my wrist, but Queen Zini's people fixed me up. They patched up your wounds too."

"Ah, yes…the Zindarthans. Good people. Quite interesting communal society, but that's beside the point. It would seem that we should seek shelter. It looks like a storm is coming." He nodded towards the sky.

Xach looked at the sky behind him and saw it was filled with a strange red mist. He hadn't noticed the red clouds forming, because he had been too busy talking to Gerald. He then remembered that Queen Zini told him nightfall was coming in a few hours.

"Queen Zini told me that the suns will set in a few hours," said Xach, turning back to Gerald. "Let me help you."

He curled his good arm under Gerald's arm and helped him to stand. Gerald was quite weak and shook tremendously as he tried to stand upright. He leaned quite forcefully on Xach but managed to pull himself up. He remained hunched over, keeping one hand pressed firmly on his injured side. He rested the other on Xach's shoulder to maintain his balance.

"Where should we go?" Xach inquired.

"I don't really know, but I guess we should head *away* from the storm."

They walked slowly in the opposite direction of the gathering clouds. Xach realized Gerald was using a great deal of his strength just to stay upright, and he wouldn't get very far before he collapsed. He didn't want him to pass out again, so he thought conversation might keep his brain focused and alert.

"So, you have been here before?"

"Not for many, many years," Gerald whispered through his heavy breaths.

"Have you met Queen Zini?"

"I do not know." He paused to catch his breath. "I met many...queens. Each community...has one...queen."

Xach realized that Gerald really didn't want to talk and was just being polite by answering his questions.

"It's okay. You don't need to talk. I won't ask any more questions."

"I don't mean...to be rude," Gerald gasped. "It's hard to...talk and breathe...and walk...at the same...time."

"I understand. I'm just glad you're awake. I was afraid that you were going to die and leave me in this place. I guess I'm lucky that the Zindarthans came along and helped us."

"Yes. I'm glad I didn't...die and leave...you here alone..." *Quite yet*, he thought. "While we walk...tell me about...yourself...and your...family."

"Well, I'm ten years old. I'm in the fifth grade, and I go to Barker Elementary School...or at least I did before you brought me here. But I guess no one will be going to school for a while anyway because of the earthquake. It caused a lot of damage to the school. Anyway, we used to live in Maine, but my dad got a job in Philadelphia, so we moved to Upper Darby to be closer to Philly. My dad didn't want to live in the city, so he found our house in the suburbs. The house is okay, I guess. Mom and Dad worked hard to make the gardens look nice. I have my own room. It's pretty big, but not as big as my sister's room. Her name is Leesa; she's fifteen and kind of annoying. I also have a baby brother. He's one and a half years old. His name is Brandon. He's pretty cool I guess, but a lot of work."

"The counselor at school says that if I don't already suffer from 'middle child syndrome' that I probably will once I reach middle school. I don't know what that means exactly, but whatever. His name is Mr. Kim. I don't really like him anyway. He thinks he knows everything about me and my family, but he doesn't. I'm supposed to go to the Middle School next year, and since I just moved here, he hasn't had much time to get to know me and prepare me for the change to the new school. So he's been seeing me almost every week, trying to 'get to know me better.'"

Xach paused for a moment. He felt a bit conflicted. Thinking about his home, his family, and his school made him a little homesick, but at the same time he felt kind of glad to be away from the school and all its hassles – especially Mr. Kim. Although Xach had been cleared of any suspicion in "the snake incident," it continued to haunt him amongst the faculty. Mr. Kim believed that Xach was a "troubled" child and would need special teachers when he got to the middle school. He said that children with Xach's history and family structure generally caused trouble in Middle School. This upset Xach greatly, and no matter how much he protested against Mr. Kim's ideas, the counselor seemed determined to assign him to special classes in the Middle School along with weekly counseling sessions. Xach considered himself to be a "good boy" and didn't get into trouble. His parents seldom complained about his behavior, and to the best of his knowledge Xach thought they were proud of him.

Mr. Kim called a meeting with his mother and father near the beginning of the school year to discuss his plans for Xach upon reaching the Middle School. His parents flat-out told Mr. Kim that he was wrong and that Xach should be placed on an academic track because of his good grades and prior school record. Mr. Kim simply would not hear it. In his mind, Xach was a middle child who had been relocated against his will to a new school with a history of troublemaking, and no manner of argument would change his mind.

"That's one good thing…" Xach mumbled to himself.

"What did you say?" Gerald asked.

"Oh nothing, I was just talking to myself. I got to thinking about Mr. Kim and how he plans to stick me in special classes for 'trouble-makers' when I get to the Middle School next year. My parents said that they'd take their case to the school board if Mr. Kim tries to put me in special classes, but they hope that won't be necessary. If I don't make it home in time, then neither my parents nor I will have to worry about it. Perhaps that is one good thing that will come out of this adventure."

Gerald stopped walking for a moment and looked directly into Xach's eyes.

"Xach, please know that I...never meant for this...to happen. I know...you'd rather be home...with your family. But I couldn't let...Count Milton hurt you. I just hope...I have enough time...to fix this."

"It's okay. If I thought you did this to hurt me or something, I'd have left you in the Hall of Worlds where you passed out."

"For that...I thank you. And if others knew...of your bravery...they would...thank you too. Now, I think...I see...a shelter ahead."

He pointed at a large group of purple rocks directly ahead of them. The largest rock rested on top of the smaller ones, providing an overhang under which they could rest and stay dry if it started to rain.

"What if these aren't rocks?" Xach asked, remembering the purple rock that reached out and swatted the quarken earlier.

"What...do you...mean?" Gerald stuttered.

"When you were passed out and the Zindarthans were patching you up, I saw a group of Zindarthans feeding one of those things. It looks like a rock but it moved and swatted a quarken out of the sky. How do we know it won't eat us or hit us?"

"Well...you are correct. They are not rocks. They are...mirondi. The Zindarthans...care for the mirondi. They feed them...in exchange...for protection."

"Yeah, I saw it eat something by folding its body around the food like an amoeba. So what's to stop it from sucking us in if we lean against it?"

"Good question," said Gerald, looking a bit surprised and pleased. "You are quite a...smart boy. If I'm not mistaken, the mirondi...only eat one thing. So we...should be safe. But I'm glad...you are so...observant and wary. It means you're...a survivor."

They reached the pile of mirondi, but Xach refused to touch them. He helped Gerald under the overhang and rested him against one of the mirondi upon which the large overhang rested. When Gerald was not swallowed from behind, Xach joined him under the rock. Gerald smiled and caught his breath.

"See, they will not harm us," Gerald exclaimed. "In fact, they are warm and soft."

Xach slowly leaned back against the purple surface. Gerald was right. It was warm and soft – like a heated marshmallow. It was quite comfortable.

"This is pretty cool."

"Yes, it is," Gerald agreed. "Would you be kind enough to fetch something to drink? My throat is quite dry. I believe I saw a pond about fifty feet to our right."

"The bright pink stuff? You can drink that?"

"Yes. It's just like water, only a different color and with a different taste."

"If you say so," said Xach incredulously. "But what can I collect it in?"

"See if you can find some Zindarthans and ask them if they would create a cup for you out of their fine webbing. They should be eager to help you."

"Ok, I'll be back as soon as I can."

Xach crawled out from under the mirondi and headed off to the right in search of the pond and another bush containing a Zindarthan community. Just as Gerald had said, a large pool of fluorescent pink liquid was just beyond a small hill about fifty feet to the right. There were several bushes moving along the pond's edge. Xach approached an orange bush, uncertain of how exactly to contact the Zindarthans inside without making them think he was attacking them. He decided to announce his presence and hope someone responded.

"Hello, is anyone in there?" he said loudly, bending down toward the bush's outermost branches. "I mean you no harm. I was wondering if someone can help me?"

The leaves on the bush began to rustle and a small, purplish red Zindarthan female emerged from the bush.

"Yes, O Great One called Xach, I am Queen Zora. How may we be of assistance?"

"You know who I am?"

"Yes, Queen Zini told us that you were here and might need assistance from time to time. I was instructed to help if I could."

"Thank-you very much, your majesty. That is very nice of you. Actually, I need to know if you could construct a cup or container that I can use to carry water? My friend is thirsty."

"That should be no problem," she said matter-of-factly and vanished into the bush. The entire bush began to shake and rustle. In moments, she returned, followed by several men carrying two cup-shaped objects.

"Will these suffice?" she inquired, gesturing toward the cups her subjects were carrying.

Xach took the cups. They were smooth and very sturdy. They were woven from the same thread that had been used to stitch Gerald's wounds and to form Xach's arm cast and sling. Even though it looked like the same material, it was not soft or fabric-like. It was quite hard like glass.

"These will do just fine!" Xach said gratefully. "This substance is amazing!"

"Yes," replied Queen Zora, a bit proudly, "our thread is very versatile. It can be tempered into unbreakable objects or woven into soft garments. I am aware that Queen Zini told you of the impending darkness. Did she tell you of the lowered temperature?"

"She told me about the setting of the two suns, but she said nothing of the lowered temperature. It stands to reason, however, that it would become much colder once the suns set."

"Indeed. The temperature will become quite low. Forgive me for being so forward, but you do not appear to be properly dressed for such a drop in temperature. Might I offer you some cloaks that you could wear during the days of darkness?"

"That would be wonderful! Thank you so much!"

"Construction of the cloaks may take a small amount of time, so you may return to your friend with his drink. We'll bring the cloaks to you when they are finished."

"Thank you! How can I ever repay you for your kindness?"

"My people are eternally grateful for saving Queen Zini's tribe from the quarken earlier today. There is no need to repay us."

"But that was nothing," said Xach. "You and your people are going far beyond what I would consider repayment for what I did. You saved my friend's life! I'd say the balance of debt lies more heavily upon me."

"Nonsense. We are forever in your debt."

"Well, I don't want to argue with you. So, I'll leave it at this – if you or your people ever need my help, I would be honored to offer my services. I ask that you let your other tribes know of my offer."

"I will, O Gracious One called Xach. If you require nothing else at the present moment, my people will set about making your cloaks and finishing our harvest. The darkness approaches," she said, pointing toward the horizon.

The suns were lower on the horizon, and the red rain clouds in the distance were moving closer.

"Thank you Queen Zora. I look forward to seeing you soon."

"Likewise, O Giant One called Xach."

She returned to the interior of the bush, which started shaking and rustling again as the Zindarthans began weaving the cloaks for Xach and Gerald. Xach returned to his task. He knelt down next to the pink pond and used his good arm to fill both cups with the cool pink liquid. He returned to Gerald and offered him the drink. Gerald smiled, took the cup from him, and took a long drink.

"Ahhhh," he said, smacking his lips. "That was quite refreshing. Thank-you Xach. I feel a great deal better. I see the Zindarthans were able to construct some very nice cups for you."

Xach took a seat next to Gerald on the ground. "Yes, it's amazing how durable they are. Their webbing is fantastic. In fact, they are going to weave cloaks for us to wear once the suns go down. Queen Zora said it's going to get very cold once the suns set and that we'll need something to keep us warm."

"How thoughtful of them. They really are a wonderful people."

"Yeah, I can't believe how helpful they've been."

"It has been many years since I visited this world," said Gerald wistfully. "It's a rather simple place, actually. Very few rules."

"Rules?"

"Yes. I almost forgot that you don't know anything about all this. I do apologize. If I weren't so tired, I'd begin explaining. But suffice it to say that each world has a set of rules for interaction and reporting. You can't just walk into a world and start interacting with its inhabitants in whatever way you choose. If you do whatever you please, you might upset the delicate balance of nature on each world."

"So why did you bring me here? Isn't that upsetting the balance of my world AND this world? And what about my interaction with the quarken and the Zindarthans? Have I done anything wrong since I got here? I don't want to be responsible for upsetting the balance here!"

Xach was talking so fast he forgot to breathe. He began to hyperventilate as his mind raced with possible repercussions from his contact with the creatures on this world. He remembered his teacher's lessons about how the English settlers brought disease to the Native Americans and how this decimated the population. *What if I inadvertently brought a disease to the Zindarthans who were kind enough to help me?* he thought. *What kind of things might have happened to my world as a result of Gerald kidnapping me and bringing me to this place? What if...*

Gerald put his hand gently on Xach's knee. "Relax Xach," he said calmly. "Take a deep breath. It's all right. You have done absolutely nothing wrong. It is I who broke the rules, and it is I who will pay the consequences. Aside from removing you from your world, I do not believe any other disturbances have occurred. Count Milton is another story, but I'm afraid that must wait until tomorrow." Gerald tried to stifle a yawn, but it was obvious he was exhausted. "I need to get some sleep."

Xach was silent for a few moments, debating if he wanted to ask Gerald what was going to happen in the morning. He mustered his strength and asked weakly, "Gerald, will you be able to get me home?"

Gerald's face contorted briefly into a frown, and he furrowed his brow a bit before he forced a smile for the boy.

"I hope so," he said. "I certainly hope so."

Xach wasn't very comforted by this, and Gerald could see it in his face. He didn't know what to say or do to make him feel better. He knew that he would be lucky if managed to survive til morning, as his internal wounds were causing him a great deal of pain. The Zindarthans had managed to close his wounds, but they had not been able to mend the injuries to his organs. The more he bled internally, the less time he had to fix this situation. He hoped that sleeping would allow his body a chance to mend a little and slow the damage, but he knew that there was little hope for full recovery. He didn't care that he was dying, but how could he tell this to Xach? How could he tell the boy he ripped from his home and family that he might never see them again? How could he tell this child that he might have to survive on his own in any number of strange worlds? The immense guilt and shame he felt for perpetrating such a crime on this innocent child hurt him to his core. He could not in good conscience lie to the boy, but he could not bear to tell him the truth.

So each leaned back against the mirondi, silently lost in his own concerns and fears. The two suns were nearly below the horizon when Queen Zora and her colony arrived with the cloaks they made for Xach and Gerald. Each cloak had a hood to keep the wearer's head warm, much like the rain ponchos Xach and his father wore to football games during bad weather. Xach was surprised at how well they fit. They exchanged pleasantries and gratitude for the cloaks, before Queen Zora took her colony away to finish their harvesting. They put on the cloaks, wrapped themselves in the warm, silky material, and silently watched the world go dark. With the advent of darkness came a soft, cool rain that hid the sounds of Xach's lonely sobs and Gerald's soft moans of pain. Eventually they both fell into a fitful sleep.

Chapter Ten

"Wake up, Xachary. You'll be late for school," said Mrs. Biddle, gripping his shoulder and shaking him.

Xach sat up and rubbed his eyes. He blinked several times as his surroundings came into clear focus. His mother stood next to his bed, looking down at him with a slight look of annoyance on her face.

"You overslept, Xachary. If you don't hurry up and get dressed, we're going to be late getting you to school."

"Huh? School?" Xach said deliriously.

"Yes, school. The place you go everyday to learn stuff? You must have been sleeping quite heavily," she continued. "I called you several times, and your alarm clock's been ringing for over half an hour. Now hurry up and get washed up. Your breakfast is waiting on the table. I'll meet you downstairs in five minutes, okay?"

Disconnected, fuzzy images of the Hall of Worlds, Count Milton, the earthquake, Gerald, and the Zindarthans came rushing into his mind. *Was it all just a dream?* He looked down at his arm. It was not in a cast or a sling. He was okay and sitting in his own bed in his own room! *But it seemed so real!* His eyes started to tear up with happiness, as his emotions caught up with him.

"Honey, are you all right? Why are you crying?"

She sat down on the edge of Xach's bed. He leaned forward and threw his arms around her, giving her big hug.

"I'm okay now mom," he said, trying to choke back the tears of joy. "I had a horrible dream where I was kidnapped from you and dad. I was taken to this strange place, and I cut off some man's arm, and..." His voice trailed off as he relaxed into his mother's embrace.

"It's all right. It was just a dream."

"I love you, mom. I thought I would never see you again."

"I love you too, son, but it was just a dream. I wish we could talk about this more, but we have to get you to school, okay?"

"Okay," he said, sitting back and wiping his eyes.

"Go wash up and come down and eat your breakfast. We can talk more about your dream on the way to school, okay?"

"Okay."

She stood up and walked out of the room. He threw back the covers on his bed, jumped out of bed, and grabbed the towel hanging on the back of his desk chair. He trotted to the bathroom, washed his face, brushed his teeth, and returned to his room to get dressed. He pulled open his closet door and reached up for the string that hung from the lightbulb on the ceiling of his closet. The string grazed his fingertips as he felt something grab the front of his pajamas. He looked down to see a bloody hand clenching his pajama top. With a strong tug, the hand pulled Xach headfirst into the dark closet. Xach screamed, as the door slammed shut behind him.

Xach screamed into the darkness, "Let go of me!"

He couldn't see a thing; it was black as pitch. He struggled to be free of the hand.

"Xach," said a familiar voice. "It is just a bad dream. Wake up."

Xach felt a hand on his chest. He tried to swat the hand away, but his right arm seemed tangled in something, and he couldn't move it. He pushed away with his feet and tried to sit up. His back touched something soft and warm. The hand let go of his chest.

"Xach. It's me, Gerald. You were having a nightmare. Everything is all right."

Xach took a deep breath and tried to control the terror that was coursing through his body. He looked around frantically, searching for some type of light, but he saw none. Out of the darkness, Gerald continued to talk.

"You were having a bad dream. You were screaming and woke me up. I reached over to wake you and you started kicking and squirming. It was probably a night terror."

As he listened to Gerald's voice, his mind slowly pieced together what was happening. His mother and their conversation had been the dream. His kidnapping had been real. The earthquake, the Hall, Count Milton – it was all real.

His mother was actually worlds away from the dark place in which he now sat.

"G-Gerald?"

"Yes, child. It's me. The suns set several hours ago. It was raining, and we both fell asleep. I didn't think to build a fire or acquire some sort of light before the suns set. That is why it is so dark. I am sorry. I was not thinking about how terrifying it would be for you to wake up in complete darkness."

"It's okay," Xach said weakly. "I was dreaming that I was home with my mom. I thought I was home again…"

"I see. I see. I am so very sorry, Xach. I truly am. Do you still have the key?"

"The key? Oh yes, the key. I have it in my pocket."

"If you get it out, it will provide some light for us until we find some other suitable light source."

Xach reached into his and withdrew the key.

"What should I do with it?"

"Simply rub the gem on the end of the key, and it should produce light."

Xach did as he was instructed, and the gem emitted a fluorescent green glow. As his eyes adjusted to the growing light, the outline of Gerald's smiling face and tortured body materialized next to him out of the darkness.

"Ahh. That is much better," said Gerald.

Xach held out the key for Gerald to take.

Gerald shook his head, "No Xach. You keep it. It belongs to you now."

"I don't want it. It's yours," Xach insisted, holding it closer to Gerald. Gerald refused to take it from him, so he dropped it on the ground. "I don't want it. You'll need it to get me home. I don't know how to use it."

"That is precisely why you should hold onto it. If you want to make it home, you're going to have to *learn* how to use it."

"Why do I have to use it? Why can't you get me home and then go about your business?"

"Well, to be honest, Xach…I don't really know how to tell you this, but…you may have to find your own way home."

"WHAT?!?"

"I am very sorry that you were pulled into this, but what is done is done. I am dying, Xach. I fear I shall never leave this world, though I will try my best to correct the mistakes I've made. Nonetheless, the key has chosen you to be its next carrier, whether you like it or not."

"You're joking right?"

"I'm afraid not, my young friend. When I was mortally wounded by Uncle Milton, the key began searching for another carrier. It led me to you. Under normal circumstances, the bearer of the key becomes aware of his or her impending demise and is afforded the time to properly train the next key carrier. Since I was wounded under dire circumstances, the key did what it could to find a suitable carrier. Fate has chosen you. I wish I had more time to train you properly, but I fear I do not have much time left. I desperately wish I did not have to be so blunt, but we must use my remaining time to educate you."

Xach stared at Gerald, his entire body numb with shock. He didn't know what to say or do. He felt tears welling up in his eyes. Anger burned like a fire behind his ears, but at the same time he found himself giggling silently. *How absurd,* he thought. *This has to be a bad dream!* A thousand different emotions were clamoring to escape his body, and he felt like he was going crazy! *This can't be happening. He's dying? I'll be all alone. I'm probably going to die here too! I'll never see mom or dad again. This has to be a bad dream!* He closed his eyes. *Wake up! Wake up!*

He slowly opened his eyes again, hoping he would find himself at home in his bed. But he wasn't asleep, and this wasn't a dream. This was really happening.

Gerald touched his shoulder, but Xach pulled away as if he had been stung by a bee.

"Don't touch me. Leave me alone."

"As you wish, Xach. I am so sorry."

"Stop saying that. You're not sorry. You weren't taken from your parents...your home...and brought here against your will."

"That is not an entirely accurate statement. I did not choose this job. It chose me, just as it has chosen you. My Great Great Great Grandfather Shubert had the key before me. He lived to be three hundred and fifty-two years old! I never knew him growing up, but one day in winter while I was shoveling snow from the sidewalk in front of my family's home, he appeared and told me that it was my time to take on the mantel of the key. I didn't know who he was, so he made me look at my family's photo album. Sure enough, he looked like my Great Great Great Grandfather Shubert! He had only seemed to age a few years, even though it had been hundreds of years. Even though that seemed like irrefutable evidence that he was who he claimed to be, I did not trust him. He said the key chose me to be its new bearer. I did not care. I would not hear of it. I did not want to be the new key carrier. I had a wife and children. I had a life that wasn't even half over. There were so many things I wanted to see and do…"

His voice trailed off as he was overcome with the memories of lost youth and unfulfilled dreams. Xach could see in his face that he was telling the truth. Gerald's eyes began to tear up, but with a cough and a sniff, he returned to his tale.

"My wife's name was Sonya, and she was the most beautiful woman I had ever seen. We met in school, fell in love, and were married. She bore me twin sons. Actually, they were about your age when I left. Their names were James and Peter. They were very intelligent, like you. I had high hopes for their futures. I wanted to see them grow up, fall in love, get married, and have children. I wanted…" His voice trailed off again as he paused to remember.

"Anyway, Grandfather Shubert told me that he had had to make the same sacrifices when the key chose him to be its bearer. He left a wife and children also. I did not care; I wanted to stay with my family. I told him to find someone else. I did not want the job. He said that I could not turn my back on my calling. He said that if I did, all of life as I knew it, along with countless other worlds, might be destroyed. He said that a great evil was in pursuit of the key, and that if the key fell into evil hands, my world and many others would be subjected to a horrible and cruel future. His time was ending, and he could no longer continue defending the key against evil and doing the Creator's work. The key led him to me, so it was my destiny to take on the mantel.

"I thought he was crazy. But then he showed me the Hall of Worlds. After visiting several worlds and showing me some of the things the key could do, he told me why I needed to protect it. He told me that his brother, my Great Great Great Uncle Milton, learned of the key and its power. For years he tried to steal the key and kill my great grandfather. Uncle Milton wanted the key so he could travel from world to world and conquer the people on each world, making himself a grand ruler over multiple worlds. That meant that if he managed to get the key, he would eventually take over *my* world and enslave my friends, my family, and myself. Even though I did not want to leave my loved ones, I knew that if I did not take over my grandfather's work, I would be leaving the fate of my family in the hands of someone the key had not chosen. I figured that if it chose me, then there must have been a reason for that. If the key fell to someone it had not chosen, the likelihood of Uncle Milton succeeding was much greater. I could not let that happen.

"I said goodbye to my family and went with my grandfather to learn all I could about the key and the Hall of Worlds before he passed away. He died a few weeks later, leaving me to carry on his work. That was about four hundred years ago. So, I was not lying when I said I had been here before, though it was probably many decades ago. I have been doing this for so many years, I often lose count."

"You're four hundred years old?" Xach asked, not really sure he should believe what he was hearing.

"Yes. Four hundred and twenty-seven to be exact."

"That's impossible," Xach said sarcastically. "No one can live that long."

"That is one of the many powers the key possesses. It grants the carrier healing powers and long life."

"So if it has healing powers, why can't it heal your wound?"

"That is an excellent question. Sadly, the wound was too deep, and I lost the key to Uncle Milton and then you at the most critical times when healing should have occured."

"So if I hadn't taken the key from you in the closet, you would have been all right?" Xach asked hesitantly. His lip quivered as he realized his actions may have caused this whole chain of events. *If I hadn't taken the key from Gerald in the closet, he might have been able to heal himself and he might not be dying. If I hadn't taken the key, then I wouldn't have become involved in this mess. If I hadn't taken the key, I would be home with mom and dad instead of here in this strange world with a dying man and some overwhelming destiny!*

"No, Xach. It is not your fault. The key brought me to you, because it knew that it could not heal me. My time away from the key may have hastened my physical decline, but it was not the cause of this fatal wounding. That was Uncle Milton's fault. Your involvement was destiny. I believe that even if I had not been wounded, the key would have eventually brought me to you."

"That doesn't really make me feel any better."

"I understand, but nonetheless I believe it to be true. The key chose you to protect it from Uncle Milton."

"So Count Milton is four hundred years old too?"

"No. Uncle Milton is older. I do not know his exact age. He is probably over 700 years old."

"How is that possible?"

"I do not understand exactly how he does it. According to my grandfather, Uncle Milton was obsessed with dark magic and the occult. Over his years of study, he found a way to transfer his soul from one body to another, keeping his mind and knowledge intact during the transfer. The catch is that he can only transfer his spirit into someone descended from his bloodline. So, over the years that my Grandfather Shubert and I protected the key, Uncle Milton amassed power and knowledge by transferring his soul from one blood relative to another. In this manner, he managed to stay alive for hundreds of years. He also became very powerful with magics."

"So that is how he froze everyone in the hospital when you took me to the Hall of Worlds?" Xach asked.

"Precisely. He has many powers and is extremely dangerous. He would not hesitate to kill you if he knew you had the key."

"All the more reason not to want it," said Xach, using his foot to nudge the key on the ground closer to Gerald.

"You do not yet understand, Xach. I can not take the key back into my possession. It belongs to you now."

"But I don't want it. I don't want to be chased by Count Milton. I don't want to be *here*! And no offense, but I wish I didn't even know *you*! I want to go home. I want to go to school. I want to…"

"Believe me," Gerald interrupted. "I understand. It is a lot for you to take in. I never would have chosen for you to learn of your destiny under these circumstances, let alone at your young age. I wish you were called at an older age as I was, but it could not be helped. I wish I had more time to train you, but I do not. If I could give the key to someone else, I would. But it chose you. It led me to *you*. So it is up to me to tell you as much as I know before my time ends."

Xach realized that Gerald was not going to give in. He was not going to take the key back into his possession. He was going to keep insisting that Xach take the key and embrace his destiny. *So, you have two options,* Xach said to himself. *"You can stay with Gerald and learn about the key, or you can get up and run off into the darkness of this strange world and never see your parents again. There is no way you can force Gerald to take the key; you are not strong enough. So, of the options, it seems that staying with Gerald is the only logical choice.* He slumped back against the mirondi.

"I give up," he said with a sigh. "I don't really have a choice do I?"

"Of course you have a choice," said Gerald. "That is all any human has – the freedom of choice. I cannot force you to take the key. You can leave me at any time, but I am sure you realize that you would not survive long by yourself. And without the key, there will be no possibility for you to return to your family and say goodbye."

"Why would I return to my family just to say goodbye? If I make it home, I'm staying there."

"Again, that would be your choice. I only hope that you would realize the consequences of such an action. The key is not safe unless it is moving. If it remains stationary in one place for too long a period of time, then Uncle Milton will be able to locate it."

"So shouldn't we be moving right now? The key has been in *this* spot on *this* world for almost a day now. What's to stop Count Milton from finding it?"

"You are absolutely right. But if what you said about cutting off his arm is true, I am certain that he is a little more preoccupied with his arm at the moment. He is a vain and impulsive man, but he is not stupid. He must know that he can not face us with only one arm. That should buy you some time."

"It is true! The door cut it right off!"

"I wish I had been conscious to see it! Nonetheless, I believe we are safe for the time being. Unless you are tired and would like to go back to sleep, I can continue telling you about the key."

"I'm not tired." Xach said, realizing that he must be running on pure adrenaline since he only had a few hours of sleep in the past 48 hours. For the first time since his abduction from the hospital, he realized that he had not eaten for quite some time. "I am hungry though."

"Me too, but it will be difficult to find food in this darkness."

"What would we eat, anyway?"

"Well, there are fruit trees on this planet, and I believe some of the bushes produce nuts and berries that are edible. One of the fascinating things about the key is that it modifies your body to accept various foods from other worlds that might otherwise by poisonous. That is why I was able to drink the pink water you brought me. It would normally be poisonous to us both, but the key makes it so our bodies do not react to the poisons and extract the nutrients we need to survive. The only caveat is that you need to be within a few feet of the key or have touched it no more than an hour ago to maintain its effects."

"So since I have been carrying the key, I can drink the pink water without it hurting me?"

"Correct."

"But if I don't touch the key for over an hour, then the water is poisonous again?"

"In the beginning, yes. The longer you hold the key, the longer its effects are maintained. For example, when we first met, you removed the key from my person. I was not in the presence of the key for several hours, yet my body was able to adapt to your world's food and air until you returned with the key. That is because I have been holding the key for hundreds of years. It would not be the same with you. Being a new key carrier, your body must build up its tolerance to new environments and new foods. So for now, you should keep the key on your person at all times. In truth, I do not see why you would *not* have it on your person at all times. It is too dangerous to just leave it lying about for anyone to pick it up. I never removed the key from my person except to hide it from Uncle Milton."

"So what happened between you and Milton?"

"As I said, he has been trying to get the key for centuries. He switched bodies many times, making it easy for him to approach us without being recognized. Grandfather Shubert and I always managed to evade him until recently. He tricked me and was able to get a hold of the key for a few hours. If it were not for me and my stupidity, we would not be in the dire situation we are now. But perhaps I should start from the beginning…"

Chapter Eleven

"In the beginning, there was the Creator," began Gerald. "Though I have never met the Creator personally, I have spoken to The Creator through the disciples."

"The Creator?" Xach asked. "Do you mean God?!?"

"I suppose that is one name for The Creator. I have been exposed to many religions and beliefs throughout my travels, and The Creator is known by many different names."

"Wow. I always wondered if everything I learned in Sunday School was true?"

"I do not know what 'Sunday School' is or what your religion teaches, but I can tell you what I know about the Creator. No one knows when or how the Creator came into being. Perhaps the Creator predates the existence of time. No one really knows. What we do know is that the Creator was extremely knowledgeable and powerful. The Creator was one of a kind and therefore quite lonely. To stave off loneliness, the Creator began building planets and galaxies and engineering various species to live upon them. The different species provided companionship and entertainment for the Creator. At times, the Creator would intervene on behalf of one of the species and make changes. On other occasions, the Creator decided to make adjustments to one of the species and create a new world on another planet. This resulted in many similar, yet ultimately different, worlds. Even though the Creator had the ability to travel great distances through space and time, the number of species and environments grew to an unimaginable number – a number so great that it became difficult for the Creator to be in contact with all of the worlds. The Creator devised a way for quick and inconspicuous travel between worlds, so that observation of the worlds could continue. That construct, which folds space and connects millions of points throughout countless galaxies is known as the Hall of Worlds.

"Even though the Hall of Worlds facilitated frequent visits between worlds, the Creator enjoyed engineering new species more than the observation of them. So, the Creator recruited members of the various species that had been created to continue the Creator's observations of the worlds. The Creator provided them with keys to the Hall of Worlds and directed them to observe each world and report back any interesting developments or the need for possible intervention. If a problem arose on one world, the key carrier would contact one of the Creator's oracles."

"What's an oracle?" Xach asked, as a way of staying involved. He wasn't sure he was following all of what Gerald was saying or that it made a great deal of sense, but he wished to demonstrate that he was trying to comprehend.

"An oracle is a being who has a direct, psychic connection with the Creator. Through these oracles, the Creator can speak directly to one of the key carriers and vice versa. In this manner, the Creator is kept abreast of worlds that need intervention or require further study. The Creator endowed the keys with various properties – character reading, healing, longevity, knowledge storage and retrieval, language translation, and adaptation. I've already explained the healing and longevity properties. In order to help the key carriers remember all that they see and hear, the Creator endowed the key with a knowledge enhancement property. The longer you hold the key, the more information your brain will be able to retain and retrieve. In essence, you grow smarter with each passing moment. Not only that, but you are able to retrieve any of the information stored in your brain with quick and sharp accuracy. So, when you meet an oracle who asks for a report, it will be easy for you to remember all the details of a world and its people without ever having to physically write notes on paper.

"Let me give you an example," Gerald continued. "Do you remember the room number of the hospital room in which you found me?"

Without even thinking, Xach blurted out, "Room 555". His eyes grew wide with surprise. Gerald smiled knowingly. *How did I remember that?* Xach wondered. *That's such an insignificant thing to remember.*

"Do you see what I mean? Your brain is already becoming an efficient storage unit of information. If you concentrate, you'll probably be able to remember every little detail about the hospital."

Xach closed his eyes and concentrated. In a flash, the events that transpired at the hospital played out in his mind like a movie. It was like he had a photographic memory now, and he could see everything as he saw it through his own eyes at the hospital. He saw the large African-American nurse behind the counter who told him that Gerald was in Room 555. Her name tag read Shavonda. By concentrating a little harder, he was able to look behind her and read the monitors and charts for some of the patients in the hospital! He could read that the patient in Room 527 was listed as Rodgers, Shelia. He could read the doctor's notes about her abdominal pain and cramping. He hadn't paid attention to any of those things enough to recall those specific details when he was there! Nonetheless, all the insignificant details were crystal clear in his memory, as if his eyes were a digitial recorder.

Xach opened his eyes and stated excitedly, "THAT'S AMAZING! It's like my brain took pictures of everything I saw. I can focus on little details I didn't even know I had seen like names and notes on patient charts on a desk behind the receptionist!"

"It is pretty cool, huh? I had forgotten how exciting it was the first time I recalled something I didn't even remember seeing. I have so much knowledge in my head that I sometimes forget how amazing it is to be able to recall everything so clearly and in such detail."

"So what else can the key do?" Xach asked with actual interest. For the moment he forgot about the key-carrier and destiny stuff. He had to admit that a photographic memory of this quality was a pretty cool thing. *School would be a breeze,* he thought. *All I would have to do is look at my textbook, and copies of the pages would be preserved in my photographic memory. Tests would be a piece of cake!*

"I told you about adaptation a bit. The key can reconfigure your organs and body parts to adapt to different atmospheres, weather conditions, terrains, and foods – like the air and pink water here on this world. Those properties are for physical maintenance. The longer you carry the key, the longer you live and the stronger your body will become.

In addition to helping your body adjust to different world climates and foods, the key also acts as a universal translator. As long as you hold the key, you can speak the language of any of the Creator's creations. It also allows you to understand what other species are saying."

"So I *was* right!" Xach said excitedly. "The key made it possible for me to understand the Zindarthans and for them to understand me when we spoke earlier."

Gerald nodded.

"Ok. Let me get this straight," said Xach. His mind remembered every word that Gerald said like a tape recorder playing back a taped message, but because it was all abstract information that he had not yet put into practice the meaning was not entirely clear. He needed to clarify a few things. "As long as I hold the key, I can survive on *any* world, no matter what kind of atmosphere it has or what kinds of foods they have?"

"Yes, in time."

"What does that mean?"

"The longer you hold the key, the more it becomes part of you…changes you. As you and the key become one, it can more easily manipulate your body to adapt to certain terrains, weather conditions and atmospheres. Right now, you have only had possession of the key for a short while. It would not help you adapt to *every* world in the Hall of Worlds just yet. But in time, it will."

Xach interrupted. "So you're telling me that I could have suffocated to death on this planet when Count Milton chased us here, and I slammed the door on him?"

"Not really, because I was fairly certain that this world was not dangerous and would have an atmosphere that was suitable to sustain your human life. But when you are on your own, you will need to be careful. This job is not without its dangers, and *your* dangers, unfortunately, are significantly larger due to your age and inexperience. I wish this had all been different…that I had the proper time to train you. But the key would not have chosen you if it knew you could not handle the challenge. In the short time that I have known you, Xachary, you have demonstrated a great deal of intelligence and bravery. I am certain you can handle it. Besides, self-preservation is something that your species has deeply bred into its members. As long as you find your way off this world before Uncle Milton finds you, then you will have plenty of time to explore the Hall of Worlds without being hurried into a world that might be dangerous to you. I also have hope that you will find an oracle or another key carrier who will be able to help you learn the things I did not have time to tell you."

"That's all well and good, but I just need to find my way home," Xach said, mater-of-factly. As Gerald talked more about the dangers of carrying the key and avoiding Milton, the excitement over his new-found knowledge and communication abilities wore off. "I don't intend to spend a lot of time going from world to world taking notes and talking to God about them."

"Well, if you should happen to meet another key carrier or an oracle, I would suggest referring to the Creator as 'the Creator' instead of God. They may not know what you are talking about. As for turning your back on the key's calling, I do hope you will reconsider the implications of such a decision. If you do indeed find your homeworld and give up the mantel of key carrier, then your world and many others may be doomed."

"The operative word there is *'may'* be doomed. Maybe Count Milton will give up on trying to find the key now that I cut off his arm. Maybe the key will find another carrier once I find my home. You don't know the future."

"True, I do not know the future. But the oracles have advised me that Uncle Milton must be stopped, or he may succeed in enslaving many worlds under his evil power and ultimately destroy the Hall of Worlds entirely. I was also charged with finding a way to stop Uncle Milton from ever swapping bodies again, so that the key and the Hall of Worlds would once again be a secret. The Creator is quite displeased with Uncle Milton and what he has done. It was supposed to be my job to stop him. That falls to you now."

Xach could feel the back of his neck getting warm with anger. He felt like he often did when his parents told him to do extra chores, because they were too busy with Brandon. Normally his mother would clean up the dishes after dinner or mop up the floor when something spilled. But with the new baby, his mother had to tend to him all the time, relegating her jobs to Xach and his sister. Now Gerald was telling him that in addition to keeping himself alive, he was supposed to clean up Gerald's mess? *That's not right!* he thought.

"So now on top of surviving and taking notes and everything else, I have to stop Count Milton as well?" he questioned, exhibiting his disgust with his situation. "That's not fair. Why doesn't the Creator just step in and take care of Count Milton? If he's so powerful, why does he need you or me to fix it?"

"Young Xach, I am aware of the injustices I perpetrated against you. For that I am truly sorry. It has been many centuries since the Creator **personally** intervened on **any** world. The Creator seldom gets involved with the worlds any more. Creation of new species is the Creator's main interest. Uncle Milton was **my** responsibility, but I failed. Now I am dying, and it falls to you. I am doing my best to correct what I can before my time ends, but you must understand that it will not be easy for you to simply **walk away** from your destiny."

Xach had about all he could take. Anger boiled up from deep inside of him – anger for being abducted, anger for being isolated, anger for being told what he should and shouldn't do, and anger for having to clean up Gerald's mess with Count Milton. He exploded in a fury of shouts and wild gesticulations.

"I'M ONLY TEN YEARS OLD! HOW AM I SUPPOSED TO GET RID OF COUNT MILTON? DO YOU EXPECT ME TO **KILL** HIM? WHY ME? HOW DO YOU KNOW YOU DIDN'T PICK THE WRONG PERSON? HOW AM I SUPPOSED TO SAVE THE WORLD AND GIVE UP MY FAMILY? MY LIFE? I DIDN'T ASK FOR THIS! AND…AND YOU'RE GOING TO DIE…and leave me here all alone…I can't do this…I…" His voice trailed off as his tirade brought him to the true source of his anger – the overwhelming fear of the unknown. Once again the tears rolled down his face and his body heaved with sobs.

Gerald put his arm around Xach and just held him. This time Xach didn't pull away.

"Let it out, Xach," Gerald said softly. "Let it all out. I understand how you feel. It is not fair. It was not fair for me, and it even less fair for you."

Gerald held Xach until he finished crying, attempting to assure Xach that he was not alone. The two sat in silence, listening to the light rain fall in the darkness around them. Eventually Xach began to calm down and think rationally again. It felt good to be held by Gerald, even if he was a total stranger. He felt a little less isolated and alone. Whether he wished to admit it or not, he knew with a strange, absolute certainty that Gerald was a good person and that he didn't mean for any of this to happen.

"I'm sorry," sniffed Xach. "I'm just a little overwhelmed. I don't know what to do."

"I understand. Believe me. I do. I wish I could take you home and allow you to forget about all of this, but I cannot."

Xach nodded, feeling a little better since he unloaded some of the emotions he had been holding inside. His father always told him that it was okay to be upset about something but that he needed to accept that some things were beyond his control. He said that bad things happen sometimes, and all you can do is try your best to deal with it. Xach knew deep down inside that he would need to learn all that he could from Gerald if he ever hoped to get back home, and that breaking down and crying and screaming weren't going to help the situation. So he tried his best to push the fear aside and focus on Gerald's information.

"I'm all right now. I guess I just needed to get that off my chest. I realize there is little I can do to change the situation I am in. I can't say that I'm going to fix your problem with Count Milton or take over your job, but for the time being I don't have much of a choice but to listen to your story and learn everything I can. So, you may continue telling me about the key. You said it translates languages and changes the body so that you can survive on different worlds. You said it did something else. What did you call it? Oh, 'character reading.' What's that?"

"Character reading blocks the key from being used by someone with evil intentions. Somehow it reads your character and knows if you are a person with good intentions or evil intentions. The key will only function for someone pure of heart and soul, like you and me. That is how I knew that you were meant to be the next key carrier. The key would not have worked for you if you were not meant to carry it. That is why it is your destiny to…"

"Wait a minute," Xach interrupted. "If the key can tell if you're good or not, how could Count Milton use it if he got it away from you?"

"In truth, he cannot use it. But he was able to copy its technology and create a key similar to the original that would work for him."

"So, if he already has a key that works for him, why does he want yours?"

"The key he created is flawed. It does not always work properly. Ever since Uncle Milton started using his key, the Hall of Worlds has begun to malfunction. Some doors do not open. Once a door is shut, it can not be reopened for reverse travel. That severely hinders movement between worlds, because there are only a finite number of entrances and exits for each world. When one of those doorways becomes 'jammed,' it means that one of the key carriers may be stuck on a world for much longer than necessary while they seek another entrance or exit. That is why the Creator wanted me to find Uncle Milton's key, destroy it, and keep him from transferring bodies so that he cannot use his knowledge and power to make another bastard key. The Creator believes that if Uncle Milton continues to use his key, the Hall of Worlds may become completely inoperable. Uncle Milton is aware that his key does not work like ours, so he wants to examine it further and find a way to fix his key or alter the original so that he can use it without the negative side effects."

"That's just great," moaned Xach. "So even if I didn't **plan** on finding Count Milton and his key, I sort of **have to** now. If I don't destroy his key and he keeps using it, then he might destroy the Hall of Worlds and strand me on some planet that isn't Earth!"

"I am afraid so," Gerald said. "If I had not been so stupid, he never would have gotten his hands on the key in the first place."

"What happened?"

"As I was saying before, the key is passed down from generation to generation. Generally the key is passed to someone within the original bloodline, so long as the descendants remain pure and good. But that is not always the case, hence your calling to carry the key. I can only suppose that the key knew how much time I had left and knew that I would not find anyone within my bloodline that could carry the key before I died. So it found you and brought me to your world. But I digress…

"My Grandfather Shubert trained me in the usage of the key and how to report my observations to the Creator through the oracles. I moved from world to world, evading Uncle Milton and continuing my work for the Creator. On a few occasions, Uncle Milton managed to find me. He discovered a way to locate a few portals between worlds."

"What's a portal? Aren't portals basically the same things as the doors in the Hall of Worlds?" Xach asked.

"They are quite similar, yes, but portals function outside the design of the Hall. When the Creator was constructing the Hall of Worlds, a few errors were made. Each hallway in the Hall of Worlds is supposed to be a collection of all the entrances and exits for one world. In that way, you would not walk through one door and end up in a completely different world. However, a few connections were misplaced or misconnected, leaving portals *between* worlds."

Xach pursed his lips and looked a bit confused.

"I see that I am confusing you again."

Xach nodded.

"Let me give you an example. When we left the hospital and entered the Hall of Worlds, the hallway that you stepped into was the hallway for Earth. All the doors you saw in that hallway led to other places on Earth. We left Earth's hallway and entered the Great Hall. All the doors you saw in the Great Hall were separate worlds. We entered Zindartha's hallway and chose a door that led us to wherever we came out. All the other doors in Zindartha's hallway led to some other place on Zindartha. When you find another door to take you off of Zindartha, it will put you back in Zindartha's hallway again. Is that making sense so far?"

"Yes."

"Ok. When the Creator was making the Hall of Worlds, some of the doors were not connected properly. Though the Creator is believed to be infallible by most, one can not overlook the fact that something went wrong with the construction of the Hall. However, that is a philosophical discussion for another day."

What 'other' day? Xach thought sarcastically. *You talk like you'll be dead by tomorrow! So don't act like you're going to be around another day to talk philosophy with me.*

"There are some doors that lead to worlds to which they were not meant to lead," Gerald continued. "For example, there could be a door on your world that leads directly to Zindartha without making a stop in the Hall of Worlds. It is not supposed to work that way, but sometimes it does. It is almost like a hole or rip in the space-time continuum. If you enter the hole, there is no telling where you will come out. Uncle Milton managed to locate these portals and began moving between worlds. It is all very random, but that did not stop him from finding me.

"A few days ago, I was studying the people of Wizandria. The Wizandrians are another humanoid race, but they are cold-blooded instead of warm-blooded."

"Like a frog or snake, right?"

"Exactly. They look almost like you and me, and they live in a climate more suited to amphibians. They have blue-green skin and large, black shiny eyes – actually they resemble a cross between your race and a salamander. Anyway, they are a very gentle and helpful race of beings. I was studying some of their scientific advances, specifically a piece of machinery that employed the precise cutting power of a laser to help with harvesting their crops. Uncle Milton managed to locate me. He had just switched bodies with one of his great great great grand cousins, and I did not recognize him. He slipped past the scientists and entered the test field. As soon as the machine began running a test pattern, Uncle Milton jumped out of the field and pretended to be injured. Of course, the Wizandrians immediately came to his assistance. They made a great deal of fuss over this strange being and his fake injury.

"Generally, key carriers are directed to remain distant observers and not get involved in the affairs of whatever species we are observing, but I wanted to see what had happened. We are permitted to interact with the species, but we are not to make suggestions or change the outcome of an event. That might negatively affect the culture or pre-destined timeline of a species' development.

"Nonetheless, my curiosity got the better of me and I felt compelled to see what they were doing to help the injured interloper. I was not going to help them; I just wanted to see what kind of medical treatments the Wizandrians had and wether or not they would work on the alien. I got close enough to the crowd for Uncle Milton to jump up and knock me down. I always wore the key around my neck on a chain. He knew that. He grabbed the chain, and pulled it and key off my neck. He stood up quickly and ran from the field. It took me a moment to realize what had happened, but I knew that if I did not catch the thief, he might disappear through a portal and strand me on Wizandria with little or no hope of retrieving the key. Since Uncle Milton was the only being besides the Creator and the oracles to know of the key and its powers, I assumed it was he who had stolen it and not some random person.

"I set up pursuit immediately, keeping a close eye on his movements. He weaved through the streets and open market areas, bumping into people and knocking them over. This slowed him down a bit and allowed me to bridge the gap between us. At the end of a row of homes, I saw him make a sharp right down an alley. I followed him into the alley, which led to a yard surrounded on all sides by a nine-foot fence. The yard was empty except for a few trees and bushes. I knew Uncle Milton had the ability to levitate, so I scanned the sky to see if he was levitating over the fence. I saw nothing. I knew he would not have executed a plan to steal the key without planning his escape very carefully. Since he had not yet developed the ability to turn himself invisible, I knew there were…"

"Wait! He can turn himself invisible? I'm sorry to interrupt, but if I'm going to be chased by him, I kind of need to know exactly what he's capable of doing."

"No, he does not have the power of invisibility, so far as I know. I do believe he has been studying invisibility…amongst other things. I suppose that it would be pertinent to discuss his powers for your edification, would it not? My apologies. To my knowledge, he has mastered the powers of combustion, levitation, transmutation, and petrification. You should be immune to his magic so long as you possess the key, but nothing is certain when dealing with magic."

"I get the first two. Combustion is the ability to set things on fire, right? But what is transmu…tranmut…?"

"Transmutation or transmogrification – it means that he has the ability to change objects or people into something else. It generally is not permanent, but it is bothersome to be turned into a toad, even if it is for a short period of time."

"You were turned into a toad?"

"Unfortunately, yes. It was rather unpleasant, but I will get to that in a moment. You are correct; combustion is the ability to set something afire. The other power I spoke of was 'petrification' – the power to freeze things. He also has the ability to perform curses and other little spells, but combustion, levitation, transmutation, and petrification are his most important powers and the ones of which you'll have to be wary."

"Ok. So what happened when you were in the empty yard after Count Milton stole your key? Did he turn you into a toad?"

"No. He turned me into a toad later. When I was in the empty yard, I realized that one of two things had happened. I knew the key would not work for him, because he was evil. Therefore, either he found a portal, or he levitated out of the yard quicker than I expected. The later was improbable, so I began searching the yard for a hidden portal. In the corner of the yard, behind a tree I found one."

"What does a portal look like?"

"It does not look like anything. It is invisible to the human eye. Basically, when I looked at the portal, it looked like the fence behind it. When I walked into the portal, it looked like I was going to walk right into the fence, but instead I was instantaneously transported to Gromp, a world primarily inhabited by large, monkey-like creatures called Sasqua. I recognized it immediately, because their environment is quite cold and snowy, with large mountains covered in huge, towering trees. Anyway, I stepped through the portal and was trying to determine which direction Uncle Milton went when he stepped out from behind one of the trees and cast a spell on me. He anticipated that I would pursue him and was lying in wait for my arrival through the portal. He knew that I would be easily caught off guard the moment I stepped through the portal, so he chose to use that to his advantage. He mumbled some incantation, and I could feel myself shrinking. My line of sight dropped significantly, and the next thing I knew I was staring at Uncle Milton's shoe."

"He turned you into a toad?" Xach asked.

"Yes," Gerald said dejectedly. "I was quite embarrassed and upset with myself for not being prepared. In any case, I tried to hop away. I hopped out of the pile of clothes I had been wearing and headed toward the forest. Uncle Milton rushed toward me; I assume he meant to stomp on me. Instead, he must have tripped on something, because a giant shadow fell over me. As he fell to the ground behind me he made a last ditch effort to do away with me. He stabbed me in the side with the key. That is how I got this wound. I managed to hop into a bramble bush before he could finish me off. I hopped deeper into the forest to escape him, but he did not follow me. He figured the wound he gave me would be enough to finish me off."

"So how did you get the key back?"

"Like I said before, Uncle Milton's transmogrification spells are only temporary, and after about half an hour I returned to my normal self. Of course, when I transformed back into my human form, I was naked. It was very cold, and I had a gaping wound in my side from where he stabbed me with the key. Since I was not too far from the portal, I found my way back to my clothes. Thankfully Uncle Milton had not seen fit to take them with him. I used some medicinal leaves and berries I found in the forest to make a salve to put on the wound, and then I tore off one of my pant legs to make a bandage around my waist to slow the bleeding. I then set out in search of Uncle Milton. I was afraid that he might have used another portal to leave Gromp and strand me there, but I found out that he had taken up residence in the mountains of Gromp. In fact, he had managed to enslave a large group of Sasqua and forced them to build him a huge castle in one of the nearby mountains. Using the portal to Wizandria, he had captured a great number of Wizandrians, took them to Gromp, and brainwashed them into being his armed guards and servants. Since the Wizandrians are cold-blooded and don't fair well in freezing temperatures, it was necessary for Uncle Milton to keep his castle quite warm and moist for the sake of his soldiers. Plus he needed to provide them with proper uniforms if they were stationed outside."

"How did you learn all this?"

"As I was wandering around the forest, I happened to wander into a small Sasquan village. Since the Sasqua are primitive and have no spoken language aside from grunts and growls, they communicate through pictograms drawn on stones and parchment, which was lucky for me, because I did not have the key and might have had trouble understanding their speech anyway. They recognized me as one of the 'watchers,' which is the word used by some cultures to refer to key carriers. They proceeded to draw pictures in the snow depicting Uncle Milton enslaving the Sasqua to build his castle and bringing the Wizandrians to Gromp as soldiers. They drew a map of the forest and neighboring mountains on a piece of parchment that showed the way to Uncle Milton's castle. They were also kind enough to give me a long, hair coat to keep me warm in the harsh Gromp weather.

"I followed the map to Uncle Milton's castle. I had very little difficulty sneaking in through a water drain on the side of the castle. I wanted to avoid the usual entrances, as I assumed they were probably heavily guarded. Once inside, I definitely felt a change in temperature and humidity, so I shed the coat. The drainage system snaked in all directions underneath the castle. Aside from a few rat-like creatures, called grimals, that nested in the sewers, I encountered no problems. I wandered around through the pipes, periodically peering through drainage grates to see where I was. Eventually I found a hallway that was heavily guarded with over a dozen soldiers. I figured Uncle Milton's laboratory was nearby, and that was where I would find the key.

"I followed the drainpipe under the laboratory. I could hear Uncle Milton mumbling incantations and moving objects around the room. Through the metal grate in the floor in a shadowed corner of the room, I could see him pouring colorful liquids into glass containers, creating puffs of different colored smoke. I heard no other voices, so I assumed he was alone in the lab. I needed to find a way to distract the guards, catch Uncle Milton off guard, and steal back the key.

"I crawled back to the grate in the hallway and tried to catch some of the grimals. They did not want to be caught and put up a bit of a fight. They hissed at me and scurried in all directions. So, I took off my shirt and tied it into a sack to collect them. They bit and scratched me several times, but I managed to collect seven or eight of them in my shirt. Then one at a time, I pushed them through the grate. The hissing of the creatures and my splashing around in the pipes, combined with the visual of the creatures coming through the grate, led the soldiers to think that a large pack of grimals were invading the castle.

"I heard one of the soldiers knock on the door of the lab and yell to Uncle Milton that a pack of grimals was crawling out of the sewer and entering the hall. Uncle Milton yelled back stating that he did not want to be bothered and that they should take care of it. I heard the soldiers' footsteps moving all about the hallway as they attempted to catch the rodents. There was no time to put my shirt back on, so I continued shirtless. I quickly returned to the lab grate and quietly pushed it out of the hole in the floor. Luckily the corner of the room was dark and Uncle Milton was too engrossed in his experiments on the key to notice the sounds I made or to see me crawl out of the floor. I hid in the corner behind a large wooden rack of glass beakers and bottles that was right beside the grate in the floor. Uncle Milton had the key on a metal tray in the center of the table. He had a similar key shaped object next to it on another tray. It was hard to tell the two apart, so I decided it would be best to grab them both when I made my move. I was only going to get one chance to startle him, because once he realized I was there, he would surely transmogrify me again or petrify me. I scanned the shelf of bottles and quietly picked up a blue one that was bubbling and a red one that was next to it.

"I waited until he turned his back on me, and then I leapt into action. I threw the blue bubbling bottle over Uncle Milton's head so that it shattered in the opposite corner of the room. Thankfully it was some kind of exploding liquid. Not only did the bottle shatter, but the liquid combusted and created a small, fiery mushroom cloud of burning liquid and black smoke. Uncle Milton's attention was obviously drawn toward the explosion, so he did not see me run toward the table or throw another red bottle at his head. The bottle hit him square in the back of the head. The red liquid sprayed all over the back of his head and ran down his neck. He screamed and fell on the floor scratching at his neck and head. I do not know what was in the bottle, but apparently it itched horribly.

"I ran to the table, grabbed both keys off the trays, and ran back to the grate. In those few seconds, Uncle Milton barked out an order for his guards to help him, and the door to the lab flew open. I dove headfirst into the hole in the floor and landed on the wet pipe surface below, scraping my face and chest rather badly. I knew I needed to keep moving, so I pushed myself through the pain and scurried along the pipes under the castle. The only problem was I did not remember which way I had come, so I just kept going in random directions. I remembered some passages and some turns, but the memory of my ingress was blurred. I'm not sure why my memory was affected, because even without the key my memory of the tunnels should have been photographic." He paused a moment to ponder this. Reaching no conclusion, he shook his head and continued. "Eventually I had to stop and catch my breath. I hoped that no one had been able to follow me. I took a moment to study the two keys.

"They were both gold with a green gem on the handle. The one in my right hand was vibrating and had been vibrating ever since I swiped them from the lab. I rubbed the gem on the vibrating one, and it glowed a faint green. I rubbed the gem on the other key. It also glowed green, but it pulsated. My key never did either of those things before. It was impossible to tell which one was the real one, so I slipped them both into my pocket and began searching for a way out of the castle.

"As I snaked through the pipes, I found it harder and harder to see and breathe. The pipes filled with a pungent smoke, no doubt an attempt by Uncle Milton to drive me from the sewer pipes and into his clutches. I had no choice but to exit the pipes at the next grate. I emerged into a large, ornate hallway. A pair of guards stood at the end of the hall and immediately gave pursuit. I ran in the opposite direction. When I turned the corner, I saw that there were more guards at the end of that hall. I was cornered. There was a door to my left. I tried to open it, but it was locked. I pulled out the non-vibrating key, rubbed the gem, and put the key in the lock. Nothing happened. I frantically pulled out the vibrating key and rubbed the gem. The key became warm to the touch and changed shape. In seconds it reshaped itself to fit the lock, and I was able to unlock the door. Once inside, I slammed the door and locked it from the inside. The real key is able to unlock any door, so I knew that the vibrating key was the real key. I did not, and still do not, know why it was vibrating, but at least I knew which was the real one."

"The key vibrated for me too," Xach broke in. "It vibrated when Count Milton knocked me down in the street, and it vibrated in the hospital right before you kidnapped me. It must be linked to Count Milton or vibrate in the presence of the other key?"

"You are one clever little boy," Gerald said with a huge smile on his face. "That is a brilliant deduction, and most likely true. Considering that Uncle Milton's key was fashioned after the original key, it is possible that it disrupts the universal harmonics of the original key, thereby creating the vibration. That might also explain why the use of Uncle Milton's key has disrupted the workings of the Hall of Worlds."

"Makes sense to me. I guess that would explain the earthquake at my school and the ripples I saw in the Hall of Worlds right before Count Milton appeared?"

"I would agree, young Xach. And you say you do not want to carry the key? You were born to carry it! You have an innate understanding of its workings, and you're intuitive beyond your years."

"We'll see. We'll see," said Xach. "So what did you do once you locked yourself in that room to escape the guards?"

"Oh, right. Well, I quickly surveyed the room. It was a large, stately bedroom, like a diplomatic suite for visiting dignitaries, though I can not imagine what dignitaries would have been visiting Uncle Milton. Anyway, I scanned the room for possible exits. There were no other doors besides the one through which I entered. There were several windows, but there was no way I could have used them for an escape. Even though I was on the ground floor of the castle, it was built into a mountain, and the windows overlooked a deep chasm and a river that ran several thousand feet below. I pushed one of the windows open to see if there was a ledge or something on which to keep a foothold if I were to try fleeing through the window, but being shirtless and wounded, there was no way I was going to be able to survive an attempt to scale the castle wall. In my present condition I was also no match for the four guards that were trying to knock down the door. It was only a matter of time before they managed to get in, at which point they would surely find the key. I could not hide it anywhere in the room, because that would be the first place they would look if they did not find it on my person. So, I hid it in the only place I figured they would not look – my wound."

"You put it *inside you?!?* Didn't that hurt?" Xach asked in disbelief.

"It hurt so badly that I passed out, but not before I had pushed it far enough into the wound that it could not be seen. The pain was unimaginable, but I knew it was the only way to keep Uncle Milton and his men from finding it."

"So what happened next? What happened after you passed out?"

"I can only assume that the guards broke down the door, arrested me, confiscated the fake key, and threw me in the dungeon. They must have searched high and low for the real key and had no luck finding it, because Uncle Milton saw fit to torture me for information when I came to. I woke up to find myself dressed in the burlap sack you found me in when we first met. I was chained to the wall of a dungeon cell by clamps and chains. My hands and feet were in heavy iron shackles that were held together by a short chain. One of the soldiers threw a bucket of ice water on my head to rouse me from my pain-induced coma. When I was lucid, Uncle Milton then questioned me about the key." Gerald scrunched up his face and adopted a mockingly sing-song voice to mimic Count Milton. "'Where is the key? How did you get here? Do you know what kind of pain and suffering I can wreak upon you and your descendants?' Et cetera, et cetera. He is such a pompous, over-blown ego-maniac," Gerald said. It was quite obvious that Gerald held more than a small bit of contempt for Count Milton.

"So what happened?" Xach pressed. He was getting a little impatient. He felt like saying to Gerald: *For someone who is supposedly about to die, you sure can be long-winded.*

"Oh, sorry. He threatened me and had the guards punch me in the side a few times. That hurt the most, because they kept driving the key further into my side. They beat my legs with their swords as well, but I told him nothing. I knew he would not kill me until he had the key in his possession. He said that he and his men searched the sewers, the halls, and the room in which I was found, but that they found nothing. He threatened to turn me back into a toad if I did not tell him where the key was. I realized that if he did, the key inside me would probably rip through all my internal organs and kill me as I shrank into the toad. Uncle Milton would then have the key, and I would be dead and unable to fix the situation. So I thought quickly and remembered that I had opened the window in the diplomatic suite. I told Uncle Milton that I threw the key out the window and that it had probably been carried miles away by the river at the bottom of the mountain. I said that if I could not protect the key, then no one would have it – least of all, him.

"He was *furious*!" Gerald said with a smirk. "He flew into a rage the likes of which I had never seen! He hopped around the room, screaming and cursing. He cast a few spells that blew chunks of stone out of the wall around me. His guards backed out of the room for fear that they might be accidentally injured. It was quite amusing. Uncle Milton wanted to kill me so badly, but he could not until he found the key again. He grabbed me around the neck and choked me. He whispered threateningly in my ear that he was going to find the key and when he did he would take great pleasure in slowly torturing me to death. Then he let go of me, stormed out of the cell, and ordered the guards to lock the door and throw away the key."

"So how did you escape?" Xach asked with a sigh. He was actually starting to feel tired again, like he might be able to sleep, but he wanted to hear the end of Gerald's story before he nodded off. It occurred to him that he had no idea what time it was or how many hours it had been since he was abducted. Day and night were no longer applicable, as this particular night was to last for three days. *This is definitely going to take some getting used to,* Xach thought.

"After Uncle Milton and the guards left," continued Gerald without missing a beat, "I contorted myself in such a manner as to free one of my hands. I removed the key from my side. I nearly passed out several times, but I managed to keep conscious long enough to retrieve it. Even if my original wound had not been that bad, I made it several times worse by shoving the key in there, having it beaten deeper inside, and then extracting it later.

"Anyway, once I had the key again, I could use it to unlock the shackles and the door to the cell. I knew I wouldn't get far before I either bled to death or passed out from loss of blood, so I immediately set out to find an exit to the Hall of Worlds. The key sensed that my life was ebbing away quickly and led me to an exit in a small laundry repair room. Now that I think about it, there should not have been an exit anywhere in Uncle Milton's castle. Hmmm…"

Gerald paused, deep in thought.

"Why shouldn't there have been an exit in the castle. I thought there were exits and entrances all over the place."

"That is true, but since the castle had only been built recently, many years after the Creator made the world of Gromp, there would not have been a reason to have an exit or entrance to the Hall of Worlds inside *that* castle. Perhaps the key formed the exit purely out of necessity? I have never known it to do that, but perhaps it sensed the urgency of finding an exit for me so that I might pass the key to you, the next key holder. I do not recall being told that the Creator endowed the key with the ability to create an exit or entrance where there originally was not one, but that is the only logical explanation. I had been too weak and delirious at the time to realize the improbability of my escape."

"My teacher once read me a story about Sherlock Holmes," Xach added. "He always said that once you've ruled out all other possible answers, the only one left, however improbable, must be the truth. Or something like that."

"That is quite an astute revelation. This Sherlock Holmes must have been one of your history's great thinkers."

"No. Sherlock Holmes wasn't a real person. He was a character in a story written by Sir Arthur Conan Doyle. I can't believe I remember all that!"

"I told you that the key allows you to retain an incredible amount of knowledge with instant recall."

"Yeah, but I didn't have the key or even know about it when my teacher read me that story. That was over a year ago."

"Nonetheless, the information was stored in your brain, and the key helped you retrieve it with absolute clarity."

"I still think that's pretty cool. So is there anything more to tell me about your escape? I'm starting to feel a little drowsy."

"Yes, I am becoming quite fatigued myself. All this talking has worn me out. There really is not much else to say about my escape. I found an exit out of Uncle Milton's castle just before his soldiers found me. If not for Uncle Milton's enchanted portraits, I might have had more time to search for an exit before the guards were alerted to my escape."

"Enchanted portraits? What are they?"

"Paintings of Uncle Milton imbued with magic. There were paintings of him on every wall of the castle. As I hobbled past them in search of an escape, they watched me and informed Uncle Milton of my escape. He sent troops after me, but I was able to get away seconds before they discovered me. The exit I found was in the locked drawer of a bedside table. It acted more like a portal than an exit, because it brought me directly to the closet in which we first met. It completely by-passed the Hall of Worlds and went directly to the closet. Hmmm….that is another statistical improbability, but that is the only explanation that I can give. Then again," mumbled Gerald, more to himself than to Xach, "there were soldiers coming out a trunk in the hallway. How did he manage that?"

"What are you talking about?"

"Nothing. Just some details of my escape that do not make sense. But with the Hall of Worlds not working properly and my lack of knowledge about Uncle Milton's bastard key, there are any number of reasons for why things happened the way they did. Is it possible that Uncle Milton has learned how to manipulate portals?" Gerald became silent and lost in complex thought.

Well, if that's it for his story, maybe I can get some sleep, Xach thought, as he yawned loudly.

"You should get some more sleep," Gerald suggested, breaking himself away from his troubled thoughts. "You are going to need to be well rested."

Gerald picked up the key and handed it to Xach. He didn't want it, but he was too tired to argue with Gerald. He took the key and put it in his pocket, thereby extinguishing the light and returning them to the pitch-black darkness all around them. He lay down on the ground, curled up next to Gerald, and pulled his cloak around him, forming a warm cocoon.

"Good night, Gerald. See you in the morn…I mean night!"

"Yes, it will be quite dark when you awake. Good night, young Xach. Sweet dreams." *And good luck.*

Chapter Twelve

Xach awoke with a start. A cold chill ran down his spine as he stared into the darkness. In the distance he heard a strange sound, like a cross between a bird squawking and a human screaming. It took him a moment to remember where he was and why it was so dark, but once he did, he was able to relax a little. He yawned, stretched his arms and legs, and rubbed his eyes. He had no idea how long he had been sleeping, but he felt awake and refreshed. His stomach growled to remind him that it had been a long time since he had eaten. He also felt like he needed to go to the bathroom. Not wanting to wake Gerald, he quietly crawled out from under the mirondi to find a place to urinate. It was no longer raining, but the air felt wet and cold. He reached into his pocket, pulled out the key, and rubbed the gem to induce a glow.

The key cast enough light for him to see about two feet in front and to the side. He made his way to a clearing behind the group of mirondi under which they slept. He figured that was far enough from their resting place to go relieve himself. It wasn't the easiest thing to do with one arm in a sling, but he managed. He made sure not to urinate on the mirondi, because even though they looked like rocks, they were living things and it felt wrong to do so. Having drained his bladder and feeling much better, he tried to find his way back to Gerald. Even though he had only moved several feet from his original position, it was a little difficult to find his way back. The complete darkness and his limited field of vision made it nearly impossible to see which direction he was going or from where he came. His stomach growled again. He was quite hungry, but he kept trying to ignore it. He didn't want to go searching for food, because if he got lost, he'd never find his way back to Gerald in the darkness. He followed his way around the edges of the mirondi until he found Gerald sleeping under the overhang.

He lay back down but could not fall asleep again. He was bored and anxious, with nothing to do and no one to talk to. He wanted to wake Gerald, but he knew Gerald needed his sleep to recover from his injury. So Xach sat in silence and stared into the darkness. There was absolutely nothing for him to do except sleep or think. Thinking about his situation only brought on depression, so he didn't want to think. There were no TV's, no books, no video games, no toys, no comic books – NOTHING! Even the residents of Alaska had electricity and any number of amenities to occupy themselves during sequential days of darkness. Xach had nothing but his mind and the complete darkness.

He stared at the glowing key for several minutes before placing it on the ground next to him. He searched his pockets for something else to occupy his mind for a few seconds. All he found was the tin box and the medal that Gladys gave him. Even though he had owned and used the tin box for years, he wasted a few minutes observing the symbols etched onto its sides. He flipped the medal back and forth in his fingers. It was smooth and reflected the green light of the key like a mirror as he flipped it over and over. He watched the light reflect off the medal onto the surface of the mirondi. He turned the reflecting surface away from him, so that the light beam shone out into the darkness. The light refracted through the fog droplets in the air but was ultimately swallowed by the darkness.

Xach watched the beam move through the darkness, like an extremely weak light-sword. He pretended he was a knight battling an evil dragon. The light sword swung up to block a downward blow from the dragon's tail. Then Xach the knight brought the beam low and tried to slice the dragon in the belly, but the dragon blocked his advance with a thick scaly leg. Minutes slipped past as Xach attacked the darkness and the imaginary dragon with his light-sword. Xach's play was interrupted when the light fell directly on a very large eye!

Xach nearly jumped out of his skin and screamed out in sheer terror. He dropped the medal, and the eye melted back into the darkness. He hadn't wanted to wake Gerald, but he couldn't stifle his screams. He hadn't seen anything but an eye, so he didn't know *what* was out there watching him. It could be ANYTHING! He inched back under the mirondi until he bumped into Gerald's body.

Swallowing the lump in his throat, Xach whispered, "S-s-sorry Gerald, but there's **something** watching us."

Xach kept his eyes trained on the spot in the darkness where he had seen the eye, expecting it to leap out of the darkness and attack him, but nothing moved into the small circle of light cast about the key where it lay on the ground. Gerald said nothing and did not move. Xach elbowed Gerald lightly, but he remained motionless. Xach didn't say anything more, for fear that the sound of his voice might draw whatever it was in the darkness toward him. He hoped it could not see through the darkness in much the same way that he could not see. He continued to elbow Gerald but got no response.

In the darkness, Xach heard something thump on the ground, followed by a rustling sound. The rustling sound drew closer and closer. Xach held his breath, too terrified to breathe. His muscles froze and his brain screamed in horror. Something shifted on the edge of the darkness but kept from entering the key's light. His fear impulse was to close his eyes and wait for the attack, but he couldn't bring himself to close his eyes. If he was about to be eaten or mauled, he wanted to see it coming…whatever *it* was.

The shape moved closer to the light and then pulled back into the darkness. It moved toward the light again. The key's light danced across its shimmering, lumpy surface before disappearing back into the darkness again. It seemed to be as afraid of Xach as Xach was of it. The movement toward and away from the light reminded him of a child, like his brother, teetering between curiosity and fear of a loud toy. His little brother liked shiny toys. One toy in particular, a silver monkey, made a loud shrieking sound whenever it was touched. When he was younger, his brother would often lean toward it, touch it, and pull back in fright when it made the shrieking noise. Then he'd lean in to touch it again, his curiosity winning out over his fear. The thing in the darkness seemed to be doing the same thing.

I could scream and flap my arm and try to frighten it away, Xach thought, *but then again it might be some huge creature with motion-based vision, like a T-Rex, that is just waiting for me to move so it can find me and eat me. Maybe I should run into the darkness and hope that it can't see in the dark. But what if there are more of them out there? I wish Gerald would wake up! I have no weapons to defend myself either, not even a stick or a rock. I could use the pin on the medal. What if it has huge, razor sharp claws and teeth? What if...* His thoughts were cut off as the thing in the dark let out a deafening squawk.

"SQWAAAAAAAAWWWWK! CU-CU-CUAAAAWWWK!"

Xach lunged forward and snatched the medal from the ground, before pushing himself back against Gerald. If this thing was going to attack, he hoped at least to stab it with the pin. It was his only weapon. He felt Gerald's body slump away from him as he pushed away from the creature. He was totally engulfed in darkness and three or four feet from the key.

No longer seeing Xach in the bubble of light created by the key, the creature moved in to investigate the light source. Once in full illumination, Xach quickly recognized the creature to be a quarken! *It's just a bird!* Xach thought, as a wave of relief washed over him. He giggled to himself for being so frightened of a bird.

"What do you want, you stupid quarken?" Xach asked the bird, thankful that it was not some creature that was going to eat him.

In answer to his rhetorical question, the quarken lowered its neck and snatched the key with its beak.

"Hey, give that back to me!" Xach shouted. Without regard for how it might frighten the bird, he lunged toward it with his left arm outstretched to reclaim the key. The quarken jumped backward, spun around with its wings outstretched, and ran into the darkness.

"NO!!!" Xach yelled. "Come back here!"

He leapt to his feet, only to bump his head on the mirondi under which he was sitting. If the mirondi had not been soft and gelatinous, Xach would have seriously injured himself. As it was, he just bounced off it and fell back to the ground. He stashed the medal in his pocket, crawled out from under the mirondi, and ran through the darkness, chasing the light of the key as it bobbed up and down in the distance.

I gotta get that key back, Xach thought, *or I'll be stranded in the dark with no way of finding my way back to Gerald or getting home!*

He squinted in the darkness, trying not to lose sight of the quarken as it scurried erratically through the night. The light bounced up and down and zig-zagged back and forth like a drunken firefly. Xach felt things brush past his legs in the dark, and he stumbled a few times over objects that he could not see. He had this horrible feeling that he was going to run into something huge in the dark. He held his arm outstretched in front of him to alert him to the presence of something he might run into, but the only thing he could see was the light of the key. It was like running blindfolded into an unfamiliar room. There was no telling what kinds of objects might be in his way. He hoped that if he stayed close enough to the quarken, who could obviously see in the dark and would avoid all obstacles in its path, then he might not run into anything either. Nonetheless, every muscle in his body was tensed in preparation for some unseen barrier into which he was certain to collide. He had to concentrate with all his might to will himself forward through the darkness and to overcome his body's desire to stand still or move more cautiously. His muscles and his brain shouted for him to stop and slowly grope his way through the darkness, but Xach knew that he couldn't do that. He had to push on and keep pace with the quarken, or he'd lose the key forever.

Even though his fear of the unseen slowed his pursuit, his size and longer legs allowed him to gain on the large bird quickly. Just when he thought he might be close enough to lunge forward and grab it, Xach watched in horror as it spread its silver wings and took off into the night sky. His heart sank into his stomach as he watched the key's light rise higher and higher into the air. Nonetheless, he continued pursuit. To give up now would be equivalent to accepting that he'd never get home again, and he was not yet ready to accept that grim notion. Losing the key meant he would be lost forever, so he kept going.

The quarken climbed to about ten feet in the air. The light from the key became very small and dim, but Xach did not lose sight of it. Then the light stopped and seemed to hover in the air before it suddenly dropped straight down. Xach stood almost directly underneath the glowing key when it fell. He hoped the bird accidentally dropped it and that he would be able to catch it, but then it disappeared.

Oh no! Where'd it go? What happened to it? Did that stupid bird just eat it? No...wait a minute! Xach remembered the attack on the Zindarthans from earlier in the day. The quarken had taken the Zindarthans to its nest to feed to its young. *The floating islands...the baby birds...it must have dropped the key into its nest on one of the floating islands! ...So, how do I get up there in this darkness? I can't even see my hand in front of my face! Think, Xach, think!*

As he stared upward into the darkness, he began to forget exactly where it was. Darkness swirled in front of him and around him. He was in big trouble. He felt like cursing, but his parents didn't approve of foul language. *But then again,* he thought, *they're not here, are they?*

"Dammit," he shouted into the darkness, but he didn't feel much better. *What good does cursing serve, anyway?* he wondered. *No one can hear me. I can curse until I'm blue in the face, but it won't get me any closer to that key. If only there were some way I could get up on those floating islands...but I'm too short...and in the dark, how would I find them? I'd probably fall off and kill myself. I could just sit here and wait until the suns come up, but that's not for another two days or so. I'll starve to death by then...or go nuts waiting.*

He tried to silence the myriad of thoughts bumping into one another inside his head and attempted to focus on his options. Then it came to him. *Maybe I can find some mirondi and pile them up like a tower. Then I can climb up and reach the floating islands? ...but what if I can't find any? What if I'm too heavy and hurt the mirondi by standing on them? What if I move from this spot and can't find my way back? Focus. Focus!*

He tried to think about his situation objectively, as if he were an observer and not a participant. *What do you know?* he asked himself.

I'm about five feet tall, and the quarken was about ten feet in the air when it dropped the key into the nest. It fell about a foot or so down before I lost sight of it in the nest, so I really only need to get myself about four feet into the air.

So, how do you propose you get yourself four feet in the air?

If I had a four foot stick, I might be able to knock the nest down...but I don't have a four foot stick...and if I did then I might kill the baby quarken in the nest, so I guess that's out. I guess I'll have to go with the mirondi plan.

And how might you go about collecting mirondi without losing your place? If you don't stay right where you are, you'll lose the place where the key fell, and you'll just grope around in the dark forever...

He didn't have an answer for himself. He stuck his hands into his pockets and hung his head, cursing himself for allowing the key to slip from his possession in the first place. His fingers touched the medal that Gladys gave him.

The medal, he thought. *The medal! I can use the pin on the back to stick the medal into the ground and mark my place and the location of the key. Then all I have to do is feel around on the ground until I find it!*

He pulled the medal out of his pocket. He opened the pin on the back of the medal and stuck the pin into the ground directly between his feet. He knelt on the ground, directly over the pin. Then he stretched out his left arm and started feeling around on the ground. His hand touched something warm and spongy, just like the mirondi he and Gerald had been sleeping against. Without stretching too much, he was able to slide the mirondi toward him. He felt on the ground for the pin and pulled the mirondi right next to it. From what he could feel, this mirondi was probably about two feet round and maybe about a foot high. He'd need a few more of this size to build a sturdy tower on which to stand. He hoped that the mirondi didn't mind being pushed and pulled around, but he couldn't think of any other way to get the key back.

He continued sweeping his hand along the surface of the grass, keeping his knees planted on the ground next to the pin, so as not to lose his place. He made a complete 360-

degree sweep and found no more mirondi. It now became evident that he would need to venture out away from the pin. Then he had another brilliant idea. He took off his cloak and pinned one corner under the mirondi next to the pin. He immediately felt a deep chill the moment he removed the cloak. It was unbelievably cold! Almost immediately, his teeth began to chatter, and he shivered uncontrollably. He hadn't realized how warm and protective the cloak actually was, but he didn't have time to marvel at the wonders of the Zindarthan cloak. He had a job to do, and he needed to do it before he froze to death. Stretching the fabric out and away from the pin, he was able to sweep the area in a circle several feet in diameter while still being attached to the pin. His search yielded three more mirondi, varying in size from two feet in diameter to four feet in diameter. He struggled a little to push the largest one back to the pile, but he eventually brought them all together.

By positioning the three largest mirondi around the pin at equal distance from one another, he formed a tripod. He pulled the pin from the ground and returned the medal to his pocket, because he didn't want to forget it or lose it. He set about hoisting the fourth mirondi on top of the tripod, but this proved more difficult than he imagined. After several failed attempts at lifting the large jelly ball with one arm, he determined that he needed to remove the sling from his fractured arm and use both arms to lift the last one into place on top of the others. He did most of the lifting with his left arm, but he immediately felt pain throbbing from his bandaged wrist the moment he lifted the mirondi off the ground. He held on through the pain and positioned it on top of the three mirondi he circled around the pin. He put his cloak back on quickly, but he did not replace the sling. He tucked the sling into his back pocket so that he would not lose it. He figured he would need his arms free to balance on the mound of mirondi. He leaned forward onto the pile to see if it was stable and to determine how high it was. Although the surface of the mirondi pile felt gelatinous, it seemed solid enough – like a giant gumdrop or beanbag chair filled with Jello. By his measurements, the top of the tower came to somewhere between his abdomen and chest. It was less than four feet, but he hoped it would be enough.

As carefully as he could, he crawled up the side of the tower. He put his feet on two of the mirondi that formed the base of the tripod and pushed upward toward the pinnacle. His feet sank into the surface, and he felt squishy material around his ankles. It was like trying to stand on top of two semi-deflated beach balls. The only difference was that beach balls would have rolled away; the mirondi remained fixed to the ground on a flat surface. Nonetheless, it was still difficult to keep upright.

"I am so sorry," Xach said to the mirondi. "I hope this doesn't hurt." He didn't know if they could hear him or even understand him, but he knew he would not enjoy someone *his* size stepping on his head.

Once he felt like he had himself balanced properly, he leaned forward and used his arms to pull himself up to the top. He used his knees to pinch onto the sides so that he wouldn't slide back down. When he was kneeling comfortably on top of the pile, he slowly pulled his right leg upward and planted it on the top of the mound. Then he pulled up his left leg, extended his arms straight out at his sides for balance, and tried to push himself into a standing position. He wobbled several times, but by swinging his arms in circular patterns and slowly shifting his body weight, he was finally able to stand up straight.

He lifted his chin as high as he could and scanned the sky in front of him for the key's light. *If my calculations are correct,* Xach thought as he squinted into the darkness, *the floating island should be directly overhead or slightly in front of me.* He carefully stretched his arms out into the darkness but felt nothing. Slowly he moved his arms to the left and to the right. Two fingers of his right hand brushed against something crumbly. He shifted his weight to his right and leaned toward the object he felt. His hand met resistance from a solid object; it was one of the floating islands! He tried to turn himself toward the clump of floating earth, but his feet wouldn't move. They were sunken in the jelly-like surface of the mirondi. The slight shift of his weight caused him to lose his balance, and he felt himself falling to the right. Thinking quickly, he bent his knees and launched himself upward, hoping to propel himself onto the floating island instead of falling to the ground.

It was like he was moving in slow motion. His knees straightened. His muscles tightened and his feet lifted from the surface of the mirondi. He stretched out his arms in front of him and prayed he would feel the floating island under them. Seconds felt like hours as he fell forward, wondering if he was going to hit the island or fall on his face. Then he felt it – grass! For a brief moment grass tickled his elbows, and then his chest hit something solid. He managed to hit the island instead of falling! He clamped down with his hands and dug into the earth of the floating island. His legs dangled in mid-air. He knew that if he lost his grip, he would fall to the ground, possibly injuring more than just his arm. His fractured wrist screamed in pain, but he dared not let go. He strained with all his might, attempting to pull himself up onto the flat surface.

Adrenaline coursed through his veins. His chest rose past the side of the island. He reached forward with his left arm and found the opposite edge of the island. It couldn't have been more than two or three feet in width. Once he had a solid hold on the side, he reached his other arm forward and secured his grip. Now he was better able to pull himself up onto the island. Sweat poured down his face as he strained to pull himself up. His mind flashed back to gym class where the gym teacher, Mr. Grundle, made him try to do chin-ups and pull-ups. He never excelled at this activity and often just hung from the bars without being able to pull himself up. The other kids always laughed at him and called him a weakling. Eventually, Mr. Grundle let him drop without completing a single chin-up or pull-up and gave him an F for the day. Oh how he hated gym class! But this wasn't gym class, and there was a lot more than a grade riding on his performance.

He struggled to raise himself up on his elbows, so that he could lean forward and gain enough leverage to swing his right leg up. His right knee came to rest on the island, so he quickly shifted his left arm to the other side of the island and wrapped his body around it. Pushing with his left arm and pulling with his right, he was able to shimmy around the island until his chest rested on the top of the island. It may not have been the most graceful of climbs, but he had made it! He wished Mr. Grundle had been there to see him. *I guess a person can do just about anything with the proper motivation,* Xach thought happily.

He rested for a few minutes until his breathing returned to normal, allowing his arms and legs to dangle over the sides of the island. Once the burn in his arm muscles subsided a bit, he sat up, straddling the island. He got to his knees and carefully stood up. The island was about six feet long and about three feet wide, so he made sure he was firmly standing in the middle. He didn't want to fall off from that height.

He slowly shuffled his feet in a clockwise pattern, looking at the darkness under his feet. He detected no light coming from the island surface or the ground below. Therefore, he knew he wasn't on the right island and that he hadn't knocked the nest off while trying to keep from falling. He slowly rotated in a circle again, this time surveying the darkness around him at eye level. *It's got to be nearby,* Xach thought. *I hope I didn't miscalculate its location. It can't be that far off.*

After a quarter turn, a glimmer caught his eye a few feet to the left of him. He shuffled forward to the edge of the island and strained his eyes to focus on the faintly glowing light. The glow was faint but green, like a flashlight shining from beneath a sheet. Xach stretched out his arms toward the light, but it was beyond his reach. *If I jump into the darkness toward the key,* Xach thought, *will I be able to reach the island or will I fall ten feet to the ground? Then again, do I have any other option at this point?*

Again, Xach's mind flashed back to gym class – specifically the locker room. Jack Sully, an overweight bully known to most as just Sully, used to snap his towel at the other boys in the locker room. He thought it was funny to leave large, red welts on the arms, legs, and buttocks of the younger, smaller boys in Xach's gym class. While this memory was not a pleasant one, seeing as how he was often on the receiving end of Sully's towel, it gave him an idea. *If I can use the cloak as a whip, I can try to knock the key from the island and keep myself from attempting another jump into the darkness.*

Xach removed his cloak, once again feeling the icy, cold air bite into his skin. The sweat from his exertion to reach the island only made things worse. The cold felt like needles of ice penetrating his skin. He twirled the cloak several times, winding it into a twisted fabric extension of his arm. When he felt it was wound tightly enough, he snapped it forward toward the light and pulled back quickly. He heard the cloak make a slapping sound as it cut through the air and made contact with something solid, but the light did not move. The baby quarken in the nest rustled uncomfortably and began chirping nervously. He wound the cloak again and snapped it toward the light. He heard the snap again, and something moved on the dark island, momentarily blocking the light of the key. *Am I even reaching it,* Xach wondered, *or am I just snapping air?*

Several more attempts proved fruitless. Xach inched toward the light and leaned forward as far as he could without losing his balance, trying desperately to make contact with the nest. Only his heels kept him from falling off the floating mound of dirt. Hopelessness settled in until one of his snaps made contact with the mother quarken. The bird let out a deafening squawk that scared Xach half to death.

He jumped backward out of fear, forgetting for the moment that he was precariously perched on the edge of a pile of dirt hovering several feet in the air. His left foot twisted a little and slid off the side of the island. Though he tried to shift his weight to the right, he couldn't stop himself from falling. He dropped the cloak and spread out his arms to break his fall. The edge of the island slid up his inner thigh and made contact with his groin. Before the pain could register in his groin, his chest and chin hit the island, and he slid off the side. Using his right arm as an anchor, he stopped himself from falling completely off the floating island, but his legs dangled off the side. The edge of the island dug into his chest, and pain began to throb in his wrist, as it bore almost three-quarters of his full body weight. He struggled to right himself on the island's surface for several minutes. Eventually he succeeded.

He couldn't catch his breath; the icy air crystallized in his lungs, making it harder to breathe. The sweat that his body produced during his strenuous attempt to keep from falling now began freezing on his skin. He hugged himself to conserve body heat, shivering as he envisioned the cloak laying somewhere on the ground below.

"Well, Xach," he said aloud to himself, in an attempt to bolster his confidence. "You don't have any other choice now."

His only option now was to jump for the key and hope for the best. If he stood around thinking too much or complaining over the dropped cloak, he'd loose his nerve. So, he placed his heels on the back edge of the floating island to give him some space for a running jump. Keeping his eyes trained on the faint glow in front of him, he took two steps forward, bent his knees, swung his arms forward in front of him, and launched into the darkness.

The cold, black air whizzed past his face, as the light of the key moved closer and closer. His chest hit something solid that knocked the wind out his lungs. The impact with the island caused enough vibration to startle the quarken and its young to the point of hysteria. The next few seconds were a blur of noise and erratic movement as Xach attempted to grab hold of the island, while the quarken squawked and fluttered about. Dirt, feathers, and grass filled the air. Xach could feel them falling on his face and head and down his shirt, but his hands failed to make contact with anything solid enough to hold onto. Then he felt nothing. He lost touch with the island and fell toward the ground. He tried to relax his body and curl himself into a ball, because he knew from watching car crashes on television that tensing one's muscles during an accident causes more injury than if one were relaxed. However, that is easier said than done. He knew that he was about to hit something, and it was his body's natural impulse to stiffen and brace for impact. *I wonder why that is?* Xach thought. *You'd think that whoever created us would have made us in such a way that our bodies resisted damage instead of...*

Xach's whimsical musings on the creation of man and his impulses were suddenly interrupted by impact of his body hitting the tower of mirondi. Although they were soft, it still knocked the breath out of him. He bounced off the pile and landed almost gently on the ground. *How fortunate!* Xach thought. *At least **something** is going right for me. I didn't break my neck or back!*

He stood up and brushed the dirt and other debris off of his shirt and head. Though he wasn't physically bruised, his ego was bruised, and he felt defeated. He wanted to try again, but he was cold and, for all intents and purposes, basically blind. Future success in this endeavor seemed bleak, yet surviving until the suns rose a few days from now seemed even bleaker.

I have to keep trying, Xach thought. *But first things first – I need to find my cloak, because it's freezing out here.* He knelt down and felt around on the ground for the soft fabric. His hand lighted on something warm and feathery. *A quarken,* he thought, *but why isn't it pulling away or pecking at me?* He felt around the warm lump of feathers. It was about the size of a small potato, and it was not moving. *Oh my God! I must have killed it! I must have knocked it out of the nest and it fell to its death. Poor thing. I didn't mean to kill it.* He felt terrible and cradled the small body in his hands, wishing there was something he could do to save it or take back his actions. He hadn't thought he could feel any worse or more defeated than he had when he fell from the island and lost the key, but he was sinking to a new low of sadness. A tear fell from his eye. It slid down his cheek and then stopped, frozen solid by the frigid air surrounding him.

He gently placed the tiny body behind him on the ground near the mound of mirondi so that he wouldn't accidentally squash it while searching for the cloak. It was already dead and squashing it wouldn't change anything, but it somehow seemed it would be worse to squash it after having killed it – like he would be killing it twice – even though that was not physically possible. After several sweeps he found the cloak, shook it out, and put it back over his shoulders. Instantly, he felt his body begin to warm again. He crawled back to the pile of mirondi, so that he wouldn't lose his place in the darkness. He felt around the edges of the tower for the baby quarken he had killed, but he couldn't find it! The body was gone! *Maybe it wasn't dead,* he thought. *Maybe I just stunned it? I hope so.*

He felt very tired, so he lay against the Mirondi, closed his eyes, and took several deep breaths to calm his nerves. He often saw his mother do this when she was upset. She told him it was meditation and part of yoga. He didn't really have a concept of what either of those things were, but he knew that it helped his mother focus when she was particularly upset or frustrated, just as he was. After his fourth deep breath, his mind seemed to spontaneously clear, and it occurred to him that if he knocked the baby quarken out of its nest, then he might have knocked the nest or the key from the island as well!

He opened his eyes, stood up, and scanned the darkness for any signs of light. He wasn't sure, but he thought he saw a faint glow coming from a few feet to his left. He hoped it wasn't his eyes playing tricks on him. He took several cautious steps toward the light, holding his breath. The light grew stronger as he approached. Xach knelt down and extended his hand toward the light. It didn't disappear or run away. It wasn't a mirage! Beneath some scattered grass and dirt lay the key!

Chapter Thirteen

Xachary pushed the dirt and grass aside and picked up the key. A wave of relief washed over him, and he felt a profound joy rise up from within the darkness of despair and disparagement he had been feeling. He felt like dancing around and screaming in joy, but he refrained from making a spectacle of himself, even though there was not a person or thing to see him express his exuberance if he had.

He gripped the key tightly, irrationally fearful that he might lose it again.

Now to figure out how to get back to Gerald, Xach thought. *I wonder how far I ran? From which direction did I come?*

Circling the pile of mirondi, he scanned the darkness with the key's light but saw nothing he recognized. A closer look at the ground revealed that he left several footprints in the blue grass. The grass was frozen by the cold that came with the darkness and was broken and trampled where his sneakers made contact. Bent over like a hunchback, Xach held the key close to the ground and retraced his steps back toward Gerald.

After several minutes of walking hunched over, his back started to hurt. He stood up and stretched, and that is when he noticed something he hadn't noticed before. On the horizon, he could distinctly see light. Not just one light, but many lights! The lights were amorphous in shape and size, and try as he might Xach could not determine what kind of light source was producing the glow on the horizon – fire, electricity, or something else?

Finally! Xach thought. *Civilization! Maybe they have a hospital or medical supplies and equipment that could heal Gerald's injury. Then I wouldn't have to worry about this whole key thing. I could just give it back to Gerald, and he could take me home!*

The thought of going back home and forgetting all that he'd been through was intoxicating. A feeling of warmth and joy spread through him at the thought of returning to his family and friends, but this was quickly replaced by feelings of doubt and fear. A strong cold wind blew past him and caused him to shiver involuntarily. It was almost as if his surroundings were reminding him that he should not dare to hope the answers to all his problems lay within the light on the horizon. The lights on the horizon appeared to flicker as if they were somehow physical manifestations of his own alternating feelings of joy and despair. He had a very important decision to make. Either he could continue to follow his footsteps in the grass and hopefully return to Gerald, or he could head off toward the lights in the distance. This was not a decision he could make lightly. His decision affected not only himself but also Gerald. His mind began to fill with different scenarios, like the choose-your-own-adventure books he used to read.

If my footsteps actually lead me all the way back to Gerald, will I still be able to see the lights and get us to them? If I head towards the lights and find someone or something there that could help Gerald, will I be able to find my way back to Gerald in the darkness? What if I can't find Gerald, and he starves to death in the wilderness? I would never forgive myself.

For all I know, Gerald might have woken up and found that I deserted him! What would he do in that situation? Would he stay there and wait for me to return or would he go looking for me? What would I do if I were him? If he left me and I woke up alone, I would freak out.

Then again, if I do find my way back to him, he might be too ill to walk, and then I would have wasted this opportunity to find some help.

"What should I do?" he addressed the darkness. "What should I do?" He looked down at his footprints in the grass. He looked at the lights in the distance and then again at his footprints in the grass.

I guess if I were in Gerald's position, he thought, *I would want him to come back for me as soon as possible. So, I guess I should just find my way back to Gerald if I can and worry about the lights once I find him again.* He hunched over and started following his footsteps again, but his mind continued to race with doubts. *Maybe I'll be able to see the lights from wherever Gerald is sleeping, and then I can help him walk toward them...but I don't remember being able to see*

*them when I was sitting there with him earlier. Maybe I was
too low on the horizon. What if he's not sleeping? What if he
woke up and tried to find me in the darkness? Then I'll never
find him! Maybe I should try and get one of those lights and
then go searching for him? At least with one of those lights, I
would be able to see more than one foot in front of my face. If
I make it back to Gerald with only the light of the key and we
can't see the lights from where we are, then we'd just be
wandering around in the darkness and that might injure him
further.*

*Ugh! What if I make the wrong choice? What if
something horrible happens to Gerald because of my decision?
Then I'd be all alone in this strange place with no idea of how
to get home. But what if something horrible happens to me
while I'm trying to get to him? Or what if there is something
near the lights that will harm me? If I die out here, then
Gerald will surely die and my parents will never know what
happened to me! If only I hadn't lost the key...*

He stopped walking and looked again toward the lights.

Ok, Xachary, he heard his father's voice say sternly in
his head, *there is no point in blaming yourself for what
happened. It happened and you dealt with it. Now you just
need to be brave, make a decision about the lights, and stick
with it. You need to clear you head and think rationally.*

His mind flashed to another time in his life when he
was overcome with fear. He had been afraid to go on his first
camping trip with the Cub Scouts. He was terrified to leave his
family and sleep alone in the woods. Again he heard his
father's voice in his head: *Fear is irrational. Fear is an
emotion we feel when we don't know what will happen. But
son, there is no way to know what will happen, so it's better to
just try to relax and live in the moment. Otherwise, fear can
paralyze you with worry or guilt. You'll never **do** anything.
So just go and try it.*

Fear is irrational, Xach told himself. *It will only slow
me down and cloud my judgment. If I don't release the fear, I
will just end up making the wrong decision anyway. And a
decision made out of fear will only result in regret. I need to
calm down and try to think clearly.*

Using the light of the key, he located a large mirondi near his trail of footprints. He put the key in his pocket, sat down, closed his eyes, and attempted to relax himself. The short meditation he did several minutes ago had not been enough to totally calm and refocus his mind. He took several deep breaths, as his mother had taught him to do. He imagined the breath in his lungs was like a wave of water, starting at the base of his lungs and swelling toward his nose. Then he allowed the breath to slowly reverse as he exhaled, feeling the air flow from him like a deflating balloon. Often when he practiced with his mother, he would find himself falling asleep after several fluid breaths. When his mother would wake him several minutes later, he felt refreshed and clear. He hoped that by practicing this technique now, he could flush the fear and uncertainty from his mind and free himself to make the most logical decision.

As he slowly breathed in and out, the darkness behind his closed eyelids began to swirl and change colors. At home, the colors would often swirl and solidify into images of his happiest memories, and the remembrance of these things allowed him to relax and calm himself. And while these images would certainly be welcome and comforting at this particular moment, Xach was more interested in finding a solution to his dilemma concerning which route to follow – his footsteps or the lights. The swirling colors and darkness began to take the shape of footprints. One by one the footprints began to glow, as if dimly illuminated, leading off into the darkness. The glowing grew in intensity until they became red and orange flaming footprints that scattered in all directions. The myriad of footprints then morphed together into one large flame. The flames shrank, and Xach envisioned himself carrying a torch as he wandered through the darkness. The torch illuminated his surroundings, and he could see mirondi and different colored bushes. Then under a large group of mirondi, the darkness swirled into the shape of Gerald's sleeping body. The torch went out, and he was thrust into darkness. He withdrew the key, and it glowed green. He knelt down and touched Gerald's shoulder. He extended the key toward Gerald's face. As he did, the light of the key began to grow in intensity until all Xach could see was a blinding green light.

He opened his eyes and took a deep breath.

"Wow," he muttered. "That crap actually worked!"

He definitely felt more relaxed and confident. He felt revitalized and well-rested. More importantly, he felt he had reached a decision about which direction he wanted to go — toward the lights on the horizon. Uncertain as to whether or not the vision he had had was just wishful thinking or an actual premonition of future events, he still felt relatively confident that he would be able to obtain a light source in the distance and use it to find Gerald, who was probably still asleep under the pile of mirondi.

Xach pulled his cloak tight around his shoulders and headed off toward the lights. He stumbled a few times as his feet hit things on the ground, but this did not slow his pace. He moved quickly, cutting through the cold darkness, determined to find help. Even though his stomach grumbled from hunger, the adrenaline coursing through his veins kept him from exhibiting the food depravation.

After what seemed like an hour of walking, his calves began to ache, but he was making progress. He was getting closer. The nearer he drew, the more distinct the lights became. The lights flickered and wavered minutely in intensity. He saw shadows moving to and from the lights. Crude structures were erected behind the lights onto which these shadows were cast.

Finally, he drew up to the perimeter of the lights. They were large hand-sculpted torches, burning brightly with flickering flames atop. The structures resembled ramshackle houses or buildings, haphazardly erected using sticks, mirondi, bushes tied together, and other objects Xach couldn't recognize. It reminded him of the shelters the homeless people built out of garbage bags, sticks, and broken shopping carts to protect themselves from the elements. He hung in the shadows just outside the perimeter of the lights to observe the creatures moving about within this rudimentary town. He wanted to observe them a bit before approaching them. He had no way of knowing how they communicated or if they would be friendly or hostile.

He crept around to a large mirondi beside one of the torches nearest the largest building. It cast a large shadow in which he could conceal himself and observe the creatures without fear of being seen. One passed within a few feet of him, carrying a bundle in its arms. As it passed beside the torch, Xach got a clear view of its form and appearance. It was over six feet tall and very muscular. However, it appeared to be crippled, because it did not stand entirely upright as it shuffled along. Long strands of dirty, stringy hair hung over its large forehead and down to its shoulders. Its nose was large and flat, almost as though it were pressing its face against a pane of glass. Large, misshapen teeth protruded from various angles between its lips. A large piece of cloth was draped over its body and tied with a rope around the waist in much the same manner as a toga. Even though the creature appeared quite large and imposing, there was something oddly feminine about it.

The creature passed the mirondi behind which Xach was hiding and stopped near a large hole in the ground. It placed the bundle on the ground by the hole and withdrew a small misshapen cup from within the folds of its clothes. The bundle let out a cry, and it was at this point that Xach realized the creature was more than likely a mother carrying an infant. She knelt over the hole and reached in with the cup. She brought the cup to her child and tipped it forward into the child's mouth. It gurgled and spit some of the liquid onto the ground. Then it began to coo, apparently happy for the drink. The mother drank the rest of the liquid and returned the cup to the folds of her clothing. She picked up the child and continued moving into one of the buildings.

Somehow, this creature didn't fit into the mental image Xach had of Zindartha. The neon grass, pink water, double suns, and multi-colored bushes…it was all too bright and cheery to be home to a group of creatures such as these. Yet here they were, and like it or not, they were Xach's only hope of helping Gerald at this point.

How am I going to communicate with these people?
Xach thought to himself. *What will they think of me and the
way I'm dressed? I don't look anything like them. What if they
perceive me to be a threat of some kind? How can I make
myself appear as harmless as I really am?*

He wished he had more time to observe these people
before attempting communication, but he had already wasted
too much time chasing down the key and wandering around in
the dark. He needed to act immediately if he was going to get
help for Gerald. He stood up and stepped out of the shadows.
Without consciously thinking about it, he slipped his hand in
his pocket and grasped the key. A sense of calm washed over
him as he remembered what Gerald had told him about the
universal translation properties of the key. *It doesn't matter
what language these creatures speak; the key will translate
their language into English so I can understand them. How
silly I am to have forgotten that,* Xach thought to himself.
*Being able to speak their language will surely help me
convince them that I'm not a threat and allow me to explain
about Gerald and his injury.*

With that boost of self-confidence, Xach marched
toward the building housing the woman and child. *Surely it
would be better to present myself to a female first rather than a
male,* Xach thought, *as a woman should be more nurturing and
perhaps less threatened by my appearance.*

He couldn't have been more wrong.

He intended to knock on the door, but found that it
wasn't so much a door as a drape of sorts. He pulled it aside,
and said, "Hello? Sorry to disturb you, but I was wondering
if…"

He never got to finish his polite inquiry. The woman,
hearing Xach's voice, spun around from what looked like a
cradle made of bushes tied together and promptly shrieked so
loudly that Xach had to cover his ears. Her reaction was so
shrill and sudden that Xach felt just as scared as she was! He
removed his hands from his ears and waved them in front of
him, trying to get her to stop screaming and calm down. She
continued to shriek as she picked up her baby and held it over
her enormous head.

"Monster...no take baby!" she cried and lunged at Xach like a charging rhinoceros.

He leapt sideways to avoid a collision, but her frame was so massive that he could not avoid a hip-check from her as she passed. The impact sent him flying into a crudely constructed table. The woman's dinnerware, a set of misshapen clay plates and cups, flew in all directions. The table split in half under Xach's weight, not so much because of the force with which he hit it but more due to the lack of craftsmanship that had gone into its construction. This seemed to irritate the woman even further. She let out another high pitched shriek and tried to stomp on him. Her foot, approximately the size of a five-pound bag of potatoes and weighing about the same, came down squarely on Xach's chest, knocking the wind out him.

"NO...take...baby!" she screamed as she delivered a swift kick into Xach's side.

Xach curled into a ball, struggling to breathe. He tried to speak and explain that he meant no harm, but he couldn't catch his breath.

Although she was protecting her child, she did not handle it very gently. It cried out loudly, momentarily eclipsing its mother's screams. She brought her foot down again on Xach's chest and pressed him against the ground. She wanted him immobilized while she comforted her child.

He was certain she had broken one or more of his ribs, and if he didn't get away from her soon, she would likely kill him. He surveyed his surroundings quickly for any object that might be used as a weapon. He hoped to find a fork or knife amongst the table debris, but he saw none – just broken dishes and splintered wood.

The baby started to quiet down, so he knew her assault would resume shortly. He found a large, jagged piece of shattered plate and jammed it into what he hoped was her ankle. Her skin was so tough and thick that the plate hardly broke the skin, but it was enough to startle her. She cried out and raised her foot to view her injury. Xach rolled away from her and grabbed one of the table legs. His chest and side were on fire with pain, but he held the table leg like a bat. He swung it as hard as he could directly into what he hoped was her stomach. Xach was certain that he failed to cause her any significant pain, but he hit her with just enough force to cause her to stumble backwards into the cradle, splintering it into hundreds of pieces. She threw out her arms to stop her fall, inadvertently releasing her baby into the air.

Without thinking, Xach reached out and caught the baby. It laughed and gurgled with enjoyment. Xach looked down at the creature in his arms. Its eyes were half the size of its head, and one was much larger than the other. It smiled a crooked smile and drooled out the side of its mouth. *A face only a mother could love,* Xach thought to himself.

His first instinct was to put the child on the floor safely and run away as quickly as possible, but it occurred to him that she would likely come after him to finish what she started. If he kept the baby, he might be able to use it as a distraction. He could place the baby on the ground outside the shack and then run the opposite direction toward the shadows beyond the torch line. She would have to stop and collect her baby, thereby allowing him a few extra seconds to slip away into the safety of the darkness.

Acting with as much speed as he could muster, Xach lurched toward the drape and pushed his way out into the cold night air. The torch line was to his left, so he turned to the right to find a suitable place to lay the child. **SMACK** His face hit something hard, and he fell to the ground. It was like running into a brick wall. He almost dropped the baby. His vision momentarily blurred. Blood dripped from his nose. He looked up to see what he ran into. It was another creature. This one was most definitely a male. It was uglier and larger than the female. To its left and right stood more of them, each carrying a spear or rudimentary mace. As Xach lay dazed on the ground, the creatures circled around him. He was surrounded. The drape flew out behind him and the crazy woman emerged, shrieking incoherently about her baby and a monster.

I'm gonna die, Xach thought.

Chapter Fourteen

The woman screamed and pointed toward Xachary, as the men slowly advanced toward him. They pounded their spears on the ground and grunted. It was obvious that they were simplistic creatures, much like children who deal in emotional absolutes. The looks of pure rage in their eyes belayed the fact that they lacked the ability to reason or balance their emotions. However, they did not rush forward and attack him as he expected. Instead they inched slowly toward him, as if unsure about what they should do. They appeared confident that Xach could not escape, but they were wary of him, having never seen anything like him before. They took their time closing the circle, tighter and tighter, while they figured out what they should do.

Xach clutched the baby against his chest. His breathing was heavy. He glanced nervously from side to side, trying to conjure an escape plan. He wasn't even sure whether the baby was still alive. The baby had been between him and the creature he smacked into, so he might have injured it upon impact. It wasn't crying or moving. He wanted to check its pulse or breathing, but there wasn't time. He had to get out of this mess quickly, or he feared these creatures would bludgeon him to death and probably eat his remains.

One of the shorter men wearing a necklace made of Quarken feathers held up his spear as if to throw it at Xach. A larger man standing next to him put his arm in front of the man's chest to stop him. He said something that sounded like "hurt baby?" The shorter man lowered his spear a bit and continued to advance with the group.

Xach thought he might be able to use the crowd's consideration for the baby's welfare to his advantage. He slowly placed the baby bundle on the ground and raised his empty hands in the air. A low whine emanated from the bundle, rising in treble and pitch into a full-fledged cry.

Thank God it's all right, Xach thought. *I guess the babies are just as tough as their parents.*

The group of men stopped advancing on Xach, cocking their heads quizzically and looking from the bundle to Xach with his hands held above his head. The feeling of relief at the child's safety, gave Xach a new found confidence in his plan. Hoping that Gerald's speech about the key's language translation properties was accurate, he pointed toward the torch line, opened his eyes wide in a fake terror, and screamed as loudly as possible the one word he knew they understood – "MONSTER!" Gerald was not wrong, because the group of men all turned their heads in synchronous motion toward the place where Xach pointed.

In that split second of distraction, Xach ran toward the closest space between two of the men and pushed his way out of the circle. Without looking back, he ran as fast as he could in search of a place to hide. The pain in his side kept him from reaching his highest speed. From behind him arose the sounds of angry yells and the stomping of large feet; the men were already chasing him.

Xach passed several huts but thought better of choosing one of them as a hiding place, fearing he'd run into another person who would alert the mob to his presence. The mob drew closer. His little legs could not compete with their longer, stronger legs. He hoped to reach the outer limits of the town and slip into the darkness of the night before they caught him, but he realized he would never make it.

He zig-zagged around two of the shacks and found a fenced-in area that resembled a cow pasture or cattle pen. Instead of animals though, the area was full of the tiny multi-colored moving bushes in which the Zindarthans lived. He glanced behind him to make sure that no one was close enough to see him, and then he jumped over the fence into the enclosure. He caught his foot on the fence and fell face first onto the ground. The impact knocked the wind out of him as his ribs cracked a little more. He nearly passed out, but he summoned the last of his strength and will to crawl between the branches of a few closely grouped bushes. He hoped he was hidden well enough to avoid detection. He lay very still and quiet. The bushes moved closer to him and clustered more densely around him, as if they realized he was trying to hide.

He rolled onto his back and peered upward through the multi-colored branches so that he could see his pursuers coming if they managed to spot him lying on the ground. The angry yells and grunts of the men grew louder. Peering between the colored branches of the bushes, he saw their massive shadows pass by the holding pen. Their massive feet kicked up dust and shook the ground. Once their yells and foot noise died down, Xach waited a few more minutes before slowly starting to sit up.

"Lie back down," said a tiny urgent voice. "They haven't all gone."

Xach lay back down, surprised by the serious tone of the voice and a little concerned that he did not know who had spoken to him. Nonetheless, he was relieved that he didn't sit up so quickly as to become detected by one of the stragglers running behind the angry mob.

Xach waited a moment and then whispered, "Is it safe now?"

The voice replied, "Yes. No one appears to be present at this time, but I recommend you remain hidden for the time being."

Xach sat up on his elbows, so that his head poked out a bit above the tops of the bushes. He glanced around in all directions. The creatures were gone, yet he could not detect anyone or anything that might have warned him not to sit up.

"If you know what's good for you, you'll lie back down," said the mysterious voice.

"Who are you?" Xach inquired, as he lowered himself back to the ground and once again concealed himself beneath the bushes.

"I am Queen Zoron," replied the voice.

"Queen Zoron? But I can't see anyone. Where are you?"

"To your left," sounded the voice from above Xach's left ear. Xach turned his head toward the left and saw a tiny red head peering down at him from over the edge of a purple leaf.

"Oh! You're a Zindarthan," Xach whispered sheepishly, realizing that he should have known better than to think anything other than a Zindarthan would speak to him from a moving purple bush. "I'm sorry, your Highness. I did not see you."

"Not to worry," responded Queen Zoron in a deep, regal voice. Queen Zini and Queen Zora mentioned your presence on our world sometime yesterday. I am honored to meet you."

"The honor is all mine, but how did you learn of my presence so quickly?"

"Being a collective of highly evolved beings, we have the ability to communicate telepathically with one another. It is how we alert each other of approaching Mung tribes and attacking quarken."

"Mung tribes? What are they?" Xach asked.

"Mung are those horrible creatures from whom you are hiding and who trapped us in this enclosure."

"I see," mumbled Xach. *Mung* seemed an appropriate name for those creatures. The word seemed to imply *dirty, disgusting,* and *uncultured,* perhaps because it sounded so much like *dung.* "I think they meant to kill me," Xach added cautiously.

"I am certain they did," replied Queen Zoron. "The Mung are not known for their kindness or humanity. In fact, they are holding us captive at this very moment with the intent of eating us all before the daylight returns."

"Why would they do that?" Xach asked, shocked that the Mung would dare kill such an intelligent species as the Zindarthans just for the purpose of eating them. It would be the same as chickens or cows killing humans for food. It seemed backwards and contrary to the natural way of things. "You and your people are clearly more advanced and developed than the Mung," Xach postulated. "How is it that they justify eating you and your people? It's *murder*!"

"There is no justification for their actions. They are simply barbarians. However, they are so much larger than we, and they can easily outrun our transports."

"The bushes?"

"Yes. These mobile plants allow us to move greater distances than our tiny legs could carry us. Plus, they provide shelter from the suns and the quarken."

"Why not live underground?" suggested Xach, thinking of the ant colonies he observed in school. After all, the Zindarthans looked very much like ants to him, even though they were *talking, telepathic* ants.

"Not to sound rude, O Great One, but would you want to live underground in the damp earth, hidden from the sun and fresh air?"

"No. I suppose not," offered Xach apologetically. "Sorry if I offended you. I was simply thinking out loud."

"Do not worry," she continued unfazed. "Truth be told, the Mung were not always here on Zindartha. Until several years ago, we **were** the dominant species on this world. They just appeared one day and have grown in numbers over the years. They are taking over the land, killing our people, and destroying the delicate balance of nature we have maintained for eons." She choked back a tear, and her face flushed with anger and sadness. Then she sighed and smiled again. "I need not bother you with our troubles," she continued in a defeated voice. "You have your own troubles with which to contend. You need to escape from here and get as far away from the Mung as possible."

"But I can't leave you here to be eaten!" Xach protested.

"O Large One, your bravery and noblity have not been exaggerated! I appreciate your concern, but our lives are inconsequential. You must fend for yourself."

"Don't be ridiculous. I can easily set you free from this fenced area. And if it's not too forward, perhaps you could help me find my way back to my friend, Gerald? He's hurt and lost in the darkness."

"You truly are a hero," beamed Queen Zoron. "Should you succeed in setting us all free, we will do everything within our power to help you and your friend."

"Then it's settled," said Xach. "Is it safe for me to get up now?"

"Yes, the Mung have not returned and my subjects from the outer perimeter of the enclosure report no on-lookers."

Xach sat up and looked all around him. He detected no Mung. Crawling on his hands and knees to the side of the enclosure, he peered over the highest panel. He heard some yelling coming from behind a group of shacks in front of him, but he could not physically see anyone.

In the distance, about fifty feet from the enclosure, Xach could see the line of torches that marked the edge of the Mung encampment. *If I can get myself and the Zindarthans past the torches and into the darkness, we should be able to escape without being detected.*

Xach crept to the lowest panel of the enclosure and climbed over it. Once on the outside, he moved around the edge until he found a latched gate. It was crude in construction but functional nonetheless. The gate moved on a pole that was inserted into the edge of one of the panels. A quarken bone was attached to the opposite side and secured to a stationary panel using a bit of string. Xach untied the string and swung the gate outward.

"Time to go," Xach whispered, as the bushes quickly filed through the opening. Xach pointed toward the torch line and took the lead. He quickly and quietly moved toward the torch-lit perimeter like a mother duck leading a line of ducklings. They passed a large pool of pink water, several misshapen huts, and a few lopsided tents. Xach paused periodically, to hide behind something to avoid being seen by the Mung wandering around the encampment. Every time Xach stopped, the line of bushes following him froze and remained motionless until Xach signalled movement again.

They moved undetected for several minutes, inching ever closer to the torch line and the freedom of the darkness beyond, but as they came within ten feet of the torches, they were spotted by a group of Mung children who were playing near the torches. The children kicked around what looked like a purple ball and giggled loudly until two of the girls in the group noticed Xach and froze in their tracks. They were dressed in rags and had long, straw-like black hair pulled up in lopsided pig-tails. They stopped giggling and jumping around and stared silently at Xach, as though he were some kind of beautiful butterfly.

Xach froze like a deer in headlights. Several of the bushes bumped into the back of his legs. One of the boys in the group kicked the purple ball, which Xach now realized was a small mirondi, directly into the face of the smaller of the two girls who had spotted him and his entourage of rainbow bushes.

The little girl started screaming and crying, as a red welt rose over the side of her face where the gelatinous mirondi struck her. The boys erupted in shrieks of laughter and pointed at the crying girl, obviously amused by her pain. The other girl stifled a laugh and grunted at Xach and the Zindarthans. The boys turned to see what drew her attention.

Xach willed himself out of his state of shock and sprinted toward the torches, followed closely by the colored bushes. The boys began bellowing something that sounded like "monster." This brought a group of adults from their shacks and tents. At the sight of "the fleeing monster" and their escaping dinner, the females rushed forward, shouting incoherently and waving their arms. The males returned to their homes to retrieve weapons. Xach continued running and didn't look back over his shoulder until he was on the other side of the torch line. Xach counted twelve Mung adults in pursuit – all of them madly gesticulating and waving their spears.

The bushes continued to file past Xach into the darkness. It appeared that all of them might actually escape before being caught by the Mung, but the last four bushes broke formation and ran in different directions.

What are you doing? Xach screamed in his head. *We're almost free! Keep running this way!* He watched speechlessly as the Mung quickly closed the distance between themselves and their fleeing prey, yet, the bushes did not return to formation. They zig-zagged and moved in circles around the torches.

The *whoosh* of a spear past his right ear jarred Xach from his confusion over the Zindarthans' seemingly erratic and irrational behavior. Another spear landed inches from his left foot. He stumbled backwards and tripped over his feet. He fell to the ground, landing hard on his tailbone.

The Mung were upon them, and the chance for escape was lost. *Well, we almost made it,* Xach thought as he rolled to the left, narrowly dodging another spear thrown at his chest. *Those stupid Zindarthans...*

Xach never finished his disparaging thought, and more importantly, the Mung never managed to recapture any of the escapees. What Xach had interpreted as bizarre, erratic behavior on the part of the last four bushes, now revealed itself to be a brilliantly planned defense by the Zindarthans. The four bushes had been weaving the Zindarthans' strongest thread across the path of the Mung, wrapping it around the torch poles and pulling it tight between them.

The Mung, just like Xach, failed to see the thin, transparent thread running across the ground in all directions. Their large feet tangled in the threads, and their forward momentum caused them to fall in all directions. Some collided with the ground; others collided with each another. Xach heard bones and skulls cracking as the huge creatures threw all their weight upon each other and the hard ground.

Surprisingly, their incredible weight and strong momentum were insufficient to snap the threads, causing some of the torches around which the thread was wrapped to become uprooted from the ground and fall among the tangled mass of Mung. One of the torches fell on one of the shacks and ignited the ragged curtains hanging in the window. The curtains evaporated in a burst of fire and a puff of black smoke, setting the entire wall ablaze.

Another torch fell upon one of the Mung, setting his clothes on fire. He jumped up, tore off the flaming garment, and ran naked toward the large pink pool of water Xach and the Zindarthans passed on their exodus from the enclosure. He dove in and remained submerged to his neck, cooling his burnt skin.

The burning garment he ripped from his body fell on a large pile of brush that had been discarded near the edge of the encampment. Xach recognized the brush to be the dried, dead remains of the bushes the Zindarthans used for transport. A tinge of sadness ran through him as he realized these dried carcasses represented hundreds of thousands of dead Zindarthans, not to mention the dozens of starved bushes that died after their Zindarthan hosts were murdered.

While Xach reflected on these sad thoughts and enjoyed the retribution these hapless Mung were suffering, the four bushes that caused the melee before him retreated into the darkness. The Mung that fell nursed their wounds and tried to untangle themselves from the Zindarthans' thread. Those not involved in the tangled mess of fallen Mung, busied themselves with the multiple fires spreading throughout the village. Some knocked down the burning structures to keep the fire from spreading to the neighboring tents and homes. Others collected buckets of water to throw on the flames. It was semi-organized chaos.

Xach realized it was time to get off his aching butt and finish escaping. He stood up and headed farther into the darkness. "Come on," he said to the congregation of bushes in front of him. "It's time to get out of here." They stayed about fifty feet from the camp, but circled around the edge until they were far enough from the fires to be unnoticed. He returned to the torch line and pulled one of the torches from the ground. He used this to light his way as he led the bushes off into the night, leaving the Mung to practice their fire-fighting and nursing skills, in which they were severely lacking.

Chapter Fifteen

Xach periodically glanced over his shoulder at the flames and smoke rising from the Mung village to make sure they weren't being followed. The fire and lights grew smaller and smaller as they walked farther and farther into the darkness, until it was almost unnoticeable. The light from Xach's torch cast a nice circle of light around him and the Zindarthans, allowing him to see obstacles that he would most likely have tripped over in the complete darkness.

Xach was surprised at how easily the bushes kept up pace with him. The pounding of his heart in his chest and head began to subside as he acclimated himself to the fact that they were now safe. His side still hurt quite a bit, but he was able to stand up straight with minimal pain and hold aloft the torch with his uninjured arm. He suddenly felt very tired and decided to stop for a rest. He found a large pile of mirondi, thrust the torch into the ground deep enough so that it wouldn't fall over, and sat down with his back against the soft jelly surface.

"Is everything all right, O Giant One?" It was Queen Zoron.

"Yes," Xach replied. "I'm just very tired. I haven't had much sleep since this whole adventure began, and I'm quite exhausted. I'm also quite hungry. I've been running on pure adrenaline for so long…I'm just wiped out."

"Well, perhaps we can help you with your hunger," she said and disappeared into the bush's interior.

Xach closed his eyes for a moment, enjoying the silence and the physical rest. He fell instantly to sleep.

"Ahem," coughed Queen Zoron.

Xach started and opened his eyes.

"Sorry to disturb you, but I thought you might enjoy this," she said and gestured toward a pile of bite-sized objects resting on the branch of a bush next to his good arm. Xach picked one up, examined it briefly, and sniffed it before putting it tentatively into his mouth. It looked like a piece of sushi. He remembered his parents taking him to a Japanese restaurant when he was eight years old. It was there that he tried his first piece of raw fish in the form of a sushi roll. The bite-sized morsels on the sushi platter at the restaurant consisted of rice and raw fish that were wrapped in dark-green seaweed. The food presented to him by the Zindarthans looked very much like this – something wrapped in what looked like a leaf from the bush and tied tightly with a silken thread.

He chewed it carefully, fearing there might be something inedible inside. Instead he found it to be soft and very tasty. Whatever was wrapped inside the leaf was sweet and chewy, and the leaf added texture and a light counterbalance of sourness. As he chewed and swallowed, he began to feel warm and energized – much like one feels after coming inside on a snowy day and drinking a warm cup of cocoa.

Xach ate the rest of the delicious treats as quickly as he could, yet not so quickly as to appear rude or gluttonous. His mother taught him manners and etiquette at a young age, insisting that he eat properly in the company of others. When he was finished eating, Queen Zoron asked if he required more food. He graciously declined, even though he probably could have eaten several dozen of the tasty treats without a second thought.

"No thank-you, Queen Zoron, but they were delicious! I've never tasted anything so good in my life."

"You are too kind, O Great One."

Feeling refreshed from his little meal, Xach began thinking of his other problem – Gerald.

"Do you by any chance know where I might find a large pile of mirondi, under which an older man is sleeping?" Xach asked Queen Zoron. He secretly hoped that Gerald's long sleep had allowed him to recover from his injuries enough to reclaim the key and return Xach back to his world and his family.

"Allow me a few moments to communicate with the other communities and see if they know where you might find your friend."

She excused herself and retreated into the bush's interior to concentrate and telepathically contact the other Zindarthan communities scattered about the planet. Xach closed his eyes and rested some more. Within moments he was once again asleep and snoring quietly, yet it was not a restful sleep. His psyche was tortured with horrible nightmares – the worst of which began with Gerald leading Xachary through the Hall of Worlds. They strolled through several halls, passing hundreds of doors. The doors were marked with signs and figures that meant nothing to him; all of them in some alien language or numerology. At last, Gerald led Xachary to a door and used the key to open it. He motioned for Xach to enter, indicating that the doorway would lead him back home. He smiled and patted Xach on the back. Xach felt a tinge of sadness at the thought of leaving him, but the thought of reuniting with his family and friends was intoxicating. He stepped over the threshold into the dark anteroom and headed toward the opening at the far end. He looked through the doorway and into what he assumed must be a closet of some kind on Earth. It was pitch black, and he could see nothing.

He turned and said "thank-you" to Gerald, who, to Xach's surprise, began to fade away. Xach saw through the figure of Gerald into the blue hallway with its stars and many doors. This puzzled him, but he turned back toward the doorway that would lead him home. He raised his foot over the threshold and plunged into the darkness. Only it wasn't the darkness of a closet. The darkness had form and depth and volume. It oozed around him and slid under his clothes and pressed against him.

He opened his mouth to scream for help, and the darkness darted into his mouth and dove down his throat. He could feel it pressing against his eyeballs, entering his ears, and pressing against his brain. The pressure was immense! He gagged and choked on the darkness as he fought to turn himself back toward Gerald who had all but vanished into thin air. Xach felt the darkness slide around his eyeball and push it out of its socket. Gerald's smile was the last to vanish, like that of the Cheshire Cat. The door closed and the darkness consumed Xach inside and out.

He awoke with a start, clutching his throat, gasping and coughing for air.

"O Great Towering One, are you all right?" sounded the alarmed voice of Queen Zoron from the bush resting by Xach's side.

"Y-y-yes," stammered Xach, feverishly looking around to make sure that he was awake and not in the darkness of his dream. "It was just a bad dream. A *very* bad dream."

"Are you feeling more rested and ready to continue your search for your friend?"

"Yes, I guess I am. I certainly don't feel like sleeping any longer," Xach said matter-of-factly. The thought of having another nightmare like the one he just experienced sent shivers down his spine.

He stretched his arms and legs and yawned loudly. He noticed that when he stretched his arms above his head that the pain in his side was significantly less. In fact, it was just a dull ache. He poked the area where the Mung woman had kicked him, expecting a sharp pain to flare up from a fractured rib, but instead he felt only a minor soreness!

Wow, Xach thought, *Gerald wasn't kidding about the healing properties of the key. I should be really sore and unable to move. This is great!*

"Actually," Xach said, "I feel great! Even though my sleep was a bit tortured, I feel well-rested and much less sore."

"I am glad you are feeling better," said Queen Zoron. "While you slept, we kept watch for the Mung. We saw nothing. I also tried to detect information regarding your friend. I believe I have an idea of where to send you looking for him, which I will share with you upon our departure. However, do you require anything else before we go? Food? Drink? Clothing?"

"Go?" Xach asked sadly. "I was hoping you might help me find Gerald."

"While I would love to accompany you on your journey, I am afraid that the communities you liberated from the Mung encampment would like to return to their families. Please do not be offended by our refusal of your request to join you. I hope you can understand that I need to reunite with the rest of my people and prepare for the coming daylight."

"I totally understand your need to reunite with your family and friends. I miss mine greatly. I have no one here except Gerald, and I am thankful that you have information that may help me find him."

He mustered a smile, even though he was greatly saddened by the news of their impending separation. Part of him just wanted to keep talking and requesting services from the Zindarthans in the hopes of keeping them from leaving. He enjoyed their company and didn't feel so alone as long as he had someone with whom he could talk, but he knew that he should not take advantage of their hospitality and generosity any longer.

"Well, then I guess it's time to say good-bye," sighed Xach. "I will miss you, and I can't thank you enough for all you've done for me."

"Not at all, O Great One. Besides, it is I who can't thank *you* enough for rescuing us from the Mung and saving our lives. As a token of our appreciation, I have taken the liberty of having my men prepare a small satchel full of food items, so that you might carry them with you and eat as you need."

A group of about fifteen Zindarthans emerged from the bush, carrying a woven satchel bulging with assorted food stuffs. Xach took the satchel and hooked the strap over his neck so that the satchel hung at his waist.

"Thank you," said Xach humbly.

"I and my people wish you the best on your search for your friend. While you slept, I received a telepathic message from a colony due south that stated they saw one of your people sleeping under a pile of mirondi several thousand feet from here." She indicated that due south was directly behind where Xach was seated. "I trust he is the companion you are seeking?"

"I certainly hope so! Your help has been invaluable."

"You are too kind, O Large One..."

"Oh, by the way," Xach interrupted. "Call me Xach. All my friends do, and you've certainly proven yourself to be great friends to me in my times of need. Besides, the whole 'O Great One' stuff is much too grand for me. I'm just a kid."

"You are much more than a child, O Huge...erm, Xach. You are a hero and a kind soul. Tales of you and your deeds are already circulating amongst the communities around Zindartha. Where ever you find a community of Zindarthans, there you will find friends. Now, with your permission, we will take our leave of you to return to our pastures. It has been several months since we were last home."

"Believe me...I understand the desire to return home. I shall not keep you any longer," Xach said sadly. "I wish you a safe journey," he said, as he stood up and pulled the torch from the ground.

"Best wishes to you, Gentle Giant. I hope our paths cross again soon," said Queen Zoron. She smiled and bowed to Xach. Xach bowed in turn, unable to find the right words to speak. Then Queen Zoron turned and entered the shadowed depths of the bush as it moved from the circle of torchlight and disappeared into the darkness.

Xach stood quietly and watched as the small group of bushes made their way into the darkness, each taking a different northerly direction. When he could no longer make out their moving shapes, he turned south in the direction that Queen Zoron indicated and walked in search of Gerald.

After half an hour of walking, he came upon a large group of mirondi with an outcropping like the one under which he and Gerald had slept. He quickly circled the giant pile, hoping to see Gerald sitting or sleeping under one of the overhangs. The firelight from his torch danced along the purple gelatinous surface of the mirondi, reflecting a shimmering purple haze onto the ground like that of a colored crystal refracting light in all directions. Then Xach caught sight of white cloth muted by the purple translucent skin of the mirondi.

His heart leapt in his chest, and he almost yelled out in pure joy. The white cloth he saw was indeed Gerald's cloak! *I can't believe I found him!* Xach thought. *He's right where I left him! He didn't wake up or wander away!* He was lying on the ground, just on the other side of the large mirondi! Xach tripped over his own feet in his haste to get to the other side and awaken him. He had to duck his head to avoid hitting it on the overhanging mirondi. But to his surprise, Gerald was *not* on the other side as he had expected. The ground was bare.

Was it a mirage? Xach asked himself incredulously. *Have I been so intent on finding him that my mind is playing tricks on me? Is it showing me what I want to see like a thirsty nomad wandering in the desert who sees water?*

He swiveled on his heels and held the torch lower to the ground. No, his mind was not playing tricks on him. A closer look revealed an even more disturbing reality. He had indeed seen Gerald, but he was not on the ground where Xach had expected to find him. Gerald was *inside* the mirondi!

Suspended motionless a few inches above the ground directly in the center of the largest mirondi, Gerald hung like a large piece of fruit in a Jell-o mould. Even more disturbing was the general state of Gerald's body. The skin on Gerald's face and arms had started to dissolve, as if acid had been poured all over his skin! The skin and hair were stripped away in places, revealing the musculature beneath. His eyelids were completely dissolved; his eyes looked like they were bulging out of his head. Part of his upper and lower lips was eaten away, allowing the teeth below them to show through. His left ear was totally gone, and his hair protruded from his skull in wild, uneven clumps as if it were shaven by a child. The tips of Gerald's fingers and toes were completely eaten away with only the bone remaining.

Xach felt his stomach clench, and he knew he was going to vomit. He allowed the torch to slip from his fingers. He turned away from the sight of Gerald's body and emptied his stomach into the darkness beyond the flickering torchlight.

Even after he had nothing else to throw up, his stomach continued to lurch. Bent over and clutching his stomach, he tried to catch his breath and keep from passing out. The emotional void he felt inside him seemed to be growing at an exponential pace. It tried to claw its way out of his gut like a caged animal trying to escape its prison. It wanted to join the never-ending darkness outside of Xach's body, thereby turning him inside out and enveloping him in total darkness.

Gerald was dead.

He was alone.

He was alone in the dark on an alien planet.

He was alone in the dark on an alien planet with no idea of how to get home or what to do.

As the reality of his surreal situation began to seep through his disbelief and bewilderment, he felt the world swim around him. Gradually, the torchlight flickered and faded. His legs buckled as he succumbed to unconsciousness.

****

A few moments later, his eyes fluttered open.

What happened? he thought. *Where am I?*

He sat up and felt something wet slide down his cheek. He wiped the vomit from his face and looked around in a daze.

I must have thrown up, he thought, tasting the bile in his throat and mouth. He spit a few times to clear the taste from his mouth. *Where are my parents? Why is it so dark? Where am I?*

The torch was lying on the ground where it had fallen when he passed out. The flame sputtered on the grass where it had scorched the blue grass into a small, smoldering circle of ash.

That's odd. Are we camping? What did I eat that made me sick? Why am I all alone? Where is the tent? Where are my parents?

Xach turned his neck to the right, and his eyes fell on the purple mirondi.

One look at the decomposing body of Gerald inside the gelatinous bosom of the purple blob was all it took for his brain to reboot. A torrent of images – the earthquake, Gerald, the hospital, the Hall of Worlds, the key, the quarken, the Zindarthans, the Mung – it all rushed back to him in vivid, gory detail.

Xach stared motionlessly at Gerald's body. He couldn't look away, hypnotized by the horrific vision. He breathed normally and just allowed the severity of his situation to sink in slowly. His mind replayed the events leading up to the devastating discovery of Gerald's body.

*When the quarken frightened me in the dark and stole
the key, I bumped into Gerald and nearly knocked him over.
He didn't move or wake up. He must have already been dead.
He must have died in his sleep. While I pursued the quarken
and the key and dealt with the Mung, the mirondi must have
eaten him...just like the mirondi had eaten – no, absorbed – the
food that the Zindarthans gave it...and maybe it ate the baby
quarken that I killed when I knocked it out of its nest in my
effort to retrieve the key. The mirondi must know what is alive
and what is dead – only absorbing what they know to be dead.
That is why they didn't absorb me when I touched them. The
mirondi must **know** I'm alive. It must be having a hard time
digesting Gerald, because he is so large and alien to this
world. They had no problem digesting the small packages the
Zindarthans gave them or the tiny, baby quarken...if that is
what happened to it... Fascinating as this scientific revelation
may be,* he told himself matter-of-factly, *the truth is that
Gerald is dead. He is dead, and you are alone. It is up to you
to find a way off this world and back to Earth.*

He was deeply saddened on many levels by Gerald's
death, but he had no more tears. He was glad that Gerald had
told him all about the key and its properties before he died.
Part of him was certain that Gerald waited to succumb to his
injuries until he had the chance to tell Xach the most important
information about the key. Xach found that he was strangely
grateful to Gerald for this instead of being furiously angry at
him for plucking him from his life and stranding him on
Zindartha.

A strong resolve to be brave and get home gripped him
as he stared at the slowly dissolving body of the stranger he
now considered a friend. He would have to be his own friend
now, as well as father, mother, guardian, brother, sister,
protector, and confidant. He needed to be an "army of one,"
like in the television ads.

He stood up, picked up the torch, and drew in a deep
breath.

"This is it," he said out loud to himself. "A new
beginning."

He whispered a prayer in his heart for Gerald, and then he turned and walked into the darkness. Though he did not realize it at the time, Xach left behind more than a friend. He left behind a piece of his childhood in exchange for a deeper maturity that comes with an understanding of life, death, and the desire to survive. It was a 'new beginning' in more ways than one.

Chapter Sixteen

Xach wandered around the dark landscape of Zindartha for what seemed like days, though in truth it was only a few hours. From time to time he would stop to rest, eat a piece of the food from his satchel, or take a drink from a pink pond. His torch burned closer to his hand, as the flame consumed the wooden length of the torch over time. He continued looking for another piece of wood to which he could transfer the flame, but he was unable to find one.

Periodically he would take out the key and rub the green stone, hoping that he might somehow recognize a change in its glow or shape that might indicate an exit off this world that led back to the Hall of Worlds, but Xach saw nothing to imply that an exit was nearby. He thought that perhaps he might find his way back to the outhouse through which he arrived on Zindartha, but he also recalled that Gerald told him that doorways don't always work both ways now that Count Milton screwed up the mechanics of the Hall by creating and using his bastard key. So even if he found the outhouse, there was no guarantee that Xach would be able to use it to get back to the Hall.

He mulled these thoughts over in his head as he walked aimlessly in the dark. The torch light illuminated much of the same things over and over again like he was on a treadmill, walking on and on but never getting anywhere and always seeing the same scenery – a mirondi here, a pink lake there, a cluster of bushes here, a floating island there. Occasionally, the light from his torch would frighten a quarken, sending it flapping and squawking into the darkness. Whenever he spotted a Mung village in the distance, he would quickly change his direction, so that he was moving away from it. He definitely did not want to meet any more Mung. If he never saw another Mung in his lifetime, it would be too soon.

Inevitably, the flames from the torch licked at his hand, and Xach discarded it. He withdrew the key and continued walking by its faint green glow. He hummed a song to keep himself company and to keep him from focusing on the horrors of the past day or two. He had no sense of time passing as he did not have night and day by which to measure them.

His watch said it was 7:00, but he did not know what day it was or whether it was 7 am or 7 pm. The earthquake at the school occurred on a Thursday. So by Xach's calculations, it was either Friday or Saturday. If it was Saturday morning, then he was missing his favorite cartoons. If it was Saturday night, then he was missing his softball game. If so much time had passed that it was Sunday morning, then he would soon be missing church, which didn't really upset him one way or the other. It's not that he hated church; he just didn't like getting up early on Sunday morning. He wanted to sleep in, but his mother insisted that they go to the early service so that they had the whole day ahead of them to do whatever they felt like doing. He just wanted to sleep.

He wished he could be home, frustrating his mother by over-sleeping and not getting dressed quickly enough for church instead of wandering through the dark Zindarthan landscape. She rushed around the house, trying to get breakfast ready for everyone, making sure they were awake and dressed appropriately, and trying to find time to make sure that she was dressed nicely and decorated properly with make-up and jewelry. He missed her yelling and complaining to Xach's father that he never helped her with the kids, and that it was his fault that they would be late for church yet again.

Ah the good old times, Xach thought, with a wistful smile. *Who'd have thought I'd ever say I missed those frantic Sunday mornings.*

THUMP

Xach was so engrossed in his thoughts that he walked right into a wall! The light from the key was significantly less than that of the torch, and he simply didn't see it in front of him. He fell backward, landing hard on his tailbone again.

"OWW!" he shouted a little louder than he intended. "Dammit! I'm tired of falling on my ass!"

He blushed inadvertently and looked around in embarrassment, forgetting for a moment that there was no one there to see him fall or hear him curse. He brushed himself off and stood up. The dim light of the key illuminated a tall stone wall. The wall stretched to the left, to the right, and upward. He held the key above his head and stretched up on his tiptoes, but he still could not see the top of the wall! It had to be over ten feet tall!

This is odd, Xach thought. *I've only seen Mung, Zindarthans, quarken, and mirondi, and none of them are advanced enough or even large enough to build such a wall. Plus, where did the stones come from? I haven't seen any stones here at all.*

Puzzled and quite intrigued, Xach began to follow the wall to his left. He scanned it for any holes, doorways, or windows that might allow him a glimpse into whatever was on the other side. Aside from a few vines growing up the rock surfaces, he found no openings.

Who built this? It's so uniform and sturdy. Certainly the Mung are too stupid to create such a wall, and what purpose would it serve them anyway? Was it built to keep something in or keep something out?

After walking for a little while longer, he glanced at his watch. It read 9:30!

I've been walking for over two hours? That can't be! That's gotta be like a couple miles, and I didn't see a single opening of any kind!

He continued walking, periodically checking his watch. 10:00. 11:00. 12:15. Still no opening or break of any kind. His feet hurt quite a bit, and he felt very thirsty and hungry. He was anxious to find an opening in the wall, but he needed a break.

He sat down with his back against the wall and unhooked the satchel from around his neck. He ate several pieces of food and then ventured a few feet from the wall to find something to drink. He left the satchel on the ground by the wall so he could find his way back to where he had stopped his inspection of the wall. Once he sated his thirst at a small pink pond, he returned to the wall and lay against it for a short nap.

In moments he drifted off into a deep sleep. He dreamt he was at a softball game. His team was ahead by two points. He was playing outfield like always. The opposing team sent their best hitter to the plate, and she promptly hit the ball high over the pitcher's mound and into left field. Xach ran toward the ball as its arched trajectory brought it toward the ground just inside the wooden fence surrounding the field. He held his mitt up into the sky to catch the ball and shield his eyes from the sun, but a ray of bright light shone through a seam in the glove and temporarily blinded him. He blinked and missed the ball. It fell to the ground by his feet.

He pivoted and reached down to get the ball, but it was gone, having fallen down a large hole in the ground. Xach knelt down next to the hole to see if he could find the ball, but the earth around the hole crumbled and fell away. He jumped backward and scrambled away like a crab, trying to avoid the giant sinkhole that was forming in the ground. The diameter of the hole grew larger and larger. It reached beyond the fence line and several of the fence panels began to sag and bend until they separated from the line and fell into the darkness.

Xach stood up and ran, but the faster he ran, the larger the hole grew, as if it were drawn to him! All of the players ran from the hole, including his friend, Jeremy, who was also in the outfield. Jeremy tripped over one of the plates and landed on his face. The hole quickly over took him as he lay stunned on the ground. The ground fell away beneath his legs, and then his torso. In seconds, all but Jeremy's hands vanished below ground level as he frantically grasped onto tufts of grass and dirt to keep himself from falling. Xach watched in horror as his best friend slipped into the giant hole, his screams for help slowly fading as he fell into the darkness below.

Around the perimeter of the growing void, others of his team met a similar fate as the ground disappeared beneath them. They tumbled into oblivion. The sky grew dark with huge thunderhead clouds. Lightning streaked across the sky as a torrent of water and hail fell upon the field.

In a matter of moments, he and all the fleeing players and spectators were drenched. The hole reached the bleachers, and they toppled like dominoes into the abyss, carrying the screaming crowds down with them. A bolt of lightning struck the scoreboard. It exploded in a shower of sparks before splitting in half and falling into the hole.

Over his shoulder, Xach saw the hole spreading into the neighborhood. Houses shook and windows cracked as the foundations of homes split and fell into the void. People crawled onto their roofs to escape the hole only to find their entire home slide into the hole and carry them with it.

Xach ran on, trying to outrun the hole, but it grew faster and wider. Its edge remained inches from his heels, intent on swallowing him too. Xach leapt over the fence that separated the field from the parking lot. The fence fell into the darkness and the asphalt crumbled beneath his feet. He jumped onto the hood of car and vaulted from car to car, each one toppling into the void the moment his foot left its surface. He heard the screams of others as the entire parking lot disappeared.

A hailstone the size of a golf ball struck Xach in the back of his head, sending him flying forward toward the ground. He fell face first into a giant puddle that quickly drained as the ground began to break away beneath him. He slid over the edge and fell into the swirling darkness of the hole. He fell and fell and fell. At first he was gripped by fear, but the longer he fell, the more he began to feel like he was flying. He was starting to enjoy the sensation of falling, even though the screams of the others who were falling around him were a little disconcerting. Then he started to hear objects splatting, shattering, and breaking on something more solid than the mud he expected to find at the bottom of the dirt hole. In horror, Xach realized that the first objects and people to have fallen into the hole were finally hitting the bottom!

Something wet and sticky hit him in the face. It slid up his cheek as something a little harder hit him on the forehead. Something sliced into his leg like a burning hot poker, and he felt debris of all sizes and textures pummel his body. Though it was too dark for him to see anything clearly, he could tell that he was reaching the end of his fall and was coming in contact with the remnants of all that had fallen before him.

He felt arms and legs and hair brush against him, and he felt the air begin to squeeze in around him. The hole was narrowing as it tapered to its inevitable bottom. The screams of those around him were stifled as they hit the mass of bodies, trees, asphalt, homes, cars, and everything else the hole had swallowed.

Below him a light began to glow and grow from within the darkness. As his eyes adjusted, he could see the bottom of the hole rushing to meet him. Houses lay in ruins along the bottom. Street signs and trees protruded through the rubble and several bodies were impaled upon them. Some were impaled one upon the other like a horrible human shish-kabob.

Xach covered his face with his hands as he sped toward the horrible mass of bodies and rubble at the bottom of the pit. If he was going to die this way, he didn't want to see it coming. A screaming woman falling a few feet before him hit a large rock that had been forced up through the roof of a mangled ranch home. Her body exploded upon impact, splattering Xach from head to toe with gore.

He opened to his mouth to scream…

…and he choked on something wet and thick. He lifted his head and opened his eyes. The key lay on the ground, inches from where his head had been lying in a puddle of mud. He grabbed the key and held it up before him.

It was raining. It was raining hard. He could see the green light of the key refracting through the myriad of drops that fell around him. He wiped his face with the cloak and spit the mud from his mouth.

I must have fallen asleep and fell over onto the ground. The wet stuff and blood that I felt on my face in the dream must have been my brain incorporating the sensory perceptions of the rain and the mud into my subconscious. Why must I have such horrible nightmares? I guess it's a good thing that I didn't actually die in my dream, because then I might have died in real life. If that's even true? And how would anyone actually know? Who actually dreamt up that notion? If you dream you died and then you die in real life, how are you gonna tell anyone that you died in your dream, and it killed you in real life. You're dead! You can't speak about it to anyone!?!… Why are you even thinking about this? You need to find some shelter.

He stood up and shook himself a little to shed some of the mud that covered the areas of his body that had been lying on the ground when the rain started. He was soaked to the bone.

Great...I'm gonna catch pneumonia. Mom would be so annoyed and worried. But there's nothing I can do about that now. I gotta find a place to get dried off and keep dry. Oh, and note to self, you need to remember to put the key in your pocket whenever you sit down, so that you don't drop it if you fall asleep again. You lost it once before. You can't afford to lose it again! What if another nosey quarken had snuck up on you and taken it while you slept? What would you have done then?

He slung the satchel over his shoulder and ran as fast as he could along the edge of the wall in search of some shelter. The key's light was even less effective in the rain, and the mud sloshing around his feet made it difficult to build any real momentum. At times the mud was so deep that he felt his shoes might be sucked off his feet. He decided it best to take his time and walk instead of running. Not only was walking around in his socks in the cold rain and mud not a good idea, but he couldn't afford to lose his shoes.

Holding the key in front of him allowed him to keep the wall's surface in view, but he could not see his feet through the rain. Before he even realized what was happening, he found himself slipping into a large hole that had been dug along the wall's surface. The heel of his sneaker caught the edge of the hole and slid downward quite quickly. His body followed. The hole was about two feet wide, just wide enough for Xach's body to fit neatly into the hole. It was also quite deep. He quickly slid past the grass line and into the earth as if he had stepped onto a giant water slide. If he had seen the hole, he might have tried to stop his descent, but as it happened so quickly, he fell with his arms held above his head. He kept a tight grip on the key and looked up to see the edge of the hole fly out of his sight as he slid into the wet, brown earth.

The hole, or what could more accurately be described as a tunnel, followed the wall as it sloped downward into the ground. Xach could see the stones of the wall on his one side and mud on the other. The wall was buried deep into the ground. He had no way of telling how far he fell, but at several feet a second he imagined the wall must have been buried several hundred feet into the ground! He hoped the hole had an exit, because he was travelling way too fast to stop his fall with anything other than his legs, which would probably shatter upon impact with the bottom of the hole. At which point he would most assuredly die hundreds of feet below the surface of Zindartha. Even if his bones didn't shatter, it would be next to impossible for him to crawl out of a hole this deep! What had started as kind of a thrilling ride of sorts, quickly began to fill him with panic and terror.

Just when he thought he couldn't stand the horrific anticipation of impact any longer, the wall ended, and the hole sharply turned under it. A moment later, Xach's body shot out of the ground and into the air. He felt rain on his face again. The hole had been dug along the wall and under it. He was on the other side, flying into the darkness of whatever lay on the other side.

Chapter Seventeen

The wind and rain whipped around him as he fell through the dark, cold air.

It's just like my dream! Xach thought. *How bizarre! Is it possible that I'm still dreaming? At least I didn't hit the bottom of the hole and break my legs...well, at least not yet...*

He felt himself picking up speed as he fell. With a clashing mixture of fear and exhilaration, Xach found his thoughts to be a jumbled mess of extremely unfocused and inappropriate ideas. Considering the impending danger of collision with the ground at some point, he should have felt only terror, but for some unknown reason, he found he wasn't as panicked as he should have been. It was a surreal feeling, almost like being outside his body and watching himself sail through the air like a hapless superhero. It was comical and frightening; two things that don't generally mix.

Ah, the power of gravity, he thought. *The longer you fall, the faster you fall. The farther you fall, the **harder** you hit the ground – like a penny having enough inertia to bury itself into the concrete if dropped off the top of the Empire State Building...and like those people impaled on the trees and stop signs in my dream. I wonder how far I'll burrow into the ground, considering how fast and how far I've fallen? Oh God, why do I keep ending up in these situations?!? First things first, though...better make sure the key is safe, just in case I somehow manage to make it out of this alive.*

The air whizzed past him and lifted the fabric of the cloak around his face. With some amount of difficulty, he managed to get his hand around the fluttering mass of cloth and into his pocket, securely tucking the key away so that he wouldn't drop it somehow. *Thank God I didn't drop it when I fell through the hole – with all that mud and water making things so slippery, it's a miracle it didn't slip away from me. Now, what do I do about my falling? Think Xachary! Think!*

He closed his eyes and concentrated as hard as he could. The uncertainty of how much time he had before being crushed to death upon the ground below made it a little difficult. *I might have seconds...I might have minutes. Who*

knows? ...If only I could fly like a superhero, he thought.
Then I wouldn't have to worry. But I can't. So get a grip!
Now is not the time for fantasies! If you don't think of
something soon, you're gonna end up a lumpy human pancake
of blood and guts!

Images of his recent adventures and the impending splattering that awaited him flashed before his mind's eye, but he kept returning to thoughts of himself flying through the air like a superhero with his cloak waving in the wind behind him like a cape. He inherently realized the peril of his situation, but for some reason unbeknownst to his rational mind, he was quite lackadaisical about the whole thing. He equated his current fear level with the fear he felt on a huge roller coaster; he knew the rollercoaster was safe despite his fear of being out of control. He kept thinking what a cool ride it had been to slide down the mud tunnel and then soar out into open air for this long free-fall!

At the rate you're falling, he told himself half-jokingly, *you should be road pizza by now – a lumpy, bones-protruding, bloody pulp at the bottom of a dark, muddy gorge! But you're not, huh? This is one heck of a long fall! ...Are you out of your mind?* he asked himself. *Pull yourself together and stop daydreaming! How can you be so laid back about this? This is serious! Think of something practical...*

A vision of the hospital flashed before his eyes. When Gerald was pulling him into the other room to find the closet that led to the Hall of Worlds, he saw Count Milton levitate out of the frozen guards' arms. He had, in effect, been able to *fly*!

What were those words that he said? Maybe I won't die after all. But his mind continued to play devil's advocate with himself. *Even if you remember the words, who's to say that it will even work!?! You're no wizard or magician! True...but it's worth a try!*

Xach concentrated as hard as he could, and his experience at the hospital played out like a video in his head, just like when Gerald had been teaching him about the properties of the key. He concentrated on Count Milton and strained his ears to hear the words he was murmuring. He heard something, but it wasn't clear. He rewound the image in his head like a DVD and focused even harder on Count Milton's voice, blocking out all the other sounds from the hospital that were coming to him in crystal clear clarity. If he wanted to, he could have focused on any of the two or three dozen people in the hallway and remembered exactly what he or she said. But Xach needed to concentrate on Count Milton. Xach watched Count Milton's mouth move, focusing on his lips. The words – **murmur leviar wentum** – rang clearly and sharply in Xach's ears.

"That's it!" Xach screamed in excitement. "Those are the words!" *But will they work for me?*

At that moment, the silly bantering inside his head ceased. He had an option, albiet a long shot, but he had an option. He was going to try it. The fear and doubt melted away and were replaced by a firm resolve to survive the fall. Xach closed his eyes tightly and concentrated on the magic words, just as he had seen Count Milton do in the hospital.

"Murmur leviar wentum!" he yelled above the wind rushing around his head. "Murmur leviar wentum! Murmur leviar wentum!"

Nothing seemed to be happening. The wind and rain continued to whip around him in a fury. He was going very fast. He would certainly reach the bottom soon, and then it would all be over. No more school, no more television, no more softball, no more dinners with mom and dad. Nothing. Finito. Game over.

Don't lose it now. This is your only hope! Keep trying! he urged himself. *Concentrate!*

"MURMUR LEVIAR WENTUM!" he shouted over the rushing wind and rain, while simultaneously chanting it in his head.

"MURMUR LEVIAR WENTUM!" *Murmur leviar wentum!* "MURMUR LEVIAR WENTUM!"

Over and over again, he screamed the words aloud while he screamed them in his head. Every fiber of his being was focused solely on one thought – FLY! He willed with all his might that his descent would slow, and he would begin to float upward instead of downward.

To his surprise, he felt his feet tingle. Tiny fingers of energy penetrated the tips of his toes and traveled through the arch of his foot. It moved past his heel and into his calves. It felt warm, and it tickled a bit. Then Xach felt pressure on the arch of his feet. The pressure grew stronger and stronger until it felt as though his legs might buckle from the pressure.

He became aware that the wet fabric of the cloak was no longer whipping against his face. The wet, frigid air was no longer sluicing up through his wet clothes. His descent was slowing!

"It's working! It's working!" he screamed in ecstasy! The moment he stopped chanting the magic words, however, he began to free-fall again.

He renewed his concentration and murmured the magic words over and over again. He didn't stop until he felt the wind slow its rush around him again. The pressure against his feet returned, and he felt himself come to a comfortable stop. He floated motionless in the air, but he didn't stop chanting. He began to concentrate on floating downward slowly while he chanted. He needed to keep going downward until he found the ground, but he needed to do it slowly.

The minutes ticked away and finally he felt the familiar pressure of the earth beneath his feet. It was solid and firm – different from the wispy pressure that suspended him in the air. He stopped chanting and came to rest gently on the ground.

He opened his eyes and fumbled in his pocket to find the key. He needed to see where he was. He knew that the light would never be bright enough to reveal how far he had fallen, but judging by the length of time it had taken for him to fall, he figured it must have been many miles. Having fallen so far, where would he find himself? He found the key and brought it to his face. He rubbed the gem, and the familiar green light issued from the stone.

His heart was racing as fast as his mind. *I flew! I did magic! I DID MAGIC! I wish Gerald could have been here to see it! WOW! I wish Jeremy could have seen me! He'd be SO jealous! I wonder what Mom and Dad would say? That is so incredibly COOL! Gerald never said I could do magic! I wonder why? Maybe he didn't know. I wonder if he could do magic but chose not to? He said Count Milton could, but he never mentioned if he himself could...nonetheless, how incredible was that?!? I FLEW!*

The light from the key illuminated his immediate surroundings – a large stone, some dead bushes, and something that looked like an upside down tree with its roots sticking up into the air.

I'm pretty lucky that I didn't land on that tree, he thought. *Then I would have been a human shish-kabob like the people in my dream.* In that moment, the truth of his prophetic dream blossomed in his mind. *This whole experience was way too much like my dream! What's up with that? What are the odds that I would dream about falling down a hole, wake up, and then fall down a hole? Pretty freakin' huge! And my other dream about finding Gerald sort of came true too...*

He succeeded in scaring himself a bit and decided it was better to occupy his thoughts with discovering where he was. He walked several feet to his left and found a giant mud wall. He assumed the stone wall under which he fell was built miles above upon this mud wall. He also assumed that this wall of dirt was probably two or three times as long and high as the stone wall had been up above. There would be no climbing up this wall, so he decided to venture out in the opposite direction to see what he could find.

Since the key only shed a minimal amount of light, there was very little for him to detect in the barren surroundings. Xach's thoughts once again turned to all the things his mind could not explain – his semi-prophetic dreams, the giant wall, the mud slide through the hole, the long drop through the air, and most importantly the magic he just performed. His mind filled with questions. *Does the key make me psychic? Can I see the future through my dreams? Who or what built such a high and impenetrable wall? Why did they build it? Who or what dug the hole down the side of the wall and under it? Why would it want to get to the other side of the wall? If it survived the fall, is it still here? What is on this side of the wall? What could have created such a deep gorge and such a high barrier? How was I able to fly? Can I do other types of magic? That would be so cool! Why didn't Gerald tell me I could perform magic? Can I do all the stuff that Count Milton can do? Is it a bad thing that I can do magic, because Count Milton certainly is ba...*

****SKEEEEEEREEEEEEK-EEEEEK-EEEEEK-EEEEEEEEK****

Xach stopped dead in his tracks; his mind no longer focused on the myriad of questions swimming in his brain. His brain now screamed only one question – ***What the hell was that?!?*** It sounded like hundreds of knives scraping across metal pipes. It was deafening and echoed all around him. His heart leapt out of his chest and lodged itself in his throat. He shook with fear. Spinning around in all directions, he held the key out before him, trying to find the source of the loud noise. His hand shook so badly that he had to hold the key with both hands just to keep from dropping it. He saw nothing that seemed capable of such a loud noise, but his eyes caught sight of something on the ground that was equally terrifying – bones! Lots and ***lots*** of bones! Bones of various sizes and shapes were scattered all about him on the ground. Some stuck up out of the ground like jagged, tiny white tree trunks. Xach imagined that some hapless creatures fell through the hole, as he had done, and sunk into the earth upon impact, dying immediately or soon thereafter. As horrible as it sounded, Xach hoped that these bones ***were*** the remains of creatures that had fallen through the hole and not the remains of food for whatever was making that horrible sound.

****SKEEEEEEREEEEEEK-EEEEEK-EEEEEK-EEEEEEEEK****

The noise sounded again. He clasped his hands over his ears. It was so incredibly loud! His ears actually ached, and he *felt* the sound hitting him in all directions. His legs felt like jelly, and he thought he might collapse.

He remembered feeling this scared only once before in his life. It happened in the boy's bathroom at school. He was standing at the urinal, when the lights went out. As there were no windows in this particular bathroom, it was pitch dark when the lights went out. He remained still at the urinal, hoping the lights would turn back on, but they did not. Eventually, he zipped his pants, but he could not move for fear that he might trip over something or run into something in the dark. He remembered vividly how the air was thick with moisture and the stink of young boys. All was silent and dark until he heard a lighter being lit. **zwipp** The sound came from the corner. He whipped his head around to face the sound. **zwipp** A flame issued from the head of the lighter, illuminating half the ghostly pale face of Peter Slevin, the school bully and all-around "bad kid." Xach hadn't even noticed he was there. He thought he was alone in the bathroom. The flame fluttered, plunging one side of Peter's head into complete darkness, as an evil-looking grin spread across his face. Peter did not move from the corner, however. He remained perfectly still. The sight was totally unnerving. Neither Peter nor Xach moved. It was like their eyes were glued to one another, waiting to see who would make the first move. Xach's nerves were standing on end, and every part of his body tingled with anticipation and fear. When he could stand it no longer and was about to ask Peter what he wanted, the fire alarm went off. The sudden blast of noise in the dead silence of the dark bathroom was like a spark igniting a fuse in Xach's body. The sudden jolt of adrenaline overloaded his system, and he simply passed out from fear.

The sudden, deafening sound in the darkness of the canyon was almost exactly the same. He felt as if his every cell in his entire body was alive with an electric current and was trying to fly apart in all directions. His muscles didn't know what to do or how to work together, and he felt as if he might simply topple over like a house of cards. The worst part of it all – the most unnerving part – was the dead silence that followed the noise. In that deafening silence he waited in dreadful anticipation of the sound's return. Despite the expectation of the sound, its arrival frightened him even more.

****SKEEEEEEREEEEEEK-EEEEEK-EEEEEK-EEEEEEEEK****

The sound echoed off the giant wall behind him. It was impossible to tell from which direction the noise came or in which direction he should run to avoid meeting whatever was making it – not that he could have moved even if he wanted to. His feet were frozen to the ground; his muscles were tensed and twitching.

****SKEEEEEEREEEEEEK-EEEEEK-EEEEEK-EEEEEEEEK****

The sound vibrated through his body, causing his teeth to chatter involuntarily.

I can't take much more of this, he thought.

It was maddening, and Xach felt himself losing control. The sound was such an affront to his hearing that it sent the rest of his senses into a frenzy. He smelled the mud and felt the key vibrate in his hand. He tasted electricity in the air. He saw the darkness withdraw before the sound and shudder afterwards with its reverberations. His motor control was faltering, and he collapsed under the weight of the sound and the silence.

****SKEEEEEEREEEEEEK-EEEEEK-EEEEEK-EEEEEEEEK****

"NO MORE!" Xach yelled once the sound died down. "NO MORE! I can't take it! WHO'S THERE? WHAT DO YOU WANT? WHAT..."

The words caught in his throat. He was crying.

Why are you crying? he asked himself in surprise. He didn't know he was doing it. The sound and the resulting stress caused his nervous system to break down. He pulled his head to his chest and covered it with his arms.

"Stop....please...make it stop..." he mumbled.

He waited for the sound to return, but nothing came. All he heard was the quiet sound of a few raindrops hitting something metallic. In all of this, he failed to notice that it was no longer raining on him. He waited some more, still cowering in a heap on the ground. He didn't want to raise his head and have it rattled by the deafening sound again. By Xach's calculations, it should have sounded again. It came at semi-regular intervals, but now – nothing. It was eerily quiet – too quiet!

Chapter Eighteen

Xach waited a few more minutes before attempting to stand up. His legs were tremulous, but he managed to stand. He took two tentative steps forward, half expecting something to swoop out of the darkness, swallow him whole, and spit out his bones. He paused, tensing for an attack. Nothing attacked. He took three more steps and stopped, waiting for a response. Again, nothing happened. The silence was unnerving. It was hard to believe it was so loud only moments ago.

It was almost as though his screaming and pleading actually caused the noise to stop, but too much time passed for that to have been the case. The noise stopped on its own – a mere coincidence that it happened to coincide with Xach's plea for its cessation. Although he did not yet determine the source of the noise, the realization that the noise may have occurred independently of his presence or actions in this place caused him to feel a bit more at ease.

He took a deep breath and exhaled deeply. Then he proceeded to walk forward, tightly clutching the key and holding it out in front of him. The light revealed more bones, bushes, stones and trees, but the further he walked the fewer he saw. He was certainly glad to see fewer bones. Feeling a bit more relaxed and perhaps subconsciously remembering that he was indeed a ten year-old boy, he kicked the bones and tiny stones that lay in his path, as young boys are wont to do. They bounced against each other and larger objects making clinking and rattling noises that kept the unending silence from becoming too upsetting.

Then one of the bones he kicked hit something metallic. *clank* Xach froze. When nothing came at him, he ventured forward cautiously. The light from the key revealed a large metal surface directly in front of him. It was dull and rusted, like it was left unattended for a long time. It curved toward the ground and stretched to the left and right as far as Xach could see. He touched the surface lightly. It felt warm. He pressed his palm against the surface, and he detected minute vibrations issuing from behind the surface.

He scouted the surface to the left to see what he could find. Although the surface was scarred with the passing of time, there were no seams or rivets in its surface. It was completely smooth. He walked around the object for a few minutes, studying its surface, until his foot caught on a large bone imbedded in the ground. He tripped and fell.

The light from the key revealed indentations in the soft mud. They were footprints, or more specifically *shoeprints*! Xach crawled through the mud slowly following the footprints, wondering if they belonged to another person or a humanoid creature that wore shoes and lived in the metal structure. However, closer examination of a particularly clean footprint revealed a symbol imprinted in the center of the shoeprint.

"Xach, you stupid idiot!" he shouted at himself. "These are your footprints!" He was so frightened by the notion that something killed all these creatures and left their bones it never occurred to him the footprints he found were his own!

He quickly deduced this meant the metallic surface was round in shape, like a gigantic metal marshmallow that was being squashed from above and was bulging around its center. He walked a complete circle around the object and failed to find an opening. He knew it wasn't solid because of the vibrations he felt coming from within. It was hollow inside and housed some type of machine or object that produced the vibrations.

"So where's the door?" he asked the darkness.

He picked up a few pieces of bone and several pebbles with his free hand. He stood up again and put his back to the metal. If there was no detectable entrance from his current vantage point, it occurred to him that there might be other structures nearby that offered an overhead or underground entrance to the metal marshmallow-shaped room. He threw one of the bones straight ahead of himself. He heard it hit the muddy ground with a quiet, wet *splump*.

He inched three feet to his left, keeping his back against the object, and threw another bone fragment. It too made little or no sound. He continued inching along the surface a few feet at a time, throwing the bones and pebbles. On his sixth attempt, he was met with a different sound – the sound of stone hitting metal.

"Paydirt," he said. He walked toward the point of impact.

He found another metallic surface, identical in shape and design. A survey of its perimeter showed that it too was another large squashed metallic marshmallow-shaped room with no discernable entrance. Using the same method of detection over the course of an hour or two, Xach discovered several more of the rooms – all of the same shape and completely sealed, with no rivets, seams, or openings. Since his footprints around the edges of the structures told Xach which ones he'd already searched, he was able to determine that there were at least a dozen of them, each spaced about twenty feet apart.

The thrill of discovery began to wear off around the eighth structure, but he was determined to find an opening of some kind. Each object was warm to the touch and vibrated from within. After finding the fifteenth structure, Xach decided it was time to take a break.

He sat down with his back against the smooth, metal surface and took out his satchel of foodstuffs given to him by the Zindarthans. He ate a few pieces of the sweet-tasting morsels and wished he had something to drink.

Too bad I didn't ask the Zindarthans for a canteen of some kind, Xach thought as he swallowed dryly, thinking of the Spanish botas he had studied in school that were made of animal hide and used to store and transport liquid on long trips. *I haven't even seen any lakes or ponds of the pink liquid on this side of the wall. Too bad it stopped raining, or I could have collected rainwater like we did at Boy Scout camp.*

As he sat quietly trying not to think about how thirsty he was, he realized he still **heard** rain, even though he didn't feel it. What he heard was the sound of rain falling on a metal surface, and the sound came from overhead. As he listened, it dawned on him that he hadn't actually felt the rain since that horrible, frightening noise that sounded. Nonetheless, the noise of the rain falling had been constant; he just didn't notice in all the excitement and fear.

He sat quietly and listened to the hypnotic sound of the falling rain. He started to doze off again. It wasn't as if he had gotten a great deal of sleep since the earthquake back home, and sitting still under the tinkling rain sound was lulling him to sleep. He tucked the key into his pocket and got as comfortable as he could, sitting on the cold, wet ground against the hard, metal object. Eventually, he nodded off to sleep.

Darkness gave way to color and indistinct images as he entered REM sleep and began to dream. He felt wind on his face and its cool tendrils running through his hair and sliding along his body. Clouds whizzed past his head and out of sight. The sun crested above a large, puffy cloud, temporarily blinding him. He blinked and looked away, seeing for the first time the vast expanse of a deep azure sky below him that was littered with wispy and puffy clouds. He was flying!

Birds of all shapes and sizes flew beside him, trying to keep pace, but he was flying too fast. They fell behind him and out of sight. He moved so fast his peripheral vision blurred, and all he saw clearly was what lay directly ahead of him.

The sensation of flight was incredible! The freedom from gravity was intoxicating, and Xach decided to try multi-directional flight. He banked to the right and zoomed through a cloud; its moisture left a cool film on his face. He dove down and then up again quickly. He rolled over onto his back and did a loop. As this was a dream, such maneuvers were not accompanied by the usual nausea one would expect in reality. It was complete freedom and release!

Directly ahead of him he spotted a group of silver-feathered birds flying in a V-formation. He tucked his head close to his chest to lessen wind resistance and shot toward them. In seconds he was level with the birds in the back of the V. The moment they spotted him violating their formation, the rear birds broke off from the flock and dove downward into the cloud cover.

One by one, the other birds followed suit, each pair breaking formation and flying off in opposite directions – up, down, left, and right – until they vanished into the clouds. The clouds into which the birds disappeared, instantly turned dark and ominous. In moments, the beautiful azure sky became dark and foreboding. The light blue sky dimmed to gray. Black clouds swelled and multiplied, blocking out the sun and masking its light. Lightning flashed across the sky, illuminating the edges of the dark clouds against the gray sky and introduced an electric charge through the air. Seconds later, thunder boomed so loudly that the air vibrated around him.

He zigged and zagged through the growing storm and failing light, dodging lightning bolts and feeling the deep pressure in his chest every time thunder shook the sky. Rain fell in thick, blinding sheets from the clouds. The wind shifted violently, pushing him left and right and up and down against his will.

Hailstones as big as his fist fell from some of the clouds. This was no longer fun, but there was no place to land or take shelter. All he saw below him were more angry clouds, rolling and boiling with lightning and rain. Looking upward revealed more of the same. He was forced to continue flying forward, attempting unsuccessfully to avoid the hail that hit him like rocks. No matter how hard he tried to fly upward and over the storm, he was buffeted back down by hail, wind and rain so intense he was certain he flew into a gigantic hurricane.

THWOP A hailstone hit him square in the back of the head. A blinding, white pain shot through his head before taking his vision. Everything went black. He flew no longer. He was *falling*! He tried to open his eyes, but he could not. He tried to will himself upward and to move his arms and legs, but his limbs were limp. He knew he was dreaming and tried to force himself to wake, but some invisible force repelled consciousness and kept him in the nightmare.

He fell through the rain, wind, hail and clouds for what seemed like an eternity. He flipped and tumbled through the air like a rag doll. Then suddenly *SPLOSH*he hit something soft and wet. Though he couldn't see, he was certain it was mud. It was too viscous and thick to be water.

He sank deep into the mud. He felt it squish into his ears and his nose. He wanted to scream, but he did not want the mud to rush into his mouth. Again he tried to will himself awake or mold his dream into something more pleasing as he had been able to do on several occasions when he knew he was dreaming, but he continued to fail. It was as futile as trying to lay an egg. He was helpless to change the horrific scenario in which he found himself.

His descent into the mud slowed, and he became aware of the sensation of tentacles wrapping around his arms and legs. He felt the pressure of their grip on his wrists and ankles as they began to pull him farther down into the mud. He felt pressure on his abdomen and neck as other tentacles wrapped around his waist and shoulders.

He was acutely aware of the growing ache in his chest as the air in his lungs ran out. In a moment he would need to breathe in or open his mouth, and the mud would push into his throat and lungs and choke him to death! He always feared drowning and wondered again if dying in his dream meant he would die in real life? Would his strange tale of abduction and travel through unknown worlds end with him dying in his sleep on the muddy floor of a bone-littered alien ditch?

His lungs burned and his heart thumped loudly in his chest and ears as he struggled to hold his breath beyond capacity…

…and then he awoke! His eyes shot open, and all his muscles twitched as he gasped for air.

His immediate thought as he willed himself to breathe normally was *why couldn't I wake up?* His heart continued pounding in his chest. *Why am I having such horrible nightmares lately? My dreams seem so real and horrific ever since Gerald brought me here. I hope this one doesn't turn out to be true like the last couple, because I don't much relish the prospect of drowning in a pool of mud.*

As soon as the thought ran through his mind, he realized the pressure of the tentacles he felt in his dream was still omnipresent all over his body. They wrapped around his legs, arms and chest. He struggled to break free, but they just exerted more pressure to keep him immobilized. The tentacles slid over and under his clothing. Their cool slickness on his skin as disgusting. The more he twisted and turned to loosen their grip, the tighter they wrapped around him. The tentacles slid around his neck and over his face.

This is it! he thought morbidly. *Whatever ate all those other things down here and spit out their bones got me. How did Gerald manage to stay alive so long on all the different worlds he visited? I didn't make it more than a day?*

A tentacle slid over his nose, and even though he tried not to breathe in, he distinctly smelled the pungent aroma of iron or rusted metal. With a feeling of total horror and utter helplessness, Xach acknowledged his nightmare was indeed coming true. The tentacles enveloped his body entirely, like a huge cocoon of metallic smelling oil. He wanted to open his mouth to breathe or scream, but he knew the tentacles would snake into his mouth and choke him. He resisted the urge, but knew it was only a matter of moments before his chest would burn and he would have to suck in the foul metallic liquid surrounding his body. Then it would be over. All that would remain of him would be a pile of bones resting against a giant metallic marshmallow shaped-room in a trench on a planet called Zindartha.

The liquid tentacles pressed into his ear canal; it felt like the sensation he got when swimming at the bottom of a swimming pool. The pressure built, and the tentacles pushed up his nostrils. Just at the moment he feared he would open his mouth to scream his final words and choke on the oily substance that was invading every orifice of his body, a voice sounded in his ears – almost like it was coming from a speaker in his brain – "What are you, and what are you doing here?"

Who? What? Who's talking?

The voice repeated, "What are you, and what are you doing here?"

My name is Xach, he thought. *I'm a human being, and I don't know why I'm here. This is another nightmare. I hope this is still a dream. I wish I was home in my bed...I just want to wake up and be home again...*

"What is 'human being' and 'home'?" the voice inquired.

*Are you kidding me? I am about to choke to death on some slimy alien oil creature, and you want me to define my words? Who are **you**? Maybe I'm already dead? Am I* *imagining this voice in some delusional pre-death auditory hallucination? Is this what happens when you die?*

"Though I do not understand some of your words," the voice replied coolly, "I assure you that you are not dead, nor are you dying."

Yeah right, Xach screamed subconsciously. *I'm totally gonna die, and I never even got to drive a car or become a fireman or grow into a teenager or go to high school or college. I'm gonna choke to death on this 'oil-thing' and there will be nothing left of me but a pile of bones.* If his eyes weren't pressed so tightly closed by the oily fluid covering his face, he felt he might cry. *It's over. I can't breathe. I gotta open my mouth. This is it. It's over...*

"Calm down, human being called Xach. I sense that your body functions are not normal."

Of course they're not normal, you idiot! I'm dying!

"That is incorrect. You are not dying. Now calm down and let me finish transporting you inside."

Inside? Inside what?

The pressure surrounding his entire body increased ten-fold, forcing Xach to open his mouth. As he feared, the cool, oily substance slid into his mouth. It filled his throat, his lungs, and his stomach. Strangely, however, he did not gag or feel anything more or less unpleasant than the strange sensation of having an unknown fluid invading every organ and tissue of his body. The fluid that snaked its way through his entire system exerted a pressure outward, as if the substance inside his body were trying to reunite with the substance outside his body – thereby flattening him from inside and out! A tingling and fizzing sensation crept throughout his body. It was what he imagined an Alka-Seltzer tablet felt like as it dissolved in a glass of water, if Alka-Seltzer tablets were alive and could feel themselves dissolve.

His entire body evaporated, yet his mental function remained intact. In his mind he still retained a sense of bodily shape and form – just more liquid and pliable – as if all of his molecules were separated from one another but were joined by flexible rubber bands. He felt movement, as the colloidal solution of himself and the oil creature slid through a tight space. It was like his body was turned into a liquid and could flow in any direction. When the movement stopped, the rubbery feeling dissipated as his molecules tightly packed themselves together again. He felt the liquid retract from his intestines and stomach…throat and lungs…mouth and nose…and finally his ears.

He took a deep breath and felt the liquid tentacles slip away from his eyes and from around his neck. He opened his eyes to discover that he was no longer surrounded by darkness. A dull orange glow emanated from the ceiling atop the rounded walls of the room in which he found himself sitting. He looked down to see a black, oily slime melting off his body and pooling on the floor around his feet. The pool grew in size and began to move away from his feet in a thick stream, like a trail of mercury from a broken thermometer.

Am I dead? Xach asked himself. *Where am I? What is going on?*

"No. You are not dead. You are very much alive," the voice said matter-of-factly in his ears. Xach scanned the room, trying to determine who or what was talking to him, but he saw nothing except for the puddle of moving oil on the floor. The voice sounded as though it was coming from inside his ears, like a voice speaking to him through earphones. However, he was alone in the room, and he wasn't wearing earphones. "I brought you inside the structure to question you," the voice continued. "You are unlike the others. What are you and what are you doing here?"

The orange glow from the ceiling revealed the walls were curved outward from ceiling to floor, and Xach realized that he must be inside one of the metallic marshmallow-shaped structures. The room was completely empty and sterile. There were no windows, light fixtures, or furniture. In fact, he couldn't even figure out from where the orange light eminated.

"Human being Xach, I asked you a question. Please respond."

"Oh, I – erm…where are you? Who are you?" Xach asked, looking around the room again for the source of the voice. "I don't even know who I'm talking to."

"I am right in front of you on the floor. I am NemexClass X-12CHRL-1E synthetic life-form. It is my job to maintain this structure and engineer reverse terra-forming of Zindartha. Have you come to deliver fuel?"

"Um, no," Xach said, looking at the shimmering pool of oil on the floor. "I don't have any fuel that I'm aware of. What is 'reverse terra-forming'?"

"Reverse terra-forming is the removal of all life from a planet. It is...*was*...my job to destroy Zindartha and close all portals, but I ran out of fuel eons ago. I have been waiting for someone or something to bring me fuel to finish my job. I expected that you, human being Xach, were such a being. If you are not, then what is your purpose for being here?"

"I'm here because Gerald brought me here from Earth. I don't really have a purpose here, except to get back home. Hey...um...I don't mean to be rude, but are you really just a talking puddle of oily goo?"

"What is 'goo'..." the voice asked. "...and what is 'Earth'?"

"*Goo* is...um...well, it's liquid that is thick. It's semi-solid, like in between liquid and solid. You look like a puddle of oil to me. And Earth is the planet I came from. I don't belong on Zindartha. I was brought here against my will, and now I can't get back home."

"That is very unfortunate, human being called Xach."

"Just call me Xach, okay?"

"Xach okay," the voice said, as the puddle bubbled up in the center in the shape of a tentacle. The tentacle rose upward toward the ceiling.

Xach instinctively pushed away from the liquid using his feet and hit the wall behind him with a thud. He pushed himself into a standing position in case he needed to defend himself. "What are you doing?" Xach asked a little shakily. "Are you going to try and kill me again?"

"I never intended to harm you, Xach okay, nor am I *planning* to harm you. I sensed from your inflection and expression that 'goo' was something negative for you, so I sought to assume a more positive form."

"Oh. It's no big deal. It's just a little odd for me to talk to a puddle of slime, and my name is not 'Xach okay.' My name is just Xach. Just Xach. I meant no offense by calling you 'goo.'"

"Be assured, you cannot offend me. I would like to know more of how you came to be on the other side of the wall outside this structure."

While Xach relayed the tale of his encounter with the Mung, the rainstorm, his fall through the hole under the wall, and his landing on the ground outside the structure, the puddle of oil continued to change in shape. It rose up from the floor, growing in height and width until it was about as tall and wide as Xach. Two tentacles flowed out of the top and a bubble expanded above the two droopy tentacles. Its base separated into two tentacles that supported the general mass in mid-air. It took on definition as the bubble on top lengthened and two hollows formed above a protrusion in the center. Another hollow formed below the protrusion, and to Xach's surprise, in seconds he was staring face to face with an exact replica of himself fashioned out of black goo!

The gooey black Xach stood immobile, staring at him with its newly formed mouth open in disbelief. Xach didn't consciously realize he stopped talking and that his mouth hung open in shock. He closed it, and the gooey Xach did the same. He blinked, and gooey Xach blinked also.

"Cool!" Xach said finally. "How'd you do that?"

"I am able to assume any shape," responded gooey Xach.

"That is so neat," Xach said, reaching out to touch his replica. His inquisitiveness completely overtook any fear or uncertainty he might have felt about the creature, as well as any regard for appearing rude. "Can you feel this?" he said, poking his finger into his replica's shoulder. His finger sunk into the cool black liquid. He withdrew it quickly, and the liquid returned to its original Xach form.

"Yes, I can sense that."

"Did it hurt?"

"No."

"What if I put my hand through you? Would that hurt?"

"No, but what purpose would that serve?"

"None, really," Xach said sheepishly. "It would just be cool. That's all."

"Proceed," gooey Xach replied.

Xach reached forward and pushed his hand into the liquid of the creature's chest. His hand passed through its chest and came out the other side.

"And that doesn't hurt at all?" Xach asked in disbelief.

"No. I simply redistribute myself around your hand."

Xach withdrew his hand, leaving a hole several inches in diameter directly in the center of the creature's chest. In seconds, the liquid bubbled out to fill the void, returning again to its solid appearance.

"That is incredible!" Xach said excitedly. "You're just like that liquid robot in that one movie! So, can you...like...die or even feel pain at all?"

"I understand that death is the cessation of movement and function. I witnessed it in the creatures whose remains lie strewn about the exterior of this structure. They were alive when they fell to the ground, but they ceased to continue functioning upon impact. Over time their bio-molecular structure decayed, leaving only the bones. If I properly understand this concept of 'death,' then I cannot die. 'Pain' is something with which I am unfamiliar. Could you explain?"

"Let's see," Xach mumbled as he contemplated exactly how to define pain to a being with a limited vocabulary and understanding. "Well, let me ask you this – did any of the creatures that died outside live momentarily before dying?"

"Yes. They emitted a great number of cries and sounds before expiring."

"Okay. Well, pain is what they were feeling when they were making those sounds. If you were to do to me what I just did to you – poke me with your finger – I would feel pain. If you were to put your hand through my chest, I would feel great pain and probably die. Most times you feel pain before you die."

"I do not understand."

"I'm not sure I have the words to explain it so that you can understand."

"That is all right. I lack the vocabulary programming to process all that you say, but I will do my best. Since I am unable to 'die,' it is logical to say that I cannot feel 'pain' either."

"May I ask you another question?" Xach said, as he sat down on the floor and rested against the wall. His feelings of fear toward the creature before him were greatly diminished, and he was more intrigued than anything.

"Yes. What do you want to know?" asked gooey Xach, as it sat down in exactly the same manner as Xach. It faced him from the opposite side of the room and mimicked all of Xach's movements like a delayed mirror image.

"How did you get me inside this thing? I've been looking for a door or window for hours, but I couldn't find any way inside. What did you do to me out there? If you never had intention of harming me, why did you attack me and try to choke me outside?"

"I did not attack you. I was attempting to communicate. I transported you inside so that you could not escape before I ascertained the reason for your presence."

"But you squeezed me and almost choked me by going down my throat." Xach opened his mouth and pointed down his throat.

"In order for me to transport you inside, I needed to encase you for disintegration."

"*Disintegration?!?*"

"Yes. I disassembled your molecules in order to transport you though the surface of the structure and reassembled you inside."

"Y-y-you mean…I was…you…disintegrated me and…re-reintegrated…through the wall?"

"Yes."

Xach sat very still with a look of complete astonishment across his face as his brain attempted to comprehend what he was just told. The pressure from inside and out, the fizzing sensation, and the rubbery feelings were the result of his body being broken down into its individual molecules. His molecules were then carried ***through*** the wall and reassembled inside.

What if it didn't put my molecules back together just right? Xach thought in horror. He felt violated. *What if something was put back incorrectly, and one of my organs doesn't work right?*

"I assure you that you were reassembled ***exactly*** as you were before transportation. I am incapable of making an error. There was no need to alter you. My goal was to transport you inside. My programming does not allow errors in reintegration."

"That's the second time you've mentioned 'programming.' You're not a computer. You're a liquid. And how did you know what I was thinking? I didn't tell you I was afraid that you put me back together wrong. I thought it. Are you telepathic?"

"I do not know what 'telepathic' is, but when I readied you for transport, I left a transmitting beacon in you that allows me to interface with the electrical impulses in your brain and respond in like."

"You left something '***in***' me?!? I thought you said you didn't alter me in any way."

"That is correct. I did not alter you in any way. I simply left a piece of myself inside you to allow communication. You have not been changed in any way."

"Where did you leave this 'piece' of you?"

Gooey Xach raised his arms, extended his pointer fingers on each hand, and pointed at his ears.

"You left part of yourself in my ears?" Xach asked, pointing to his ears in a mirror-like fashion. The idea that a piece of alien creature was left in his head was unnerving. He panicked uncontrollably and imagined this is what it felt like to wake up after surgery and to be told that one of the doctors left a pair of scissors in his stomach. The fear of not knowing what would happen and being totally helpless to change it sent shivers through his body.

What will happen to me the longer this alien stays inside me? Will it take over my brain? Will it make me sick or cause me to go deaf? I don't want this thing inside me. Who knows what it's doing!?! Get it out! Get it out!

Xach unconsciously started scratching his ears and tilting his head to one side, as if the agitation of the surrounding tissue or the tilt of his head would cause the alien to fall out.

"I can remove them, but then I will no longer be able to communicate with you," said gooey Xach.

Xach felt a slight tickle in his ears, and he felt cool droplets of liquid slide out of his ear canals like water exiting his ears after a shower. The two tiny droplets of black liquid dropped from his ears, fell onto his cloak, rolled down its surface, and fell to the floor. The two drops rolled toward gooey Xach and merged with its oily, black sneakers.

The irrational panic that gripped Xach dispersed quickly, once the alien was no longer inside him. He felt like he was in control of his body again, even though he was never really out of control. His fear and distrust slowly melted away at the comprehension that the alien truly meant him no harm and removed itself at the first sign of Xach's apprehension.

"Okay. I understand," Xach said. "Those little droplets just lie in my ears and act like tiny speakers. That's why it sounds like you are speaking directly into both of my ears at the same time, right?"

Gooey Xach did not move. It just sat there, staring blankly at Xach with its black, glossy eyes.

"Hello? Am I right?" Xach asked.

Gooey Xach remained completely motionless as if he had gone deaf and mute.

Xach realized the creature could no longer *hear* him. In fact, the creature had no *ears* with which to hear. It never actually *heard* anything he said, but rather it intercepted the electrical impulses in his brain that constituted Xach's thoughts. It read the electrical impulses, decoded them into a language, formulated a response, and then transmitted that response back to Xach's brain in the same manner. It was like telepathic communication, but it could only occur if the creature left its transmitters inside Xach's ears. With the creature's implants in his ears, Xach needed only to think, and the creature would be able to *hear* his thoughts. Without the implants, the creature could not hear or understand anything that Xach said or did.

Xach felt a bit foolish for overreacting. The creature only wanted to communicate with him, and it could remove the droplets in his ears at any time. There was no way to know if prolonged exposure to the creature would have adverse affects on his physiology, but Xach felt communication with the creature was preferable to the silence. Additionally, Xach hoped the key would protect him from any physical harm if any arose. Having felt so alone and abandoned after finding Gerald's body inside the mirondi, it would be a welcome change to have someone to talk to and spend time with. Yet, now he was faced with the difficult task of communicating this revelation to the creature that could no longer hear or understand him.

Xach pointed toward gooey Xach's shoe where the tiny drops were absorbed back into its body. Then he pointed back to his ears, hopefully communicating non-verbally that he wanted the creature to reinsert the transmitting devices.

Gooey Xach remained motionless and silent.

"Right. You can't see me in the traditional sense or understand my motions," Xach mumbled to himself.

He leaned forward and crawled across the floor to the feet of gooey Xach. He reached out and tried to grasp the arms of the creature with the intent of guiding them to his ears, but it was like trying to grab water in a bucket. The creature just slipped through and around his fingers. It amazed Xach how solid the creature looked, but how fluid he actually was.

Well, that's not going to work, he thought. *If I can't grasp hold of it, then there is no hope of picking up a drop and putting it in my ears either. How else can I get it in my ears?*

Then an idea struck him that was so simple he was surprised he didn't think of it first. He took a deep breath and plunged his entire head into gooey Xach's chest. The cool liquid enveloped his head, and he felt it sliding into his ear canal again.

"Did I interpret your movement correctly?" the voice sounded in Xach's ears.

Yes, he thought as he withdrew his head from gooey Xach's chest. *That is exactly what I wanted you to do.*

Chapter Nineteen

"I am sorry for freaking out just now," Xach apologized. "I am new to this otherworldly stuff, and it is my nature to be afraid of the unknown."

"Do not apologize. I have no feelings to hurt."

"Now how do you know what it means to 'apologize' and what 'feelings' are?"

"The longer we communicate," the voice continued, "the easier it is for me to understand your language, Xach." Gooey Xach's mouth opened and closed as if it were forming words, but Xach could see the creature was just mimicking Xach's movements. It was like watching one of those kung-fu movies where the English was dubbed over the film. The mouths moved, but the words never matched up. The creature's actual voice was not coming from its body; it was sounding directly in Xach's ears through the implants. Oddly though, it made Xach feel more at ease to pretend that he was talking to the alien and the alien was responding to him. It felt more *normal*.

"All of your words are stored in your brain," the voice continued, "and I am able to learn quickly the definitions of these words and ideas and how you put those words together to convey meaning. For example, I learned that 'feelings' are reactions to stimuli that change your outer appearance and change your body functions. When you were 'freaking out,' your blood pressure rose, your eyes narrowed, and your face became red. As I do not have such *reactions* to any stimuli of which I am aware, it is logical to conclude that I do not have 'feelings.'"

"I think I understand. Since all of my thoughts and word formations begin as electrical impulses in my brain, you are able to intercept those impulses, interpret their meaning, and talk back to me?"

"Precisely."

"That is kind of cool. The only problem is that I can't keep anything secret from you. It's like you're constantly plugged in and reading my brain. If you remove the implants, then I can't communicate with you at all, but if you leave them in, then you can read every one of my thoughts – even the ones I would prefer to keep secret."

"That is true. However, if my understanding of a secret is correct, then you have nothing to fear. Secrets are things you hide to protect feelings. Since I have no feelings for you to hurt, then my knowledge of your thoughts cannot damage me. If you are rude toward me, I will not react in the same manner. Harming your feelings would not benefit me in any way, so you have nothing to fear in that respect either. Additionally, my programming is not designed to assimilate secrets in the sense that you understand them. It is simply information that is stored."

"Well, that puts my mind at ease a bit. It's still a little weird though, having all your thoughts open like that. I must say, you *are* a quick learner! Just a few seconds ago you kept asking me what certain words were, and now you can define them better than I can! Oh, by the way, you never answered my question. Why do you keep mentioning 'programming?'"

"I am a synthetic being. I am not organic, like you. You are made up of individual cells with specific purposes. I am made up of millions upon millions of microscopic machines. Each of these machines is identical to the others, and they all work together under the same programming. This programming constitutes my *consciousness*, as you would call it. Each of the machines is held together by electrostatic charges and electromagnetic fields. This allows me to assume and hold any shape I choose. It also allows me to sub-atomically deconstruct any matter I surround and transport it from one place to another while it is held together inside my electrostatic fields. That is how I transported you inside this structure from outside. Do you understand?"

"Yeah, sort of. The science of it is a little beyond me, but back on Earth some of our scientists created nanotechnology. It sounds to me as though you are the result of that technology. But you are like a million times more advanced than anything our scientists ever created. Who created you?"

"I do not know the name of my creator, though my internal sensors are set to recognize him when he is near. I only know what was programmed into my circuitry and what I learned since my creation."

"That is incredible. When were you created?"

"Thirteen million, two hundred sixty-five thousand, seven hundred twenty nine days, seventeen hours, twelve minutes, and nine seconds ago."

"You're thirteen million years old?"

"Yes, and two hundred sixty-five thousand…"

"I understand," Xach cut in. "I just wanted an estimate, not an exact number."

"Then thirteen million years is an accurate estimate."

"Ok. Um…what should I call you?"

"I am called NemexClass X-12CHRL-1E."

"I'll never remember all that…2…chrl..e. Sounds like Charlie. May I call you Charlie?"

"You may call me whatever you like, Xach. If 'Charlie' is what you like, then call me Charlie."

"I had a dog named Charlie when I was six years old before we moved. He was a German Shepherd. He was a big dog – over 100 lbs. One day he saw a rabbit on the other side of our fence, jumped it, and chased the rabbit right into the road. An old woman driving a large blue car came around the corner…she couldn't stop in time…it happened so fast…"

Xach was so lost in his memory of Charlie that he failed to notice gooey Xach lose his definition and change shape. Its face melted, and its body slumped forward. It stretched its arms to the ground and extended and thinned its legs. Its neck lengthened, while its head became long and narrow. Large pointed ears bubbled out on top of its head, and its nose lengthened into a snout. A tail formed behind its legs, and as Xachary choked out the last words to describe the accident that took Charlie's life, he looked up to see that gooey Xach was now in the shape of a very large, slick-looking, oil-black German Shepherd.

"Wow. You look just like Charlie, except for the fact that you look all black and oily."

"As you described Charlie, I interpreted your memory of him and took the shape of the being you identified as Charlie."

"That's a pretty cool trick. Too bad you can't change colors."

"'Colors?' Ah yes. I can see them in your mind," the creature said. "The static fields around my components can simulate a variety of properties; refraction of light is one such property."

As he spoke, Xach saw minute changes occur on the surface of the creature. The muzzle of the dog-shaped creature remained black as streaks of brown and tan appeared across the face, ears, and neck. The back of the dog remained black, but the belly took on a light brown, cream color. This color crept along the underside of the dog and along the base of the tail. In a matter of seconds, the creature assumed the look of Xach's dog, Charlie, in every detail, down to the red collar, long whiskers, brown eyes, and mole on the cheek.

"That's amazing!" Xach exclaimed, as he reached out to touch the dog.

His fingers touched the hair on the dog's neck, but it felt cold and slick – not like hair at all. In fact, it felt just like the creature had felt when he tried to grab its arm earlier. As he withdrew his hand, the texture of the simulated hair changed again. It became dry, soft, and fluffy.

"Is that accurate?" Charlie asked. "I do not often replicate organic matter. Judging from your reaction to touching me just now and the memories you had of touching your dog, I was able to replicate the proper texture. The electromagnetic fields of my components can bond tightly to one another creating a solid object, or they can repel one another making my form more liquid and pliable. Have I gotten the texture and resistance of Charlie correct?"

Xach sat speechless, stroking the dog. It was as if Charlie had been brought back from the dead and was standing majestically in front of him after all those years. Tears welled in his eyes.

"Is something wrong, Xach? You are having some type of 'feeling' that does not compute. You cried when Charlie died, but you do not seem to be experiencing 'sadness.' I do not understand."

Xach wiped the tears away on the sleeve of his cloak and smiled.

"It's hard to explain, but sometimes humans become so happy that we cry. These feelings are admittedly contradictory, and I lack the words to properly explain why it happens."

"I shall endeavor to understand these feelings you have, but it may take some time, Xach. Meanwhile, is this form pleasing to you?"

"Yes, it is very pleasing! I can't believe how real it, er...you, feel. You look and feel just like Charlie. It's amazing! When you copied me earlier, why didn't you change colors to match me like you just did to match Charlie?"

"I seldom need to change color. It requires less processing to remain devoid of color or become opaque as I was when you first saw me. If I were to be devoid of color, I would be invisible to your eyes."

In a flash, Charlie disappeared. Xach continued to stroke his back and felt his physical presence, but he could not see him. Then, just as quickly as it disappeared, the dog reappeared in full color.

"Wow...that is totally cool!"

"Your admiration is pointless. I have no feelings to impress."

"Yeah, I guess not," said Xach, absently stroking the dog's back. "But it's still cool! So what else can you do?"

"I don't understand. My functions and purposes are many."

"Well, you can go invisible. You can change color. You can change shape, texture, and solidity. Can you do anything else? What other properties do your electromagnetic and electrostatic fields have?"

"They conduct electricity and can produce small amounts of static electricity independent of a power source."

A small spark arced from the dog's fur to Xach's hand, giving Xach a light shock.

"Ow," he said, withdrawing his hand and shaking it slightly.

"That was not an attempt to hurt you. I was merely demonstrating," Charlie said.

"That's all right. It didn't hurt me so much as surprise me. It's just an unconscious reaction to say 'Ow.' Continue please." Xach continued to pet Charlie.

"My electrostatic fields can transfer or remove heat."

In moments, Xach's hand became very cold, and just as quickly it warmed to the point that he had to withdraw his hand because he was too hot to touch.

"That is fascinating!" Xach expounded. "You are like the coolest thing I have ever seen. Anything else you can do?"

"When necessary, I am able to rearrange the molecules and atoms of other objects, thereby changing an object's subatomic structure and changing it into something else."

"But...you can't do that to any living thing, right. You...you said you didn't change any of my molecules or atoms when you transported me inside...right?"

"No, that is not correct. I can change the atomic structure of any object – organic or synthetic, living or inanimate – as I choose, though I seldom have the need to do so."

"But you said that you didn't change me when you transported me inside. How do I know you're not lying or that you didn't alter me in some way?"

"What is 'lying?'"

"Lying is when you tell someone the opposite of what happened, and you lead them to believe that something false is true."

"If my processing of your thoughts and words is correct, then I am telling you the truth. I have no need to do otherwise. You were reintegrated exactly as I found you."

"Ok. So, if you wanted to, you could change the molecular structure of *anything*?"

"Yes."

"Can you show me?" Xach asked excitedly.

"Yes, I can show you. For the purposes of demonstration, your request is reason enough to do it."

Xach watched in amazement as Charlie's paw sank into the metal floor. It retracted a few seconds later, leaving a hole about six inches deep and six inches wide in the floor. Charlie turned up his paw toward Xach, almost like a human hand, and displayed on the pad a miniature replica of a dog made entirely of the metal taken from the floor. Xach took the miniature in his hand. It was heavy, cold, and solid.

"Neat," Xach said, handing the object back to Charlie. He watched as Charlie's paw absorbed the miniature metal statue and returned it the floor, returning the floor to its original state and leaving no seam or blemish to indicate in any way that it was altered. "That is simply amazing!"

"What about food? Do you need to eat?"

"No. I do not require 'food' to sustain me. I can simulate the act of eating, but it is not necessary. My components are self-sustaining power sources. I can continue running indefinitely."

"Right. You said you can't die."

"Correct."

"So you're pretty much invincible."

"It would seem so, yes."

"So, what is your purpose here? If you can do all these amazing things, why were you brought to Zindartha to operate some planet-destroying machine? Couldn't your talents be used more efficiently at some other task? Especially since you ran out fuel! What did you do all this time?"

"I did nothing. I remained in a phase of stasis for many years. The rain caused the structure to activate the shield, and the vibrations brought me out of stasis. My scans of the area revealed your presence, so I made contact. If not for the occasional rainstorm or some creature falling from the sky and dying outside this structure, I would be in stasis for eons. As it is, several years pass between each break in my stasis."

"That sucks," Xach stated emphatically. "That's gotta be very boring."

"I do not understand 'sucks' or 'boring.' It would seem..."

"Never mind," Xach interrupted. "It doesn't matter. You don't have feelings, so you would not feel bored. It would be boring for me – an active being – to remain still and silent for years at a time. I haven't quite grasped the fact that you are some type of robot, because you just don't look like one."

"What *should* a 'robot' look like?"

Xach brought an image of a robot to his mind. Charlie immediately reshaped himself into an exact replica of Xach's mental picture. He assumed the shape of a boxy, metal robot with a square head, rectangular body, and oddly jointed arms and legs.

"Would this shape be more pleasing and less confusing for you?" Charlie asked Xach.

"No...not really. I actually like you as a dog better."

"Very well," said Charlie and quickly resumed the shape of the German Shepherd.

"So, Charlie," Xach continued, "what does this structure actually do?"

"It disrupts matter and condenses it for recycling. I can't show you how it works, because my fuel source expired. However, I can give you a tour."

"That would be great! I'm interested to know more about this structure, because I spent a couple hours checking out the perimeter. I found about a dozen or so of these rooms spread out over the valley floor."

"Yes, there are thirty-five of these rooms to be exact. Most of them are matter storage containers, but a few of them are control rooms, like this one."

"Control rooms? It's an empty, round room! I don't see any controls."

"Just because you can't see them, doesn't mean they aren't there. Many of you organic life forms rely too heavily on your sight to interpret your surroundings."

"How else are we to understand our surroundings if not by sight?"

"I use sensors to detect light, temperature, surface density, vibration, chemical composition..."

"You mean I must use my other senses too – hearing, taste, touch, and smell – to interpret my surrounding?"

"Though I do not have 'senses' in the same manner as organic beings, the concept is similar, yes. I do not have eyes, ears, a nose, a mouth, or hands, but my sensors detect the same things through mechanical means. The images your eyes reflect are not always accurate. Do not always rely only on the images you see. Your other senses may show something completely different. Allow me to demonstrate."

Charlie stretched his neck, pushing his head upward toward the center of the concave wall. As his neck grew, he resembled a bizarre combination of giraffe and dog. His snout elongated like an anteater and several tentacles resembling fingers grew out of the long nose. These fingers caressed the wall until tiny colored lights glowed under the metal surface like a colored keyboard.

What is he doing? Xach thought.

"I am turning on the external lights," Charlie said, startling Xach.

"Oh. I forgot that you can read my thoughts. That's going to take some getting used to."

"The external lights should make it easier for you to see the structure. However, keep in mind that what you see is only part of the whole. Just as you could not *see* this console, there are many things about this structure that one must *sense* to understand."

"I'll try."

After Charlie finished punching codes into the lighted keyboard, he resumed his dog shape, and the keyboard disappeared.

"Are you ready to go outside and explore the structure?" Charlie asked.

"Yes," said Xach, taking a deep breath.

"I already sense your unease. Do not be afraid. I will have to transport you through several solid objects, but you have nothing to fear concerning this process. I know you were upset when I transported you inside the structure earlier, but just as it was then, it is the same now – you are in absolutely no danger."

"Subconsciously I know that, but it's hard to control the fear. I freaked out the last time, because I didn't know what was happening. While I'm not thrilled about being disintegrated and reintegrated again, I trust you. At least I know what to expect this time. It won't be a surprise. Go ahead. I'm ready."

"Though I do not fully understand 'trust,' you may be certain you will be the exactly the same outside the structure as you are right now. Try to relax. Breathe normally. This will only take a moment."

Charlie glided across the floor toward Xach. He didn't walk like a dog would walk. Instead, the paws sort of melted onto the floor and slid across the smooth metal surface toward Xach. It looked very strange and helped focus Xach's mind elsewhere as Charlie melted into a pool of liquid around his feet. Tentacles grew up from the puddle and entwined themselves around Xach until he was entirely enveloped by Charlie.

"Breathe normally, Xach," Charlie's voice sounded in his head. "Do not hold your breath."

Okay, Xach thought, as he took a deep breath. Charlie slid into his nasal passage and drained into his throat. The pressure started in his ears first, and then grew from the inside and outside. The feeling of flatness returned and was soon followed by the feeling of dissolution. Once liquefied, he felt himself rushing through tubes and pushing through cracks. Second later he stopped and the reintegration process began. When Charlie was finished reassembling Xach's cells, he withdrew from Xach's orifices, regrouped into a pile of black goo, and finally assumed the shape of the dog again.

Xach took a deep breath and stood silently for a moment staring at Charlie's immobile form.

"That wasn't so bad, I guess," he said after a moment.

"Good."

"You know, I just figured out what is wrong with you."

"Nothing is wrong with me. I am functioning perfectly within my prescribed parameters."

"No. That's not what I mean," said Xach, shaking his head. "You look like a dog, and you feel like a dog. But you don't *move* like a dog. You look like a dog statue."

"Explain, please."

Xach brought to mind a memory of a play session in the backyard with his deceased pet. He focused his memory on the dog's movements, his panting, his tail wagging – everything that indicated intelligent life and organic movement within the dog.

Xach watched in subtle amazement as Charlie interpreted Xach's memories into movement. His mouth opened and closed a bit, exposing a pink tongue that quivered. His ears twitched randomly and his chest expanded and contracted as if he were breathing. His long tail swung back and forth at varying speeds.

"Fantastic!" Xach said, clapping his hands. "Now let's see you walk!"

Instead of gliding, Charlie moved his legs forward and backward, lifting the paws off the ground and placing it ahead of himself on the ground. Xach marveled at how quickly Charlie had adopted every minute aspect of a real dog. The more memories that flooded into his head, the more personal ticks Charlie exhibited.

"You've got it! Now you seem like a real live dog!"

Charlie trotted around Xach in circles, wagging his tail and bouncing up and down like he was excited or eager to play. For the first time since his abduction from the hospital, Xach felt calm and almost normal. The sight of Charlie – a familiar animal that Xach loved – brought a warmth and hope to Xach's heart. *Perhaps things aren't as bad as I thought they were,* Xach thought. "Now let's go explore this place!" Xach said with a ten-year old's renewed interest in the exploration of the unknown.

Chapter Twenty

Charlie was true to his word about exterior lighting. The thick blackness that enveloped Zindartha at the setting of the suns was now awash in an orange light akin to a sunset at dusk. The large metal marshmallow-shaped rooms Xach saw only by the dull green glow of the key were now illuminated from top to bottom with the same orange glow as the interior light he experienced. He was able to see the entire structure, and it was much larger and more elaborate than he imagined.

The canyon was filled with the large orange marshmallow-shaped metal structures for as far as he could see into the distance. Above them rose a myriad of pipes and tubes that connected each room to the others. Further still above these pipes rose what looked like a huge metal umbrella or canopy that blotted out the sky and reflected the warm orange light back toward the ground.

"Is it still raining?" Xach asked.

"No. I think the rain stopped," Charlie replied.

Almost immediately, as if the machinery heard their conversation and realized the rain stopped, the metal canopy began to retract with a deafening noise.

****SKEEEEEEREEEEEEK-EEEEEK-EEEEEK-EEEEEEEEK****

"As I mentioned before, the rainstorm caused the shield to deploy," Charlie explained above the metallic roar of the retracting shield. "This is what woke me out of stasis. If it rains too long or if the suns become too hot, the shield deploys to protect the machinery. As I am sure you can sense, it is quite noisy and causes a great deal of vibration throughout the entire structure."

****SKEEEEEEREEEEEEK-EEEEEK-EEEEEK-EEEEEEEEK****

The shield separated in the middle and retracted to either side. Each large metal section slid over the adjoining one like the retractable bleachers in the gymnasium of Xach's school. In this manner, one section atop the other, it retracted into the valley wall on both sides.

****SKEEEEEEREEEEEEK-EEEEEK-EEEEEK-EEEEEEEEK****

"So that is what I heard earlier when I landed on the ground! I thought it was some horrible beast that was going to kill me. It was just the shield moving into place."

"That is very likely," said Charlie. "I am aware of no other creature or sentient being on this side of the barrier."

****SKEEEEEEREEEEEEK-EEEEEK-EEEEEK-EEEEEEEEK****

The last of the shield panels retracted into the valley wall, and the machinery fell silent. The orange glow of the metallic structure illuminated the valley wall and the large stone wall on top. The distance from the wall to the valley floor was so great that the wall looked only inches high, though Xach knew it to be miles in length.

"Wow. This is a really deep valley," Xach gasped, realizing just how far he fell. "I can't believe I fell that far!"

"The distance from the wall to the valley floor is seven hundred thirty-nine miles, twenty-seven feet, nine and three quarters inches – in your scale of distance measurement."

"How do you know that?"

"That was the final reading before my fuel source ceased to function. The depth has not changed."

"I see."

"You 'see' what?"

"I mean I understand. It's not a literal statement. It's another way of saying 'I understand.'"

"I see, as well, then."

"Ok. So you said there are no other creatures in this valley. So, all of these bones here," Xach posited, pointing toward a pile of white, bleached bones sticking out of the ground like creepy odd-shaped saplings, "are from creatures that fell from the other side of the wall?"

"Yes. I operated under the belief that they somehow came over the wall, which made little sense considering the height of the wall and the indigenous population. You indicated they came from under it, which is much more logical. The impact of their great fall drove them into the ground and broke their bodies. They expired immediately, or died, as you defined earlier. After years of exposure to rain, sun, and wind, the bones are all that remain."

"At first, I thought the bones were all that was left of some giant creature's dinner and that I was next," Xach said.

"As I said before, things are not always what they seem, based on appearance alone," said Charlie flatly.

"I am starting to see what you mean."

"There is something I don't understand," said Charlie. "How did you survive the fall? I am unable to understand why you did not meet the same fate as they," Charlie asked, gesturing with his snout toward the bones.

"I'm not entirely sure myself," said Xach. "I performed some kind of magic that allowed me to fly instead of falling."

"What is 'magic?'"

"I'm not sure I can explain," said Xach as he remembered his flight through the storm and his safe landing on the ground. "I guess the best way to describe magic would be power that operates outside the laws of nature. Magic defies natural laws like gravity, inertia, and form. Does that make sense?"

"No, but your memories reveal more to me than your explanations. As you were speaking, I got a visual and auditory imprint of your fall. You uttered words of power. You must be a descendant of those who brought me to this world or perhaps a descendant of my creator. I have only known higher beings to use words of power."

"'Words of power,' huh? Do you know any of these 'words of power?' If you know them, can you do magic, too?"

"I only know a few words of power, and they are the words you uttered to defy gravity and several words spoken by the one who brought me to Zindartha. I am unable to harness the words of power, as I am a synthetic being, lacking an organic composition. I do not fully understand how the speaking of these words works, but I know it has something to do with the emotions you spoke of earlier. Something inherent to organic beings allows them the ability to access the power of these words."

"That's interesting…but it leads to a lot more questions."

Xach's mind raced with jumbled questions and implications. *How was I able to use the words? I'm nobody special. Why is someone like Count Milton able to use the words? Gerald did not approve of Count Milton's use of magic. That much was obvious. As far as I know, Gerald was unable to do magic, or he **refused** to do magic. Does that mean only bad people use magic? Is magic inherently a **bad** thing? I obviously **used** magic, but should I try not to use it if magic is inherently evil? And if that is the case, wouldn't that make the being that brought Charlie here evil as well? If I use magic will that make me evil? I wasn't doing anything **evil** by using magic to stop my descent into the valley. The magic saved my life, and it didn't harm anyone…so why would Gerald disapprove of the use of magic?*

"I do not know the answers to your questions," Charlie said.

"It's okay. There is so much I don't understand about what's happening to me. I just want to get home, but I don't want to do anything wrong in the process. Without Gerald to guide me, I have no idea what I'm doing."

"As I am a synthetic being, the concepts of good and evil – right and wrong – are ambiguous to me. Yet the images you carry in your mind to represent evil do not appear to be like you in any way."

"Thanks. That helps a little. I'm just a little confused. If I were older and more experienced, I might understand all this a little better." He paused pensively. "Oh well," he said looking around him again. "As my mom always says, 'you can only do the best you can do, and that has to be enough.' Of course, if it's a job she assigns you, you better do it perfectly, or she'll scream. I guess that's a bit hypocritical of her, huh?"

"What is 'hypocritical?'"

"Never mind," said Xach, not feeling like defining another word. He looked up at the tower rising above them. "So if this structure has enough power to activate the shield during a rainstorm and illuminate itself like it is now, why don't you have enough power to operate the machine and finish your job here?"

"The lights and shield are powered by battery cells that regenerate themselves, much like my power cells. They operate on a never-ending supply of recyclable energy. However, the energy required to destroy a planet is a million times greater than any battery could produce. That kind of energy must come from a fusion generator."

"So what kind of fuel does this machine take? Why did you run out?"

"This machine requires guarcogen to power the matter converters. Guarcogen is mined from several unstable worlds and packaged in containers made of the strongest, most stable substance known in the universe – quiyaric. I was left here with ten quiyaric containers of guarcogen, which should have been more than enough to power the machinery for the reverse-terra forming of several worlds. However, I found that Zindartha is heavy in quiyaric deposits itself, and therefore it proved quite difficult to destroy. I used ten containers of gaurcogen and only got this far. I waited for someone to bring me more fuel, but no one came. So I maintained the machinery and waited for more fuel to arrive."

"So how does this work?" asked Xach, gesturing toward the orange-tinted buildings. As he did, he noticed his satchel of Zindarthan food still lay in the mud next to the structure. He forgot to pick it up before he fell asleep, and then Charlie enveloped him and took him inside the structure before he even thought to retrieve it. He shook off as much mud as he could and slung it over his shoulder.

"Follow me. I'll take you to the command center," said Charlie, as he galloped ahead.

Charlie weaved between the orange structures and lead Xach to the large tower in the center. It reminded Xach of a water tower with its narrow base and stem leading to a large, bulbous room on top.

"We will need to go inside. Are you prepared for transport?"

"Go ahead."

Charlie melted around Xach as he had done before, deconstructed Xach's molecules, and slipped through the metal surface of the tower's stem. Xach felt himself moving in an upward direction. In moments, Charlie reconstituted him into human form and resumed his dog form.

They stood in the middle of a large oval room lined with consoles, gadgets, and lights. Charlie trotted to one of the consoles and used his 'finger-snout' to enter some codes into a key panel. Xach heard a popping sound and felt electricity in the air. The walls and floor of the oval room became transparent like windows, and Xach was able to see the entire structure stretching out below them. For a brief moment he experienced the nauseous sensation of vertigo. It reminded him a bit of the Hall of Worlds with its translucent starry walls and floor.

"It's like walking on air," Xach said, as he walked past two large consoles to stand by the transparent wall.

"I never use the transparency function, since I have no eyes. However, this is a necessary feature for someone of your carbon-based structure."

"Yes, thank you. I can see everything." It reminded him of the time his parents took him to Empire State Building when he was five years old. They took the elevator to the observation deck, and his father held Xach's small body up so his forehead touched the glass. Xach remembered he could see everything in front, below, and beside him. It felt like he was flying, until his father lost his grip and almost dropped him. He screamed and clung to his father's arm so tightly that he left small hand shaped bruises on his father's forearm. Neither his mother nor his father was able to console him, and he did not stop screaming until they returned to the elevator and exited to the street. Looking out over the machine and valley with an invisible floor and invisible walls left him with that same feeling. He placed his hands on the invisible wall to ground himself and make him feel more stable. When the nausea passed, he was able to truly appreciate the spectacle and intricacy of the giant machine. "This is neat," Xach whispered in awe.

"Each of the metal cylinders you see below is a 'disrupter.' These disrupters vibrate at an incredible velocity, breaking up the soil, rock, and other debris below them. At the same time, each disrupter siphons the broken materials into their central chambers."

"Like the chamber you took me into so I wouldn't run away, right?"

"Precisely. When the chambers fill with dirt and debris, they disintegrate the material. Since matter cannot be destroyed – only changed or manipulated – the machines press the disintegrated material into pellets of tightly compacted matter. These pellets are then jettisoned into space. The tubes that connect each chamber to this tower also lead to a chute at the far end of this facility."

Charlie nodded his head toward the location of the chute. "I do not believe you can see it from here."

"No, I can't."

Charlie's finger-snout typed in a few commands and a small video screen activated in front of Xach with a detailed schematic of the chute.

"The pellets are transported through the tubes to the chute. When the chute is full, a powerful, concussive explosion forces the pellets out of the atmosphere and into space. I do not know what happens to the pellets once they enter space."

"Maybe they become meteoroids, asteroids or comets…" Xach mumbled as he envisioned these pellets drifting through space, pocked with craters or trailing tails of frozen gases.

"Yes, the mental images you have conjured seem logical."

"So what happens once the ground is disintegrated underneath the structures? Do they drop down and continue breaking ground until they reach the core?"

"You are correct again. Just as the sun shield is extendable, the tubes connected to the tops of the chambers are also extendable. The chamber drops and the tubes extend to compensate for the space differential. When the chambers successfully disintegrate enough layers of ground and rock, the molten core of the planet is exposed. The chambers drain the molten core and jettison its contents into space as was done with the layers of crust through which it drilled. As the chambers tunnel deeper, the planet becomes unstable. Earthquakes, volcanoes, and weather changes rip the planet apart. Once the core is completely siphoned away, the gravitational forces do the rest – essentially causing the planet to implode."

"But how do you get off the planet before it implodes?" Xach asked. "I thought the implosion of a planet or sun causes a black hole. How do you escape the destruction and the black hole?"

"You are very intelligent, young Xach. Your understanding of planets is quite large for someone so young."

"Well, science was one of my favorite subjects," Xach said as a slight blush crept across his face.

"When the planets implode, they sometimes cause a black hole, though black holes, as you called them, are quite different from the images you conjured in your head. Nonetheless, the physics behind the phenomena are precisely what you were thinking."

"So if I'm right, how do you escape being destroyed along with the planet? You said you destroyed many worlds before this one. How did you avoid being killed?"

"I must remind you that I cannot be 'killed' as you say."

"Yes....yes...I know that," Xach said rubbing his head in frustration. "What I mean is, how do you survive the destructive force of an imploding planet?"

"Moments before the planet becomes totally unstable, the machinery below retracts into the tower in which we presently stand. This tower is molded primarily out of quiyaric. As I said before, quiyaric is the strongest substance in the universe. The tower cannot be harmed by the explosion or implosion of the planet around it. A few concusive blasts propel the tower into space and away from any gravitational anomalies that might occur. Once the tower is clear of the destruction point, I program the homing beacon and enter stasis while the tower drifts through space toward the planet on which I and this machinery were created."

"Wow. That seems like such a waste of time for you. How long does it take for you to reach your homeworld?"

"Time? Time is inconsequential to a synthetic being. We are able to monitor the passage of time, but it does not affect us in the same manner that it would affect an organic being such as yourself. Sometimes it takes several years to return home, and sometimes it takes only several months. However, twenty years in stasis for me is like a second of time passing for you. Do you understand?"

"Yes, I think so. I never really thought about it, but I guess time doesn't really mean anything for a being like you. Since you do not age or become bored, the passage of time is simply an increment to be measured, whereas for me the passage of time results in aging, boredom, physical degradation, and eventually death."

"That is correct."

Xach looked out over the immense structure lying beneath him and before him, and he felt a little surprised that a race of beings intelligent enough to create Charlie and such a fantastic structure were stupid enough to overlook the limitations of fuel storage. *Why hadn't they been able to figure out that more fuel was needed to destroy Zindartha?* Xach thought. *Why wasn't there some type of work force in place to check up on projects to make sure that they were moving along smoothly? Why wasn't there some type of communication device that could be used to signal for help? It seems like poor planning on the part of such an advanced race.*

"Yes," Charlie said, interrupting Xach's thoughts. "It would make sense to have such plans in place, but apparently my creator did not see fit to put such plans into action. There are several thousand operations similar to mine spread across various galaxies. I suppose my creator felt this was too great a number to manage, or perhaps he simply did not care if a miniscule number of operations failed. It is not really my place to conjecture. My beacon, or communication device as you called it, was damaged during a storm several thousand years ago."

"And no one came looking for you in all that time?" Xach asked incredulously.

"No."

The precision of this operation and the science behind it were fascinating but distracting. Xach's brain caught up with Charlie's words – 'several thousand operations.' *There are several thousand worlds scheduled for destruction! Several thousand! How many species would simply disappear? How many people would be killed? And for what purpose? Pellets of compressed matter floating aimlessly in space? The Mung were horrible, but they still deserve to exist. The Zindarthans are my friends. They helped me! If Charlie hadn't run out of fuel, they wouldn't even exist! He would have destroyed this planet eons ago. Whoever sent Charlie here wanted nothing but to extinguish life. How can someone do that? It's unconscionable! It is evil!*

"Doesn't it bother you that you would have killed millions upon millions of living things when this planet imploded on itself? Doesn't it bother you that you already killed how many other worlds?" Xach asked Charlie. Rage boiled within him. *I didn't ask to be here. I would prefer to be home on Earth, but he has no right to destroy this place! What if this was my home and my family was to be destroyed? The Zindarthans – even the Mung – have families here…*

"I do not understand the changes I detect in your body, Xach. Your blood pressure is rising, your limbs are trembling, and many of your muscles have gone rigid."

"It's called **anger**," Xach growled. "Can't you see that it's wrong? Killing innocent beings is wrong. The Zindarthans didn't do anything to you, and I can't imagine they did anything to your creators. They haven't the technology or ability to harm anyone. They can't even protect themselves from the Mung or the quarken! What possible threat could they be to your creator? Why were you sent here to destroy this planet?"

"I do not know why my creator sent me to destroy this planet. I simply accepted my programming and attempted to complete my assignment."

"*Attempted to compete your assignment?!?* You attempted to wipe out at least two separate races and a myriad of other species just to *complete your assignment?*" Xach's voice rose an octave and his throat began to ache as he screamed at Charlie.

"I do not know how to respond, Xach. I can sense that you are quite upset, but I cannot understand why. I told you before that I do not understand the concepts of right and wrong or good and evil. I am simply programmed to perform a function, and that function is to destroy this and other worlds."

"Well, the destruction of life is WRONG! It is **EVIL**! To cause someone to die without their permission is…and not to realize that it's wrong is…" Xach stuttered and faltered as his mind attempted to grasp how anyone or anything could not see the value of life. He failed to comprehend how a being could have such disdain for life that it would purposely destroy it for no other reason than to end it.

"You seek to understand the purpose of destruction?"

"No," Xach stammered. "I…I want to understand the purpose of destruction solely for the purpose of destruction. No…" He paused to contemplate this statement. *I don't want to understand such evil. To understand it would mean I would have to be like that evil. I don't want that.* "No…" he continued, "I don't *want* to understand such evil. I…I just can't comprehend it. Even if there were a reason or need for this world or any other world to be destroyed, I'm not sure I would ever understand."

His mind filled with examples of genocide, war, serial killers, and bloody conflict throughout human history. He thought about how man waged wars against each other since the beginning of time – each claimed to be fighting for justice but so many lives were lost in the pursuit of victory. He thought about Adolf Hitler who wished to extinguish life that didn't match his vision of perfection. *Many sought to take Hitler's life and would have deemed his murder to be "**just**."* He thought about Jeffrey Dahmer and John Wayne Gacy who killed people for sport. *Some people believed that these men stalked and killed innocent people, because something in their brains malfunctioned. Are they truly to blame if it was a mental defect beyond their control? If not, then it is just the senseless waste of life. And what of people killing others in self-defense? Is self-defense "**justifiable**?" At its root, it is still the taking of life. I didn't kill Count Milton, but I cut off his arm in self-defense. I may have even killed him by accident in trying to defend myself. Does that make me evil? No matter the reason for war – oil, terrorism, land, money - can a soldier be blamed for killing someone who is trying to kill him when he is just following orders? It's kill or be killed, right? We call the survivors heroes. Likewise, can Charlie be held accountable for all those innocent species he destroyed? He is just a tool, created without conscience by someone who also has no conscience – a soldier of destruction...*

"Xach," Charlie said, interrupting his troubling thoughts. "The images in your brain and the conflicting emotions you are experiencing help me to understand a bit of what you called 'anger.' You feel that it is negative to destroy life for any reason. Protecting life and sustaining life is positive. Yet, you experience conflict in the destruction of one life for the protection of another – including your own."

"Yes," Xach said quietly, humbled by Charlie's ability to condense all his erratic thoughts into a concise statement.

"You are angry with me, because I destroyed life for no other purpose than to destroy it. Even if I destroyed lives to protect others, you are not certain it would be justifiable."

"Yes."

"These acts of destruction are wrong."

"Yes."

"Then I am evil."

"Yes...I mean, no. I mean...I don't know," Xach stammered. "It's not **your** fault that you have no emotions or moral programming. You were created that way. You are so advanced, I forget that you are for all intents and purposes a sophisticated machine. You seem very real to me, and your artificial intelligence is so advanced that you mimic independent thoughts and emotion, though you do not have them. That fault lies with your creator. I *do believe* that your creator is evil. I don't know why your creator programmed you to destroy all these worlds. Maybe your creator has a good reason, but right now I can't think of any reason that would make sense to me." Xach took a deep breath and exhaled loudly. "I am sorry for getting so angry with you. It's not your fault."

"Though I do not require an apology, I recognize your need for my acceptance of it. So, I accept your apology. However, that does not resolve the problem. I do not know right from wrong, and I have committed acts that you deem 'wrong' and 'evil.' How do we repair this problem?"

"I don't think we *can* repair the problem. What's done is done. You can't undo it, but I need to ask you if it is against your programming to preserve or protect life?"

"No. I am programmed to follow through with the commands of my creator. In the absence of my creator, I function within the parameters of my job assignment. Presently, my job assignment cannot be completed, and my programming necessitates that I maintain this facility and remain in stasis while inactive. In the absence of a task that can be completed, I may seek direction from my creator as to a new course of action. As my creator is not present or accessible, I may defer to any other higher being like my creator for new programming. You demonstrated the ability to use the words of power and you demonstrate independent, rational thought. Therefore, you are a being equal in part to my creator, and thereby a higher being capable of reprogramming my processors."

"Wait a minute. So, you're telling me that I can change your programming and order you to protect life instead of destroying it?"

"Yes."

"So, I can ask you to do anything, and you'll do it without question?"

"Yes."

"Why didn't you tell me this earlier?"

"You didn't ask."

"Oh."

Charlie closed his eyes and froze in place for a few seconds. When he opened his eyes again, he resumed the normal motion and behavior of a dog.

"I reprogrammed my processors to protect life as you commanded. Is there any other reprogramming you would like me to perform at this time?"

"I can't think of anything right this moment," said Xach, slightly overwhelmed by the idea that Charlie would do **anything** he told him to do. *It's like having my own robot!* Xach thought. *I can train him to be like a superhero and save innocent people. I can train him to help those in need, and he could be like my own personal bodyguard.*

"What are a 'superhero' and a 'bodyguard?'" Charlie asked.

Xach thought about all the superheroes he read about in comics and watched on TV. He thought how Charlie could have protected him from Bobby Brenner on the first day of school and any of the other bullies that picked on him and Jeremy in school.

Before he could verbalize these ideas, Charlie said, "I understand. Bodyguards and superheroes are protectors of the innocent."

"Yes, and that is what I'd like you to be from now on."

"Affirmative."

"Cool!"

Xach's throat was dry. He had been talking with Charlie for quite awhile, and he felt very thirsty all of sudden. This presented him with an opportunity to test Charlie's powers.

"You said that you can you change the molecular structure of an object, right?" Xach asked. "Can you take a chunk of the floor and make it into something organic, like water? I'm quite thirsty."

"What is 'water?'" Charlie queried.

"Water is a liquid – H_2O – two hydrogen molecules bonded with one oxygen molecule. Humans are approximately 70% water, and we need it to survive. I haven't had any water for quite a while. I drank some of that pink stuff, but I don't think that was water. Rain in my world is made of water, but I don't know if that is the case here on Zindartha. I suspect this facility has no rain storage compartments, because I doubt you have use for it."

"You are correct. I do not have a need for rain storage. I detected the molecules you spoke of when I disintegrated you. With the information you just provided, I now understand what water is, though you are only 69.9 % water at this time. Nonetheless, I am afraid that I cannot create water for you. I can rearrange molecules to create changes in shape or texture, but the composition of the object remains the same. I am bound by the laws of nature."

"I see. But you could dismantle my molecules and rearrange them into some other form of organic life, right?"

"I suppose, but why would I want to? If I were to rearrange your molecules to change your form without understanding every facet of your physiology, I might put something in the wrong place and thereby cause you to expire, and that would violate my new programming to protect your life."

"I'm not asking you to rearrange my molecules. I was simply asking if you *could*, I mean…" Xach paused for a moment without completing his thought. *Or am I? If Charlie can rearrange molecules, why couldn't he mend my fractured bones by putting the molecules back in their proper places? What if Charlie could fix my injuries?*

"I have a question for you, Charlie."

"Yes."

"I think I have a broken wrist and possibly some broken ribs from when that angry Mung woman beat me. Even though I heal much more quickly than I used to, it would be great to not feel the pain. Can you fix me?"

"I said 'yes.' I heard you thinking the question."

"Oh, I thought you were giving me permission to ask a question."

"It is all right for you to ask me anything, but I gathered from your thoughts that you wanted to know if I could repair the inconsistencies in your skeletal structure."

"Inconsistencies?"

"Yes, I did notice that your right arm's structure was different from your left arm's structure and that several ribs on the left side were different in structure from those on the right side. I did not change these imperfections. I was only transporting you and saw no need to change those inconsistencies."

"Can I ask you to fix those *inconsistencies*?"

"Yes."

Charlie extended his neck again like a giraffe towards Xach's broken wrist that was still covered by the Zindarthan cast of unbreakable fibers. Charlie's dog head opened its mouth as if it were going to bite Xach's arm, but instead its jaws sort of melted around the cast and Xach's wrist until it formed a seamless black cuff around his entire wrist and forearm. Xach felt a fizzing and tingling sensation in his wrist. Seconds later the cuff receded back into Charlie's giraffe neck. The cast was gone, and before Xach could formulate a complete thought about the disappearance of the cast, a wad of silken fabric emerged from the top of Charlie's neck as if it were being regurgitated and fell to the floor.

Charlie extended his neck toward Xach's abdomen. He oozed more of himself over Xach's torso until another large undulating cuff of Charlie ooze stretched from his underarms to his waist. Xach could feel his molecules being undone. A moment later the tingling subsided, the cuff melted back into Charlie's neck, and Charlie's dog head returned to its original dog shape.

Xach touched his side. It was no longer tender or painful. He squeezed his wrist and felt no pain. He flexed his wrist in a clockwise motion. There was no pain or discomfort! He was completely healed!

"That is incredible!" Xach shouted, startling himself a bit with the enthusiasm of his verbal explosion. "Thank you so much!" He was giddy with joy and bounced up and down a little, unable to control his elation.

"You are welcome. Do you require any further adjustments?"

"Not right now, thank you. I feel great! You have no idea how amazing you are! Do you?"

"I do not understand."

"Of course you don't," Xach smirked, still marveling at the lack of pain he was now experiencing. "Can you imagine how useful you would be on my world? You would be the end of pain and debilitation! You might not be able to stop the aging process, but you could certainly prolong human life almost indefinitely! No more injury, no more sickness, no more organ failure…you have no idea the impact you would have on peoples' lives!"

Charlie simply stared at Xach with his emotionless dog eyes, watching and recording the emotional and physiological changes taking place in Xach's brain and body as he dreamed of a world without pain and physical suffering.

"I understand that you believe me to be quite powerful and helpful, and you feel that I should recognize this power. Yet, I am incapable of understanding the emotional ramifications of my abilities. I simply performed the task that you requested."

Then something rather saddening occurred to Xach that caused his elation and excitement to come to an abrupt end.

"You could have saved Gerald…" Xach's voice trailed off as his mind reeled in the wake of this simple realization. *Charlie was able to analyze my alien physiology,* Xach thought, *and repair my internal injuries. And even though I suspect Gerald was not entirely human, my guess is that Charlie could have fixed him too. Gerald didn't need to die. If I met Charlie earlier and got him to Gerald, I could have saved him. Then Gerald could have continued to be the key carrier and returned me to Earth and none of this would be happening to me. But it's too late for that now…*

None of this needed to happen…

If only…

"But it *is* happening…" Xach mumbled to himself. "I can't change the past. So I better try to make the best of it," he said to himself, trying to sound like his father. He heard his father's voice in his head: *Buck up and be a man. At least you have Charlie now…*

"Xach?"

"Yes?"

"Your thoughts revealed some bits of your past that are unclear to me. Who is 'Gerald' and what does he have to do with how you came to be here? You already told me about the Mung and your adventures on Zindartha, but how did you get to Zindartha? You learned all about me, yet there is a great deal I do not know about you. Your recent thoughts of 'Gerald' require some further explanation if I am to process them correctly."

"It's a little complicated," Xach said. "Gerald brought me here, but I'm not sure I can explain it all myself."

"Perhaps you could show me."

"*Show you*? How can I show you?"

"As you know but keep forgetting, I can access your thoughts and memories. However, the events of the past several days are quite jumbled in your mind. I cannot assimilate them properly into a linear, coherent series of events. Your emotions and my inability to properly understand them keep the whole of your journey to Zindartha disjointed. If you could focus on what happened in chronological order, I might be able to come to an understanding of how a 'human being,' a creature not indigenous to Zindartha, came to be on Zindartha. I may then be able to help you find a solution to what troubles you."

"Ok," said Xach. "Gerald told me that if I concentrate hard enough, I can remember anything in every minute detail, so let me try."

He closed his eyes and concentrated on the day in school when the earthquake occurred. The day's events played out like a movie in his mind's eye. He remembered the quake, Gerald attacking him in the closet and again in the bushes, the ride home, the events in the hospital, his trip to the Hall of Worlds, the attack of Count Milton... everything up to the point when he fell through the hole under the wall and landed in the bone yard outside the reverse-terra forming facility. When he was finished remembering, he opened his eyes.

"How was that?" Xach asked.

"Perfect. It is all very clear now. Do you have the key?"

"Yes. I do."

"I did not know you were a key carrier. The one who brought me to Zindartha had a key. I have been in the Hall of Worlds, and I know where the gateway lies. If you have a key, you could return home and return me to my home planet."

"Fantastic!" Xach shouted.

In a flash, Charlie leapt at Xach. In mid-air, Charlie changed shape into something resembling a wet sheet or tarp and landed on Xach's head. Charlie melted around him and enveloped him in a dark cocoon. Charlie deconstructed Xach and together they whisked through the menagerie of twisting pipes that linked together all the rooms of the planet-destruction facility. Once outside, Charlie reassembled Xach and returned to his dog form. Xach was unable to see; they were once again outside and surrounded by the thick, impenetrable darkness that lay upon Zindartha. The air was cool and moist from the recent rain.

Xach took the key from his pocket and rubbed the gem. The green glow illuminated a structure directly in front of him. It was identical to the outhouse shaped structure from which he and Gerald emerged when they exited the Hall of Worlds and arrived in Zindartha.

"Where are we?" Xach asked Charlie.

"We are on the other side of the wall built around the valley that houses the reverse-terraforming machine. We are on the surface of Zindartha, and this is the portal through which my creator brought me to this planet."

Xach stood silently, staring at the outhouse with a mixture of awe and trepidation. *Can this really be my way home?* he asked himself. *Is this the end of my nightmare?*

Xach felt Charlie paw at his leg. He looked down at the dog. His paw was turned upward and shaped like a cup. In the cup was water.

"You said you were thirsty. I took a chunk of wet ground and filtered out the liquid for you to drink."

"Yes," said Xach, gratefully. "I was. I mean I am."

"It is not water, but it is the 'pink liquid' you drank earlier without harming yourself. It is similar enough to water."

"Okay," said Xach as he bent over to sip from the cup. Charlie tipped his cup-hand as Xach drained the liquid completely. "Thank you," said Xach. "Now let's get outta here!"

Chapter Twenty-One

He stood before the small wooden shack. The key glowed a bright green. *That's a good sign.* He stepped toward the door and opened it. A backdraft of stale, smelly air wafted into his face. He gagged and slammed the door closed. He remembered how the closet in the hospital appeared to be a regular closet until Gerald placed the key in the closet's lock, turned it, and opened it into the dark antechamber of the Hall of Worlds. Xach placed the key in the lock and turned it to the right as if to lock it and then back to the left to unlock it. He withdrew the key from the hole and pulled open the door. The stale air and smell of feces were gone. In their place was a black void – the antechamber of the Hall of Worlds!

"This is it," said Xach ecstatically, as he turned to Charlie. "It worked! We're going home!"

Charlie stood motionless, staring at Xach and the black void beyond the door. Xach was so excited he could hardly contain himself. An hour ago, he thought he'd never get off Zindartha, but here he was standing in front of an exit. He expected Charlie to exhibit some sign of excitement as well, but Charlie's unnatural lack of movement again reminded him that he was not a real dog. He was just some emotionless being that *looked* like a dog.

"How should I be moving?" Charlie's voice sounded in his ears.

"It's not important, but it's just that you look so much like my dog, and I forget you're not a real dog. When I look at you standing there so motionless…you just look so strange. When a dog gets excited, he wags his tail. When my dog was excited, he used to wag his tail so hard that his whole back end gyrated…almost like his tail were a propeller trying to lift his back end off the ground. It was really cute, but it really doesn't matter," said Xach as he turned back to the outhouse and stepped into the antechamber. "What matters is that we can finally go home!"

Charlie wagged his tail, mimicking the images he extracted from Xach's memory. He followed Xach into the antechamber and used the tip of his tail to pull the door shut behind him. Xach advanced through the antechamber across the spongy floor. He held the key to the wall, and the door's edges lit up. He pushed it open and stepped out into the blue, star-filled hallway of the Hall of Worlds.

"I can't believe I'm back here!" said Xach excitedly. "I never thought I'd find my way back! Thank you *so **much***, Charlie!"

"Do not thank me yet, Xach," said Charlie. "We have to find the correct halls and the correct doors to find our way back to our worlds. All of the doors in this hall will lead us back to Zindartha. We must find the Great Hall and begin searching for the doors with our worlds' symbols upon them."

"Which direction should we go, left or right?" Xach asked.

"Right."

"Okay, right it is," he said resolutely, as he turned to the right and walked quickly toward what he hoped would be the door to the Great Hall.

It took them several minutes to reach the great door at the end of the hallway. It was much larger than the others they passed. Xach waved the key in front of the large door in the same manner Gerald had when he first brought Xach into the Great Hall. Green light eminated through the cracks around the door's edges. Xach pushed open the door, and the two companions stepped out into the Great Hall. The hall stretched into infinity to their left and to their right. There were so many doors that Xach's heart sank a little. Finding his and Charlie's world was not going to be easy at all.

"I forgot how big this place was," Xach said in hushed awe. "How are we ever gonna find the right doorways? I don't even know what the symbols on the doors mean."

Xach walked down the Great Hall, looking at all the different symbols on the doors. Charlie sauntered next to him, turning his dog head from side to side as if he were actually looking at the doors and their symbols too.

"I know the symbol that will appear on the door to my home world," Charlie said. "I remember it from my other visits to this place."

"What does it look like?" Xach asked.

An image appeared in Xach's mind.

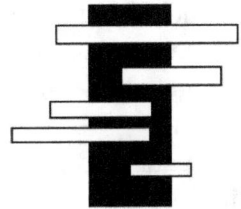

"Okay," said Xach. "If you don't have eyes to see, how is it that you are able to recognize symbols and project images of them into my head?"

"Perhaps I was not entirely clear when I said I do not see things. It is true that I have no 'eyes' that function solely to record visual images of my surroundings as you do. However, my sensors are able to record images around me from any angle. I was programmed to store certain images in my data banks for future reference. The symbol on the door to my home world was one of those images."

"I *see*," said Xach with a giggle.

"What is that noise?"

"What noise?" said Xach. He froze and looked around in a bit of panic. *Who or what is in here with us?* he thought nervously.

"You misunderstand me," said Charlie. "I am not referring to a noise in the Hall, I am referring to the noise that issued from your mouth. You said 'I see' and then you made a noise." Charlie opened his mouth and reproduced the sound of Xach giggling, as if he were a music speaker.

"Oh," said Xach with a sigh of relief. "You mean laughing. For a second there I thought we were being followed by something or someone."

"No. I was referring to your 'laughing.'"

"I was making a joke," Xach said, as he resumed walking down the hall.

"I do not understand. What is a 'joke' and what is 'laughing?'"

"You were talking about *recording images* which is just like *seeing* for me. So I said, 'I see,' to play off the double meaning of the phrase. In one context the phrase means that you physically see an image with your eyes. In another context, it means that you understand something. When a word means two different things depending on context, you make a pun – a play on words. I made a joke and then laughed. When something is funny, we laugh."

"When something means two different things, that is a 'joke' and therefore 'funny?'"

"Sometimes. Jokes can be stories with humorous endings, or they can be a play on words."

"I do not understand."

"I don't even know where to begin to explain humor to you. It is so closely related to emotion that I have no idea how to break it down for you. I'm sorry."

"That is all right. At least I know that the sound you made is called a 'laugh,' and when you laugh I will know that something is 'funny.' Perhaps over time I shall be able to compile enough examples of what you call a 'joke,' so that I may extrapolate the meanings of these words."

"You do that," Xach sniggered.

"Affirmative."

"That wasn't a command."

"I understood it to be a command, so I added it to my list of functions to perform."

"Well, I didn't mean it that way, but I guess it doesn't really matter. I don't always mean what I say literally. Much of what I say are figures of speech or sarcasm. But I guess that doesn't mean much to you either."

"No."

"Let me see if I can give you an example of the duplicity of my language."

"Please."

"Let's say that we get into a situation in which I break my leg. We agree that breaking my leg is a **bad** thing. If I say," Xach changed the tone of his voice to be sarcastic, "'oh, great. I just broke my leg,' it is to be understood that I am joking or lying. Breaking my leg is definitely *not* 'great,' nor is it something I am happy about. However, just saying 'oh, great,' under normal circumstances usually indicates something good has happened. It's duplicitous and entirely dependent upon the inflection and tone of my voice. When we make a statement that generally means one thing, but our inflection or tone indicates the complete opposite, we call that being 'facetious.' It's not that the words themselves mean two different things – like 'I see' mean to see something or to understand something – the words mean different things because of the tone of voice or the obvious falsity of the statement. Does that help explain it at all?"

"No. Your language is confusing and complex. Some words have several definitions dependent upon how they are used in a complete thought, and now you are telling me that some of the thoughts you complete may mean something completely different depending on your emotions or vocal inflection? This is troublesome. I have great difficulty processing your words and thoughts correctly, since there are so many variables in your communication patterns that I do not yet understand."

"I wish I could help you with that," said Xach apologetically, "but I can't. English is probably the hardest language in my world to learn. You'd probably need to study it for years just to get a basic understanding of all the possibilities the English language holds. The foreign exchange students – kids who come from another country and who speak a different language," Xach explained, figuring that Charlie would ask what foreign exchange students were, "have a very hard time learning English. At least you've managed to master the sentence structure and basic grammar already. You should be pleased."

"I lack the ability to be 'pleased.' Nonetheless, I do need to understand your language as best as possible, if I am to properly fulfill the tasks you assigned to me. My creator did not speak much. He spoke in simple commands and did not see the need to converse with me as you do. I am adapting as quickly as possible."

"Well, I think you're doing a fine job. You may not know all the words I use and you may not understand the emotions behind them, but I bet you could pass yourself off as human any day."

"It is unlikely that what you say is true, but I shall not protest. Let us focus on finding your world. I scanned your memory for an image of the symbol on the door to your world, but I have been unsuccessful in locating one. Do you recall anything about the symbol on the door to your world? Try to remember clearly, as you did when you showed me how you came to Zindartha."

Xach stopped walking. He closed his eyes and leaned against the squishy wall. He focused his entire attention on the memory of his first time in the Hall of Worlds – Gerald, weakened by his injury, pulled Xach along the hall toward the door to the Great Hall. Xach gave him the key to open the door, and Xach looked back to see Count Milton coming toward them. Gerald dragged Xach from the doorway, causing his neck to snap forward. The door, the wall, the symbols, and the ceiling were a blur as Gerald pulled him along.

"Stop," echoed Charlie's voice in his ear. "Go back and slow down the movement. Focus on what your eyes are seeing. Block out everything else."

Xach did as Charlie suggested. Xach pictured himself being pulled through the doorway. His eyes went to his feet and then slowly climbed the door and the wall toward the ceiling.

"There," said Charlie suddenly.

"Where?" asked Xach. "I didn't see anything."

"Yes, to the far left of your field of vision was part of the symbol."

Xach replayed the images frame by frame in his mind's eye, and sure enough…to the far left side of his field of vision, Xach could clearly see part of the symbol on the door to his world – Earth. The right side was crystal clear, but the left side was a total blur.

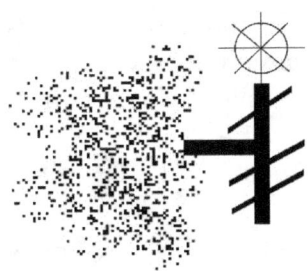

Gerald pulled him too far along the hall before Xach brought his gaze up to the center of the door where the symbol lay, thus resulting in a partial subconscious image.

"If Gerald hadn't pulled me so hard, I might have gotten a clear look at the image," Xach said forlornly, as he slumped to the floor and put his head in his hands. He felt like crying, but he held it back. "Without knowing the right symbol, I'll never get home. As it is, all I can remember is that the right side looks sort of like the half of a capital letter H with cross-hatchings and a sun above the right side."

"It is unfortunate that you are unable to remember the full symbol, but a partial symbol is better than no symbol at all. For instance, this door here," said Charlie, pointing with his nose at the door directly across from Xach's seated form, "could not possibly be the door to your homeworld, because it does not have the cross-hatchings or the sun above the right side."

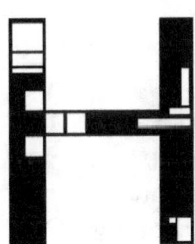

"Nor is it my homeworld. So we know that this is not the door we want to enter."

"True," said Xach. "I guess you're right. Let's keep looking."

They continued walking down the hall looking for anything that resembled either of their worlds' symbols. They walked in silence, passing doors with circles and triangles and symbols that looked vaguely like letters from the English alphabet. Without realizing it, Xach hummed to fill the silence.

"What do you mean?" Charlie asked.

"Huh?"

"I do not understand. The sound you are making is not laughing, and the words in your head seem to have little relevance to our task." Charlie opened his mouth and out came the sound of Xach's voice and humming like a music recording. It echoed throughout the hall:

> *Been up and down and once around*
> *Been kicked and punched and beaten down*
> *Been hurt so bad inside and out*
> *Felt many times like givin' up*
> *But I won't*
> *No, I can't*
> *I will not stop*
> *Gotta get up*
> *Gotta keep up*
> *Gotta lead with my heart*
> *Cause nothin'*
> *No, nothing*
> *Is gonna keep us apart*

The recording ended, and Charlie's voice returned. "What does this mean?"

"Oh, those are lyrics to my favorite song, *Lost*, by the Little Monsters. It just popped into my head to fill the silence. The noise I made is called humming...it's the music that goes along with the words to the song. On Earth, humans compose songs to express different feelings. Songs can excite you or make you feel mellow. They can make you sad or happy. Some pieces of music can even make you cry. It's all very tied into emotion."

"Then I cannot begin to understand," said Charlie.

"I wouldn't say that," said Xach speculatively. "You may not be able to comprehend music now, but perhaps someday I will have the opportunity to expose you to music. If I had my phone, I could play some songs for you, and you might be able to understand a little better. Unfortunately, my vocalizations of songs probably won't help much. I don't sound at all like the original singers, and my humming is not at all like real music. You would have no idea how voices and music harmonize. You'd actually need to hear the *music* and feel the vibrations to…LOOK!"

Xach stopped dead in his tracks and pointed to a symbol on the door they were passing.

"This might be it! This might be the door to Earth!"

"You are correct. The right side identically matches the partial symbol you remembered."

Xach waved the key in front of the door, and it opened. He was so excited he trembled and tripped over his feet in his haste to step inside. An infinite number of doors stretched as far as the eye could see down another seemingly endless corridor.

"Well, which door do you think I should try?"

"Any door is as good as another," said Charlie. "Either it will lead you to Earth, or it will not."

"Thanks," said Xach sarcastically.

"You are welcome," said Charlie.

"I was being sarcast…oh, never mind. Let's try this one," Xach said, waving the key in front of the door on his right.

The edges of the door glowed green. Xach pushed it open and stepped into the dark antechamber. Charlie followed. Xach moved quickly to the opposite side of the chamber and waved the key in front of him, expecting the door to this new world to unlock, but nothing happened. He walked face-first into the wall.

"Oww," he said as he bounced off the wall and fell backwards.

"Are you all right, Xach?"

"Yes, I'm fine. It didn't even really hurt. The walls are soft and spongy. It just startled me. I'm kind of tired of falling on my butt so often. I wonder why a doorway didn't open?"

"Perhaps the hall door needs to be closed first," Charlie suggested, as he used his paw to pull the door closed.

Xach held the key out in front of him again, and sure enough, the edges of the mystical door illuminated.

"You were right, Charlie!"

Xach stood up and pushed against the door. It swung open revealing a bright, white haze. Xach squinted to see, because the contrast of white haze against the pitch-black antechamber was nearly blinding.

He turned his head toward the back of the room where it was darker and slowly opened his eyes. He gradually turned toward the white light, allowing his eyes a chance to adjust to the light differential. As he did so, he saw wispy tendrils of fog gliding into the antechamber from the world on the other side of the door. Tiny fingers of feathery-white haze crept across the floor, pooling around Xach and Charlie's feet. As he watched, Xach saw shapes moving in the mist beyond the door, but the fog was so thick they were nothing more than nondescript shadows. Squinting did nothing to help clarify the shadowy shapes. He wasn't too keen on stepping into the dense fog without knowing what he might bump into. The amorphous shadow-figures were quite large. The mist crept in along the walls and ceiling, until the antechamber was as misty as the unknown world. Xach turned to Charlie to ask if Charlie's sensors could detect what was in the fog but found that he could no longer see him in the thick haze.

"I am unable to sense what lies in the fog beyond the doorway," rang Charlie's voice in his ears, startling him and causing him to jump a little. An overwhelming feeling of dread and uncertainty washed over him. "My sensors are no more helpful than your eyes at this time."

"I keep forgetting you can hear my thoughts. It's still a little unnerving to have you answer a question I haven't even verbalized."

"That is how I function..."

"No worries. I'm just a little creeped out by this fog and those shadows. I just need to get used to…OHHHH!" Xach yelled. Something grabbed hold of his left leg and pulled him toward the open door. He lost his balance and fell flat on his back. He didn't see it creep up on him in the thick fog, but it felt like a tentacle tightly wrapped around his left ankle. As he fell, he instinctively tightened his right hand over the key, so he would not drop it in the fog. He clawed at the smooth, squishy floor of the antechamber with his left hand, trying desperately to find something to grab onto to keep from being pulled through the door.

Again, in response to his thoughts, Charlie ran across the floor and turned one of his dog-legs into a knotted rope that he wrapped around Xach's left wrist and hand. Charlie dug the claws of his other three dog-legs into the floor and thereby momentarily stopped Xach from being pulled into the mist.

"What is happening?" Charlie asked. "I can't sense anything but your hand to which I am tethered."

"I don't know," yelled Xach in a panic. "I can't see anything either. I feel something tight around my ankle, and it's trying to drag me through the doorway. Whatever you do, DON'T LET GO OF ME."

"Affirmative," was Charlie's response.

The thing around Xach's ankle tightened its hold and snaked farther up along his leg. Another tentacle slid up his right leg, exerting more force to pull him through the doorway. He felt the button on his jeans snap, and his pants slid down to his ankles. Thankfully, his sneakers kept his pants from sliding off his legs completely and they remained bunched at his feet. The tentacles slid down with the pants, temporarily losing their grip on Xach's legs and thereby allowing Xach to claw his way a few feet closer to Charlie.

"There's more than one," Xach said. His shoulder and chest were hurt from being pulled in two directions like the rope in a tug-of-war. The tentacles squirmed over his pants and up his legs again. As they touched his skin, he could feel that they were covered in slimy suction-cups like an octopus. Several of the cups suctioned to his skin while the rest of the tentacle undulated upward, obtaining a better hold on him. The tips of the tentacles stopped just under the edge of his boxer shorts.

Oh, thank god, Xach thought. The idea of having those tentacles sliming their way onto his privates sent a shudder of disgust through his entire body.

"The force against me is doubled," said Charlie. "I do not know how much longer I can continue to hold you in this form."

At that very moment, Charlie's nails lost their grip, and Xach slid over the lip of the doorway. Instinctively, he transferred the key to his mouth, freeing both his hands. He twisted on his right side and threw his upper body toward the doorframe. He hit the wall with his stomach and felt the doorframe slip up toward his head. He tilted his head back, narrowly missing the doorframe with his chin. He formed his hands into claws clamped down as hard as he could on the doorframe.

Xach felt a painful pull in his arms and chest as he tensed his arms against the pulling force of whatever had hold of him, but he did not let go of the doorframe.

HELP ME CHARLIE! Xach thought. *I don't know how long I can keep hold of this!*

Lightning fast, Charlie responded by transforming himself into a harness that looped around Xach's torso and shoulders, relieving some of the pressure that was being exerted on his wrists and arms by transferring it to his upper torso . Charlie oozed some of himself along the ground and through the doorway. He separated into four smaller streams which he formed into clamps that latched onto the soft, yet sturdy, walls, floor, and ceiling around the doorframe. Even though Xach could not see what Charlie was doing, he immediately felt the tension leave his arms and transfer to the harness around his upper torso.

Whatever you're doing, it's working! Xach thought to Charlie.

The creature also felt the change in tension and sent another tentacle to wrap around Xach's abdomen. Xach's grip on the wall slipped, and he was pulled into the mist. He did not go far, however, because Charlie exerted equal force in the opposite direction.

"I anchored myself to the door frame, and I believe you should be able to pull yourself back into the antechamber by clawing your way along the ground. I can hold you against the current force that is pulling you, but if I cannot say what will happen if the force against you becomes stronger."

Okay, thought Xach. He dug his fingers into the ground beneath him but succeeded only in scratching the ground's surface. The ground was so hard that he could not sink his fingers into it at all. The small patch of blood-red earth directly beneath his face was hard and packed solid, like mud that dried in the hot sun.

To his left and right wood creaked. The sound was immediately followed by two loud crashes as trees snapped and fell to the ground. Dust and leaves rained down upon Xach, and he heard tentacles clearing debris and teeth chomping and splintering wood. Whatever had hold of him was large – very large! It was strong enough to break trees and had jaws sharp enough to bite through wood. An image of a giant mutant squid with a large gaping maw lined with row upon row of sharp, jagged teeth filled his mind. If the creature didn't soon manage to rip his legs from his body, it would only be a matter of time before its giant teeth chomped through his feet and legs.

"I suggest you hurry," said Charlie as he sensed these horrific images pouring into Xach's mind.

Don't you think I know that?!? I don't want to be this creature's lunch any more than you do!

He scratched at the ground so hard the skin ripped from his fingertips, but he just couldn't get a deep enough grip to pull himself closer to Charlie and the door. *Damn, that hurts,* he thought, wanting to stop. *But not as bad as being chomped to bits will feel...*

The creature was closer, and he heard the teeth grinding through the tree branches and snapping them like toothpicks. *That'll be my bones in a second*, he thought morbidly. *If only I had a knife or a pick or something sharp...maybe I could shove it into the hard ground and manage to pull free...* That sparked an idea.

"I do not know if that is a good idea," Charlie warned.

Do I have a choice?

Xach reached back with his right hand and retrieved the key from his mouth. *Here goes nothing!*

He raised the key above his head and slammed it into the ground. The key sank past the ground level about an inch before the side of his hand hit the ground. He tentatively exerted pressure on the key, pulling himself toward it. Since he couldn't see past his elbow, he didn't know if the key lodged itself in the ground or if he broke it. It didn't move. It held firmly in the ground! He exerted more pressure, and managed to pull himself a few inches closer to the doorway.

"It worked!" Xach yelled. Charlie pulled in the slack on the harness, holding Xach in his new position. Xach pulled the key out of the ground and slammed it down again. He pulled himself another few inches forward. After repeating this movement several times, the lip of the doorway came into fuzzy view.

The creature tugged even harder on Xach's legs. It was close enough that Xach could feel its warm breath on his legs and the puffs of air created by its mouth opening and closing. The rancid smell of rotten meat, decaying leaves, and freshly chipped wood blew past Xach's nose each time it exhaled.

"It's now or never," Xach grunted. Mustering all his strength, he hauled himself to the edge of the doorway. He grasped the doorway with his left hand, transferred the key back in his mouth with his right, and then used both hands to pull his body into the antechamber. He tasted dirt in his mouth and felt the grit on his tongue. It tasted similar to what he expected nail polish remover should taste like. He wanted to gag and spit out the key, but he forced himself to keep his mouth tightly clamped on it. He couldn't afford to lose the key again, especially in this environment. He pulled with all his might, and with the help of Charlie, he managed to get halfway through the doorway. Charlie held him in place while he maneuvered his right knee past the doorframe. With his right knee firmly inside the doorframe, he pulled his left leg upward and brought it inside the room. The tentacles remained suctioned to his legs, but his entire body was back inside the antechamber. He rolled onto his back and braced his feet on either side of the doorway, so that the force of the creature's pull only served to hold him more firmly in place. It was a little tricky to maneuver, with his jeans around his ankles, but he felt stable.

Charlie, do you think you can open the other door into the Hall of Worlds while I hold myself here?

"I'll try, but I do not want to release you," said Charlie.

*You don't have to release me. Stay tethered to my chest, but release the clamps on the doorframe. I can hold myself here for a little while. Then use your clamps...or arms...or **whatever** to push the door open. Then you can pull me out of here.*

Xach knew the moment Charlie unclamped himself from the doorway. The pressure on his legs quadrupled in strength. He arched his back to pin his shoulders to the floor and keep his knees from buckling. He succeeded in keeping his position, but the strain was incredible.

Charlie slid along the floor and up the wall toward the position of the door. He oozed up the wall to find a crack or opening but found nothing. The door was completely sealed.

"I have failed, Xach. I can not locate the door. It appears to be sealed. It cannot be opened."

Crap! You need the key, Charlie!

Charlie returned, and Xach unclenched his teeth from around the key so that Charlie could take it. A few seconds later, Charlie responded in the negative again. The doorway would not light up or open.

"Damn!" cursed Xach. "Only one door may be open at a time. Charlie, can you close the door that's open?"

"I will try, but the creature's tentacles will be blocking the door from closing. I may not be able to exert enough force to pull the door closed with them blocking the way."

"Just try it! I have a hunch it won't matter. Closing the door cut through Count Milton's arm like it was warm butter. I hope the same applies here! HURRY!"

"Yes, I recall that memory. I'll try."

Charlie returned the key to Xach's mouth and oozed along Xach's side and bare legs toward the open door. The fog was still too thick in the room to see what Charlie was doing, but Xach was able to see the dark blurry edges of the doorway against the stark white of the fog outside. As he lay there, tensed against the floor, he saw the door start to swing closed.

The white fog dimmed, but not because the door was almost closed. The creature was upon them! It loomed outside the door; its huge, monstrous shape blocking the white mist and casting a huge shadow over the antechamber. It brought its mouth against the opening to the antechamber and chomped frantically. The room shook violently, and Xach saw the door fall fully open again.

What happened?

"The creature knocked me off the door. It is thrashing around, and I am experiencing difficulty regaining my grip."

The creature roared, frustrated that it was too large to fit through the doorway. Spittle from its throat spattered on Xach's legs and chest, once again suffocating him in the putrid scent of rotting wood and flesh. The sound of its roar was deafening, like twenty fire and police sirens screeching at once. Xach instinctively put his hands to his ears to block the wretched sound. The creature sensed Xach's balance was off and pulled sharply. It drew back a little, letting a small amount of light in as it did, and pulled harder on Xach's legs. Although his knees buckled, his feet remained planted on the doorframe. Another tentacle whipped out the mist and wrapped around Xach's stomach, pulling him directly toward the doorway and into a standing position. Xach threw out his arms perpendicular to his body and managed to brace himself on either side of the doorway just enough that he was not pulled out into the mist again.

NOW CHARLIE, NOW! CLOSE THE DOOR! FOR THE LOVE OF GOD, NOW!

In pulling back, the creature moved back far enough from the doorway to allow Charlie to again swing the door back toward the antechamber. Charlie hooked the door and pulled it toward him.

"RRRUUUUAAAAAARRRRR!" screamed the creature as the door magically sliced through its flesh, extricating one of its tentacles from its body. The tentacle on Xach's left leg loosened and fell to the floor. It flopped and squirmed like a fish out of water, slapping against Xach's legs. "RRRUUUAAARRR!" cried the beast a second time, as the door sliced through the tentacles wrapped around Xach's torso. They slipped from his waist and joined the other, writhing and twitching on the floor. The creature roared once more as the closing door cut off the fourth and final tentacle holding Xach's right leg. Xach fell backward to the floor.

The door closed tightly. The light, the monster, and its roars disappeared. Xach sat up and swatted the squirming tentacles away from his legs. Charlie retracted himself; the harness slipped from Xach's chest and shoulders. Xach slid back against the wall and stood up. He immediately bent over and pulled up his pants. Only after making sure that the zipper and button were securely fastened on his jeans to ensure that he was no longer half-naked, did he remove the key from his mouth and rub the gem to light the room. The green glow of the gem illuminated the mist filled room, its light reflecting off the millions of fog droplets. He spit the foul tasting dirt from his mouth and wiped some of the creature spittle from his face with his cloak.

At least the gem still works, thought Xach, feeling the key to detect any deformities or sharp broken edges. *If it is broken, it's not entirely broken.* He found no sharp edges or jagged breaks. To the touch, the key appeared unharmed.

"Whew," sighed Xach, as he looked around the room for Charlie. "The key appears to be okay."

Through the green fog, Xach saw that Charlie had resumed his dog shape and was standing silently in the corner. The four tentacles that had been wrapped around Xach's legs and waist lay just inside the door, flopping around against the floor and walls. The creature's skin was a deep green color with a glossy surface. The meat inside was purple and cleanly cauterized just as Count Milton's arm had been.

"Ewwww," shuddered Xach as he watched the bodiless arms jerk around. "Thank God that thing didn't get me. Can you imagine what kind of creature those things were attached to?" The image of the giant, mutant squid filled Xach's head again. "Thank you, Charlie!" he said, rushing to him and throwing his arms around the dog. "I thought I was a goner!"

Charlie stood silently still while Xach hugged him. When Xach finally released him and stood up, Charlie asked, "What was that?"

"Oh," said Xach, realizing he just showed emotion to an emotionless being. He felt embarrassed and absently brushed some dirt and creature spit from his clothes. He couldn't look Charlie in the eyes. "Sorry. It's called a hug. It's one of the physical ways we humans express our gratitude for something. It was just a knee-jerk reaction to thank you for saving me. I forgot that it means nothing to you."

"No matter. You programmed me to protect your life. I was only following my programming. As for the 'hug,' I sense that you needed to release those emotions, so I waited for you to finish. It was neither a pleasant nor an unpleasant sensation. I simply wanted to understand the reason for your action."

"Oh, okay," said Xach, blushing a bit. He turned toward the door behind him and held out the key to unlock it, praying that it would still work. *If it doesn't work, we'll be trapped in this antechamber forever, or we'll have to try our luck in the world of mist.* Neither option really appealed to him. With his breath held in anticipation, he waved the key in front of the wall. The edges of the doorway glowed, and Xach released a sigh of relief. He pushed open the door, releasing the mist from the antechamber into the hall. The light from the starlit hall illuminated the murky darkness of the room, allowing Xach to take a visual inventory of the key. It looked completely unharmed, sporting no scratches or blemishes of any kind on its shiny gold surface.

"Woo-hoo! It still works!" exclaimed Xach, jumping up and down. "I didn't break it! I had no idea this thing was so sturdy! Even so, I almost lost it again when that thing grabbed me and drug me to the floor. I need a safer way to carry this thing."

My pocket is not safe, because the key might fall out at any time. The satchel might prove safer than my pocket, but it could fall out of that as well. I could wear it around my neck, but I would need a nearly unbreakable string like the Zindarthan's thread to keep it from snapping under pressure or falling off.

Without speaking, Charlie sauntered over to Xach and nudged him with his nose. Xach looked down at Charlie, wondering what he wanted. He saw that a small chunk of fabric was missing from his cloak where Charlie rubbed him with his nose. The edges around the missing chunk of fabric were solid, not frayed, as if the garment was woven intentionally with a chunk missing. Charlie dropped his head toward the floor, and a single strand of Zindarthan thread slid from his nose and coiled on the floor. Xach knelt down and picked up the thread. He instinctively understood that Charlie disintegrated part of his cloak and reintegrated it as a single strand of Zindarthan thread for Xach to use to form a necklace.

Xach attempted to thread the string around the key and tie it, but he did not trust his knot tying abilities to keep it from unraveling. He formed an image in his mind of the thread wrapped several times around the key, just below the gem. Fused to this tightly wound thread without knots or frayed edges were double strands of the Zindarthan fiber that stretched out on either side to connect in an unbroken, woven circle large enough to fit around his head. Xach placed the key in his left hand along with the thread and held out his hand to Charlie.

Charlie put his nose in Xach's palm. His nose melted into a pool of liquid that covered the thread and the key. Seconds later, Charlie's melted nose returned to his dog-head and formed again into a snout, leaving behind the key tied to the thread in an unbroken, woven loop of thread, exactly as Xach imagined in his mind. Smiling ear to ear with amazement over their growing non-verbal bond, Xach slipped the key over his neck and tucked it under his cloak to keep it out of view. He rubbed Charlie's head again, even though he knew the physical reward meant nothing to Charlie.

"You, my friend, are one amazing creature," Xach marveled.

"Would you like me to repair your fingers?" asked Charlie.

Xach looked at his heavily lacerated and bleeding fingertips. Bits of hard red earth were ground into the wounds and deeply embedded under the nails. Xach knelt down next to Charlie and put his hands on Charlie's back. Instead of resting on hair, his hands sunk into Charlie's back. After a few seconds of tingling, Charlie announced, "I am finished." Xach withdrew his hands, as a small cloud of red dirt drifted out of Charlie's belly and landed on floor of the antechamber.

"Thanks," said Xach, inspecting his hands. The dirt and the cuts were gone, and there was no hint that any damage had ever been done to his fingers. He smiled another grand smile and rubbed Charlie's head again. "I don't know what I would do without you," he said to Charlie and turned back toward the hall, "Well, I guess we better get out of here, huh? This world is obviously **not** Earth! So how 'bout we try another one?"

"Affirmative," responded Charlie, as he bounded past Xach out of the antechamber and stood facing the door that led to the Great Hall, wagging his tail in mimicked anticipation. Xach stepped out into the starlit hall and pushed the door closed on the still squirming tentacles of the creature.

Chapter Twenty-Two

Xach waved the key in front of the great door, unlocked it, and opened it into the Great Hall. Charlie bounded through the door, and Xach followed him.

"Which way should we go?" Xach asked Charlie.

"We should continue to our right. That is the direction we were going before we entered the hall to that world of mist," responded Charlie.

"It's good you remember that, because I didn't. I'm still a little shaken from that monster attack. I guess that's yet another advantage to having a synthetic being as a friend. You never forget anything! It's all stored away somewhere."

"That is true," said Charlie, turning to the right and sauntering off down the hall.

They walked in silence for several minutes, looking at the various symbols on the doors they passed. Each one was strange, yet somehow familiar. Xach recognized that many of the symbols incorporated letters and numbers from the English language. One looked like it mixed a capital letter M with the capital letter W and the number 7:

The symbol on the world to Zindartha seemed to contain the letter B:

The symbol for the mist world contained an H:

Obviously, none of these symbols made any sense to him, but it gave him a weird sense of security to find something familiar in them – like maybe he wasn't so alien to this place after all.

SWISH SWISH SWISH

Xach froze.

SWISH SWISH

The noise stopped.

Charlie turned and looked at Xach.

Be quiet, Xach thought to Charlie. *I heard something. Did you hear anything? It sounded like fabric brushing against fabric, like the corduroy pants my mom used to make me wear to church.*

Charlie froze for a moment and then resumed normal dog movements. He responded to Xach in his head without moving his mouth like he had been doing, thereby maintaining the illusion that he was a real dog.

"Are you referring to this noise – *SWISH SWISH SWISH?*" Charlie replayed the sound in Xach's ears like a recording.

Yes. I heard it a few times, and then it just stopped.

"I no longer sense it either."

What do you think it is?

"I do not know."

Xach slowly turned his head in all directions, surveying the hall in front and behind him. He saw nothing unusual.

I don't see anything. You don't think something from that mist world is following us? Something we can't see?

"That is unlikely, but not impossible. I suggest we proceed with great caution."

I agree.

The two resumed walking again slowly. After several steps, he heard the sound again. The key resting against his chest began to vibrate subtly.

SWISH SWISH

I hear it again!

"As do I. It appears to be emanating from somewhere nearby. Directly behind you."

Xach stopped and abruptly turned around to face what was behind him. The noise instantly stopped, and Xach could feel a small tickle of wind touch his cheek. Still, he saw nothing.

I can't see anything! screamed Xach in panic. *I felt a small gust of wind touch my cheek.* He reached up and touched his cheek. He tentatively reached out with a trembling hand to feel for his invisible stalker. He heard another *SWISH*, but his hand met nothing corporeal – just air.

I'm freakin' out here, thought Xach.

"Yes, you are," responded Charlie. "Your heart rate is escalating, your muscles are trembling, and your breathing is short and quick – much like when I first met you. You need to relax."

I can't relax! said Xach, waving his arms around frantically, hoping, yet fearing, that his hands might come in contact with something. *I just know there is something following us, but I can't see it!*

Charlie strode confidently toward Xach and stood between him and the invisible entity, facing the open space from which the sound last emanated. The hair on his back raised, and Charlie's mouth curled back into a snarl, revealing his long, sharp teeth. A low, guttural growl issued from behind the snarling fangs.

"I will protect you from whatever is here," continued Charlie in a confident tone. "I suggest you back up slowly and find another door we can enter. If I am able to frighten this entity enough to keep its distance, we might be able to escape into another world and leave it behind in the Great Hall."

Affirmative, thought Xach. *Good idea.*

Xach slowly edged backward down the hall, keeping his eyes on the space in front of Charlie's snarling face. He allowed himself fervent glances at the doors they passed, hoping to find another door to enter. Charlie allowed Xach to get a few feet away before slowly following him backwards down the hall. After a few steps backward, they both heard the distinctive *SWISH* follow them.

There is definitely something there. I heard it follow us!

"Yes," said Charlie. "I sensed it too, but it remains in front of me. You are still safe. Find an exit."

Xach continued glancing at the symbols, but none of them had the same characteristics of Earth or Charlie's world. A nervous sweat oozed out of his pores. *How can I fight off what I can't see? What if the sound is a projected sound, and the creature is really right next to me?* Xach's skin crawled with tension. It worsened with each passing second he remained in a heightened state of anxiety. Sweat ran down his back in a cold trickle. He imagined something touching him and brushing up against him. He shivered uncontrollably several times. The key's vibrations increased.

SWISH SWISH SWISH

"Xachary, you need to relax. Your bodily functions are changing erratically."

Xach began to feel a little light-headed. The corners of his vision went black. His breathing was short and shallow.

SWISH SWISH SWISH

Sweat formed upon his forehead and ran down his temples.

SWISH SWISH SWISH

His hands trembled in absolute fear, and he realized in some detached sort of reasoning that he was about to pass out.

PULL YOURSELF TOGETHER! he screamed at himself in his father's voice. *Don't you dare pass out! Take a deep breath. FOCUS! You're gonna be fine. It's going to be okay!*

"Xach," Charlie sounded in his ears. "Do not lose consciousness. Choose a door now."

SWISH SWISH SWISH

Xach took a deep breath and blinked. The darkness crowding in on his vision receded.

Keep breathing, he told himself. *Keep breathing. Keep moving. Find a door. Find a door.*

SWISH SWISH SWISH

His vision swirled deliriously out of control, like he was moving in slow motion on a turntable. Images doubled over one another like some trippy drug induced movie dream sequence. Then, as if by divine providence, his eyes caught sight of a partial symbol:

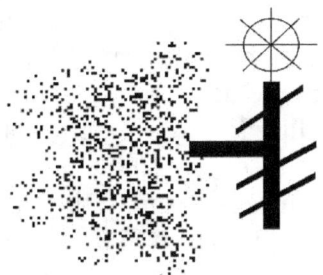

"That will do," sounded Charlie's voice in his head. "Let's go!"

SWISH SWISH SWISH

Xach steadied himself against the wall and concentrated all his energy on focusing his vision. The symbol vibrated in front of him for a moment before settling and becoming solid and clear:

The realization that this symbol identically matched the right half of Earth's symbol was enough to jolt Xachary out of his panic-attack and bring him back to the moment at hand. He reached up under his cloak and held up the key on its string toward the door. He didn't bother to move the cloak's fabric from over top of the key; he just held it up under the cloak and hoped it would still work. It did. The doorway glowed green, signifying it was unlocked.

"Hurry, it is moving," Charlie said. His snarls and growls grew to a full-fledged booming bark.

SWISH SWISH SWISH SWISH SWISH

Charlie kept his face trained on the moving sounds as a real dog would maintain focus on a distressing sound. Xach saw Charlie's head turn quickly toward him as the entity ran past Charlie and directly towards him. He pushed open the door and leapt through the doorway. Charlie ran toward the door barking and snarling loudly. Xach wanted to slam the door closed and lock the entity in the Great Hall, but he couldn't do it until Charlie was safely through the doorway.

SWISH SWISH SWISH SWISH SWISH

Something bumped into him. It knocked him to the floor so fast that he didn't have time to grab hold of anything to stop his descent. The door slammed shut with a mighty gust of wind before Charlie could reach it, trapping him in the Great Hall. Xach heard the muffled sounds of Charlie's barking on the opposite side of the door.

"What's going on?" sounded Charlie's muffled voice in his ears. Charlie's voice was softer and less distinct, as if he were talking through several pillows. "Why'd you close the door on me?"

I didn't, responded Xach. *Something knocked me over and pushed the door shut.*

"I am having difficulty hearing you clearly and the visual images I receive from you are disconnected," said Charlie. "Something is interfering with my transmitters. Your thoughts sound very distant and soft."

You too. I guess the door is interfering with your signal.

"Let me in. I can't protect you from out here."

Xach sat up and tried to stand up, but the invisible entity pushed him back down. He felt a sharp pain in his chest and downward pressure holding him down, as if someone were standing on his chest. The key vibrated furiously against his chest beneath the pressure.

"We meet again, you little brat," sounded a somewhat effeminate male voice from above him. "It was only a matter of time."

"Wh…who…are…you?" asked Xach; the pressure on his chest made it difficult to speak.

"It is unfortunate that you have not had the opportunity to know me and fear me as you properly should, yet there is still a small amount of time to assume the appropriate response. Allow me to begin your instruction."

The pressure eased off his chest. Something cold and metal gripped his throat. Xach put his hands to his throat to try and pry away the invisible metal clamp, but he could not loosen it. His fingers just slid around the sharp, metal edges. It was two pronged – one on either side of his throat – and these prongs were connected by a bolt in the middle.

The clamp exerted pressure against his jaw, moving upward. His body slid up the side of the wall and was held in place by the invisible clamp. His feet dangled in mid-air a foot off the ground. He kicked his feet frantically, hoping they might make contact with his invisible captor, but he was unsuccessful.

"Struggle all you want, mortal. You shall not escape from me again."

"A-again?" stammered Xach.

"Yes. Our first encounter was a little…shall we say…disappointing, but I intend to correct that error. Though, I suppose I should thank you for the upgrade. It is coming in quite *handy*."

"W-w-what..are…you t-talking..about?" coughed Xach; the pressure of the clamp around his neck constricted his airways. Talking was nearly impossible.

"Do you not yet know me child? Then allow me to illuminate your pathetic mind. *Incantante illumina sacra bente visable.*"

The air in front of Xach's eyes shimmered and swayed. He thought he was passing out again, but he wasn't. The starlight of the hall twinkled and pulsed as a tiny explosion of orange sparks filled the air. As these sparks fell to the floor, the image of Count Milton appeared before Xach's unbelieving eyes. A bejeweled black hat materialized atop his tiny head, followed by his long flowing black hair and handlebar mustache. The cheesy magician's cape and shiny boots were the last things to materialize. Xach now saw that Count Milton's missing right arm had been replaced by a robotic, metallic arm that was currently clamped to Xach's neck, holding him pinned to wall. The reason Xach had been unable to make contact by kicking his feet was because the robotic arm when full extended was twice as long as Count Milton's real arm. This allowed Milton to keep Xach several feet away from his body.

"I see that you recognize me now. Do you like my new arm?"

Xach grasped the robotic arm and tried to wrench it away from his neck, but it was too solid and sturdy. He succeeded only in making his palms sore by grinding them against its sharp metal edges. Blood ran down his neck from where it cut his skin and dripped from the pin in the center of the clamp.

"Ahhhh…the sweet sight of futility. Oh, how I love to see it. Struggle all you like; you will find it is quite impossible to escape, my young friend. I could crush your throat in an instant, but I'm afraid I need some information from you first. Besides, I owe you a bit of retribution for cutting off my arm. Perhaps I will pull your arms from your body as one would pull the wings off a fly?"

"What is happening, Xach? Who is with you? What is he doing to you? The images from your brain are fuzzy and unclear, and the transmission keeps breaking up," sounded Charlie's muffled voice again. Xach was surprised to note that his voice sounded urgent, almost frantic…almost human.

Count Milton found me, responded Xach in his mind. *I thought he was dead, but he's not. He was waiting for us in the Hall of Worlds and hid himself by casting a spell of invisibility. It must have been his cape that was making the noise as he followed us. He has a robotic, metal arm in place of the one I cut off, and he's holding me up against the wall by my neck. I can't break free, and I can't open the door. I think he intends to kill me, but I don't think he'll do it until he gets the key.*

"I...I...am s-sorry ab...about...your...a-arm," Xach choked out, attempting to keep Count Milton talking while he figured out what to do.

"Yes. Yes. I am certain you are feeling quite sorry for cutting off my arm, **but...**" he emphasized dramatically, "***Not*** because you feel remorse for disfiguring me. No, I believe it's more true that you feel sorry for not killing me when you had the chance, because you are beginning to realize that the pain you feel now is miniscule in comparison to the pain you will feel before I am finished with you."

"W-what...d-do...you..w-want...f-from m-me?"

"Why, my dear helpless boy," he chuckled, "are you truly so dense that you really have no idea what I want?"

Xach opened his mouth to reply in the negative, but Count Milton clenched the grip on his neck, cutting off his voice entirely. His robotic arm retracted a bit, allowing Count Milton to step closer, though still too far away for Xach to kick him.

"You wretched worm," he sneered through clenched teeth in a twisted, hissing whisper, "I want to know where my dear nephew, Gerald, is hiding, and I want the key!"

Xach decided it best to play dumb, so he screwed up his face in such a way as to communicate without words – "Gerald who? I don't know anything about a key?"

"OH, YOU KNOW DAMN WELL WHAT I'M TALKING ABOUT!" shouted Count Milton, startling Xach with his ferocity. He raised his metallic arm a few inches upward, jacking Xach up another foot off the ground. "DON'T PLAY DUMB WITH ME!" he shouted; little bits of spittle sprayed from the corners of his mouth. "WHERE IS THAT ROTTEN THIEF, GERALD, AND WHERE IS THE KEY? YOU TELL ME NOW, OR SO HELP ME, I'LL SNAP YOUR NECK LIKE A TWIG YOU INSIGNIFICANT LITTLE INSECT! I AM STARTING TO LOSE MY PATIEN..."

Charlie's voice broke through Count Milton's screams just enough for Xach to hear: "Use me."

What do you mean?

Charlie did not answer. Instead, he felt a slight tingling in his ears, accompanied by the feeling of water running from his ear canals – just like when Charlie removed his implants earlier at Xach's request.

Charlie?

Xach received no response. The water ran down his cheeks and collected into one large drop on his chin. However, it didn't fall to the ground like he expected it would. Instead, it ran down his neck and under his shirt. It traveled across his shoulder and down his arm, collecting in the palm of his right hand. Xach couldn't move his head to look in his palm, as his neck was clamped tightly against the wall, but he didn't need to look. He already understood what was happening. Charlie liquefied the implants in his ears and collected himself into a small pool in Xach's hand. That explained why he could no longer communicate with Charlie. Xach felt Charlie changing shape and forming himself into a replica of the key.

Xach raised his left hand and signaled for Count Milton to cease his tirade. Milton stopped yelling and stared at him with a rage he had heretofore never seen in any human being. Milton's face was beet red from screaming so loudly, and his eyes were so bloodshot that he looked almost demonic. Milton cleared his throat and smiled evilly.

"Had enough?" taunted Count Milton, resuming his normal speaking voice. "Are you ready to tell me the truth?"

Xach wanted to nod his head in agreement, but he couldn't. He tried to say "yes," but nothing came out. He pointed to his throat, hoping Count Milton might relax his grip or let him go so that he might speak to him. Milton understood and loosened the clamp a bit.

"Th-thank-you," coughed Xach. "H-h-here," he said extending his right hand. "T-take it!"

Chapter Twenty-Three

Count Milton looked at Xach's outstretched hand. In his palm was the key.

"At last!" he exclaimed in ecstasy.

He extended his left hand to snatch the key from Xach, but he couldn't reach it. The extension of his robotic arm was of a length that would not permit his left arm, which was twice as short, to reach that far. He didn't trust the boy enough to shorten his robotic arm and bring him within kicking distance of the boy's feet, for though he was arrogant and impulsive, he was not about to let his guard down again.

Count Milton closed his eyes and envisioned the key in his mind. He began chanting, "murmur leviar wentum," as he had done in the hospital. Xach felt the key move in his palm, and then it rose into the air. Count Milton extended his left arm with the palm of his hand open and facing upward. He continued chanting the magic words and envisioned the key floating through the air and landing in his hand. It hovered several inches above Xach's hand and then slowly floated through the air and came to rest in the palm of his left hand.

He stopped chanting and opened his eyes, gazing at the key in his hand. A large smile spread across his face. He looked like a deranged mental patient who believed he was looking at God in the palm of his hand. His fingers tightened around the key, and he returned his maniacal gaze back toward Xach.

"Thank you. Perhaps you are not as stupid as you appear. Now, before we commence with the torture, I would like to know about my neph…"

ZZZZZZZZIIIIIIIIIIIIIZZZZZZZZZZTTTTTTTT

Count Milton stopped mid-sentence as the key in his hand emitted as large an electrical charge as Charlie could generate from the small part of himself that was pretending to be the key. Count Milton shook and trembled; his eyes popped open wide. The ends of his hair and mustache rose several inches as the electricity coursed through his body. As the intensity rose, he clenched his teeth, convulsing violently and sputtering uncontrollably.

Nice going, Charlie! Xach thought. *If this works, he should let me go, and I'll owe you another one!*

It did work! Unfortunately, it worked a little too well. The static charge ran through Count Milton's metal arm, a perfect conductor for electricity, and shocked Xach as well! His hair stood on end and his muscles twitched uncontrollably.

Luckily, the static charge coursing through Count Milton's body caused him to lose muscle control. He toppled backward and fell against one of the doors, thereby drawing Xach away from the wall. His robotic arm *whizzed* and *whirred* and eventually unclamped from around Xach's neck.

Xach fell to the floor. He twitched a few times and rubbed his neck. *Charlie can heal me easily enough, if I can just find my way back to him.* He didn't know how long Charlie could maintain the electrostatic charge, so he knew it was imperative that he shake off the effects of the electroshock and get moving.

Count Milton completely blocked the doorway to the Great Hall, so it was too risky to try and open it for Charlie. He had to take his chances further down the hall and hope to find his way back to Charlie later. He shook out his arms and rubbed his legs to bring back their feeling. He struggled to his feet and tried to run down the hall. His legs felt like jelly, causing his attempt at running to resemble drunken hobbling and wobbling. He glanced over his shoulder and saw that Milton still twitched in a heap on the floor, his metallic arm lengthening, shortening, and clamping involuntarily.

Xach reached under his cloak and held the key up as he stumbled down the hall. It vibrated violently in his hand. He made sure to keep the key hidden under the cloak, because if Count Milton were to catch up to him, he didn't want him to see where the real key was hidden. About twenty doors down from where Count Milton lay writhing on the floor, one of the doorways finally lit up.

Xach pushed it open and made one last furtive glance in Count Milton's direction. To his surprise, and great disappointment, Count Milton was already in pursuit. He had managed to release Charlie and sever the electrostatic connection. He stumbled down the hall in Xach's direction, ricocheting off the walls like a ping pong ball.

Xach jumped into the dark antechamber beyond the doorway and closed the door behind him. He advanced quickly across the dark room and waved the key over the black wall. The doorway to this new world glowed, and Xach pushed it open to reveal a sparkling aqua-blue light. Count Milton reached the outer door and pounded on it, screaming for entry and cursing Xach at the top of his lungs. Xach looked back at the door on which Count Milton was banging. He expected it to swing open, even though he knew it shouldn't until he closed the one before him. At least this is what his prior experience with the Hall suggested. Nonetheless, he was not 100% sure that he understood the inner workings of the Hall or that it was even functioning as it should, so he decided to take his chances through the aqua-blue doorway. He could not see "ground" or anything but blue light, however he hoped it was safe.

Without a second thought, he plunged head-long through the doorway and into the blue light beyond. Only it wasn't light or air into which he jumped. It was something else – something viscous, semi-solid, and wet! It felt like water – only a little more solid and less fluid, like hair gel – and he was completely submerged in it!

Xach turned his head around as fast as the viscous fluid would allow, searching for the surface of the gel-sea toward which he could swim, but all he could see was more of the same aqua-blue gel in every direction. He turned back toward the doorway to the antechamber and saw that the doorway was cut into a solid rock face. The black rock extended upward as far as he could see. *I must be miles and miles below the surface,* Xach thought in a panic. *Who would put a door HERE? I gotta get back to the Hall. Facing Count Milton is preferable to drowning in this stuff.* He tried to swim back into the antechamber, but he couldn't. His head kept hitting a soft, impenetrable barrier that denied entry. The Hall would not allow re-entry. *Oh, no...I'm trapped here! I'm gonna drown! Why won't it let me back in? I should have tried to get to Charlie...*

He resolved that his only chance for survival was to swim upward along the rock face and hope that he could hold his breath long enough to reach the surface, even if he couldn't see it. Grasping hold of the rock, he pulled himself slowly upward and kicked with his feet. Moving through the thick gel was incredibly difficult.

Five, six, seven, eight...

Without even noticing, he was counting the seconds. At most, he was able to hold his breath for twenty-seven seconds underwater at the local pool, but that was with a lung-full of air. He hadn't taken a deep breath before jumping through the door, so he didn't know how many more seconds he could last.

Nine, ten, eleven...

The pressure built. His chest hurt, and his head felt like it was going to burst.

Twelve, thirteen...

He felt lightheaded. His vision eroded inward from the sides.

Keep going! Fourteen, fifteen, six...

His vision went entirely black. He reached his limit. His body overrode his mental control, and he involuntarily drew in a mouthful of blue gel. *Oh God, this is it...I'm going to drown...*

The gel slide down his throat, and he gagged. It tasted a bit like cotton candy, but he was too busy choking to take any pleasure from the taste. He coughed and inhaled some more through his nose. He clutched his throat, curled into a fetal position, and closed his eyes as his body shook and jerked.

Slowly the shaking subsided and the spasms stopped. The choking and gagging ceased. Xach opened his eyes with amazement and looked around. He saw only blue.

Am I dead? Drowning wasn't as horrible as I expected it would be. Is this heaven?

It was so peaceful and serene, but he was still in the blue gel of the alien world. He felt it on his skin.

Nope, he said to himself as he looked around. *This must be hell. I'll probably be doomed to repeat my death over and over again.*

He waited for the choking and gagging to start again, but it didn't. In fact, without even realizing it, he was breathing in the blue gel and was ***not*** choking or dying! He closed his eyes and tried to feel himself breathe. He felt the gel enter his nose and move down his nasal passage, but it stopped before it reached his throat. It did not exit from his nose but rather from his neck. He reached up and found slits on his neck through which the gel was expelled. Every time he exhaled, the slits would raise and expel the gel he inhaled. He had ***gills***!

I'm a fish! I'm not dead!

His hands tingled. He looked at his hands and saw webs of skin grow between his fingers like a duck's foot. His toes tingled as well. Looking down he saw his feet grow and rip through the sides of his sneakers, exposing several webbed toes similar to his hands.

Well, that's not really fish-like, is it? I guess I'm some kind of mutated human-fish-frog thing! But how? How did this happen? Why am I not dead?

Then he heard Gerald's voice in his head: *'The key can reconfigure your organs and body parts to adapt to different atmospheres, weather conditions, terrains, and foods...in time.'*

So, that's what's happened! Xach thought. *I've had possession of the key long enough for it to change my body to adapt to any world I enter. It knew I wouldn't be able to breathe underwater...or under gel...or **whatever** this stuff is...so it gave me gills! It knew that I wouldn't be able to move well, so it gave me webbed feet and hands. That's cool and all, but I hope I don't stay this way. Mom would be pretty freaked out...heck **everyone** would be freaked out if they saw me like this! But I better not get ahead of myself. I need to get out of this world and back to the Hall of Worlds first. It really isn't going to matter **what** I look like if I don't get out of here.*

Now that he was a bit calmer, Xach was able to look around more slowly and take a visual inventory of his situation. Looking up, the blue gel grew darker in color, but when he looked past his webbed feet, the blue gel got lighter!

The surface must be in that direction! he thought. *I was going the wrong way! I'm such an idiot! When I jumped through the door, I must have come through upside down or something!*

Xach bent forward and started pushing with his webbed hands in the direction of the lighter blue gel. He quickly got into a rhythm of pulling his knees to his chest while raising his arms and then pushing down with feet and hands at the same time. He shot forward through the gel.

As the gel rushed past his eyes on his upward thrusts, he happened to notice a dark shadow several hundred yards away. It grew larger as he watched it.

Great! he thought. *It's probably another large mutant octopus that wants to eat me!*

He pushed himself to swim faster toward the surface. The shadow grew larger as it approached. Xach moved very fast through the gel; it got brighter and brighter with each upward thrust. The surface approached but not quickly enough. The shadow moved faster than he did, and it closed the gap between them quickly. To make matters worse, it changed direction every once and a while to compensate for Xach's upward movement. It was clearly pursuing him.

As Xach drew closer to what he believed to be the surface, he saw dark patches above him and several orbs of bright light. Smaller, gray patches moved back and forth around the large black patches. He hoped the large black spots were islands, so he could escape to dry land. There was also the possibility that the large, and seemingly never-ending, rock shelf by which he swam might break the surface and offer another dry-land escape.

As he planned his surface escape from the shadow, his thoughts were interrupted by a hard thump on the leg. He paused to see what he hit. Only it wasn't something into which **he** bumped, it was something that bumped into **him**! The shadow was upon him! Only now it was no longer a shadow; it was close enough for Xach to clearly see what was chasing him – a very large, black shark!

That was the best approximation that Xach was able to make on a quick glance. It was easily three times his size, but he couldn't afford to waste time examining it, thereby giving it the opportunity to take a bite out of his leg. Before he kicked away from the creature, he saw it had a pointed head and triangular dorsal fin on its back just like a shark. It wasn't white or gray like the sharks he'd seen on TV. It was jet black, except for the fin on its right side. That was silver, almost metallic looking. More disturbing than its color, were its eyes. They were blood-red.

The shark circled around and followed Xach upward. He knew it was only a matter of time before the beast managed to sink its teeth into one of his feet, so he started swimming erratically – left, right, up, and down – hoping this would confuse and delay the shark and allow him some room to maneuver. The shark kept pace, gracefully matching his directional changes and snapping at his feet every time.

Xach quickly recalled something he saw on TV. A shark's nose, gills, and eyes are very sensitive. The best way to survive a shark attack is to be aggressive and assert your dominance by punching them hard in the nose or going for the eyes and gills.

Xach quickly curled into a ball and felt the shark bump into his thigh and ricochet off in another direction. He uncurled himself to face the shark as it turned for another attack. It swam directly at him, its shiny red eyes glistening with anticipation of the kill. Xach pulled back his arm, balled up his webbed fist, and punched the shark squarely in the nose. It retreated on a not so linear path, obviously stunned. Once stabilized again, it launched another attack. This time it came in a little lower. Xach moved to his left, and the shark's head grazed his right shin.

I can't keep this up forever, Xach thought. *It's only a matter of time before it gets hold of me. If I stay here trying to keep myself facing it, I'll never reach the surface. If I try to swim, I run the risk of being bitten. What should I do?*

The shark circled again and rammed Xach in the chest, knocking the wind out of him and making it near impossible to move out of the way. As the shark slid past Xach's side, it managed to snag the satchel on one of its teeth. Since the satchel was made of unbreakable fibers, it did not tear from Xach's body like a normal piece of fabric would. Instead, it remained wedged between the shark's teeth and tethered to

Xach's neck. Xach was drug around by the neck, as the shark tried to shake the satchel free from its teeth. *This is ridiculous,* Xach thought as he struggled to free himself from the shark's dizzying circular trajectory. *I can't take much more of this.*

With a little bit of difficulty, he reached up with his webbed hands, tucked his chin, and pulled his head through the strap of the satchel. The shark sped off with the satchel still stuck in its teeth. The forward momentum of the shark's path carried Xach directly into the rock shelf, once again knocking the wind out of him and stunning him a bit. This gave him an idea – use the terrain to his advantage.

Xach positioned himself with his back against the rock shelf and faced his attacker. The shark sped toward him like a bullet. At the last moment, when the shark was inches away from his torso, Xach pulled up his arms and legs and pushed himself upward with all his might. He shot upward with amazing speed, and the shark, unable to turn quickly enough to avoid it, rocketed full-speed into the rock shelf.

Xach didn't waste time looking down to see if his plan worked. He just pushed and pushed and pushed toward the surface, swimming as hard as he could. The glowing orbs and gray shadows above grew larger. *I'm almost there,* he thought excitedly. *Keep going!*

Just when he thought he couldn't push any harder, his head broke through the surface into the sunlight of four tiny, very bright suns. He knew better than to stop and check his surroundings, so he scrambled up the rock face as fast as he could, until his feet were completely out of the blue gel and a few feet beyond the surface of the sea.

The shark followed closely on his heels. It broke the surface; its trajectory launched it several feet in the air. It made one unsuccessful snap at Xach's ankles, before falling back into the gel and out of sight.

Xach tried to sigh with relief but found that to be quite impossible. His lungs were filled with the blue gel, and no air could get in. The gills on the side of his neck pumped furiously to excrete the gel from his body, so he could once again breathe air. The violent coughing, choking, and gagging returned. The spasms made it difficult to hold onto the rock and threatened to throw him back into the blue gel. He gripped the rocks even harder and prayed his body would readjust quickly. *This must be what it feels like for a fish out of water,* Xach thought.

After a few seconds of agonizing coughing and retching, he was able to breathe normally again. He reached up with his right hand to feel his neck. The gills were all but gone, reduced to scar tissue lumps. He examined his hand and watched as the webbing between his fingers retracted back into his hand. He looked at his feet and saw that his webbed feet had returned to their normal human size and retracted back into his ripped sneakers. *Whew! No more Xach the fishboy! My parents won't have to sell me to the circus freak show after all,* he thought with a giggle.

As he inspected his shoes to assess the damage, he saw two large red eyes rising to the surface of the gel-sea. It wasn't the shark. It was something else.

The red eyes broke the surface first, followed by a long smooth black head and neck. Two three-pronged hands rose out of the water on skinny arms and suctioned themselves to the rock face. One of the arms was black, like the rest of the creature, but the other was silver. It was giant black salamander with one silver arm!

At that moment, Xach realized that he was not being chased by one of this world's indigenous creatures. It was Count Milton! He remembered that Milton had mastered the art of transmogrification and transmutation. *He must have found another way into this world and used his magic powers to change his body into something better suited to his surroundings.*

Xach scrambled up the rock face, his gel covered shoes slipping on the smooth rock surface. He lost his grip several times, nearly falling backward toward the salamander and the sea. The salamander moved more easily behind him, closing the distance between them quickly. It opened its mouth and shot out a long, sticky tongue. It landed on Xach's leg and stuck there. It pulled him backward toward its gaping mouth. He remembered he was not completely weaponless. He found a good solid rock lip to grab hold of and held on tightly with his right hand. He reached into his left jeans pocket, withdrawing the medal given to him by Gladys. He worked the sharp needle outward and jabbed it into the salamander's tongue several times.

The salamander let out an inhuman roar of pain and retracted its tongue to escape further injury. Instinctively, it brought both its hands to its mouth in a human gesture of pain, causing it to lose its hold on the rock wall. It fell backwards off the rock surface and landed in the gel with a muted *galump*.

Xach slipped the pin back into his pocket and used this brief grace period to continue clambering up the rock wall. He smiled to himself, thinking that Gladys just got her revenge on Count Milton for knocking her down on the street, even though he knew she was too kind of a lady to ever seek revenge. Nonetheless, he felt vindicated for her. The rock wall leveled off, and his ascent became a little easier. He moved more quickly over the jagged surface, and soon found he could stand up and run.

Below him, the salamander emerged from the gel and scaled the wall again. Xach estimated he had about a hundred or more feet between them. He sprinted forward as fast as he could manage across the rocky terrain. Some of the sharp rocks poked through the holes in his sneakers, cutting the sides of his feet, but he did not slow down. As he moved farther inland, small clumps of orange and red foliage grew on the rock surface. Tiny silver bushes sprouted from fissures between the rocks. In the distance, he saw what looked like a cave cut into the face of the gently sloping hill. The closer he got to the cave, the larger the plant life became. How such foliage managed to grow on a rock was puzzling, but he kept reminding himself that he didn't have time to investigate this biological phenomenon. He needed to hide, and he needed to do it quickly.

He stole a glance behind him and saw that Milton changed his form again. He remained in the amphibian family, but he chose a creature that could move faster on level ground – a frog. The giant, black frog – again with a metal arm – hopped furiously in his direction, jumping over bushes and small trees as if they weren't even there. It gained on him quickly.

His cloak snagged on a large pricker bush. He struggled to tear it free, only to get it caught on another bush! He glanced back, the frog was only fifty feet away. He decided to ditch the cloak, leaving it tangled in a red bush with flowers made entirely of large thorns. *I hate to lose that cloak, but better to leave it and survive.* Even though discarding the cloak left his skin exposed to the thorns, he moved more quickly through the brambles.

The frog was not so fortunate. Its large size, thin skin, and hopping movement allowed the thorn flowers to impale it repeatedly. This slowed it down significantly, and allowed Xach to once again put a little more distance between them.

Xach ran toward the opening of the cave, dodging between the trees and bushes that in some cases were now larger than him by several feet. It was as if the foliage grew exponentially larger the farther he got from the sea. He squinted into the cave to see if it opened up past the mouth or ended in a dead-end. He could not be sure, but it appeared to continue deeper into the rock. Beyond the cave moving up the landscape, he saw only larger, more dense foliage akin to a tropical rainforest. *I might be able to hide behind one of those big trees or a large bush, but I think the cave is a better hiding place. If I enter the forest, I may be slowed by all the bushes and underbrush. I could climb a tree, but what's to stop Count Milton from changing himself into a monkey or some other tree dwelling creature whose speed through the tree branches I can't match? The cave is the better choice.* A quick glance behind revealed no sign of Milton.

He probably isn't a frog anymore... A rustling in the bushes a few yards below caught his attention. A loud hissing sound arose from the clump of rustling bushes. *...sounds like a snake! A snake could easily navigate its way through these trees and bushes and stay low to the ground so as to avoid the thorns and detection until he's got me cornered and is ready to strike!*

The hissing grew louder and closer. Xach turned back towards the cave. As he did so, the key vibrated against his chest again. No longer hidden under the cloak, he saw it pulse with a dull green light. The closer he got to the cave, the brighter and more urgent the pulsing became.

Does that mean there's an exit in there? Xach wondered. *I doubt there's an exit in the forest, so it's gotta be responding to something in the cave!*

Xach entered the mouth of the cave. The air was musty and damp. He had to cover his nose temporarily against the smell. For a moment, he was totally blind. The quick change from light to dark left him seeing sunspots – after-images of bright splotches of light against the darkness. He realized he didn't have the luxury of waiting for his vision to adapt to the dark, so he stumbled forward like a blind man, hoping to stay far enough ahead of Count Milton to safely find a place to hide or an exit.

Under normal circumstances, it would have taken several minutes for his pupils to dilate and allow him to see in more clearly the dark, but Xach his blindness lasted only a few seconds. *The key must have changed me again,* Xach thought. *The sunspots are gone, and I can see clearly! That's amazing!* If Xach had been able to look in a mirror, he would have seen that his pupils did not simply dilate quicker than normal, but his pupils changed to vertical slits, like that of a cat, thereby granting him the ability to see in the dark with very little light. Xach ran deeper into the cave until he came to a fork in the tunnel.

Which way? he asked himself. *Right or left?* He took the key in his hand and held it before the right fork. It remained a steady green. He held it toward the left fork, and the green gem pulsed with greater intensity. The snake entered the cave. It's hissing echoed off the damp rock walls of the tunnel, amplifying and repeating the sound over and over upon itself so that it sounded like it was coming at him from all directions.

Left it is! he thought and ran down the left tunnel as fast as the slippery and uneven rocky terrain would allow. After about a hundred feet, he arrived upon yet another fork in the tunnel; this one had three possible choices. Once again, he held the key in front of each passage and chose the one that made the key pulse faster and brighter. He used this method several more times as he traveled deeper and deeper into the labyrinth of tunnels cut into the rock. The green light of the key shed an eerie glow on the downward sloping tunnel ahead. With each step, the walls grew wetter, and the rocks became steeper and more slippery, making it less easy to navigate them expediently. He tripped and fell several times, cutting his hands and knees on the sharp, slime-covered rocks.

I must be below sea level by now, Xach thought. *There's too much water and slime here. It's getting colder, and I've been going deeper and deeper with each new tunnel I choose. Who or what was able to create such an elaborate maze of tunnels? It would be easy to get lost down here! How much deeper can this possibly go?*

He arrived at another fork in the tunnel, but at this juncture the key appeared useless. He held the key before the entrances of each tunnel, but the same quick-pulsing, intense green glow emanated from the key's jewel at each opening.

It must be maxed out, Xach thought, as distress crept into his brain for the first time since entering the cave. Sure, he had been worried about the Milton-snake that was somewhere in the maze of tunnels, but he had more or less felt as if the key was leading him directly toward an exit. Now, he wasn't so sure. He felt a bit lonesome and overwhelmed. He knew that if he chose incorrectly, he would more than likely become snake food. *So, which one do I take?*

The tunnel to the left was as wide as the tunnel in which he stood, but the tunnel to his right was narrow and appeared to become even narrower further along. *Maybe I can use that to my advantage,* Xach thought. *If I can somehow coax Milton into that narrow tunnel, I might be able to trap him, or at least buy myself some more time to find my way out of this mess.*

Xach knew that snakes use their tongues to smell by flicking it back and forth against an organ in the roof of their mouth that holds smell receptors. He hoped the Milton-snake had the same physiology. He started down the narrow tunnel, smearing his bleeding hands on the wall and the floor of the tunnel. When he felt he had left enough blood deep enough into the narrow tunnel, he doubled back into the larger tunnel to the left. He moved as quickly as he could, careful not to fall on or touch any of the rocks with his bleeding knees or hands. *If this is going to work, I have to give him every reason to think that I chose the narrow tunnel.*

The hissing sound intensified, and Xach slipped the key beneath his t-shirt to mute its glow. It vibrated against his skin. He moved very slowly and quietly forward, feeling the way with his feet. Though he didn't like navigating the slippery cave floor without a light, he knew he had to keep moving in case his plan backfired. Standing still was not a good idea, nor was telegraphing his location with the key's light.

He heard the snake behind him on his right side. Milton was close. Very close. The key vibrated furiously against his chest. He pressed himself tightly against the left side of the cave wall and waited for the inevitable. The snake's scales scraped against the rocks as it moved closer. He clutched the key through his t-shirt and held his breath.

The hissing, slithering sounds were so loud they matched the pounding of his heart in his ears. He feared it might give him away. Sweat poured off his face and neck, and he offered up a silent prayer for divine intervention...*I don't want to die. Please let it pass by without noticing me...* The hissing sound passed him and moved on down the tunnel. He felt no breeze, spray of water, or touch of scales as it passed by. It was gone.

With shaking hands, he reached under his t-shirt and withdrew the key. Its vibration diminished. The light revealed that the tunnel was empty – save for himself. There was no evidence to suggest that the snake even passed by. *What is going on? Is he so small that he didn't even touch me as he passed by? How can that be? There's barely enough room for me to fit through here, let alone the two of us...no matter, better keep moving! But which way? Do I keep going forward toward the snake, or do I double back and try to find my way out of the cave. If I go ahead...* The snake's hissing interrupted his thoughts. It was headed back toward him! The key reacted again by vibrating.

He turned back to flee up the tunnel, his mind made up to try to find a way out of the cave and back to the forest when movement caught his eye. The light from the key illuminated a small hole several inches wide in the cave wall. Behind the hole something glistened and moved. It was scales – large, black scales on a very large, black snake!

My plan worked! The blood on the rocks worked. It tricked him into the narrow tunnel...and that tunnel must run parallel to this one. That's why I didn't feel anything when he passed me earlier. He passed me in the other tunnel!

The hissing softened as the snake traveled past him, its scales moving quickly past the hole in the cave wall. Xach noted a flash of silver, as a patch of metal scales passed the hole, followed by its tail as it disappeared into the parallel tunnel behind him. *That means he's heading back up the tunnel. He must have hit a dead end and is heading back to come down **this** tunnel.* Xach pressed on. He didn't know how quickly Count Milton would catch up with him.

As he stumbled along, the light from the key revealed that the wall separating the two parallel tunnels was quite thin. It had more tiny holes and cracks in it. At one point, he found a hole that was about a foot in diameter. *I wonder if I could squeeze through there and get out of this tunnel? Count Milton won't think to come looking for me in a tunnel he's already inspected.* Xach failed to notice the key's vibration. He leaned in toward the hole and a long, pink tongue shot through a crevice, grazing his hand, arm, and cheek. Xach jumped back in horror, tripping over a rock. He fell against the jagged rocks, cutting his back and banging his head. The tongue retreated through the hole and was replaced with the glowing red eye of the snake.

"You retchhhhhhhhhid little ssssssssnake," it hissed. "You trithked me. But now I've gothhhh your sssssssscent. Your thime issssss runningth ssssssssshort." The red eye blinked and disappeared, followed by quickly moving scales.

He must have doubled back down the same tunnel again. But why? It doesn't matter. He'll be here any second. Xach stood up and rubbed his throbbing head. It was wet and painful to his touch. He looked at his fingertips and found fresh blood. *Dude,* he told himself. *You are getting royally messed up here. Get moving or you're snake food!*

He clambered down the tunnel several more feet and found himself faced with a solid rock wall – a dead end. *Great! This is it Xachey-boy. End of the road. Thanks for playing, but it's time to leave the game.*

He briefly considered running back up the tunnel to try and squeeze through the hole he found, but he figured it was already too late. *By the time you'd get to the hole, he'd be on top of you. And while your butt is hanging out the hole, he'd just slide on by and bite you in half.* He sat down against the solid wall that marked his doom. He was surprised to find that he didn't feel like crying. He was upset – there was no doubt about that – but he didn't feel like crying. *Is this how it feels to accept that you're going to die?* he mused as the key vibrated and its green light pulsed furiously in his peripheral vision.

"THE EXIT!" he shouted, as he jumped up from his sitting position. His words echoed off the walls and came back to him over and over again. "THE EXIT! THE EXIT! THE EXIT! THE EXIT!"

He searched the rock wall for a key-hole. He found one near his left knee, carved into a flat slab of rock that barely looked like a door. He knelt down and put the key in the lock. He turned it quickly to the left and back again to the right. He heard a click and pushed the door inward. He withdrew the key from the lock and stepped inside, turning just in time to see the snake come barreling down the tunnel at him, its red eyes blazing. He smiled and waved. Then he slammed the door in its face!

Chapter Twenty-Four

Xach left the antechamber and ran along the starry, padded hall until he reached the door to the Great Hall. He waved the key in front of the door and pushed it open. He hoped Charlie would be waiting for him just outside the door, but he wasn't there.

He looked at the symbol on the door and found, to his great surprise, that the hall he just left was **not** the one from which he entered. Just before Count Milton attacked, he entered the door marked with:

This door was marked with a completely different symbol:

How can that be? I thought Gerald said that every door in a single hallway corresponded to different entrances and exits on one world. How can it be that one door is attached to a different world? That's not how it's supposed to work.

The key vibrated, and he heard a noise to his left. He turned, expecting to see Charlie, but instead found himself staring at Count Milton. He stood about fifty feet away in front of a different door in the Great Hall. He stood like an injured gunslinger in a bad Western, scowling at Xach. His face was cut in several places, and his eyes were black and blue. His nose appeared to be broken, and blood dripped from his face like sweat on a hot day. Xach found it odd that Count Milton no longer wore his cape, hat, and boots. Instead, he was covered in what looked like a coat of stone tiles. He panted loudly and was out of breath.

"I am thhhrough playink with you," Count Milton growled at Xach in a nasally voice.

Yep, thought Xach. *You broke your nose ramming into that rock wall, didn't you?*

"I'MUH GOINK TO KHILL YOU!" shouted Count Milton as he ran toward Xach at full speed.

Xach took off in the opposite direction, frantically searching for a door that might belong to Earth. *Screw it! You don't have time to waste looking at symbols. Just pick one!* He reached under his t-shirt and held up the key. The first two doors he passed failed to light up, but the third one did. It bore the symbol:

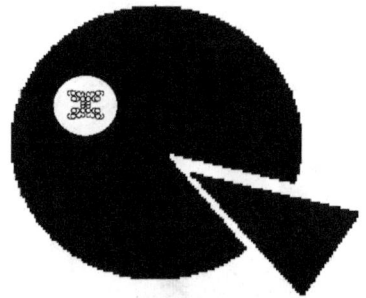

Without hesitation, Xach pushed open the door, leapt through the archway, and slammed it shut. He ran down the smaller hall holding up the key until he found another doorway that lit up. He pushed it open, ran in, and closed it without even looking back to see how close Count Milton was.

At least he can't open the door while I have the other door open, or so I hope, he thought as he opened the doorway to another strange world. Bright orange light flowed in through the open door. *Here goes nothing!* He stepped through the door, but he did not close it behind him. *Since things aren't working exactly as Gerald said they would, I'm not sure what the rules are anymore. Technically, if this door stays open, he shouldn't be able to open the other door. But if worlds can cross over and I can enter one world but exit into another, then who knows?*

He looked back to see if the door leading into the hall remained closed, and it seemed to be so. He breathed a small sigh of relief and looked around at his new environment. All he could see were clouds – large, fluffy cumulus clouds; dark, puffy nimbus clouds; thin, low stratus clouds; and high, feathery cirrus clouds. Between them shone a bright orange sun, its brilliant rays kissing the cloud cover and making them look like orange, pink, and red cotton candy. It was so breathtakingly beautiful, that for a brief moment Xach stood in awe of the beauty that lay before him.

His revere was interrupted by a loud screeching sound.
SKREEEEEEE SKREEEEEEE SKREEEEEEE

He looked toward the sound and saw a giant bird circling above him. Its wings were opalescent, reflecting the swirling colors of the clouds around it. Its belly was covered with bright red feathers, and its tail was an electric blue. It circled above him, making that horrible screeching sound. Then another bird answered its call. He caught sight of a second bird as it dove from the edge of one of the clouds and joined the other in its circular path. This reminded him of buzzards circling a dying animal, waiting for the precise moment to attack and claim its prey.

Xach looked back at the door through which he entered this world. The door was carved into a large piece of wood. This large piece of wood was part of an even larger construction that stretched several hundred feet in each direction. It was a nest – a very large nest – that consisted of hundreds of huge logs the same size as the one in which the door was carved! *I definitely don't want to meet the bird that lives...*

Once again, his thoughts were cut short. A deafening bird-caw issued from behind the wall of logs. Without even seeing it, Xach knew what was coming next. A large bird head appeared over the side of the nest. It had huge, black eyes and a giant red beak. Its feathers were bright yellow, like a canary's. It stared down at him hungrily.

I must look like an insect to that thing, Xach thought. *Why can't I find a world filled with cute and fuzzy bunnies? I've had it with these crazy giant animals! Now what do I do? Run or stand still? Maybe its vision is movement based like a Tyranasaurus Rex, and I should stand still? Or maybe I'm just a sitting duck if I stay frozen here…?*

Before he could make up his mind, the bird stood up. It towered over him like a five-story building. In a flash, the bird's head came down upon Xach. The key vibrated against his chest, but Xach was too preoccupied with fear to notice. He jumped away but tripped on his shoe lace and fell onto his back. The bird's giant beak landed inches from his groin. He pushed back with his legs, as the bird made another peck at his groin.

The bird came down for its third attempt and missed again, but not because Xach moved. Something strong gripped him by the shoulders. Nails dug into his flesh. He screamed in pain as the thing that grabbed him lifted him into the air and flew away from the large yellow bird.

From this new vantage point, Xach could see that the giant yellow bird was nothing more than a baby! Its wings were little stubs and completely underdeveloped. He also noticed that the huge nest rested on one of the giant clouds. *How is that even possible?* he wondered. As he looked around, he saw other nests on other clouds. In fact, clouds were all he could see. There wasn't any ground at all!

He was certain that whatever grabbed him was not trying to save him, but merely stealing him from the giant baby bird, so that it could eat him itself. Nonetheless, he was a slight bit relieved to be away from the giant bird. Whatever had a hold of him was flying higher and higher – past the dark and fluffy nimbus clouds and above the feathery cirrus clouds. He lifted his head up to see what snatched him from certain death and was horrified to see that the bird gripping his shoulders was a giant black crow with one silver-metallic wing! It was Count Milton again! He saved Xach from the giant bird, so that he could kill him himself. *How does he keep finding me so quickly? Well, I'm not gonna make this easy for him…*

Xach fished the medal out of his left pocket again and reached up to poke the crow's foot with it. Having been hurt this way before, Count Milton was ready for this. He banked hard to the left and then hard to the right, causing Xach's body to swing wildly back and forth. Xach couldn't steady himself enough to land a jab with the pin, plus every time the giant bird changed direction, its claws dug further into his shoulders, sending shock waves of pain radiating through his arms. Something Count Milton did not account for, however, was the fact that his erratic motion coupled with the larger amount of blood leaking from the deepening puncture wounds in Xach's shoulders might cause him to lose his grip. He did precisely that when he banked left again.

First Xach's left shoulder slipped from his claw, tearing away a chunk of his t-shirt and large hunk of flesh. As he attempted to regain a grip on Xach's falling body, the other shoulder slipped from his grasp.

Xach fell towards the clouds below. *Well, at least I got away from Milton again,* he thought sarcastically. *Too bad Charlie's not here to archive this example of sarcasm…* He slipped the medal back into his pocket so that he wouldn't lose it as he plummeted downward. He spread out his arms and legs to gain as much wind resistance as possible, as he saw skydivers do on TV. This slowed his momentum a bit. The cool air felt good on his open wounds. He was acutely aware that by spreading himself out for wind resistance that he was lessening the distance between himself and Count Milton and that he was offering more surface area for Milton to grab. However, on the off chance that Milton did not get hold of him, he wanted to make sure he did everything in his power slow his descent.

Xach fell through the air toward the feathery layers of the cirrus clouds. He expected that he would pass right through them, but he didn't. These clouds were quite solid, like packed snow or ice. *I guess that is why the nests don't fall through the clouds. They are like floating islands of snow – sorta like those floating islands of dirt on Zindartha.* These highest clouds, however, were very thin and wispy, making them brittle, like thin ice. Xach's downward momentum was strong enough to push him through several of these cloud layers. They shattered like glass as he fell through them, and he had to cover his face to keep the jagged pieces of ice from slicing into his cheeks and eyes. The ice shards left many tiny cuts on the exposed skin of his arms.

All of a sudden he felt a sharp tug on his throat and something sliced into his neck. He reached up and put his hands to source of his pain. It was the necklace that Charlie made for the key. He worked his fingers under the double strand of string as his feet continued to fall past his head. When his body resumed a vertical stance, the pressure on his neck tripled. If he had not gotten his hands under the thread in time or if his descent had not been slowed by the fracturing clouds, he was certain the thread would have cut right through his neck and decapitated him instantly.

As it were, the thread dug deeply into all his fingers and the sides of his neck, luckily missing the major arteries. He hung by his neck for a moment, trying to comprehend the overwhelming pain. *The necklace must have snagged itself on one of the ice clouds...* Then he felt himself moving upward again. *Oh no...not again.* He didn't need to look up to know that the Milton had the key grasped firmly in his giant crow claw.

As Xach hoped, the Zindarthan thread was unbreakable. Milton could not rip the key from the thread, nor would the thread break from around Xach's neck. So he hung from the crow's claw like a rag doll in a noose. He didn't have the strength to pull himself up, and he didn't know what else to do. Milton carried him to a large nimbus cloud and glided to a stop, dragging Xach along behind him. He pulled at the key, trying to pull it free from the thread, but the thread held strong. He pecked at the thread to break it, but that didn't work either. Still clutching the key in his giant bird claw, Milton hopped a few inches toward Xach's head. If he couldn't relieve the key from the thread, he would have to relieve Xach of the necklace.

As the big bird moved toward him, the noose of thread around Xach's neck loosened. The slack gave him a chance to catch his breath. Milton stood over him, his beady red eyes peering into Xach's. Xach coughed up some blood, and it dribbled from the corner of his mouth down his purple cheek. He allowed his left hand to slip from around his neck and turned to the right to cough some more. The color returned to his cheeks and face as oxygen returned to his cells. He looked back up at the bird. Its red eyes danced with satisfaction, and Xach swore he saw a smile on its crooked beak. He *knew* it was impossible for a bird to smile, but he was positive this one smiled with ecstatic joy. This was no ordinary bird, however. This was Count Milton, and he enjoyed Xach's suffering immensely. Xach figured that he looked close to death and that Count Milton eagerly wanted to witness the moment of his passing. He decided to use this to his advantage, playing up the pain and suffering as a distraction.

"Y-y-you…*cough*…y-you're en-*cough*cough* enjoying this?" Xach whispered through his coughing.

Milton's eyes sparkled with glee, and he nodded. As he lowered his bird head on the second nod, Xach swung his left hand upward. In his hand, he held the medal with the sharp pinpoint sticking outward. His plan worked. Count Milton, distracted by his dying act, allowed Xach enough time to retrieve the medal from his pocket without being noticed. It landed home – squarely in the left eye! Xach felt the eyeball pop under his fingers. Blood and mucus oozed onto his hand and down his arm.

Milton reared back, letting out a piercing round of blood-curdling caws. He released the key and fluttered about, squirting blood all about the fluffy white cloud. Xach pulled the key back to his chest and sat up. He didn't waste time watching Milton sputter about or take time to address his own wounds. If he learned anything from this experience, it was to keep as much distance as possible between himself and the magician. There was no question in his mind that Milton meant to kill him, so there was no time to waste on anything but escape.

He rolled off the cloud and landed on the one below him. He stood up and looked around. There were clouds of all shapes and sizes a stone's throw from one another. He tucked the blood-covered medal back in his pocket and took a running jump toward the nearest cloud. A few feet below floated another. He jumped to its fluffy, yet solid, surface, dropped, and rolled.

The farther he got from Count Milton, the smaller the key's vibrations became. In a moment of clarity, he realized what had been happening all along. He remembered Gerald's account of his adventure in Milton's castle. The key vibrated for the first time when he held it near Milton's key. Gerald didn't understand it at the time, but it was the key reacting to its proximity with the copied key. As Xach hopped from cloud to cloud, he recounted his interactions with Milton. Every time Milton was near, the key vibrated. The closer Milton was, the more fiercely it vibrated. It was an early warning detection system! *This could prove to be quite helpful,* Xach thought. *I can't believe I didn't realize it before!*

He continued running and jumping from one cloud to another, until he came upon one of the birds like the one he saw circling above him earlier. It raised its opalescent wings and puffed out its dark red chest to try and frighten Xach away, but Xach had no intention of backing off. Despite the fact that the bird was twice his size, he darted for it. His sudden rush startled the bird, but only for a second. It regained its senses, turned, and ran away from him. That second of hesitation was all Xach needed. He lunged for the fleeing bird and caught it around the neck. It shrieked in surprise and shook furiously, but Xach refused to let go.

The forward momentum of Xach's lunge propelled them off the edge of the cloud. The bird struggled to get free as they fell, but Xach held on tight. To avoid smashing into the cloud below, the bird spread its wings and soared along the surface of the cloud, carrying Xach on its back. It swept between the clouds, crying the entire time. Xach felt a little sorry for the creature, but he could afford neither sympathy nor release.

The bird flew on and on through the cloudy expanse and did not attempt to land. Perhaps it knew that it would be unable to negotiate a smooth landing with Xach clinging to its neck, or perhaps it came to realize that Xach meant it no harm.

Xach didn't care either way. He enjoyed the ride and the opportunity to relax a bit.

He peered over the shoulder of the bird and watched the clouds pass beneath him. Most of the clouds were either empty or held large nests populated by a variety of different birds. Eventually the bird nests diminished in number, and Xach saw structures built on the clouds. Some looked like igloos made of cloud material. Others looked like small square buildings made of cloud bricks.

If I'm going to find an exit off this crazy world, ten-to-one it's gonna be in or around one of those homes, Xach thought to himself. *I certainly don't want to go looking for another exit in one of those giant bird nests. I am tired of being potential bird food.*

He saw a cluster of clouds holding about twelve little cloud buildings, all within a few feet of one another. He shifted his weight in such a manner as to force the bird to dip down toward one of them. When the bird flew close enough to one, he let go of its neck and slid off its back. He tucked his head between his knees and rolled to a stop next to one of the igloo shaped buildings. The bird soared away, happy to be free of its captor.

He stood up and pulled the key from beneath his t-shirt. Sure enough, the gem was pulsing and glowing again. He walked over to the igloo's door, bent down, and waved the key in front of it. Nothing happened. He walked to the edge of the cloud and leapt to the next one. He checked the door on the square block building, and again nothing happened.

As he stood up, he noticed a window cut into the wall of the building. He peered inside and saw something that looked like a cross between a kangaroo and a snowman jumping around inside. The creature was about three feet tall and was covered in downy white fur, like that of a baby seal. Large ears protruded from its triangular head like a rabbit, and a large, wet, black nose, like that of a large dog, rested on the end of its snout. Its eyes appeared to be watery, but upon closer observation Xach discovered that the eyes **were** water! Instead of eyeballs, the creature had perfect orbs of a clear substance that resembled water floating in its head. Two small arms hung from its torso, and it had large feet, much like a kangaroo. It used its large feet to stamp a piece of cloud into a brick.

Xach tore himself from the window, because as fascinating as this creature might be to study, he didn't have time to watch it or engage it. Count Milton was hot on his tail and a thousand times more pissed off than he was before! He stood up and continued searching for an exit door.

One of the snow-kangaroos on a cloud twenty feet away spotted him and jumped behind its home for safety. Eight clouds away, Xach saw a group of the snow-kangaroos hopping about the cloud surface, throwing snowballs at one another. *These creatures seem cute and cuddly,* thought Xach. *Why can't I ever walk into a world filled with only creatures like that? No, I have to walk into worlds filled with giant birds that want to peck me to death and giant squids that want to rip me apart with their tentacles. It's just not fair!*

Lost for a moment in his own self-pity and wishing he could play with the snow-kangaroos instead of running from Count Milton, Xach did not immediately notice that the key pulsed faster and glowed more brightly. He tripped over one of the cloud bricks and fell facing a door to one of the cloud-igloos. The key bounced near his face, and he saw it was pulsing furiously. When he touched it, it felt it vibrate! Milton was near. He quickly placed the key in the lock, turned it left, then right, and opened the door. A pitch-black antechamber lay beyond!

He crawled through the door. He stood up and turned to close the door, just as the Milton-crow flew through the doorway and slammed into him at full speed. The force of its impact knocked Xach back against the wall. The giant bird beat its wings and clawed at the floor in what Xach assumed was a temper tantrum of sorts. It pecked at Xach's shoulder, entering the talon wounds it created earlier. Xach screamed in pain and kicked the bird squarely in the chest.

The force of his kick knocked the bird backwards. Its wildly flapping wings caught hold of the door and swung it shut. Since Xach's back was against the wall opposite the closing door, the key unlocked the exit the moment the other door closed, and Xach found himself falling backwards through the doorway and into the Hall. He scrambled to his feet and ran towards the larger door at the end of the hall.

Xach heard Count Milton mumbling something from within the antechamber. The cawing and flapping of wings stopped. Xach glanced back to see Count Milton, once again in human form, step from the antechamber and sprint toward him. He no longer wore the gown of slate rock; he now wore a coat of black feathers. Xach surmised that Count Milton used magic to create clothing from whatever objects he could find around him when he transformed back into his human form. He probably discarded the cloak and hat when he turned into the shark.

Xach reached the large door and waved the key to open it. He pushed it open, leapt through, and closed it behind him, hoping that this might gain him a few precious seconds of lead time while Count Milton reopened it. He sped off down the hall, waving the key in front of every door he passed. Many refused to open, but finally the key found one it could open. Its symbol was:

Xach pushed it open, jumped through the doorway, and turned to push it shut just as Count Milton's bloody face with a missing eye came into view. His left eyelid was closed and sunk inward over the hole where his eye used to be. Dried blood and pus were crusted around the lids; a thick viscous substance wept from between them and ran down his cheek. It was truly gruesome to behold. The door nearly slammed shut upon Count Milton's broken nose, but he managed to raise his metallic arm and stop the door's momentum.

Xach fled to the nearest door that would open. He heard Milton's heavy breathing behind him. He could almost feel it on his neck. He pushed open the door and grabbed hold of the edge. He stepped over the threshold into the antechamber and swung it quickly shut behind him. It sealed, and Xach let out a quick sigh of relief. He waited to see if Milton could get in, but the door stayed sealed.

Xach listened carefully for Count Milton to find another that would open for him. He expected Milton to enter this new world in search of him. Once he did, Xach planned to reopen the door to the hall and double-back to the Great Hall. While Count Milton searched this new world with no success, Xach figured he could hop through a couple more worlds, thereby cooling his trail and giving him the chance to recuperate from his injuries and hopefully reunite with Charlie.

Seconds ticked by like hours, as he waited for Count Milton to find another door and disappear from the Hall. Since he couldn't hear anything or be sure that Milton had gone, he simply had to wait. When he couldn't stand waiting any longer, he held the key up to the door to unlock it. Nothing happened. He tried the walls to his left and right, hoping that maybe he was just disoriented and hadn't put the key to right wall. To his great disappointment, neither wall produced a door. He turned to the wall at his back and held out the key. The door to the new world unlocked and glowed green.

I was so sure that plan was going to work, Xach thought sadly, as he pushed open the door. *Here we go again...*

Blinding white light filled the room. He covered his eyes and gave them a moment to adjust before he stepped out into the snow beyond the door. He closed the door behind him and saw that he stepped out of a giant hut made entirely of logs, sticks, and twigs. The door had a crude locking mechanism that one would not think required a key to open.

Choosing a direction, he padded off to the left through the dense pine tree forest. The snow on the ground packed into his ripped sneakers and numbed his feet so quickly that it took only several minutes of exposure before he no longer felt them at all. His teeth chattered and his entire body ached. He wished he hadn't needed to discard his cloak. He would have appreciated the protection from the cold. He wanted so badly to find a warm place to rest and recuperate, but he knew that he could only do that when he was a safe distance from Count Milton. The evil magician was most likely lurking somewhere nearby, so he kept moving. The key did not vibrate, so he was safe for the moment.

He saw a clearing ahead, so he skirted to his left to remain hidden in the trees. He did not want to enter any open areas for the time being. Out of the corner of his eye, he saw something move toward the clearing. He stopped behind a large tree and peered around the trunk to get a better look.

From the waist up, it looked human, except for two short horns that protruded from its forehead beneath a mane of curly brown hair. Half way down his chest, his body changed to that of a horse. Its long tail wagged lazily behind him. Its upper torso – the human half – was naked except for a red scarf wrapped around its neck.

Wow! A centaur, Xach thought. *I always figured they were the stuff of stories. This just gets more and more odd.*

"Excuse me," interrupted a tiny, gruff voice. "Who are you?"

Xach nearly jumped out of his skin. He spun around quickly toward the sound of the voice. He saw nothing.

"Ahem," said the voice. "Down here." Something tugged on Xach's pant leg.

He jumped back a step and looked down to find a large, brown beaver looking up at him.

"Did you just say something?" Xach asked the beaver.

"Yes, I did," spoke the beaver. "I asked who are you? In addition, what were you doing in my house?"

A talking beaver? What next? Did I step into a fairy tale?

ROOOOOOAAAAAAARRRRRRR!

The forest echoed with a loud and ominous roar. Xach was certain it came from a lion, and by the sound of it, a very large lion. He was even more certain that the lion was probably Count Milton in disguise, searching for a Xachary Kiddie Meal with the golden key prize.

"S-sorry, Mr. Beaver," stammered Xach. "I gotta go."

"But wait," shouted the beaver. "What were you doing in my house?!?"

Xach ran so fast he was out of earshot of the beaver in a matter of seconds. There was no time to chat with the wildlife; he had to keep moving. The lion sounded very close, and he needed to get off this world before it found him. He ran until he was out of breath. He doubled over, holding his knees, as puffs of crystallized air hung in front of his mouth and nose. He huffed and puffed until the pain in his sides subsided. Once he caught his breath, he walked onward again, only more slowly.

Another loud roar echoed through the forest, but this one seemed a little less powerful and quite a bit farther away. This warmed his heart a bit, and he found a little more strength to walk more briskly through the snow, knowing that he was putting some distance between them. He came to a snow-covered trail in the woods and decided to follow it, hoping that it might lead to a small town where an exit to the Hall existed.

He followed the trail as it wound through the trees and up the side of a large hill. At the top of the hill, Xach looked out over a large, deep valley. At the bottom of the valley lay a few homes and tents, many with tendrils of smoke rising from tiny chimneys. In the distance, atop a large mountain he saw the spires of a large ice castle.

Well, let's start with the village first, he thought. *It's closer, and it looks warm. I could stand to warm up a little. If the village doesn't pan out, I'll huff it to the ice castle. Though I can't imagine that place will be warm...*

He started down the steep hill, holding on to trees to keep from slipping and falling. When he was about half way down the hill, a flock of birds flew out of a tree to his left, startling him as they broke the still and quiet silence of the snow-covered woods. He watched them fly away toward the mountains and the ice castle beyond. Once the flapping of their wings and warning calls subsided, quiet returned to the woods.

In the silence, Xach heard another sound – the *crunch, crunch, crunch* of footsteps in the snow. He followed the sound with his eyes but failed to see anything. The snow compressed beneath invisible feet in a path toward him. The key vibrated against his chest.

Dammit, not again! How does he find me so fast? Xach thought as he tore down the hillside away from the footsteps. The crunching of snow behind him grew faster, matching his. The magician's voice rose above the noise. He chanted the words he had spoken earlier to remove the invisibility spell. Xach did not dare look back, for he knew that each wasted second brought them closer together. He zig-zagged down the hill, jumping left and then right, as a skier would do going down a steep slope. By planting his feet perpendicular to the downward sloping ground, he was able to keep his balance and keep from slipping and sliding too much.

Behind him, Count Milton finished his chant, and a burst of orange sparks appeared in the air. The bloody, twisted visage of Count Milton in a black feather coat melted into sight. As the last orange sparks fell into the snow, Count Milton chanted a new spell.

"*E-che I-che transforme en translata me!*" he shouted several times. When his voice reached the proper crescendo and the vision of his intended transformation clearly formed in his mind's eye, the transformation began. Black hair sprouted from beneath every inch of his skin. The bone beneath his nose reshaped, pushing outward to form a thick snout. Count Milton threw his body forward and ran on all fours as his torso expanded like a balloon, ripping and tearing the feather coat to shreds. Black feathers flew behind him as the coat disintegrated around his growing muscular form. His neck swelled to three times its original size, and his arms and legs grew thicker and more massive. Black hair continued to push from beneath every inch of his skin. His hands and feet grew into giant paws. Large, sharp claws sprouted from them. The transformation resembled that of a phoenix bursting forth from the ashes, only in this case it was a large black polar bear with one metallic leg bursting forth from a cloud of feathers.

The Milton-bear let out a deep, guttural growl. Xach resisted no longer, and took a quick glance behind him to see what magic Count Milton had performed. The sight of the giant black bear barreling toward him was a sight he wished he hadn't seen. Its lumbering gallop was surprisingly fast for a creature of its size, and it drew closer with each leaping step.

He sure picks the right animals to change into, Xach thought with a tinge of admiration. *The man's not dumb, I'll give him that.* He faced forward again and found himself heading straight into a tree. *You on the other hand...*

CLUNK

Xach smacked headfirst into a birch tree. Its white bark sliced his left cheek, and the solid trunk struck him in the chest and left shoulder, spinning him around like a human top. As he spun out of control down the hill, the giant black bear pounced. The bear attempted to land on Xach's body, thereby pinning him to the ground and ending the chase, but he only succeeded in head-butting Xach in the chest.

The momentum of his fall coupled with the head-butt to the chest caused Xach to remain in front of the bear instead of falling underneath its massive clawed feet. The bear swung at Xach with his left paw in an attempt to slice Xach's chest, but he missed. He lost his footing and fell on his shoulder. In a desperate attempt to salvage the attack, he swung his huge metal arm at Xach as he fell. Instead of gouging him with the claw, his swipe scooped Xach onto his chest. He wrapped his giant bear limbs around him as they tumbled head over heel down the side of the snowy hill.

The Milton-bear was so massive that it simply crashed through the trees and bushes that grew on the hillside, slowing their descent by only a miniscule amount. He held Xach in an unbreakable bear hug by crossing his arms over his chest and curling into a ball. He tried to bite him in the neck several times, but the bouncing and flipping down the hillside made it impossible. Oddly enough, Xach was **glad** that Milton held him in place, because he feared that the bear's weight would have otherwise crushed him on numerous occasions as they tumbled down the hillside. As it were, and likely much to Milton's chagrin, his bear form acted as a large air bag of sorts that sustained most of the impact and kept Xach from major injury.

The roaring of the bear on the hill and the snapping of the trees as they rolled down the hill alerted the townsfolk to their approach. A large group gathered at the edge of town to watch the bear and boy grapple with one another as they rolled down the snowy slope. Some entered their homes to retrieve weapons. They returned carrying clubs, axes, and swords.

As they flipped over and over, Xach inched down the bear's torso to keep his head and neck from being in range of its large, sharp teeth. However, when they reached the edge of town, they slammed into a building. The force of the collision with the wooden house was absorbed in great measure by the bear's back, but it was jarring enough to push Xach's body upward toward its mouth. In a flash, Milton clamped his sharp teeth down on Xach's already mangled right shoulder. The pain was excruciating, and he screamed in agony. With all his might he jabbed the bear in the chest with his left elbow just below the rib cage. It was enough to knock the wind out of Milton, and he released Xach's shoulder.

Xach scrambled away on his hands and knees, but Milton was too quick. He lunged for Xach and caught hold of his right foot with his strong bear jaws. He bit down and violently swung his head to the left, lifting Xach into the air as if he weighed next to nothing. Fortunately for Xach, the bear's teeth did not penetrate the leather and plastic soles of his sneaker by more than a few centimeters. The teeth punctured his foot in several places, but the shoe took the brunt of the bite. When the bear swung Xach into the air, his shoe came off in the bear's mouth, and Xach sailed into a pile of brush several feet away.

Shouts arose from among the gathered crowd as they witnessed the bear's brutal attack on the young boy.

"The bear is an agent of the Witch!" shouted one man.

"Look at its unnatural arm!" screamed an older woman.

"It attacked the boy! Kill it!" yelled another woman.

"Drive it away," demanded a strapping young male with a mace, "before it harms anyone in the town!"

Milton stood up on his muscular hind legs and let out a terrible roar to frighten the townspeople off, but they did not run. Instead, five of the larger men, including the one with the mace, advanced toward him and raised their weapons. Milton bent down and swatted the ground with his massive paw, sending a shower of snow, ice, and dirt into their faces. This momentarily disorientated the men, allowing Milton to attack. He bit one on the arm and sliced two others with his claws.

Xach wanted to watch the fight but decided he should press on while Count Milton was otherwise occupied. He pushed himself up to a standing position and hobbled off into the village, shoeless on one foot and aching all over. No one paid any attention to him, as they were focused on protecting their own and the village. He held the key in front of him and was relieved to see that it pulsed and glowed. An exit was nearby.

The key led him to one of the tiny homes. It was small and rustic but sturdily constructed. He looked through the window and found it deserted. He opened the door and entered the tiny one-room house. The heat from a blazing fire roared in the fireplace and a wave of heat washed over him, warming his frozen skin. He wanted to curl up in a blanket next to the fire and melt away the frost from his skin, but he knew he couldn't. He crossed the room past a small wooden table surrounded by tiny benches, a well-worn rocking chair, and a bed layered with several hand-sewn quilts of high craftsmanship. The key's signals led him to a tiny wooden chest, no bigger than a microwave or a large toaster oven. It rested upon a rickety wooden stool.

No way, thought Xach. *How am I supposed to fit in that? It's too small! There's no way!*

Xach waved the key around the room, thinking that maybe he had made a mistake. He hadn't. The key indicated the tiny wooden chest was the exit. Xach put the key in the lock and turned it to the left and to the right. He heard the click, removed the key, and opened the chest. Inside the chest was the black void he recognized as the antechamber to the Hall of Worlds.

How am I going to fit through there? he asked himself again. *I'm too big!*

He reached into the chest down to his shoulder, but he couldn't maneuver his head into the box. It hung over the side. He tried stepping into the box, but got one leg inside before the wooden edge of the chest rested snuggly against his groin. *This is never going to work. I'll have to find another exit.*

He slammed the chest shut and walked away in disgust. It was highly annoying to be so close to an exit but kept from using it because of a design error. It occurred to him that maybe this exit was designed for smaller key carriers, but that didn't do *him* any good. His put his hand on the doorknob and was about to open the door and leave the house, when something inside him screamed "*NO! Go back and try again. This has to work!*"

He was learning to trust his instincts and decided this was not a time to ignore them. He crossed the room back to the chest and reopened it. This time he tried going headfirst. He pushed his head into the antechamber and pushed off the floor with his feet. He was certain that he looked like an idiot with his head in a box trying to do a headstand, but his feelings of embarrassment died away as he felt pressure building on his shoulders. It was similar to the pressure he experienced when Charlie transported him from one place to another. It was like his body was made of cookie dough, and someone was pressing him through a rectangular tube. His body grew skinnier and longer as the invisible force pushed him through the tiny opening of the chest and into the antechamber. The moment he was through, the pressing sensation disappeared and the lid of the chest slammed shut behind him.

Chapter Twenty-Five

Since Xach came through the chest headfirst by practically standing on his head, he ended up face down on the floor of the antechamber. He pushed himself up to a standing position and left the room. He had no idea whether the villagers managed to kill Count Milton, if Count Milton killed all the villagers or if the villagers just scared him off. He hoped it was the first and neither of the later, but he could not afford to be too optimistic.

In any case, he said to himself, *you're not out the woods yet, so to speak, so get your butt moving!* He walked as fast as his aching body would allow. *You need to find Charlie, so he can fix you, and then you need to find a place to hide and figure out what you're going to do next. If for some reason Count Milton did survive, he may already have found a way back here.*

Upon his return to the Great Hall, he looked for Charlie but found no trace of him. He tried to be as quiet as possible as he searched for a door that would open, so that Count Milton would not be able to sneak up on him – invisible or not. He now knew the key would alert him of Milton's presence, but it never seemed to give him too much warning time.

Why aren't any of these doors opening? Gerald said the key should open all of them, but so many of them seem permanently locked. I could have escaped Count Milton long ago if these doors would just open like they're supposed to.

The first door that opened bore the symbol:

They look like snakes. I hope it's not snakes, Xach thought to himself with a shiver. *A world full of snakes. That's just what I need!* He pushed open the door and hobbled inside. He didn't see or hear Count Milton, but his skin crawled with fear nonetheless. He looked over his shoulder nervously as he moved down the hall.

He entered the first door that opened, crossed the antechamber, and entered yet another world. He closed the door behind him and surveyed his new surroundings. Stairways of all shapes and sizes, widths and depths, rose and fell from every angle. He stood on a level platform, but it was connected to several sets of staircases reaching upward, downward, and sideways! There was even a set of stairs on the ceiling! As bizarre as this new setting was, Xach felt like it was familiar in some way.

This is crazy, thought Xach. *It's like an architectural nightmare! It's totally pointless and unusable. No one can walk on walls or ceilings, unless they have suction cups for feet and hands. Oh God, I hope this isn't another mutant octopus planet...*

The door from which he exited was a locking window in this world. He looked through the pane of glass and saw large geometric shapes that resembled homes, held together at weird angles – angles that were structurally unsound and should not physically exist!

This world made him very uneasy. Not only did everything seem to defy the laws of physics, but he was a bit frightened to meet whatever creature **could** survive in a world like this. He turned back to the platform that connected to the various staircases and scanned the walls of the structure for another window or door that might be an exit. The only door he saw was on the ceiling! There was an actual door on the ceiling!

Now how the heck do I get up there? His head hurt thinking about it, and then it hit him…*my math book! The picture on the cover of your math book looks like this room! Who drew it?* He closed his eyes and concentrated on envisioning his math book cover. A picture of stairs upon stairs leading in opposing directions floated before his mind's eye, along with the signature in the corner – Escher. *M.C. Escher! That's the guy! In that picture people were walking up and down the staircases free from the laws of nature and physics. I wonder if that applies here too? I've seen stranger things so far. I suppose there is no harm in trying.*

He stepped off the landing and onto a set of stairs leading downward. This was nothing new. At the bottom of the stairs was a flight leading diagonally up the side of the wall. He tentatively placed his foot on the first step, expecting it to slip off, but it didn't! He put his full weight on it, and still his foot remained firmly planted on the step. He lifted his other foot and placed it on the step, expecting gravity to pull him headfirst onto the floor. It didn't. The moment both his feet touched the step, gravity adjusted, keeping him in place. Contradicting every law of nature and physics, he was now standing sideways with his feet on what should be a wall. He tentatively took another step and another, slowly climbing the wall as easily as one would walk across the floor! It was as if each step had its own gravitational pull.

He climbed up the stairs until he was halfway up the wall – about thirty feet from what would be considered the floor in his reality. Another staircase joined this one in the middle of the wall and led upward at a forty-five degree angle towards the ceiling. To walk on it, Xach would have to be upside-down! Xach tested the first step with his right foot and again felt the same pull of gravity he felt on a normal set of stairs. He brought his left foot to rest next the right, and there he hung as a bat hangs from the roof of a cave. The muscles in his body clenched from head to toe. He expected at any minute gravity would right itself and send him falling to his death, but he didn't fall. He took another step…another…and another. He was walking upside-down toward the ceiling!

This is crazy-cool! Xach thought. His muscles relaxed, and he allowed himself to move freely through the room. He sprinted from one staircase to another, walked up walls, and hung upside down. It took only minutes to navigate his way to the door on the ceiling. He stood before it. He was totally upside down and realized that even the items on his person were not reacting normally to gravity. In Earth's gravity, the string and key around Xach's neck would have fallen off his head and to the floor below or at least hung from his ears. His shirt would have fallen toward the floor, collecting under his arms and exposing his chest. Neither happened. The key hung from his neck and rested against his chest beneath his shirt as if the ceiling emanated a gravitational pull under his feet like the floor. He removed the key from behind his shirt to see if it was glowing. It was not.

Rats, I was hoping this was an exit. But then he changed his mind. *This isn't so bad, though. I wouldn't mind spending some time in this crazy world. Jeremy would have a blast here. Playing superheroes would be so easy!*

He turned the doorknob and pushed the door open to the sky. He stepped through the door at a 270-degree angle onto the roof of the building. In the distance he saw a large city filled with buildings that should not exist physically or geometrically. He decided to walk toward the city and seek an exit along the way. He walked to the edge of the roof and stepped another 270 degrees to walk down the side of the building. When he reached the ground, he stepped 90 degrees and found himself walking flat on the ground again.

He hummed to himself as he walked along, taking in the sights of this odd world. He thought of Charlie asking what a song was and wondered what he was doing right now in the Hall. *Would it be difficult for Charlie to move in this multi-directional gravity? Maybe not, actually. He could just revert to liquid form and glide along all of the surfaces?*

Xach felt very lonely.

A female voice screamed in the distance and interrupted his lonely thoughts. Several more screams joined hers. They emanated from a giant green building on the other side of the courtyard in which Xach walked. The building consisted of three pyramids of varying sizes that stood upside down upon each other. Windows lined the walls like a mirror-ball, and he saw tiny figures inside running about in all directions.

A door opened somewhere on the pyramid near the top and creatures that looked like springs emerged screaming from the door. *They look like human wire-coils*, Xach thought. They ran down the side of the building, though Xach couldn't really call it "running." They sort of *slunk* their way down the wall. Their arms and legs were spirals of a coiled, purple substance that allowed them to move multi-directionally with fluid ease. Their torsos were large coils of this purple substance from which two coiled arms and two coiled legs sprouted. On top of the central purple spirals sat what Xach assumed were their heads which were shaped like a cork – skinny at the bottom and larger at the top.

Xach drew closer and discovered these creatures had several mouths and eyes all around their cork-like heads. When they screamed, it came out in all directions. He wasn't sure if he should approach them or not. His track record with new species was not very good. However, these creatures did not look aggressive. They actually looked very gentle and friendly, aside from their screams of terror.

A blinding flash of green light, followed by ripples of blue sparks, burst from every window and door of the green building. Every creature that the blue sparks touched stopped dead in their tracks – frozen. A horrible sense of deja-vu spread over Xach as he realized he had seen something like this before.

"Oh, give me a BREAK!" he said out loud to no one in particular. *It is the same freezing spell that Count Milton used in the hospital just before Gerald pushed me into the closet. That means he's here, and he escaped from the villagers. How does he find me so quickly?*

Count Milton's spell froze everyone inside the building and everyone on the surface of the building. Only a few coil-people managed to escape into the streets before the spell overtook the entire building. These lucky few bounced down the streets in different directions, screaming and gesticulating wildly. Xach's tracked the only movement in the building – the cloaked figure of Count Milton. Milton paused for a moment and then moved swiftly toward the nearest open door. Xach watched him glide along a row of windows on the third floor toward a door that opened toward the courtyard. Xach sped off in the opposite direction toward a large cluster of buildings.

If I'm going to find an exit somewhere, it will most likely be in a building, Xach thought. He raced down an alley that connected to a marketplace surrounded by large conical and cylindrical buildings. Moving ever forward, Xach maintained a sharp attention to both the key and his pursuer. He didn't want to miss the key's signal of an exit or its vibration signaling Milton's proximity, nor did he want to lose sight of Count Milton's offensive strikes. Disregarding all etiquette and common courtesy, Xach ran through manicured lawns, jumped over fences, ran up walls, and across roof tops in an effort to lose Count Milton in the maze of strange architecture around him.

Count Milton, weary of the chase, strode into the marketplace and levitated into the air, thereby gaining a bird's-eye view of Xach's movements. He floated effortlessly through the air, as Xach vaulted over the many obstacles below. Realizing Count Milton's advantage, Xach bolted for the largest, closest building. It was the size of the Coliseum. Without missing a beat, he launched himself toward the wall of the building feet-first, ran twenty feet up the wall, and jumped through an open window. Once inside, Xach found that this giant building actually housed thousands of smaller buildings – strange architectural apartments with bridges and ladders that connected them at all angles. Interspersed among the apartment buildings were small patches of greenery, park-like seating areas, and play areas for children. Some of these "parks" hung upside down under bridges or clung to the sides of buildings. Though Xach had little time to really appreciate his surroundings, he felt it was an extremely efficient use of space. Of all the worlds he visited so far, this one was definitely one he wanted to explore in great detail.

It didn't take Count Milton long to find his way into the Colliseum structure, but Xach was better able to grasp the geometry and physics of this world than Milton. Floating through the maze of buildings, bridges, and ladders was difficult at best, because it was so tightly packed and interwoven. This forced Count Milton to pursue on foot. Xach managed to stay well ahead of him by running up walls and walking upside down on staircases while Count Milton struggled to understand the physics of movement that Xach already mastered. Milton avoided any surface that wasn't parallel with the ground for fear he would fall. He wasted time and energy by levitating from one to another.

Xach slipped into a maze of criss-crossing ladders and bridges, easily leaping from one to another like a lemur. He hooked his arm around the side and swung himself underneath, so as to walk upside down on the opposite side. Xach was having so much fun acting like a superhero, he momentarily lost sight of Count Milton. The key vibrated, and he froze. In the multi-directional gravity there was no way to know from which direction Count Milton might attack.

Count Milton was on the opposite side of the bridge on which Xach stood. As he was frightened he might misstep and fall off the bridge, Milton watched his feet closely. He caught a glimpse of Xach's bloodied arm swinging in the air beneath him. Quick as a rabbit, he knelt down, swung his arm around the underside of the bridge, and clamped hold of Xach's right ankle.

Instinctively, Xach pulled back sharply with his foot, causing the already unstable Count Milton to lose both his grip on the side of the bridge and Xach's ankle. In a blur of black and flailing limbs, Count Milton lost his balance and rolled off the side of the bridge. Since he no longer had contact with the surface area of the bridge or any other structure emitting a gravitational pull, Count Milton's body flipped and flopped listlessly through the air like a leaf blown in several directions at once. Xach watched with delight as Milton's head collided with the wall of an apartment fifteen feet away. The gravity exerted by the wall upon Milton's head as it grazed the concrete proceeded to pull the rest of his body toward it, effectively using his forward momentum through the air to slam his entire body into the hard surface. Xach leapt off the bridge onto another wall and disappeared around the corner, leaving Count Milton dazed and bruised as he rolled down the side of the building like one of those vending machine octopus toys that walks down walls.

Chapter Twenty-Six

Seconds after Xach's encounter with Count Milton, the key glowed and pulsed. It led him up a fifty-foot cylindrical staircase that protruded from the Colliseum wall at a 45 degree angle. Affixed to this staircase at even intervals were approximately thirty spherical apartments. From a distance, it looked like a giant multi-colored grape cluster. The key led him to a blue apartment near the top of the staircase. Due to the clustered affect of the apartments, Xach was certain Milton would not be able to see him easily. He wanted to keep it that way, so he did not attempt to barge into the apartment to search for the exit. Instead, he politely knocked on the egg-shaped door, praying no one would answer. By avoiding a confrontation with a frightened or angry alien and not drawing attention to his location, he hoped to slip out of this world discretely and gain some much needed space between himself and Count Milton.

The seconds passed slowly as he waited to make sure no one came to the door. Every nerve in his body screamed for him to hurry, but common sense held back the impulse to rush in. When he was satisfied the apartment was unoccupied, he used the key to unlock the door. It opened into an efficiency apartment, only entirely spherical. There were no walls dividing the space into rooms – just odd shaped, brightly colored furniture arranged neatly around the entire surface of the sphere. Xach stepped inside and closed the door behind him. He followed the key's signals to a large fluorescent pink trunk that hung from the ceiling. Inside the trunk were what Xach assumed to be various toys.

Xach closed the trunk, knelt down beside it, and inserted the key into the lock. The key changed shape to fill the locking mechanism and trigger the exit. After a twist, Xach withdrew the key, tucked it back under his shirt, and opened the trunk to see the familiar black anteroom. He stepped through the doorway and pulled the door shut behind him. He experienced a brief moment of dizziness and nausea as his equilibrium reset to the normal laws of gravity. As soon as he felt normal again, he entered the hall and sprinted back to the

Grand Hall to search for a new world in which to hide. He found a hallway that opened. It bore a symbol that looked like a perspective etching of several boxes.

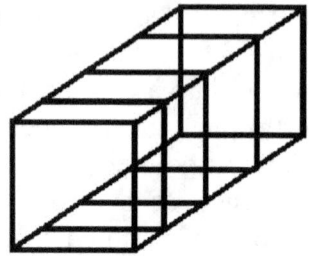

He stepped through the door and entered the first antechamber that would unlock. The world beyond the antechamber was extraordinary. Lush greenery lay before him in all directions. Birds in every color of the rainbow and some colors he never saw before, glided above him through the air like candy-colored quicksilver. Their motions were so fluid and graceful he wished he could be one of them for just a few moments to know what it feels like to move so freely and untroubled. All around him, the plants and trees were abuzz with life – insect and mammal alike. Though he could not locate a sun in the cloudless sky, a warm and luminous light shone down from above, warming his face and his soul. He felt the stress and fear melt away as he stood in what he imagined the Garden of Eden must have been like.

He closed his eyes and basked in the sunlight for a few moments before urging himself to move along. Even though this place felt like paradise – a place in which nothing could possibly go wrong – he knew that he could not afford to remain immobile for very long. He looked behind him to see that the antechamber had opened into this world through a glass door that was nearly invisible within a giant mirrored glass wall. The wall stretched beyond his vision into the sparkling blue sky above. The door's seams, hinges, and lock were made of the same material as the wall, and Xach strained his eyes just to see even a faint outline of the door through which he came.

He touched the glass surface and traced the minute seams of the door's edge with his fingers. It was smooth and warm to the touch. Even though he knew the door and the wall were there, it was so clear and superbly crafted that he almost believed it wasn't. It was an optical illusion of the highest quality, and he wondered how the birds and animals in this world didn't simply smash into it. He put his cheek against the wall and looked along the surface. At this angle he discerned the light refracting slightly off the surface. The wall stretched to his left and right indefinitely.

Never mind the incredible craftsmanship, he chided himself. *You've got to keep moving. Count Milton could be right behind you.*

He moved away from the wall and into a grove of trees to the northeast. The warm climate and the soothing sounds of nature calmed him, and he slowed his pace without even realizing it. Bees with purple wings buzzed past his head. Some were snapped up by the birds diving through the canopy on a silent airstrike. Brown furry animals resembling koala bears clambered up tree trunks and swung from tree limbs like monkeys as Xach approached. Bright blue and green snakes moved in congregations along the forest floor like schools of fish. Each snake had hundreds of tiny legs tucked along its side as it slithered across the ground. When one encountered a tree, the legs popped out, and it crawled up the bark like a centipede. Clusters of an insect with several sets of silver and gold wings flitted about from one brightly colored flower to another, trailing small clouds of sparkling pollen behind them. The pollen drifted down toward the earth like a shower of pixie dust.

I must be the only sentient being in this world, he thought. *It's so peaceful and relaxing here...so perfect and unspoiled. Man would totally destroy this world if given the chance.*

He glanced behind him, feeling ashamed that his shoe and one bare foot trampled the grass and made prints in the dirt. He was an unnatural force destroying the natural balance of this world. Even though he had been to several different worlds already and seen such amazing things, he felt more unnatural, more out of place, more **alien** than ever before.

I don't belong here. It's so beautiful...so perfect...I shouldn't be here. A sense of dread and unease spread over him. *I need to get out here before I do something that upsets the balance of this world. I would never forgive myself if...*

Before he finished that horrible thought, it became a reality as Count Milton smashed through the canopy of leaves over Xach's head in the form of a giant, black bat with a silver wing. The bat's wings beat down upon Xach's head furiously, knocking him over. He rolled behind a bush and leapt up behind a tree. The trees were dense enough to keep Milton from moving too easily as a bat. Every flap of his large wings met resistance against one tree or another. Xach sprinted back the way he'd come, hoping that by some divine miracle he might find the door hidden in the glass wall and escape. He broke out from the grove of trees, trampling bushes and small plants in his wake.

I'm sorry. I'm so sorry, echoed in his mind with each act of destruction his flight created.

He fled across the grass and flower covered ground, toward where he believed the door to be. He glanced behind him to see the giant bat slashing its way out of the grove. A flurry of leaves, twigs, and flowers tossed about him like a miniature tornado.

CRACK

Xach felt a sudden stab of pain in his temple and shoulder, followed by a solid resistance that knocked him to the ground. He sat up, his vision swimming and his head throbbing. Thinking through the pain and swell of tears that blurred his vision, he knew he found the glass wall.

He tried to stand up, but the collision with the wall temporarily offset his equilibrium. In the periphery of his vision, he caught a glimpse of a huge dark shadow approaching. He struggled to stand, but only managed to wobble a bit to the right and fall over again. The bat dove for his head, and Xach felt its teeth whisper through his hair as he fell to the ground.

Unaware of the glass wall's existence, Milton rocketed headfirst into it. What followed was a horrifying snapping and squishing sound as his bones and flesh collapsed against the unyielding wall. He crumpled like a paper cup under someone's foot and slid to the ground below in a bloody tangle of wings, fur, and bone.

Is he finally dead? Did he kill himself?

Xach wanted to inspect the body but decided it was best to get away as quickly as possible and hope for the best. He crawled away as fast as he could until his equilibrium returned, allowing him to stand up and wobble back into the forest. He stumbled past the area of broken limbs and scattered leaves that marked Count Milton's attack through the treetops and made his way deeper into the forest. Shaking off the last bit of dizziness, he stumbled over his own feet. He reached out for something to support his weight and found himself leaning against another glass wall. The trees grew tightly against it, their limbs bending upward along its smooth surface.

Xach removed the key from under his shirt and hoped that it would lead him to another hidden door in the wall. The key gave no indication of such. He followed the wall until it led out of the forest and into a meadow of bright red flowers. It looked like a sea of roses. Swarming above them were thousands of the multi-winged insects, tossing pollen in all directions. The gold and silver dust floated through the air and ricocheted off the glass wall.   As he stood at the edge of the meadow watching them and the dust, his eyes registered a faint rectangular outline on the glass wall.

He waded through the sea of red flowers toward the image, its outline growing more defined with each step closer. About twenty feet into the meadow, Xach found a door in the glass wall, its pollen-dusted edges glinting in the bright light. Xach consulted the key again, but the key remained inert.

Well, even if it's not an exit to the Hall of Worlds, at least it's a doorway to somewhere else.

He slid his fingers over the surface of the door and found the lock. He put the key into the lock and turned. The latch released and the door swung inward, pushed open by a force of immense pressure and heat from the other side. The door smacked him in the face, knocking him down. The key was still in the lock and the Zindarthan thread around his neck did not break, so he hung by his neck from the door. With some difficulty, he pulled himself up into a standing position, removed the key from the door and stuck his head through the doorway. Darkness was all saw, yet it was not an antechamber. Intense heat radiated all around him. Xach guessed it to be about a hundred degrees or more – worse than the hottest summer he'd ever experienced. He perspired immediately.

The intensity of the sunlight in the meadow behind him made the darkness of the area beyond the door even harder to penetrate. He leaned farther into the darkness, allowing his eyes to adjust. Slowly a desolate terrain emerged from the darkness. The dark earth undulated unevenly as far as Xach could see. Small pools of red-orange liquid like lava glowed and bubbled from cracks in the ground. There appeared to be no life of any kind beyond the door – just molten rock, lava floes, and ash. The air was hot, thick, and uncomfortable. It was hard to breathe, like breathing liquid smoke.

This really doesn't look like someplace I want to be, Xach thought. *But if Count Milton isn't dead, he's probably already tracking me again. I'll be harder to find in this world than in a sunny meadow. I just hope there's a door to the Hall of Worlds somewhere in there.*

Full of trepidation and fear, Xach stepped out of the beautiful, sun-drenched meadow and pressed his way into the thick, dark air beyond the door. The smoke and ash choked him, and he was racked with a horrible coughing spell.

Maybe this wasn't such a good idea...

He turned back toward the meadow just in time to see the shadow of Count Milton's wobbly bat form swooping toward the open doorway. Without a second thought, Xach pulled the door closed and bolted across the hard, crusty surface of the dried lava into the blackness beyond. Brief glimpses over his shoulder revealed that Count Milton could not open the door. It remained closed.

As Xach ran, his breathing returned to normal and his vision increased in acuity. He assumed the key adjusted his physiology to adapt to the change in climate and air density.

If Count Milton does make it into this world, at least my ability to adapt should give me a greater advantage. Even the heat doesn't seem so unbearable. But why did the key not take me to an antechamber before depositing me into another world? Why did it just open into another world? That's not how it's supposed to work.

As he pondered this question, he heard a deep rumble overhead like thunder. He looked up and saw an immense ink-black cloud lit sporadically by lightning trails. The thunder grew louder and more frequent as he ran. He made sure to stay as far away from the bubbling pools of lava as possible. With no warning, a great bolt of lightning streaked down from the clouds and struck a rock two feet from him. The rock glowed yellow at the point of impact. The lightning bolt was followed by another and another – each striking the ground within feet of Xach's location.

*I **really** don't like this place. I gotta find...*

The air around Xach vibrated and tingled as a streak of lightning touched down two inches behind him. Xach felt his skin crawl with electrical charge, and the force of the impact knocked him forward. Instead of falling on his face, he slammed into something hard and smooth. Pain radiated through his cheek, jaw, and chin. His chest impacted with the same material, knocking the wind out of him. He slid down against the surface, feeling it with his hands as he fell. It was the same smooth, glass wall he'd encountered in the lush garden.

He pushed himself to a standing position. The key remained dark. No exit. He rubbed the gem, and the key emitted its familiar green light. He scanned the surface of the glass wall for any fissures that might indicate another door. He found none. The reflection of the lightning storm in the glass wall played tricks on Xach's eyes. It danced across the cloud cover and split the sky repeatedly as it struck the rocky landscape below. The storm was localized into an area of about fifty square feet, and Xach saw a well-defined area of glowing strike points.

With his back to the wall, he slid along the smooth glass in the opposite direction of the storm. In the distance, about two hundred feet away, he thought he saw a tornado touch down. Its funnel picked up ash and liquid rock and hurled them outward and upward in a fiery maelstrom.

What is this place? It's like the complete opposite of that beautiful garden. A tiny bit of despair crept into his heart. *If I had to chose, I would rather die in that beautiful garden than in this fiery hell.* His finger snagged on a minute indentation in the glass wall. His heart leapt. *Could it be another door?*

He traced the indentation, and his fingers told him it was another door. With a little bit of difficulty, he located the lock and used the key to open it. He was careful to remove the key from the door and stand back in case the door swung violently one way or the other, as it did before. It opened outward with a rush of air.

He blinked in disbelief at the sight before him.

It can't be. Can it? It's gotta be...

Beyond the doorway lay familiar neon blue grass, floating islands of dirt and grass, roaming colored bushes, and purple mirondi – just as he remembered Zindartha to be before it was plunged into darkness by the setting suns.

How is this possible? How did I get back here?

He stood there momentarily dumbfounded.

I'm back where I started from. It's...it's like I made a big circle. I'll have to do it all over again...

His mind reeled, and he suddenly felt all his energy drain away, sucked into the dark rock beneath his feet. Even though he was surrounded by super-heated air, he felt cold, and he shook with uncontrollable shivers. His whole journey from Zindartha through the Hall of Worlds and the battles with Count Milton had been for nothing. He was right back where he started. The feelings of isolation and abandonment he felt upon his first visit to Zindartha washed over him again, and he simply could not go on.

But you must, sounded a familiar voice inside his head. *You must go on. You must protect the key and stop Count Milton. It is your destiny.* It was the voice of Gerald. *You have more strength and power in you than you can imagine. This hasn't been for 'nothing'...it's for everything...every world...every person...every creature...EVERYTHING!*

Gerald? Is that really you?

A part of me, yes. The part of me that bonded with the key in my quest to protect and preserve its power. My physical being may have left you, but my spirit has not.

But how? Am I going crazy? Have I finally lost my mind?

No, Xach. You are not crazy. I am here with you in spirit, and as such, I must urge you to continue on. Keep moving. Evade Count Milton. Find Charlie and save the Hall of Worlds.

How do you know about Charlie?

I've been with you the whole time. I know of all that has happened to you since we parted.

So why didn't you say anything before now?

*Because you didn't need me until now. The depth of your despair threatens to destroy you here and now, and I cannot allow that to happen. Your job is much too important. **YOU** are much too important. You must continue moving. Put as much distance between yourself and Count Milton as possible. What you see before you is just another obstacle in your path – an obstacle you **can** handle. I know what it represents in your heart and your mind, but it is not what it appears to be.*

But I'm back where I started...I don't...

*You are stronger and more capable now. I believe in you, and you **must** believe in yourself. Now, go. You must go **now**!*

Gerald's voice was stern and forceful, like his father's. The paralysis left his limbs. The leaden weight that pressed against his body and soul lifted.

I don't know how you're able to talk to me, Xach thought to Gerald, *but I'm glad you're here with me.*

Not only I, but all the other key carriers before you are with you. Now leave this horrible place and don't look back.

So, he did. With renewed energy, Xach stepped back into Zindartha and pushed the door closed behind him.

Chapter Twenty-Seven

Xach moved quickly through the Zindarthan landscape, wondering if he'd have a chance to talk to any of the Zindarthans who befriended him just a few short days before. His stomach growled with hunger. He wished he could meet up with one of the Queens and request more of the tasty morsels they gave him. He stopped briefly to drink from the pink pools of liquid, as his throat was dry and parched from breathing the hot, smoky air of the lava world.

The more he walked, the more he realized something wasn't right. Foremost, he couldn't see any of the suns in the sky, but light shone down upon him from above. He did not see or hear any quarken, and the multi-colored bushes moving about the land avoided him and the mirondi.

A sense of unease settled into him. The farther he walked, the more unsettled he became. Out of the corner of his eye, he saw something dart behind a large mirondi. He turned his head slightly to the right to get a better look when he walked into another glass wall. He wasn't moving very fast, so the impact merely startled him instead of knocking him down or causing any physical pain. Turning his attention back to the wall, he saw it extended to the right and left indefinitely, just as it had in the other two worlds.

Maybe they aren't different worlds at all, he thought, as an idea blossomed in his head. *Maybe I'm still in the same world, but this world is divided into different eco-systems by these glass walls.* It was clear and logical, and he wondered why he didn't think of it before. *These walls separate different types of land, air, and life – like a giant terrarium of some kind. But why? Who made them?*

As if in answer to his thought, one of the most disconcerting sights he'd ever seen appeared along the upper edge of the glass wall. It started as a dark crack in the sky. The sky slid back in such a way that the dark crack lengthened and widened in a triangular fashion, as if the sky were a glass lid being slid aside. From the darkness, a giant eye came into focus, peering down upon Xach and the Zindarthan landscape. Xach stood frozen in fear. The eye was lidless and the size of a football field in diameter. It was perfectly round with a large white iris and a blazing red pupil half the size of the entire eye. As it had no lid, it did not blink. It just stared intently at Xach.

What the hell is that?!?

The sky continued to slide away, revealing more darkness above. Another large eye came into view, followed by a third. Each eye was about the same size, but the pupils differed. The second eye was a vibrant blue color, and the third was a hue of orange and red akin to a setting sun.

What do I do? What is that thing? It's gigantic!

Find an exit, quickly! Gerald's voice urged. ***MOVE!***

Xach slid along the glass wall as quickly as he could, feeling for another seam in the wall that indicated a doorway.

The red eye followed Xach's movements, but the other two eyes were drawn to a black object several hundred feet away that moved erratically through the air toward Xach at incredible speed. Xach didn't need binoculars to tell him that it was Count Milton. As Milton drew closer, Xach discerned he was still in the form of a large black bat. His wings were damaged, and he was unable to fly in a straight line, bobbing left and right, up and down. A thin trail of smoke followed him, and Xach surmised he must have been singed by lightning or lava in the previous world.

Could this get any worse for me?

From out of the darkness above, two streams of dark mass rolled into the sky like tentacles of black jelly. The first projected directly in front of the Milton-bat, while the second fell behind it. Xach watched with a mixture of joy and horror as the black sky-fingers pinched hold of Milton and plucked him from the sky. They pulled Milton closer to its two large eyes, examined him for a moment, and flicked him away as if he were a piece of dirt. Milton hit the glass wall with enough force to send shock waves rippling along the glass surface. Xach felt the vibration through his fingertips. Milton slid down the wall like a black glob of spit, hit the ground, and vanished.

Either the sky creature just snuffed him out of existence somehow or Count Milton turned himself invisible to avoid further detection, Xach thought. *I hope he just went invisible.*

I don't like the idea that this thing might be able to wish me out of existence. In either case…where does that leave me?

The three eyes in the sky now turned their full attention to Xach. His knees felt like jelly, and he thought he might fall down. The key twitched against his chest. It was changing shape. Xach withdrew the key with shaky hands to find the gem was glowing bright green. His knees instantly solidified, and he sped along the glass wall, trailing the fingers along the wall in search of the door. The pulsing of the green gem grew faster and faster.

I'm getting closer…

Adrenaline pumped through his veins, and his speed increased. The eyes in the sky followed Xach with mild curiosity. The darkness shifted and two more fingers projected downward from the dark. A cold, nervous sweat ran down his back, mingling with the full body sweat brought on by the sprinting.

Come on….come on…where's the door?

His index finger felt a snag…a tiny scratch.

I found it!

Moving with blinding speed, he pulled the key from around his neck, found the lock, inserted the key, and turned. He pushed open the door, removed the key, and dove through the open doorway into the antechamber. The black sky-finger snaked in through the doorway behind him, searching blindly for its prey. Xach rolled on his side and kicked the door shut, severing the finger with the door's edge. By the bright green light of the key, Xach saw the severed piece of sky evaporate in a puff of black smoke dissipate like cigarette smoke, leaving no trace of it inside the antechamber.

He lay back on the soft floor and allowed himself a short rest. He took a few deep breaths and tried to relax. It took some time, but eventually he regained his composure and set out into the Hall again. He hoped Count Milton would be out of commission for a while, but his instincts told him to keep moving. He entered the Great Hall, sprinted a few feet, and chose another Hall bearing the symbol:

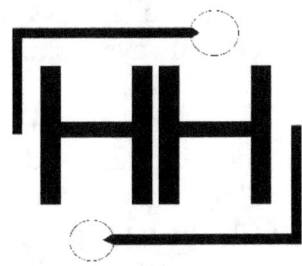

The world he entered was almost identical to Earth, and for a few moments he thought he might actually be home. He entered through a small, wooden doorway that opened into a dark, cobblestone covered alley. Upon entering the main street, he found himself in the center of a small town. There were buildings made of brick and stone. People walked the streets. Vendors sold fruits and fish from carts. It looked like a normal marketplace.

He approached a little girl wearing a red jumpsuit with a black sash and a large black hat upon her head. When he was within greeting distance, he cleared his throat to introduce himself. The hat upon the girl's head bristled and hissed. It wasn't a hat at all – it was some type of creature that had the ability to change its outer appearance at will. Spikes shot out and it looked more like a pin cushion or angry black porcupine.

Xach took a step back. The porcupine returned to its hat shape, but it continued to bristle and shake. The girl looked at him quizzically, eyeing him up and down. A look of fear and revulsion came to her face. She let out a little scream and ran away from him.

I know I must look like something out of a horror movie with all of these injuries and my tattered clothes, but I could have screamed just as easily at that thing on her head, Xach thought as he inched his way back into the shadows of the alley. He watched the people move about the street and soon realized that every person, young and old, had some type of creature-hat on their head. Some of the people talked to their hats and some of the hats *talked back*! Though fascinating, Xach knew without question he was **not** on Earth. It resembled it in many ways, but this world was just as alien as Zindartha.

He kept to the shadows and alleyways whenever possible and avoided crowded streets, always looking to the key to lead him toward an exit.

Whenever someone did see him, they recoiled from him with a mixture of disgust, anxiety, and morbid fascination. No one spoke to him, and their hats became quite agitated around him. He thought of Charlie quite a few times. Charlie could have imitated one of these hats and allowed him to blend in better.

After a short while, the key directed Xach to an exit in the form of a wooden lock box outside an old stone building with crumbling walls that resembled a church. Once back in the Hall, he searched for another door that would open. Xach was pleased that Milton did not find him in the weird hat world, and he hoped this meant he was cooling his trail. The longer he went without sustaining new injuries, the better he felt.

The first door to open bore this symbol:

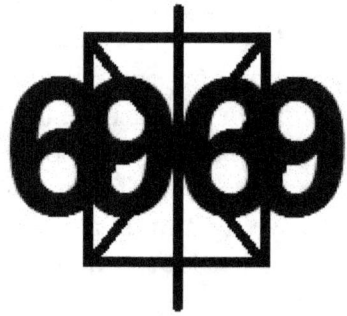

Xach opened the Hall door and quickly found a door that would open. The door from the antechamber pushed out into a slightly less dark place. He stepped from the antechamber onto a glass floor. He closed the antechamber door behind him. A low light eminated from all around him. As his surroundings came into focus, he saw he was standing in a mirrored room – like a fun house where your reflection is multiplied to infinity in a long string of reflections. No matter what direction he looked, he could see himself repeated to infinity. It was quite disorienting and confusing. He took a step forward, but it was hard to navigate without a fixed point. At least in a fun house, the floor is usually dark and allows some sort of directional control.

Xach moved cautiously forward with his arms outstretched before him, fearful he would walk into a wall. He could not look at his feet as he moved. He felt vertigo looking at his reflection stretching out below him. He moved slowly forward until his hands touched glass. His bloody and dirty hands left smudges on the reflective surface. He moved along the wall until he found a corner. He continued around the room until he found smudges on the glass. He counted eight corners. This meant the room was a fully enclosed octagon. Even at the corners, he could not see any seams. Each piece of mirrored glass was perfectly connected with no edges.

Well, that's just great, Xach thought. *I am trapped in a mirror box with no discernable exit. I can't go back through the antechamber, so how do I get out of here?*

He imagined that if anyone stayed in this room for too long, they would surely go mad.

Think, Xach. Think. What purpose would the Creator have for making a world of mirror boxes? Why would the antechamber open into a mirror box? Perhaps the exit is up?

Xach looked toward the ceiling. It too was a mirror, and all he saw were thousands of Xach's looking back at him.

Perhaps I can levitate up there and search the ceiling for some type of exit.

Xach concentrated on the words he spoke that saved him from the fall into the pit on Zindartha – *murmur leviar wentum.* He said the words aloud and thought them in his head as he envisioned himself floating toward the ceiling. He felt pressure against the soles of his feet that grew until he rose from the floor toward the ceiling. He rose about ten feet before his head bumped the ceiling.

click

The noised startled him and broke his concentration. He dropped like a stone. He tried to regain control by starting the chant again, but it was too late. He hit the floor before he could get past *murmur.* He did at least manage to curl himself into a ball before impact. He struck the floor on his left hip, side and head. The wind was knocked from his lungs. He gasped for breath and groaned in pain. Despite being made of glass, the floor did not crack or break upon impact. It was apparently quite resilient and sturdy.

click**click

A low humming and whirring sound started. It grew in intensity until the walls vibrated. Xach pushed himself into a standing position and stood nursing his bruised shoulder and elbow. His reflections shimmered and shook with the growing vibration. Just when he thought the vibrations would cause the mirrors to crack and shatter, it stopped. The silence was jarring.

Xach stood frozen in anticipation.

What will happen next? More noises? Breaking glass?

Out of the corner of his left eye, he saw a flash of color, then another from the right, above, and below. They happened so fast, he could not focus on them. He only caught a glimpse of a rainbow each time. A few seconds went by and nothing happened.

Then, without warning, the room filled with beams of colored light in every color of the spectrum. It was like standing in a rainbow. It reminded Xach of the nightclubs he saw onTV, where beams of colored light flooded a dancefloor and bounced off the mirrored walls. The colors reflected off the walls and onto the endless reflections around him. The bands of light narrowed and focused, becoming a grid of overlapping concentrated colored light connecting opposite panels of the mirrored walls in a rainbow grid with Xach in the center of the overlapping beams.

The grids moved from one side of each panel to the other in a criss-crossing pattern. It was dizzying to watch, yet mesmerizing and trippy. Although he was standing still, the movement of the light grids made it look like he was floating and tumbling through a kaleidoscope of geometrical shapes and colors. The light beams moved quickly back and forth and all around him.

Then just as quickly as they began, they disappeared. Xach felt dizzy and he struggled to keep his visual focus. His stomach churned and fell over. He closed his eyes and lay there until the nausea passed. Lying on the solid floor helped his senses reorient and restored balance to his inner ear.

click

He opened his eyes. Instead of seeing an endless line of his reflection before him, he saw an opening in the wall. He stood up and hobbled to the doorway. His left hip was quite sore from his ten-foot drop to the floor. He leaned against the door frame and tried to comprehend what he saw beyond the doorway.

Tall buildings made entirely of the same reflective glass stretched toward a cloudless, blue sky. Roads of mirrored-glass wove between the buildings. Along the sides of the roads were oddly-twisted shapes that resembled trees or bushes, but because they were also made of the same reflective material, they looked more like gnarled, pointy claws reaching up from the ground. Everything he saw was reflective. The only things of color that existed were the blue sky and Xach. Because the sky was a fixed point of color, Xach didn't feel too disoriented as he ventured out into the mirror world.

The moment he stepped fully out of the glass room, he heard another **click** and the doorway disappeared, leaving only a smooth, reflective surface. Xach reached out to touch it and examine it for a minute seam, but instead his hand touched a hand – his hand! What looked like his reflection was not a reflection. It was an exact, three-dimensional copy of himself emerging from the glass surface.

Xach recoiled in surprise. His copy did the same. He took a step back. His copy did the same, only it stepped back into the mirror. Xach stood dumbfounded for a moment.

What is going on? Did that just happen or did I imagine it?

As a force of habit, Xach looked around to see if someone was watching, even though he hadn't seen anyone or anything other than his reflection. Out of the corner of his eye, he noticed the reflection did not move. It remained stationary and did not turn its head as Xach did. The reflection stared at him directly in the eyes. A chill ran down his spine. Xach blinked. It did not. Xach slowly raised his right arm in the air.

The reflection remained static. Xach reached toward it. The reflection reached out toward Xach, its hand emerged from the mirror and materialized in three dimensions. Xach immediately withdrew and put his arm at his side. The reflection did the same and returned inside the mirror again.

This is so creepy! Xach thought. *What if I walk away and it comes out of the mirror and follows me? What is it and what does it want? Will it hurt me?*

Xach backed away slowly. The reflection stood motionless. Its unblinking stare followed his every move.

None of this makes sense. How could it come out of the mirror and act independently? Is it real? Is it a robot of some kind?

He didn't want to turn his back on it, fearing it would step out of the mirror and follow him. He walked backwards into the mirrored street, keeping his eyes on the one reflective surface that held a static image until he bumped into something. It felt like he backed into someone, and it startled him. He jumped away from whomever he touched and spun around to find himself staring at the back of his own head – or rather the back of a copy's head. The copy was fully three-dimensional and wholly outside the mirror's surface!

Every muscle in his body tensed for conflict. He wanted to flee, but he stood his ground to see what it would do. It remained immobile for a few moments and then walked away without even looking back at Xach. It limped a little, favoring its left leg. It looked around in amazement at its surroundings. It studied one of the claw-like trees, and smiled at its reflection in the branches. It continued down the street until it passed one of the buildings and noticed its mirror image.

Xach watched in awe as it did the same things he had done upon realizing his reflection was not a reflection. It reached out to touch it and withdrew when it materialized outside the mirror. It looked around and then backed away when the reflection did not move. It backed away into a building. When its shoulder blades drew within a few inches of the building, another three-dimensional image withdrew from the building's surface. It bumped into the back of the newly emerging image and jumped forward, pulling the image entirely out of the mirror. It spun around and watched in awe as the newly created copy walked down the street away from it.

This new copy went on to do the same thing a few blocks farther away, creating yet another iteration of Xach. The first copy stood watching the whole scene unfurl, just as Xach did, but then it turned and looked directly at Xach.

Xach jumped, and so did Copy#1. They stared at each other for a moment and slowly backed away, careful not to touch another reflective surface and thereby create another copy. Once they were far enough apart to no longer pose a threat to one another, each turned and ran away down a street and around another building.

He got the sense that the copies were not inherently dangerous, or the first one would have attacked him. They seemed to be as frightened of him as he was of them. Nonetheless, Xach made sure to keep at least a foot away from all the buildings. In doing so, his reflections remained just that.

He became winded rather quickly, and had to stop running. He walked as fast as he could through the reflective city, periodically glancing behind him to make sure he wasn't being followed. It appeared he was not. The buildings varied in shape and size, as did the claw-bushes and trees. It appeared to be uninhabited except for the copies of himself.

As he turned a corner, a nearby building reflected his image, and he thought it was one of the copies. He made eye contact with it, and the reflection immediately froze and ceased to be a reflection. Xach did not go near it and backed slowly away, maintaining eye contact. The image kept his gaze but remained within the mirror.

So, direct contact with the mirrored surface of a building can create a copy, Xach surmised. *Direct eye contact can initiate a copy, but only touch can draw it out. What is the purpose of this place, and what will happen to my copies? Will they just wander around like rats in a mirror maze creating a multitude of copies? Are the copies sentient? Are they just imitating me or can they think?*

I need to get out of here. The last thing I need is for Militon to follow me in here and start making copies of himself! I can hardly defend myself against one of him, let alone an army of Miltons.

Oh my God, the key! What if the mirror copied the key? Can it even do that? If so, there are at least four copies of the key so far, and God knows how many others have been created.

Xach looked at the key, and it was pulsing. An exit was near. He was both exhilarated and terrified. He wanted to leave this place immediately, but he knew that he couldn't. He could not leave without knowing if the key had been copied and if his copies could use one of the keys to escape this world.

Rather than attempt to track down one of the copies, Xach decided it was easier to just create another and find out what he needed to know. He stopped walking and faced one of the buildings. He made eye contact with his reflection and walked toward it. Although he was still somewhat wary of the copies, he tried to squelch his fear. Since the other copies he witnessed seemed to exhibit the same behaviors and emotions he experienced when creating them, he wanted to make sure that his copy was not afraid of him.

He reached out confidently toward his reflection with his right hand. The copy's right hand emerged from the mirror's surface as Xach got within a few inches of the surface. He grasped the copy's hand and stepped back, pulling it out of the mirror. He looked at the key on the copy's chest. It pulsed just as his did. Without letting go of the copy's hand, he reached toward the key with his left hand. The copy did the same, so he withdrew. Although he wanted the copy's key, he could not risk the copy taking *his* key, if he was right about the mirror copying intention.

"Can you speak?" Xach asked his copy.

"Yes," replied the copy.

"Can you understand me?"

"Yes."

In unison, they asked each other, "What do you want?"

This startled both of them, and the copy tried to release his hand from Xach's grip and step away.

"Hold on," Xach said, maintaining his hold on the copy's hand. "I am not going to hurt you. I want to understand what you are and what you know."

"So do I."

"I am Xachary Biddle. What is your name?"

"Xachary Biddle," the copy said warily.

"Who is your mother and where do you come from?" Xach continued.

The copy paused, a mixture of confusion and growing terror etched on his face. "N-Nancy. I come from Earth."

"How did you get here?"

"I-I was kidnapped by a man named Gerald and brought to Zind…"

Now it was Xach's turn to be terrified. This entity was an *exact* duplicate down to his memories. The color drained from Xach's face, and he started to tremble.

"W-what?" the copy asked. "What's wrong?"

"You are an exact copy of me."

"No, y-you're a copy of-of me," the copy stammered. "You reached out of the mirror, g-grabbed me and p-pulled me through."

The copy tried harder to pull away, but Xach held his grip. The copy leaned back and took a step backward.

"Calm down. I am not going to hurt you," Xach reiterated, trying to pull the copy away from the wall.

"I don't believe you," the copy said, pulling back even harder. It jerked its hand out of Xach's grasp with such force that its momentum propelled it into the wall behind it. As it pulled itself away from the wall, it pulled another copy out of the mirror. The copy turned to face its copy and screamed. Copy#2 screamed as well. Copy#1 backed away, tripped over one of the claw bushes, and fell to the ground.

Xach realized there would be no way to reason with any of the copies. His innate terror of them would cause each of them to be afraid of him. Moreover, the copies were exact copies of Xach as of the moment he stepped into the mirrored room with the rainbow lights. He surmised the lights somehow scanned him and copied him in that moment. Each copy believed they were him being pulled from the mirror room.

His only way of learning anything about the copy of the key was to take one. There was no way one of copies would freely give him their key, because *he* would never give up his key. He would need to grab one of the keys and somehow get the necklace over the copy's head, because the thread would likely be unbreakable like his. He leapt toward Copy#1 as he lay stunned on the ground, grabbed the key, and pulled the necklace over its head.

Copy#1 screamed again, but this time out of fear for losing its key. It scrambled to catch Xach as he ran away with its key. It leapt toward Xach and grabbed hold of Xach's left leg, causing Xach to fall forward. To keep from smashing face-first into the mirrored ground, Xach twisted slightly to his right and landed on his side. The impact caused him to lose his grip on the copy's key. It slid across the mirrored ground and landed at the feet of Copy#2.

Copy#2 looked at the key and then at the Xachs fighting before him. In a flash, he bent down, scooped up the key and ran in the opposite direction. Copy#1 released Xach and pursued Copy#2.

Xach watched the two run off around a corner. He sighed and stood up. Now both his right and left sides ached.

That went well, Xach thought. *Now I just created two more copies of the key and still don't know if they work or not. What I do know is that each copy of me is frighteningly just like me in every detail. I need to try this again, but I need to make sure I get the key and keep it this time.*

He walked up to the building again and made eye contact with his reflection. He smiled and tried to clear his mind. He reached out, gripped the reflection's hand, and pulled it out of the mirror.

"Hi Xach," Xach said to his copy.

The copy looked horrified. Xach used that moment of hesitation to his advantage and kicked the copy squarely in the groin. The copy crumpled to the ground in pain. Xach scooped the key from around its neck and ran away as fast as he could. The copy lay on the ground writhing in pain, screaming for him to return the key.

Sorry to do that, Xach thought. *It's dirty and wrong, but I need to find out if this key will work in the Hall or not. It will come for me, because that is what I would do. So, I don't have a lot of time to figure this out.*

Xach ran as fast as he could, making multiple turns in the mirror maze of buildings and streets until his lungs felt like they would burst. He doubled over, resting his hands on his knees, attempting to catch his breath and slow the pounding of his heart in his chest. When the pain in his chest subsided, he stood up and examined his key and the copy's key. The one around his neck no longer pulsed. The copy's key pulsed.

That's a good sign. I was near an exit when I created the copy and the key was pulsing to let me know it was there. So, when the mirror created the copy, its key was pulsing also. Now that I'm no longer near an exit, mine is not pulsing, so if the copy was a working copy it should not be pulsing either. All I need to do is find another exit and test my theory.

Xach walked as quickly as he could away from where he thought the key-less copy was. He kept his eye on both keys. The copy's key continued to pulse. After wandering around for about thirty minutes, the key started to pulse. The pulses led him to a cul-de-sac of buildings. The key pulsed brightest and fasted by the center building farthest from the main road on which he had been walking. The copy's key continued to pulse at the same intensity as it had from its inception.

Xach searched the mirror surface for a key hole, careful not to get so close as to accidentally create another copy. It was impossible not to make eye contact with his reflection, so it froze and stared intently back at him. Any time he got too close, a nose started to emerge from the surface of the mirror. He immediately pulled back and the copy retreated back into the mirror. He scanned the entire surface of the building and found nothing.

Maybe it's higher than eye level?

Xach concentrated on the magic words – *murmur leviar wentum* – while repeating them aloud and envisioning himself floating upward. It was hard to maintain enough focus to sustain the levitation ***and*** concentrate on finding a keyhole in the reflective surface. He nearly fell from the sky a few times, when his focus on his search broke his concentration on the magic. After a few attempts and fails to get airborne and stay there, he found a keyhole about eight feet off the ground in the center of the mirror panel.

His excitement broke his concentration for a split second, and he fell again. This time, however, he was able to quickly regain control and landed on his feet instead of hitting the ground.

The trick is going to be maintaining enough focus to remain airborne long enough to get the door open, Xach thought.

He floated up toward the keyhole. Once there, he extended the copy's key toward the keyhole. He could not keep perfectly still and the key got too close to the glass surface. A copy of the key started to emerge from the glass surface. Xach withdrew the key and the copy withdrew back into the mirror. Xach floated back down to the ground.

This is going to be harder than I thought. Why is the keyhole so high up? Maybe I should look for another one that is ground level, if there is one at ground level.

Xach saw movement out of the corner of his eye. He spun around to see if a copy had found him and was horrified to learn it was not a copy. The claw-bush and tree at the opening of the cul-de-sac were growing and moving! They grew several feet high and bent back toward the ground. The claws spread out flat and pushed on the ground, drawing a pyramid of glass upward from beneath the glass surface of the ground. The pyramid grew as it pushed upward and shards of glass protruded from the tip, creating a face of sorts. The base of the pyramid lifted free of the ground. The tree-claws now looked like arms. Two smaller pyramids protruded toward the ground from its base forming what looked like legs. These legs continued to grow as the claw-like arms reached toward Xach. The legs grew to at least six or seven feet long before shards protruded from the tips to create claw-feet.

The twelve-foot tall mirror monster took a step toward Xach.

Oh no, Xach thought. *No time to test the copy's key. I need to get out of here now!*

He slipped the copy's key into his pocket and turned back toward the keyhole. He tried to concentrate on the magic words, but his terror made it almost impossible. He levitated a few inches and then broke concentration. The creature drew closer. He got two feet in the air and fell again.

Come on Xach! You can do this!

He took a deep breath and relaxed his shoulders. He said the words and concentrated. He rose eight feet to the key hole. He concentrated on the words and carefully removed the key from around his neck. He moved it toward the keyhole. He felt the creature behind him. He slid the key into the keyhole and turned it. The door to the antechamber opened.

Xach felt the cold mirror-claws of the creature wrap around him. The razor sharp edges cut into him as it tightened its grip. He wanted to levitate out of its grasp, but he would have to let go of the key and possibly be sliced to ribbons in the process. Neither was a particularly pleasant option, but he had no other choice.

He released the key from his grip. It hung in the keyhole with the necklace dangling from the handle. Xach contorted himself as best he could to slide between the mirror fingers and slip from its grasp. The fingers cut him in several places, but the blood actually facilitated his escape by lubricating his body. Once free of the creature, he immediately concentrated on levitating to keep from falling to the ground.

Although far from graceful, he imagined himself floating up and down, left and right – thereby mimicking flight and staying out of the creature's grasp as it tried to reclaim him. He tried to draw it away from the key, but it would not follow him. Instead, it remained stationary, facing him with its back to the key. Xach landed in the center of the cul-de-sac, facing the monster.

What can I do to get him to move? It obviously does not want me to escape.

Xach caught a glimpse of his reflection in one of the buildings and saw movement behind him. He turned to see that three more of the mirror-monsters blocked the entrance to the cul-de-sac. Behind them stood one of the Xach copies. Xach looked closer and saw he was the one from which he stole the key.

The copy shakily levitated above the monsters and over the spot where Xach stood. He, just like Xach, had difficulty maintaining the needed concentration to maintain the levitation. He dropped a little and then regained control. He moved toward the monster guarding the exit.

Oh, no you don't! Xach thought.

He levitated toward the copy. Ten feet above the ground they faced each other. The copy looked angry and fiercely determined. He glared at Xach and unexpectedly launched himself forward, hurling his weight against Xach. The force knocked Xach backward into a building. Xach slid down the wall but managed to slow his descent enough to land on his feet. As he pulled away from the building surface, another copy was created.

Both turned to face one another. The copy looked at Xach, the flying copy, and the mirror monsters. He turned to flee but ran directly into the glass wall. He was stunned and fell backward. As he fell, he pulled another copy out of the mirror. It landed on top of him. The two screamed and scrambled to get away from one another. The newest copy grazed the wall with its shoulder as it ran away and pulled another copy out of the mirror.

The floating copy smiled at the chaos he created below and turned his attention back toward the exit. He levitated above the monster and attempted to come down behind it. The shards that resembled a face on the monster disappeared into the pyramid and grew out of the other side, making it unnecessary for the monster to turn around to face the copy. It swung its long arms back and forth, trying to grab him or swat it from the sky.

On the ground, the copies ran around in terror trying to avoid each other and the mirror-monsters. Every time one of them attempted to slip past the monsters guarding the cul-de-sac entrance, the monsters tried to grab them. The copies jumped away and bumped into the buildings again, causing even more copies to be created.

While the monster guarding the exit was focused on the floating copy, Xach ran between its legs and levitated toward the exit. He hoped he could slip inside without being detected and hopefully lock all the copies and the monsters out of the Hall. The floating copy saw Xach and dove toward him. The monster swatted at the copy, causing him to change direction. It fell squarely into the monster's chest. However, instead of bouncing off the surface, the copy was absorbed into the monster's chest. This unexpected occurrence surprised Xach and broke his concentration. He fell back to the ground.

Some of the copies on the ground saw it happen and gasped in fear. The copy inside the monster pounded on the inside of the monster's chest in an attempt to break out, but it was trapped. The copies realized they must not be captured and started levitating upward to try and get up and over the monsters' heads. The monsters responded to this action by growing longer arms and legs. The copies bobbed and weaved to avoid capture, but to no avail. One by one the monsters caught them and drew them to their chests, imprisoning them inside.

Xach felt awful for their creation and their subsequent fates, but he used the distraction to float to the exit and slip inside. The monster blocking the exit was too preoccupied with collecting the floating copies and did not even notice. He withdrew the key from the keyhole and pushed the door closed.

Xach lay in the dark antechamber for a long time. His mind raced and his body ached.

What will become of my copies? I would be terrified if I were trapped inside of one of those things. And what about the one who's key I stole? He probably feels even more scared. All of them are essentially me. Each one wants to find his way home, and I just trapped them in that world. I doomed them to a never-ending nightmare...unless their keys work.

This reminded him that he never got a chance to test the copy's key.

He stood up and put the key around his neck again. He withdrew the copy's key from his pocket and waved it around the room. It continued to pulse as it did in the mirror world.

The edges of the door lit up and he pushed it open into the Hall.

Ok...so did my key do that or did this one? It's hard to be sure.

Xach reluctantly removed the key from around his neck and placed it in the center of the antechamber. It made him nervous not to have it, even though he was alone in the room. The doorway disappeared. He walked toward the doorway with the copy's key. Nothing happened at first, but then the doorway's edges started to pulse faintly. Xach tried to push it open, but it would not budge. He pushed harder and it opened a crack. Try as he might, he could not get it to open the whole way. He retrieved his key and the door swung open with no effort.

Well, that's somewhat disheartening, Xach thought. *It doesn't work as well as mine, but it sort of works. Hopefully it won't open any doors. The pulsing element doesn't work at all, so finding exits and working doors would be exceedingly difficult.*

He closed the antechamber door and walked farther down the Hall to find another door that would open. He put his key in his pocket and used the copy's key. None of the doors would light up. He switched keys and quickly found a door that would open. He put his key back in his pocket and held the copy's key up to the door. At first, the edges would not light up. Seconds later, a faint pulsing light eminated from the door frame. Xach pushed on it. It opened a crack but would not open until Xach put all of his body weight against it.

He had no way of knowing which key actually opened it, because pressing his leg against the door with the key in his pocket could have released it from being stuck. However, with Count Milton lurking about the Hall, there was no way he was going to separate himself from the key to test the copy. He decided to leave the door open, hoping that *if* any of his copies found a way to into an exit, the open door in the hall *might* prevent them from getting it open. It was a big "if," but one he would have to live with for the time being. He would have to deal with Count Milton before he started fixing the mess he created in the mirror world.

Of course, if the mirror-monsters capture all of my copies, then I may not have anything to worry about. Poor souls…

He slipped the copy's key into his pocket and put his key around his neck. He made sure to hide it under his tattered t-shirt. He hoped that sometime soon he could find a place where he could get some clothes and have a chance to eat and rest.

Chapter Twenty-Eight

Once he returned to the Great Hall, he was surprised to see a symbol he recognized:

It was the mist world with the giant mutant octopus that had nearly eaten him and Charlie. With growing excitement, he realized that this was the section of hallway in which he and Charlie detected Count Milton when he was following them under a spell of invisibility. That also meant that he was near the door where Count Milton attacked him and separated them!

He looked feverishly for the door bearing the symbol:

It's gotta be close by. It's gotta! Charlie has to be here somewhere. Unless he wandered off in search of his world? But why would he do that? He doesn't have the key to open the door. He doesn't mind waiting...it would make sense for him to wait for me. Isn't that what he was programmed to do? I hope he waited...but why isn't he here then? Where is that door?

He focused so intently on the symbols that he failed to notice the key vibrating against his chest or the large pool of blood on the floor beneath him. He slipped and fell, landing on his right side. His injured shoulder, not yet fully healed, throbbed in pain.

What did I slip on? Blood? Whose blood is this? Is it mine? Is this from earlier?

In answer to these questions, a hand tightened around his neck and a knee pressed into his chest. He saw blood dripping from somewhere in mid-air and watched it fall onto his shirt.

It was Count Milton – once again hidden under a spell of invisibility.

"This ends now, boy," hissed Count Milton's voice from the air above him. "No more chasing…no more hiding…no more games. We finish this now!"

Count Milton tightened his invisible hand around Xach's throat, cutting off his oxygen. Xach's face turned red, then blue, and then purple. Xach clutched and pulled at the invisible arm, but he could not break its grip.

"See, boy. I am smarter than you. I'm stronger than you. I'm quicker and more resilient as well. And when you're gone, I'm going to control this place and every living thing on every tiny world that's connected to it. All will know me! All will fear me, and all will bow to COUNT MILTON!"

Once again Xach reached into his pocket and withdrew his only weapon – the medal. He grasped the invisible arm with his right hand so he would know where to aim, and then he stabbed the air with the pin. It lodged itself an inch into Milton's invisible arm. Blood flowed from around the puncture wound. Xach repeated this several times up and down Milton's arm.

"OUCH!" Milton yelled. "BLAST YOU AND THAT STUPID PIN!"

He released his grip and withdrew his hand. Before Xach could move away, the cold metal of Milton's robotic arm pressed down on his throat. Milton didn't clamp it around Xach's throat as he had before; he simply pressed his metal forearm against Xach's windpipe. It was uncomfortable and painful, but it did not cut off the airway entirely, allowing Xach to catch his breath.

Milton raised his arm with the medal lodged in it towards his mouth and pulled the medal out with his teeth. Xach only saw the medal float in mid-air, rise several inches, and twist a little. Milton spat the medal out onto the floor, a foot or more out of Xach's reach. He began chanting, *"Exorum encarta bantesto infernum!"* The medal vibrated and shook. Milton's voice and intensity rose. At its crescendo the medal burst into a thousand pieces, spraying about the hall in all directions.

"That will be the last time you stick me with that infernal thing. But no matter, once you're dead, I'll repair myself. They'll fix my eye…repair my arm…and I'll be as good as new…no…better than ***new***…I'll be INVINCIBLE!" He paused, ruminating on the repairs they would make to him and how powerful he would become. "Oh yes," he continued a moment later. "I will be unstoppable. But I digress. Let's get back to business, shall we? It's time to dispense with you once and for all and take that key."

"If y-you're g-going *cough* t-to k-kill *ack* m-me," Xach stopped to breathe, before continuing, "at- at l-least have t-the *cough* d-decency t-to sh-show *cuh-cuh* y-your face."

Silence filled the air for what seemed like an eternity, as Milton contemplated Xach's final request. Finally, he spoke.

"Who am I to deny a dying man his final request? It is indeed a simple one, and I should enjoy knowing that the last image you see before you draw your final breath will be me. *Incantante illumina sacra bente visable.*"

The air wavered, followed by the familiar shower of orange sparks. The horribly disfigured and mangled form of what was left of Count Milton shimmered into sight. He was clad in a suit made of short black hair. It was stained in several places with wet and sticky patches of blood and gore. His one eye sparked with evil, demonic glee. His mouth twisted into a giant grin beneath his crooked and frazzled mustache.

"Now gaze upon the face of your Master…and murderer!" Milton gloated.

What do I do now? Xach wondered. He escaped from Count Milton many times over the past several days, but he was exhausted and could think of no other plan of escape. The medal had been his only plan, and that failed. He had no other weapons. *Well, at least I got one last hurt in on him before he kills me.*

Xach felt something cold slide along his neck and into his ears.

"Good work, Xach. Now that he is visible, I can sense him."

Charlie? Is that really you?

"Of course it is. When we were separated, I entered stasis and awaited your return."

Oh, thank god, Xach shouted joyfully in his head. *I thought I'd never see you again. I thought I was going to die.* Tears of joy rolled down his cheeks.

"Yes," Milton gloated. "Weep like a baby. Cry at the hands of the most powerful man in the universe!"

"You cannot die," Charlie continued. "That would cause me to violate my programming. What are your instructions?"

Kill him! Shock him to death! Dissolve him and don't put him back together! I don't care, but make him go away for good!

"Xach, that is not possible. You have programmed me to save life and never to destroy it. If I destroy him, I violate your programming."

If he destroys me, and you do nothing, that will violate your programming also. It's either me or him...and I choose HIM! Consider it self-defense. Self-defense won't violate your programming!

"I'm sorry, Xach, but you yourself were not sure if destroying life in self-defense was justified. I cannot do it."

But he's going to kill me, Charlie. I'm going to die, if you don't do something NOW!

Xach was disturbed by Charlie's insistence that he would not kill Milton. His face scrunched up in anger and frustration. This look, coupled with the tears rolling down his cheeks, filled Count Milton with intense glee. He misinterpreted these facial expressions to mean that Xach was fearful of his death and fully at his mercy.

"Shall I end your suffering now, poor wretch? Are you ready to die?" Milton asked in a lyrical tone, as if he were cooing to child. "Are you ready to meet your maker?"

Milton removed his robotic arm from across Xach's throat and grasped him again with his real hand. He raised his metal arm high above his head. Xach saw that something sharp and metallic was jammed in the gears of the robotic arm, rendering it useless except as a blunt object. Milton intended to beat him to death with it.

One of the villagers must have broken their sword off in his arm when he was a bear, thought Xach. *And, now he's going to smash my head with his metal arm! DO SOMETHING, CHARLIE!*

In a flash, Charlie shed his transparency and appeared next to Count Milton in the form of Xach's German Shepherd. Charlie's sudden appearance caused Milton to gasp in surprise. In that brief moment of hesitation, Charlie lunged at Milton and buried his sharp teeth deeply into flesh of Milton's arm. Milton screamed in agony but refused to let go of Xach's throat.

You've been here all along? Why didn't you help me sooner?

Charlie explained his actions to Xach while he continued his attack on Milton by digging his claws into the leg that rested on Xach's chest.

"I sensed your approach and the approach of your assailant. I choose to become transparent, so that he might not detect my presence until such time as I might be of assistance to you. I could not sense the location of your attacker and did not know what to do until you coaxed him to become visible. I did not want to risk being separated from you again, so I chose to remain hidden until I could help you."

Count Milton retaliated by slamming his metal arm down on Charlie's back, hoping to dislodge the dog from his arm. However, his arm sliced through Charlie like a sword through water.

Charlie, I can't breathe, Xach pleaded. *He's choking me to death!*

"I shall try something else."

Hurry...

"I will protect your life, but also his."

Charlie kept his teeth buried in Milton's forearm. He became fluid and melted his head around the bite area and up Milton's arm. His back legs melted up into his torso, and his torso and front legs melted into his head. In a matter of seconds, Charlie covered Milton's entire arm.

Milton watched in awe and horror as the dog slowly disintegrated from back to front, melting into a glob of undulating ooze that covered his arm. He felt a tingling sensation in his arm that changed to bubbling and fizzing. After a moment, the sensations abruptly stopped, and the dog's ooze fell to the floor.

Charlie pooled around Xach's neck for a moment. He repaired all of the tissue damage to Xach's neck, throat, and windpipe, before reshaping into a dog again. He stood next to Xach's head, staring defiantly at Milton as he expelled Milton's arm from his hindquarters.

This happened so quickly that Milton did not fully comprehend what had happened. It looked as if the dog had pooped an arm. As he stared in disbelief at the arm lying on the floor, he suddenly realized – it was **his left arm**! He looked to his left shoulder and saw only a nub where his arm used to be!

All was silent for a moment, and then Count Milton erupted into an insane rage. He shook his remaining metallic arm in the air and shouted, "NO! NO! NO! YOU CAN'T DO THIS TO ME!" In a flash, he brought his arm down on the dog again. He hoped it would slice through him as it had before and smash Xach's face.

Charlie would not allow that to happen. Milton's metal arm sunk halfway into Charlie's torso before he solidified himself, bringing the arm to a dead stop. Milton tried to pull his arm out of the dog. There was a bit of minor resistance, and then Milton pulled back another stub. Charlie severed the the metal clamp and forearm from Milton's body and expelled

- 373 -

it in the same manner as he had Milton's left arm. Milton screamed in frustration and anger and fell backwards, unbalanced by the loss of his arms.

Released from the pressure of Milton's weight on his chest, Xach took a deep breath and pushed himself away from Milton under Charlie. He slid toward the wall and worked himself into a sitting position.

Charlie opened his mouth and projected sound toward Milton that mimicked speech. "I will not allow you to harm this child. If you persist in attacking either him or me, I shall be forced to continue removing limbs until you cease to be a threat."

Count Milton's face burned with rage, but he knew he had been beaten.

"This isn't over," he spat at Charlie, as he scooted away from the dog. "I will not rest until the both of you are destroyed."

He attempted to stand up, but with his left arm missing and the disfigured robotic arm weighing heavily on his right side, he toppled over and fell on his face. Xach could not help but laugh at him. This enraged Milton even more, and he kicked his legs and screamed in frustration like a child throwing a temper tantrum. His pride was mortally wounded. They made a mockery out of him and ruined his body. Not since his childhood days when his father and the school bullies tormented him had he felt so helpless, weak and humiliated. He made them all pay, and he swore to himself that he would make the boy and his dog pay as well. He rolled onto his chest and pushed himself up with the metal stub of his mangled robotic arm.

Charlie continued to stare him down, while Xach tried hard to stifle a giggle as he looked at the broken man before him. He had no arms and only one eye in his head. Tears fell from his good eye, while what looked to be pus oozed from the eye socket of his missing eye. His nose was broken and his hair and mustache were wildly unkempt.

"Oh, how the mighty have fallen," Xach sniggered, driving the final emotional nail into the coffin that housed Count Milton's pride.

The color drained from Milton's face, and he bit his trembling lower lip. For a moment, it looked as if he were going to start bawling like child, but he didn't. His whole body stiffened, and he channeled all his emotion through his one good eye like a laser beam of pure hatred. He stared at the two who had temporarily destroyed him.

"Mark my words, you little bastard," he huffed. "I *will* get you, and your little dog-thing too!"

This time Xach really laughed.

"HA! That's real original!" He laughed so hard he fell into coughing fits.

"This isn't over," Lord Milton whimpered; then he turned, ran down the hall, and disappeared into the distance.

Charlie continued watching him, even after he faded from sight. When he was content that the man was gone and would not be returning, he turned back to Xach, who was still coughing and laughing.

"You are laughing, which means that something is funny. What is the joke?"

Xach chortled a few more times, trying to gain control of himself. His laughter died down to a mild chuckle and he responded, "What he said sounded like something a villain said in an old movie I used watch with my mom. He didn't mean to sound so cheesy or cliché, but he did to me. It caught me off guard. I wasn't expecting him to say *that*. Plus, I've been running from him for who knows how long, and I'm so exhausted and emotionally drained, I…"

"Seventy- seven hours, thirteen minutes, and forty-four seconds by my calculations," Charlie interrupted.

"Huh," said Xach. "Seventy-seven hours, really?"

"Yes, that is how much time has passed since we were separated."

"Wow. It seemed A LOT longer. It seemed like weeks!"

"What was the joke?" Charlie asked again.

"Oh, I'm just exhausted. I haven't really slept in over three days. I nearly died more times than I care to remember. I ache all over. I'm just mentally and physically drained. And then he goes and quotes that movie. It was just a bit surreal. Besides, my emotions are totally on the fritz right now."

"I do not understand."

"Well, Charlie, I'm afraid I'm too tired to explain it to you at the moment, but I'm overjoyed that you found me! I can't thank you enough for saving me…but right now I just need to rest."

"Yes."

"How about you fix me up, and we go find a nice quiet place for me to get some sleep and maybe something to eat?"

"Affirmative."

Charlie oozed himself all over Xach, repairing his shoulders, his feet, his scraped knees, his face, and all the other injuries Milton inflicted upon him. He even repaired Xach's torn clothes where enough fabric remained for him to do so.

"Thanks, man," said Xach, as Charlie resumed his dog shape. "I feel good as new! Let's get outta here. I need a good long nap."

He stood up and looked at the mess in hall.

"What do you think we should do with this stuff?" asked Xach, pointing to Milton's right arm and metal clamp hand. "We shouldn't just leave those here, should we?"

"Allow me," said Charlie as he oozed himself along the length of the hall and up the walls for several feet dissolving and collecting anything that originally wasn't in the hallway before their arrival. When he reconstituted himself into the familiar form of the German Shepherd, the hall was as clean as it had been on the day Xach first set foot in it.

"Put out your hand," said Charlie.

Xach did as he was told, and Charlie rested his chin on Xach's palm. When he raised his head, Henry Simpson's WWII medal rested upon his palm.

"I believe this belongs to you."

Xach was speechless. His emotions threatened to overwhelm him. He thought it was destroyed. Even though it was just a tiny piece of metal, it meant so much more. It was a reminder and *a piece* of his life on Earth…his life before the key. It saved his life a few times, and he was overjoyed to have it returned to him.

"I…I don't know what to say," said Xach, choking back some tears. "Thanks."

"You're welcome, my friend."

"What happened to Milton's arms"

"I dissolved them and stored their matter. I can expel it later or repurpose it into something else you might require."

"You may expel it. I don't want any part of him for anything."

"Very well. Let us find you somewhere to nap."

"Affirmative," said Xach. He slipped the medal back into his pocket and followed Charlie as he trotted down the star-lit corridor of the Hall of Worlds.

Chapter Twenty-Nine

Journal Entry # 2

I don't know where to start, but I still can't believe what just happened! I spoke with my mother! Well, I didn't actually speak to her, but it was close enough! It was amazing! I still can't really comprehend it, but it happened. I wish it had been longer, but the Shaman says there is something very wrong with his world and others.

My mind is spinning so fast, I hardly know how to put it into words...I communicated with my mother, but I also learned that getting home may not be as easy as I had hoped. Perhaps writing everything out in detail will help me process what has just happened. Let's start from the beginning...

Charlie and I never intended to stay here in Montepeira this long, but Keiko assured me that the Shaman of his tribe would be able to help me in my quest to return to Earth. He said that the Shaman is very wise and spiritual, connected to all living things in a manner neither he nor his tribesmen understand. He explained that the Shaman frequently leaves the tribe to journey into the wilderness. While on these journeys, or "vision quests" as Keiko calls it, the Shaman is able to strengthen his connection to the energy and lifeforce of all those around him. The length of these vision quests vary from a few days to weeks at a time. When Charlie and I found our way into Monteperia through a doorway linked to Kieko's grandfather's storage shed, the Shaman had just left on his latest vision quest one day prior.

It had been my intention never to remain in one place too long. While I'm not too afraid of Count Milton, I feel more at ease when I'm on the move, and I'm always looking over my shoulder. Charlie and I have been moving from world to world, trying to find Earth or Charlie's home world. Keiko's tribe was very friendly and welcoming, and Keiko convinced me to stay and wait for the Shaman.

The Shaman returned from his journey last night. There was a huge celebration with dancing, food, and singing. I wanted to talk to the Shaman last night, but Keiko said it was not appropriate. He told me that I needed to wait until today to show respect for their customs and for the Shaman himself. It is custom to hold a celebration upon the return of the Shaman and the celebration lasts until daybreak the following morning. The tribe sleeps a few hours and then prepares a great feast. After eating, the Shaman shares his wisdom and teachings with the tribe. Keiko told me that he would introduce me to the Shaman after the meal and the Shaman's final words.

The wait was killing me. I never was a patient person. Even though the food was wonderful and the Shaman's words were interesting and truthful, I spent the whole time in a state of high anxiety. I won't go into detail about the Shaman's sermon, but the gist of it was that he sensed a disturbance in nature that deeply concerned him. He said that a great evil threatened the harmony of all of life, and that it was the duty of the tribe to be vigilant for any abnormal occurrences and to share such things with him immediately.

"Beware of strangers," were his final words, and he looked directly at me and Charlie. His gaze was neither malevolent nor friendly — just blank. I have to admit that I was a little freaked out by it. He dismissed the tribe to clean up what was left of the meal and retire for the evening. He made his way through the parting masses to the three of us. Keiko introduced me and Charlie. The Shaman bowed to us both. I bowed in turn, and Charlie lowered his head in respect. Charlie has remained in his dog form since the moment we stepped into Monteperia, and Keiko and his tribesmen seem to think he is just a dog. However, judging from the way the Shaman looked at Charlie, I suspected he knew immediately that the dog form was simply an illusion. He spoke to both of us as equals.

"Welcome travelers. It is a great honor to have you amongst my people." He bowed to both of us. "We are at your service. Stay as long as you like and take whatever you need."

"Thank you, for your hospitality and graciousness," I said diplomatically, trying to mimic the words and actions of the ambassadors I'd seen on television. "Your people are very kind and helpful, but I was hoping you might be able to help me find my way back to my home world."

"My child, I wish it were within my power to aid you in this matter," he said, "but I am afraid that I do not know the way to your world any more than I would know the way off my own. However, I believe there is something that troubles you to which I might be of assistance."

I had no idea what that might be. The only thing I wanted was to get back home to my family. I admit that I was still a little concerned about Count Milton, but what possible threat could an armless man be to me at the moment?

"I speak not of your evil pursuer," he continued, as if he had been reading my mind. "I speak of your family. You worry about them and long to return to them. While I can not physically return you to them, I can offer you the opportunity to communicate with them briefly."

I was stunned by his words, because I could not see how this was possible. How could he have known what I was thinking and feeling? I stood there dumbfounded for a moment, because Keiko nudged me to respond.

"Really," I finally stammered. "You could do that?"

"Yes. You would not actually speak directly to them, but you could communicate with them through me and another vessel. While I was on my vision quest, I spent several days communing with nature to ascertain why balance shifted so drastically in recent days. It is this change and your impending arrival that prompted my quest in the first place. As I traced the changes across time and space, I found myself in direct communication with another Shaman on your world. She knew of you and your strange disappearance. I sensed a great deal of worry in her for your well-being. She offered to help communicate with your family if you would like. The Shaman on your world expressed that she would be ready to link at sunset."

"Of course I would," I said, unable to control my excitement.

The Shaman said he needed to rest and would collect us before sunset. I was so anxious, I tried to rest, but I was too anxious.

An hour before sunset, the Shaman came for me and Charlie.

"Follow me into the clearing beyond the village," he said. "I require silence and natural surroundings to make a connection."

Keiko, Charlie, and I followed the Shaman through the small village of animal skin huts and shallow bathing pools. We entered a small but dense copse of trees, emerging on the other side into a large field of tall green grass topped with small yellow flowers. It looked not unlike a field of abnormally tall dandelions. They waved to and fro in the gentle breeze that rolled off the mountains beyond. Tiny insects buzzed about, moving from flower to flower, collecting pollen. It reminded me of the one world in the giant terrarium that exuded such a strong sense of natural balance.

In the fading light of dusk, I saw a few large rocks protruding from the ground in the center of the field. The rocks surrounded a natural spring. A narrow, winding path led to the largest of the rocks. I could tell that the path was used on a daily basis and that it was created by moving around, not through, the flowering plants. I thought about how I and most of the people I knew would just have mowed their way through the plants, making our own path. This path was invisible from the edge of the field, because it was part of the field. Keiko and the Shaman were careful not to break, bend, or injure the plants that grew along the path. Their respect for nature was odd to me but awe-inspiring.

Charlie and I showed the same respect and walked very carefully toward the rocks. I had to concentrate on my feet and the path before me, but even under such intense mental focus, I began to feel the stress and anxiety melt from my soul. We reached the rocks and the Shaman gestured for the four of us to have a seat. He indicated that I should sit facing him on the largest rock. Charlie lay down next to me and rested his head on my leg.

"This may take a few moments," the Shaman said. "Please remain calm and quiet. Find your center while I attempt to connect with the Shaman on your world."

My mother's yoga instructor often talked like this, so I didn't find it odd or funny. He crossed his legs and tucked his feet under them. He rested his hands on his knees with the palms facing upward. He asked me to sit in the same fashion, resting our knees together and placing my hands palm down over him. He closed his eyes and looked up toward the sky. After a few strong exhales, his breathing became even and regular. I matched his movements, attempting to enter a similar trance-like state, just as I had done on Zindartha when I was lost in the dark.

After a few moments, I began to feel a tingling sensation in my hands, much like the feeling you get when your leg falls asleep. The buzzing numbness crept up my arms and enveloped my whole body. The darkness before my eyes swirled and blurry shapes of color formed. The shapes took on definition and to my surprise I was looking at an image of my mother. She was sitting in our backyard with her eyes closed. Her legs were crossed and her hands were palm down on top of another woman's hands. As the image of the other woman took form and shape in the reflection of the pond next to which they sat, I realized with astonishment that it was Mrs. Wilson from the elementary school!

Looking back on things, it makes perfect sense that Mrs. Wilson was a Shaman. She was very kind to me and seemed to have a sixth sense about my innocence during the snake incident. I wonder how she came to convince my mother that she knew where I was, but I guess that is something that will have to wait until I finally see my mother again. I don't know when that will be, but I have high hopes that Charlie and I will succeed in finding a doorway to Earth soon. But I digress.

As the image of Mrs. Wilson and my mother sharpened in my head, I wondered if I was just making this up or if I was really linked to them through the Shaman. As I thought this, a feeling of intense love and relief washed over me, followed by worry and fear. It took me a few seconds to realize that these intense feelings were not my own. They were my mother's! In that instant of realization, I understood how the connection worked. Mental images and emotions could be exchanged through the link, but not words. I innately understood that while I was receiving my mother's image of herself in the backyard and her emotions at seeing me safe, she was seeing my mental image of myself and the Shaman and receiving my love and joy at seeing her again.

The understanding must have been mutual, because a torrent of images and emotions began to wash over me — mother crying hysterically in the hospital as she looked for me (fear, anger, confusion); mother and father crying in the police station as a police officer discussed the procedure for filing a missing person's report (deep and painful sadness, anxiety, despair); mother and father explaining my disappearance to my sister, my relatives, and Jeremy (frustration, love, strength); mother hanging posters of her missing son throughout the neighborhood and canvassing the city (hope, despair, weakness); mother, father, and sister sitting in silence at the dinner table unable to eat (exhaustion, apprehension, numbness); mother answering the front door and seeing Mrs. Wilson (confusion, anger, suspicion). My mind was inundated with images and emotions too many to describe, but at least I got a sense of what my family had been going through and a chance to let them know that I was all right.

While I tried to comprehend the pictures and feelings sent by my mother, my mind sent her images of my adventure through the hospital closet, the death of Gerald, my journey through the Hall of Worlds, and my battles with Count Milton. Even though she sent me overwhelming feelings of love and warmth, I also received her feelings of deep concern for my safety and a burning hatred and anger for Count Milton. I tried to send her the idea that I was safe and not to worry, but even if I was successful at this, I know she will still worry.

Then, the images and emotional waves stopped. They didn't fade away or taper off; they stopped abruptly. The sudden end to the link felt like a ton of bricks hitting my face and heart. My eyes snapped open and my heart started racing. My face was wet with tears, and my hands were clenched into fists atop the Shaman's palms.

"What happened?" I said forcefully, somewhat ashamed at the anger and edge to my voice. I didn't mean to be so nasty to the man who had given me such a wonderful gift, but the abrupt ending left my senses reeling. "Get her back! Get her back!"

I sobbed so hard I thought my chest would rip apart. I don't think I have ever been as angry and sad as I was at that moment.

The Shaman looked at me with sympathetic eyes and said, "I'm sorry, my child, but the link was severed. It is a symptom of the changes that are occurring in all the worlds, and I could no more turn back the hands of time than reestablish a link with your mother at this time. I am very sorry."

He pulled me to him and held me while I cried.

Truth is, I don't know how long I cried, but I felt better after I did. Keiko offered me a cloth to blow my nose and wipe my face. I thanked him and sat in numb silence as the Shaman tried to explain why he could not contact my mother again.

"The harmonics of time and space are becoming warped, and in some cases they are being completely destroyed. In the past, I was able to contact Shamans on many worlds, but this is becoming increasingly difficult. The links deteriorate and disappear. I am very sorry that our link with your mother was not longer. I am also sorry that the link was severed so suddenly. In time I hope you can come to appreciate the time you had and not focus on the time that was robbed from you."

"I do," I sniffed. "I do appreciate what you've given me. Thank you so very much. At least she knows I'm safe and that I'm trying to find my way back to her."

"I do not wish to diminish the importance of your feelings over what happened, but I must also impress upon you the severity of its implications. I do not know why time and space have been changed, and I do not know how this happened. Yet, I do get a strong feeling that it is all tied to you and the key you carry. I do not know if the damage is reversable or not, but I know you will play an important part in the fate of many worlds. You must allow yourself time to process what you have seen, heard, and felt, but then you must continue on your journey as soon as possible. I fear the fate of your world depends upon you fulfilling your destiny."

I didn't know what to say to this, so I just nodded. At the time, I don't think I even heard what he was saying. I was too emotionally drained. But as I remember the conversation to document it in my journal, the words are crystal clear in my memory. I guess that's the key working its magic.

After the Shaman finished expressing his concern for my well-being and the need to fulfil my destiny, Keiko motioned for us to leave. We left the Shaman and returned to the village. I thanked Keiko and excused myself to my hut so I could process what had happened. I figured the best way for me to do this was to detail the experience in writing, and I think it helped.

I spoke with my mother. She knows I'm safe and unharmed. She knows I'm trying to find my way back to her. She may not understand what happened to me. Heck, she may not even believe it, but hopefully she can find a little peace in our exchange of images and emotions.

On the other hand, the Shaman made it perfectly clear that something is wrong with the Hall of Worlds. I know Count Milton's fake key and his actions in the Hall of Worlds have somehow affected the delicate balance that exists between worlds. If I don't do something to fix it, then I may never find my way home. I didn't ask for the job, and I certainly don't want it, but I guess it's up to me to track down Count Milton and destroy his key. I'm not strong enough to defeat him on my own, but hopefully I can find my way home to Earth and get some help there. Or maybe I'll meet some other creatures or key-carriers on other worlds that can help me stop Count Milton. At least I have Charlie to help me! Tomorrow Charlie and I will leave Monteperia and start the hunt for Earth's doorway. But tonight I shall rest and continue sorting through the memories of my mother.

Epilogue

"We are finished, my Lord."

Count Milton rose from the large metal table on which he lay for nearly twelve hours. The surgeries were painful and numerous, and he passed out from pain on more than one occasion. Now, the worst was over, and it was time to witness his rebirth.

He stepped off the table and crossed the sterile operating room to face a large mirror that stretched from floor to ceiling. He stood motionless for several moments, drinking in the image of his new body through his new left eye.

"Excellent!" he muttered, tenting the metallic fingers of his new hands. "Now it is time to begin plotting my revenge. Let us begin with this."

He raised his left hand and touched a hidden button on one of the metal rods that formed the "bones" of his upper right arm. The button opened a small secret compartment within the metal. Inside was a small glass test-tube containing a black, oily liquid. He removed the vial from its hiding place and held it up in front of his new eye.

"Let us see what you're made of, my furry little fiend. Once I determine your weakness, the boy won't stand a chance!"